DOCKER'S DAUGHTER

Also by Sally Worboyes

Wild Hops

DOCKER'S DAUGHTER

Sally Worboyes

HEADLINE

First published in 1995 by
HEADLINE BOOK PUBLISHING

10 9 8 7 6 5 4 3 2 1

All characters in this publication are fictitious and any
resemblance to real persons, living or dead, is purely coincidental.

British Library Cataloguing in Publication Data

Worboyes, Sally
Docker's Daughter
I. Title
823 [F]

ISBN 0-7472-1342-9

Typeset by Avon Dataset Ltd., Bidford-on-Avon, B50 4JH

Printed and bound in Great Britain by
Mackays of Chatham PLC, Chatham, Kent

HEADLINE BOOK PUBLISHING
A division of Hodder Headline PLC
338 Euston Road,
London NW1 3BH

For my family
– Pete, Esther, Duncan and Robin

Acknowledgements

I am indebted to Geraldine Cooke for her vision and encouragement, Jenny Page for her patience, and Divisional Commander, Phillip Hagon, Metropolitan Police Service, for his help and advice on how to deal with Kay's arrest.

Chapter One

London 1962

It was two in the morning when the shrill ringing of the telephone pierced the dark silence of Kay's bedroom. Instantly awake, she was filled with panic. Why would anyone ring at such an hour? Blanking horrid thoughts from her mind, she listened for sounds from her parents' bedroom. Not afraid of the dark but of what might lie behind the phone call, she pulled herself up in bed and waited, hoping it would stop. Maybe someone had dialled a wrong number.

Three rings later she shot from her bed out of the room and along the passage, her hand sweeping the wall until it found the light switch.

'Hallo?' Kay's voice was quiet but her tone almost dared the caller to give her bad news.

'Kay . . .' It was her aunt Liz. The heavy pause that followed told her something terrible had happened to her uncle Bert. That wonderful, healthy, lovable man who had just celebrated his birthday. Pushing her long blonde hair from her face, Kay composed herself before asking what was wrong.

'Get Daddy for me, there's a good girl . . .' Liz's weak voice trailed off.

Jack being a heavier sleeper than Laura moaned and turned over as Kay's urgent voice woke her mother. 'Was that the phone?' She was still half asleep.

Before Kay had a chance to say who it was, Laura was out of bed in a flash. Just awake but alert enough to realize that only grave news came at that hour, she repeated over and over to herself, *Please don't let anything have happened to Dad.* Grabbing the black receiver with one hand, she steadied herself with the other, gripping the back of the chair, feeling light-headed and giddy from getting out of bed too quickly. Her heart was thumping as the dread of hearing her ageing father ask for help swept through her. She had asked him many times to give up his cottage and move in with the three of them.

'It's Aunt Liz,' Kay whispered as she stood in the kitchen doorway waiting to hear the worst.

'Liz – what's wrong?'

'I think Bert's . . .' her voice trailed off.

Slipping on to a kitchen chair, Laura drew her feet up off the cold linoleum and tucked her thin cotton nightdress under her toes. 'Liz, please . . . what is it?' A cold chill ran through her. 'What's happened?'

'I've phoned for an ambulance.' Liz's voice sounded thin and empty. 'He called out—' She broke into a high-pitched cry, 'I thought it was just a nightmare! I thought he'd gone off again. I went back to sleep.' Another tense pause filled the space between them.

'I went back to sleep, Laura! May God forgive me . . .' Her pained voice struggled to control the sobbing. 'I went back to sleep.'

Backing away from her mother along the narrow passage, Kay leaned against her bedroom door and tried to control her breathing. She knew that something serious had happened. Gripping the handle to the door of her room, willing her hands to stop shaking, she stared back at Laura. She didn't want to hear what was coming. She wanted her mother to smile and relax her face.

'It's your uncle Bert. I can't protect you from this, Kay. And it's going to hurt.'

At that moment, Kay knew by instinct that this was going to be a turning-point in her life. Her mother was admitting that she could not protect her from everything that life threw her way. She had no choice but to deliver the crushing blow which was hovering like a weapon between them.

'He's dead,' Laura murmured, 'gone.'

Turning away, Kay threw herself on to her bed and screamed into her pillow. 'It's not *fair*! He's my uncle, Mum! My uncle Bert!'

Liz had taken Bert's sudden death very badly, and was unable to cope with anything, especially having him laid out in her front room as was the East End custom. She had been given tranquillizers, and could only just manage to drag herself through the days leading up to his funeral. Her round, smiling face which so often lifted those around her, was now ashen and drawn as she sat in her small, quiet living room with her younger brother, Jack. Her hair seemed to have gone from grey to all white in just a couple of days and her red-rimmed eyes were swollen from crying.

'If only I hadn't gone back to sleep Bert might still be alive.' She gazed into her cup and pushed a floating tea leaf to one side.

'Stop tormenting yourself, Liz. You heard what the doctor said, it was all over in seconds. There wasn't anything you could have done about it.' Rubbing his eyes, Jack sighed heavily. 'We have to be thankful he died in his sleep.'

'The house is so quiet. I'll never get used to it.' She sipped her tea which had been laced with whiskey.

'Why don't you stay with me and Laura for a couple of weeks? Till the funeral's over and you've had a bit of time to get used to the idea of being on your own,' he said, believing she would turn him down flat.

'That'd be nice, Jack. I would like that.'

Pleased that his sister offered no resistance, Jack thought he might as well touch on the other idea he had been turning over in his mind. Finding the right words was the most difficult part.

'Lizzie, I don't quite know how to say this.' Turning his head to avoid her searching eyes, he caught sight of Bert's polished boots in a corner of the room. 'I can see why it would be too much for you to have Bert's body . . .' he took a deep breath. 'Why don't we have him laid out in my front room instead of the chapel of rest?' He reeled the words out quickly. A painful silence hung in the room.

'His mates could come and go, and —'

'Yeah,' Liz cut in, making it easier for her brother. 'I would prefer that.' She slipped one of her heart pills under her tongue to ease the pain.

'Good. That's good.' He was relieved to have got that over with. Reaching for his hand, Liz squeezed it and looked into his grief-stricken face. 'Thanks, love. I would never 'ave got through this without you and Laura.' She gave him a weak smile. 'Laura won't mind having me there, will she?'

'What d'you think?'

'Yeah. Silly question. We're like sisters really.'

'Too right.' He leaned across and tipped a little more Irish whiskey into her cup. 'We'll soon 'ave some colour back in those cheeks of yours.'

'What about our Kay?' Liz asked sadly. 'How's she taking it?'

'She's young. Seventeen. Still a baby. She'll get over it quicker than we will.' Jack lowered his head, praying to God he was right.

* * *

Laura had hardly entered their spare room since Jack had moved out of it and back in with her. With Kay by her side, she scanned the room in silence.

'Let's make it nice and bright for Aunt Liz, Mum,' Kay said.

'Yeah.' Laura swallowed hard. 'Good idea.'

'I'll make a pot of tea.' Laura felt her daughter squeeze her arm before she left the room, and was thankful for the natural warmth she gave.

Standing by the window, the daylight falling across the pale blue candlewick bedspread, Laura imagined Jack lying there all those nights by himself and wondered why they had let it go on for so long. They had spent over four years living under the same roof but not sharing the same bed, until Kay was nearly drowned in Kent two years previously, and both she and Jack were brought sharply back to reality.

The pale blue cover was significant for another reason. This third bedroom had been intended for their second child, Baby John, who had died in his sleep when he was no more than three months old. Neither Laura nor Jack had forgiven themselves for not waking when, as they believed, their baby would have made some small noise for attention. The cot had been placed as close to their bed as possible, yet neither of them had heard a thing.

Pulling the blue cover from the bed, Laura decided she would buy a new brightly patterned one for Liz. The curtains could come down too; she would run up some more on her new electric sewing machine. It wouldn't take her long and it would be worth it for more reasons than one. She didn't want to be reminded any more of the time when her marriage had almost broken down and she had done little, if anything, to stop it happening.

Had it not been for Kay's accident, she and Jack might not be together now. They did love one another, and probably always had. Pride and other people had got in their way and almost ruined it for good.

Sighing, Laura folded the bedspread and squeezed it on to a shelf inside a cupboard. The blue lampshade would go too; and so would the multicoloured rag mat. They could all go to the charity stall at Bethnal Green market. She silently thanked Bert for giving her the courage finally to bury the saddest time of her life.

'Goodbye, Baby John,' she whispered as she unscrewed the light bulb from the lamp and lifted the soft-blue shade from the stand. 'God bless.'

She closed her eyes and willed herself to be strong. After all, that tragedy had happened a long time ago.

As Laura held the shade close to her, she looked out of the window and up at the sky. The sun was just coming out from behind a grey cloud and its rays streamed in and lit up the room.

'Look after Baby John for us, Bert.' The sun was on her face now, and its warmth seemed to flow through her body. Smiling, she sat down on the edge of the single bed, trying to recognize the new sensation filling her being. If she could have given it a colour it would be pale gold. Warm comfort seemed to fill the room as if someone who loved and cared were there.

'My God,' she whispered. 'You've found him. You're with him!' Leaping up from the bed, she pulled open the bedroom door. 'Kay! Kay!'

As Kay appeared in the kitchen doorway at the end of the passage, she and Laura stared at each other.

'It's Baby John,' she finally managed to say, 'he's alive. Your brother's alive.' She waited for the pained look on Kay's face to dissolve.

'Not here, not in our world, but somewhere else,' she said reassuringly as Kay came slowly towards her. 'He's happy. He's with your uncle Bert and they're both happy.'

Kay reached out and pulled her close, burying her face in her mother's thick, sweet-smelling hair. 'It's all right, Mum, it's all right.'

Laura pulled away and gazed at her. 'Kay, something just happened.' She swallowed hard and wiped the tears that were streaming from her hazel-green eyes. 'It was wonderful. I don't know how to tell you, but I've just been allowed to see into another world.'

'Come on. You'll be all right.' Kay led her into the kitchen, hardly daring to look at her for fear she would break down too.

'But these tears ain't grief. Don't you understand?' she said, emphasizing each word, as if Kay were too young to take it in.

'I'll put a little drop of brandy in. We could both do with it.' Still Kay couldn't look at her mother.

Then Laura realized. The experience had been meant for her and her only. It wasn't something she would be able to share. She would have to settle for that, and not go shouting it across the world.

Kay awoke to the sound of her dad sobbing in his sleep in the next room, and his tormented face sprang into her mind. She wondered whether she should go in and shake him out of the nightmare, knowing that once he stirred, he would not get back to sleep again. She decided against it. She didn't want herself or her mother to see her dad's sad eyes which had often been referred to as 'laughing blues'.

Having made up her mind to leave him, believing that dreams only lasted seconds, Kay climbed out of bed to make herself a cup of strong tea. She could always catch up on sleep.

Warming herself by the two-bar electric fire in the kitchen, she tried not to think about her uncle Bert lying so still on the other side of the wall, and started to make a mental list of the food she and her mum would need to buy for the funeral guests. It wasn't until the sound of birdsong began to break the silence that Kay felt brave enough to go into the front room and put the cut flowers in water. She caught a glimpse of her pale, freckled face in the mirror and grimaced at her red puffy eyes and lank hair. She vowed to catch up with herself soon and pay a little more attention to the way she looked. Her own mother, her fortieth birthday approaching, still took pride in her appearance and Kay didn't want to let the side down.

As she slowly pushed the door open, the array of colourful blooms delivered courtesy of the florist brought a lump to her throat. She thought that if her Uncle Bert's spirit was in that room he would be touched at the kind gesture made by their local shop. With this thought in mind, Kay took great care in arranging the flowers in glass vases.

Adding a light blue iris to red and white carnations, she felt lighter in mood as the early-morning April sun presented itself, shining through the net curtains and across Bert's open coffin. Up until then, she hadn't been able to look at him lying there so peacefully, but the sun seemed in an instant to have lifted her spirits, and Kay went over and looked down at the uncle she had loved, not caring that her tears were dropping on to the crisp white gown he was dressed in. Her dad had been annoyed about that. Jack had wanted Bert to be buried in his dark blue serge suit, but it was the last thing he had thought to tell the undertaker, and now it was too late.

When the day of the funeral finally arrived, Kay and Laura were busy all day pouring cups of tea and forever cutting more sandwiches for the stream of relatives, friends and dockers who arrived. Numberless bottles of brandy, whisky and beer found their way into the flat. Every man brought a bottle of something, knowing how much they would all need the drink to help them through the day.

As the time drew nearer for the hearse to arrive, the noise reached a crescendo. A mixture of crying and laughter filled the flat as stories unfolded about Bert and some of the things he had unwittingly got himself into. Kay heard it all from the kitchen and smiled to herself. This was more like it. This was what Uncle Bert would have wanted, everyone enjoying a good drink on his behalf.

She caught Laura's eye and smiled back at her. She had said earlier that she didn't want her seventeen-year-old daughter to wear black. Kay lowered her head and hugged herself, perched on a chair in the crowded kitchen. The sharp contrast of her long blonde hair against the little black dress she was wearing looked wrong. She was too young to be in mourning but respect had to be paid.

Weaving among the guests, Laura reached Kay and took her by the shoulders, gently guiding her out and into her bedroom. Sitting her down on the edge of her bed, she lifted Kay's chin and smiled bravely into her face. It was just a couple of weeks ago that Laura had said how grown-up Kay was, but now the expression on her mother's face showed that she was seeing her as a baby again.

'I know it hurts, Kay,' she said gently. 'It's the first time for you . . . well, apart from your brother, but you were too young to remember that.'

She hadn't been too young. She did remember it. But this wasn't the time to say so. 'Will it ever go away, Mum, this feeling inside? This pain that doesn't hurt like a pain usually does?'

Unable to answer, Laura moved across the room and looked out of the window, anything to avoid Kay's searching blue eyes.

'BERT, BERT, I LOVE THAT SHIRT!' The suddenly booming voice of good old red-faced Harry the insurance man, and the robust laughter that followed, took them by surprise.

'Mum, how could he?'

'I knew it wouldn't be long before they'd have to say something about them white frills,' Laura chuckled through her tears.

'WHERE DID YOU GET THAT SHIRT? WHERE DID YOU GET THAT SHIRT?'

Now it was the turn of Bert's brothers, Frank and Freddie. The song resounded through the flat, and there was no doubt in Kay's mind that the entire block could hear it. Shrugging, a wan smile on her lips, she joined in and encouraged her mum to do the same. Within seconds, they were singing at the tops of their voices and crying at the same time.

While the mourners braced themselves inside the flat, ready for the undertaker to arrive and screw down the lid of Bert's coffin, wreaths and tributes were arriving, and neighbours dutifully laid them outside the block of flats until the tarmac where the children usually played was covered in flowers, with only a driveway left for the funeral cars when they arrived. A wreath had even been hung over the *No Spitting* sign.

There were hearts, crosses, footballs. One arrangement was shaped like a docker's hook. It was a farewell fit for a king. Bert's family were known and liked in the East End, even by men who had connections with the underworld.

Kay watched proudly as her dad slipped his broad shoulders underneath the front of the coffin, and together with Bert's three brothers, carried it out of the flat and down the flights of stairs while the official pallbearers stayed close by, ready to move in should any of the intoxicated men give way. They need not have worried; these were strong men, full of pride, and nothing in the world would have stopped them fulfilling their role of carrying Bert to the hearse.

'Chin up, Liz mate,' one of the neighbours called out as the women stepped into the funeral car.

'Take care of 'er, Laura!' called another.

Through her black veil, Liz's tear-stained face could only manage a weak smile as she showed a hand to the crowd that had turned out.

The procession following the family mourners seemed to go on for ever, until they had left the council estate. The funeral cortège made its way along the narrow backstreets, passing several elderly gentlemen who stood with their heads lowered, caps in hand, as the cars continued towards East India docks, where they would pause to allow the rest of the dockers to pay their last respects.

'So when we remember our dearly departed Albert, let us not forget that God has always been there, from the moment of birth until death. And in our hearts we shall always remember that . . .' the vicar glanced down at the papers in front of him, 'that . . . Albert—'

'Bert!' Jack cut in impatiently. 'He was known as Bert!' His voice echoed around the silent church and was followed by mumbling from the rest of the congregation. Some were embarrassed by his outburst, some agreed with Jack, others just wanted to get the whole thing over with.

'He was christened Albert, Dad,' Kay whispered.

'I know that!' Jack's angry face turned away from her and glared up at the vicar in the pulpit. 'Just get on with it, will yer! You've bin up there for twenty minutes telling us what a lovely man we're about to bury. D'yer think we don't know that?'

'Shush, Jack. Show some respect.' Laura gripped his arm. 'The man's only doing his job.'

Jack swallowed, ran his fingers through his hair and shook his head slowly at the vicar. 'You said the same things—' there was a crack in his voice, 'two years ago, when we buried Alf the Overcoat!'

Whether it was from drink or delayed shock Kay had no idea, but she found herself giggling at her dad's remark. When she heard other people trying to stop themselves laughing she let herself go. Adding insult to injury, a mourner in the back pew then relieved himself by evacuating a long, psalmodic gust of wind.

'God, that's terrible.' Kay was deeply embarrassed by the way the vicar was losing control over his drunken congregation. The service was quickly turning into a farce.

'I'm sorry, Kay,' Laura chuckled, 'but you're gonna have to get used to the idea that this lot won't put up with hackneyed sermons. Especially not at a time like this.'

Turning her head to look at everyone, a faint smile appeared on Kay's lips. 'You're right,' she murmured, 'and so are they. And Uncle Bert would 'ave been the first to say so.'

Kay squeezed Laura's hand, then looked from her mother up to the perplexed vicar and wondered how he would manage to conduct the rest of the service. She needn't have worried; as if by telepathy, her uncle's brothers, Frank and Freddie, were making their way towards the coffin with her dad and a family friend close behind. As they lifted it on to their broad shoulders, the vicar quickly signalled to the organist to play.

A respectful hush fell upon the church as everyone softly sang Liz's chosen hymn:

Abide with me: fast falls the eventide;
The darkness deepens; Lord, with me abide:
When other helpers fail, and comforts flee,
Help of the helpless, O abide with me.

With Liz, Kay and Laura following closely behind, the men walked in a stately manner along the aisle, carrying the much loved Bert to his final resting place.

Chapter Two

'Freelance docker? There'll be bloody murders, I'm telling yer! Once the word spreads. Then we'll see. Sly bleeders.' Jack pinched the smouldering tip of his roll-up between his thumb and finger and dropped the dog-end into an ashtray. 'Giving Bert's job to an outsider? They knew what they were doing, all right.' Pushing open the lid of his tobacco tin with his thumb, he pulled out a few strands of Golden Virginia. 'They'll get more than they bargained for, you mark my words.'

Curled up in an armchair, gazing up at the ceiling, Kay couldn't help thinking about her uncle and how his name might be used to stir up more anger and add another wharf to the growing unofficial dock strike that was spreading through London. Only two weeks out of this world and not allowed to rest in peace.

'Does it really matter, Jack?' Laura said. 'At least they took someone on. One more off the dole queue.'

Jack's light blue eyes glared back at her, his high cheek-bones flushed with anger. 'You can't see it, can you? The reason the strike started up in the first place was because they did the very same thing at another wharf! A supervisor died and they gave his job to an outside man. They've done the selfsame thing to Bert. If that's not deliberately pouring oil on the fire, I dunno what is.' He flicked the top of his Zippo and lit another roll-up.

'And now more and more cases are coming to light. Most of them casuals don't hold union cards.'

Turning his back on Laura, Jack stared out of the veranda windows and sighed. 'Six regulars applied for that job, and it goes to a casual labourer.' He turned and looked her in the face. 'How d'yer reckon Bert would 'ave felt about that, eh?' He swallowed hard and pressed his lips together, willing himself not to break down.

'Leave him out of this, Jack. You'll only upset Liz. Best she doesn't know about it—'

''Course she'll get to know about it!' he barked, not bothering that she hated to be interrupted. 'You think I'm the only one who's livid?' He stormed towards the living-room door and pulled with vengeance at the handle. Turning back to her he said, 'Our blokes'll come out now; join the other wharves on strike, and if you ask me, it's about time as well!

'Once Jack Dash gets the bit between his teeth, you'll see, we'll bring this government to its knees.'

The slamming of the door behind him sent a shiver down Kay's spine. In her heart she felt that her dad was right and secretly believed that the Import Trades Committee wanted to break the trade union and eventually would. As far as she could tell from listening many times to Billy, her grandfather, who had been a stevedore for a good part of his working life, some union officials were inclined to push management too far too fast, and their demands could lead to the end of the London docks.

Slipping her feet into her shoes, Laura sat upright on the sofa, where she had hoped to have a little doze on her afternoon off. Thursday was the day she looked forward to all week. A time when the flat would be empty and she could spend an hour or so thinking.

'What time d'yer think you'll be in for dinner?' she called after Jack.

'Don't know! Leave it on steam if I'm late. And if any of the men drop by – tell 'em I'll be in the Carpenter's Arms later on!'

Relieved that Jack would be out for the rest of the afternoon, she kicked off her shoes again and lay down, flinching at the sound of the front door banging behind him.

'I wish he wouldn't slam the door like that,' Laura said, closing her eyes.

'I'm going out for a walk, to the museum.' Kay kissed her mother lightly on the cheek.

'I thought you'd grown out of that,' Laura smiled as her eyes glazed over. She was remembering. 'You used to spend hours in that place, gazing at that big doll's house . . . you must know every nook and cranny.'

'I won't be long. Enjoy your catnap.'

Resting her head on a cushion, Laura closed her eyes and tried not to think about the turbulent weeks that lay ahead. For Jack to walk out of the docks as soon as he heard about Bert's job going the way it had meant that a few others would have followed him. It was just over an hour since he had thrown down his docker's hook in a temper. The entire wharf would have heard about the business and there would be pandemonium.

It was all a far cry from the dreams of tranquillity and country living she had been caught up in just over two years ago. Allowing the face of Richard, her ex-lover, to move into her imagination, she wondered if they would ever see each other again.

While Liz sadly packed her few belongings into a small suitcase, Kay sat on the edge of the bed studying a holiday brochure. She had given up trying to persuade her aunt to stay on another week until she had had more time to get over Uncle Bert. Looking up from the colourful pictures of sand, sea and sunshine, Kay studied Liz's face. She was caught up in another world.

'Why don't you come to Spain with me, Aunt Liz? I'll look after you.'

A faint smile swept across the ageing face. 'I couldn't take that foreign food, Mog. I've only just got used to the idea of eating chicken chow mein. Besides, they eat horse meat over there, don't they?' She chuckled, carefully folding her mauve cardigan and laying it on top of a grey skirt.

'Dad always goes on about that, but I never know if he's kidding or what.'

'Your dad's all right about you going, then?'

Knowing how her dad had first reacted to the idea of her going away with her friends, and abroad at that, Kay knew that he wouldn't give in on this one. 'He'll come round.' She couldn't keep the touch of defiance from her voice.

'I wouldn't bank on it.'

Kay laid the brochure on top of her aunt's open suitcase. 'Look at that. He can't have anything against me going there. It looks like paradise!'

'Yeah. So do all the pictures in them magazines.'

'It beats hop-picking though, don't it?' Kay smiled, turning over the pages, hoping to impress her aunt.

Sitting on the edge of the bed next to Kay, Liz became pensive, staring at nothing. Kay knew she was thinking about Uncle Bert. She had a vision of him herself, bending down by the fireplace outside the huts, setting it up ready for cooking the Sunday pot- roast.

'He was a good picker.' Liz smiled. 'Loved the smell of them 'ops; and the flavour it added to his cheese sandwiches.'

'Didn't put hops in with the cheese, did he?' Kay said, trying to lighten the atmosphere.

'No. The taste came from handling 'em.' Liz looked down at her own hands and thumbed her wedding ring. 'Poor old Bert,' she whispered, 'two years of saving up for that caravan and now he'll never get the chance—'

'But you will, Aunt Liz, and that's why he bought it in the first place,' Kay cut in. 'For you. To make up for no more hopping. You know he did.'

'Yeah.' Liz patted her niece's hand, 'You're right there, Mog. He would 'ave died a little bit easier knowing he'd left me that hut on wheels.'

'Liz!' The bedroom door flew open and Laura stood in front of them grinning from ear to ear. 'That was the employment officer at Hammond's on the phone! You've got the job! The crotchety old cow's turned out to be human after all.'

'Oh, Laura. I 'aven't worked for over five years.' A worried expression came to Liz's face.

'You'll fit into that canteen like a glove. The women are great, you'll love 'em.'

'What will I 'ave to do?'

'Serve the staff with tea and sandwiches. Couldn't be easier.'

'It will get you out of the house, Aunt Liz,' Kay added.

Sighing, Liz rolled her eyes. 'When do I start?'

'Monday.' Laura grinned.

'What do I wear?'

'They'll give you a pink and white check overall and a little white hat.'

'But will they 'ave one in my size?'

'Will you care if it's a bit loose?'

'Do me a favour, Laura. Whose uniform will I be slipping into, two-ton Tessie's?'

Laura gave Liz a quick once-over. 'You've lost at least a stone Liz, I bet you're down to ten now.'

Liz liked that. She stood up and examined herself in the mirror. 'You could be right there, Mog. This frock's hanging off me. Reckon I'll 'ave to use a bit of the insurance money to buy some new clothes.'

An encouraging cheer went up from Kay and Laura as Liz turned away, embarrassed. 'To please Bert, of course,' she added quickly. 'He wouldn't want me looking like a sack of potatoes.'

Making fun of her own position in the fashion department at Hammond's, Laura stood behind Liz and pulled at the spare fabric of her dress until it was skin-tight. 'This dress was simply *made* for modom! A little tuck here and a little tuck there.'

'Think I might 'ave a little rinse when I go to the hairdresser's. What d'yer reckon on a Deep Chestnut?' Liz was beginning to sound like her old self again.

'Only if you let me pay,' Laura said.

'You're on. Manicure?' she asked, pushing her luck.

'A bottle of nail varnish. If you behave yourself.' Laura turned to Kay and the smile drained from her face when she saw the holiday brochure in her hands.

Letting go of Liz's dress, Laura looked at the reflection in the mirror and raised an eyebrow. Then picking up one of thc brochures she flicked through the brightly coloured pages and slowly shook her head.

'It's no good, Kay. Your dad won't budge on this one. No way he'll let you go abroad.'

'No?'

'No!'

'Pamela's parents can't seem to understand his attitude. She's ready and waiting to book. Waiting for me to make up my mind.' Kay was feigning indifference, determined to get her way in the end.

'She'll be going with a proper travel agent, Laura.'

'Talk to Jack, Liz, not me. She can go to Australia for all I care!' Laura stormed out of the spare room.

'She doesn't want you to go either, then?'

'No.' Kay was close to tears.

'It's only because they're worried about you. You're all they've got. You mean everything to 'em.'

How many times that thought had gone through Kay's mind she couldn't say. One thing was clear though. She was beginning to feel trapped by their devotion. Somehow she would have to make them realize that she was a person as well as their only child.

'I only wanna go for two weeks. And to Spain, not outer space.'

'Perhaps next year, eh? Give 'em time to get used to the idea that you're growing up.'

'Don't you mean *grown*-up?' Turning away Kay lowered her voice. 'And still a virgin, in case that's what's bothering them.' Before Liz had time to butt in, she continued, 'And if they think I'm going all that way just to lose it to some Spaniard they need their brains looking at.'

'I don't think that's what's on their minds.' Liz couldn't help smiling.

'Oh, of course it is! Why else would they want to stop me?'

'You don't listen to a word I say, do you?'

'I heard what you said but I don't agree. It's not because I'm an only child!' She hid her face behind the pages and murmured, 'Anyway I'm going, no matter what they say.'

'You think I don't know that? You'll be forging his signature on your passport, knowing you.' With that risky remark, Liz quietly left the room.

Staring into space, Kay suddenly felt lighter inside as she remembered an article she had read in a woman's magazine. An astrologer had written that while some people felt trapped by invisible bindings others put on them, what they failed to realize was that all it took was an invisible knife to cut themselves free.

Turning back to the picture of white sand and turquoise sea, Kay knew that it was time for her to do just that. How that could be achieved and when was something else. But do it she would, before they suffocated her.

Reversing into the edge of the kerb outside Liz's house, Jack's face fell as he caught sight of the white blinds on the windows. A reminder of what they had left behind. 'You sure you'll be all right on your own, Liz?'

'You are gonna come in?' She tried to cover the concern in her voice.

''Course I am. I'm talking about once I've left.' He pulled the brake on and turned to face his sister. 'I would stop the night, but I've got the meeting—'

'I don't want you to stop the night,' Liz cut in. 'I've got to start fending for myself sometime.' She looked back into Jack's face. 'You can stay for a cup of tea though, can't yer?'

''Course I can. Don't 'ave to be there for another hour.'

Liz sat her handbag square on her lap and sighed. 'I hope you know what you're letting us all in for, Jack. If this strike spreads the way you want it to.'

'It will,' he cut in. 'We'll go for an all-out if the managers don't back down. Hundreds 'ave joined us already.'

'Yeah, and hundreds of wives will be wondering 'ow they're gonna feed their kids on strike pay.'

Jack leaned back in his seat and stared out of the window. 'I'm telling you, Liz, this is the beginning of the end. If we let the London Port Employers get away with this one, they'll be replacing registered dockers with non-union and casual labourers in no time.' He looked her straight in the eye. 'I've got a horrible feeling that the Dock Labour Board might welsh on us. So far it's just their attitude, but it all starts with a look, don't it? I reckon they'll approve listed men to unload vessels. They'll be condoning this "unofficial strike" next; you see if I'm wrong.'

'You're spending a lot of time on this strike, Jack. Kay and Laura's not seen much of you, if anything.'

'I know that. But this is our livelihood, Lizzie. If we don't safeguard it, who knows what the future'll hold?' He gave her one of his cheeky winks. 'Our Kay might marry a docker for all we know. For all 'er grand ideas, she might just settle for living by the docks in the end.'

Liz didn't want to get into that conversation right then. She had argued enough with her brother that he should encourage Kay to see a bit more of the world.

'It's a changing world all right,' she said instead, shifting the subject. 'Remember I said it would be different in the sixties? There's a strong feeling in the air. It's as if someone's messing about with the electricity; new lights coming on and old ones going out.'

'Well, all the more reason then to make sure our light bulbs stay right where they are and linked to the power!' Jack reached out and pulled one of Liz's carrier bags from the back seat. 'Now get out and get in there! I'm gasping for a cup of tea.'

Once inside the small terraced back-to-back, Jack took the stairs two at a time, saying he needed to have a pee. Slowly pushing open Liz and Bert's bedroom door he took a deep breath and went inside, making for the double bed. With one swift movement he pulled both pillows together, centred them and laid the special sympathy card he had bought that day on the silky gold eiderdown. Jack knew that going to bed alone was going to be a crippling emotional experience for his sister. At least she would have his letter, which he had slipped inside the card to help her through that first night.

With his invisible blinkers firmly in place, Jack strode out of the room. The last thing he wanted was to see Bert's personal bits and pieces around. Had he looked down, he would have seen the brown socks beside the bed that his brother-in-law and best friend had peeled off the night before he died.

'You know, it wouldn't hurt you to get yourself a decent-sized telly out of the insurance money, Liz.' Jack had been racking his brains for what he might suggest could fill his sister's lonely evenings. 'I know someone who'd snap up your old set.'

'We'll see, Jack, we'll see.' Liz didn't want to think about the insurance money. 'Don't rush me, eh?'

'I just don't like to think of you by yourself.'

'Are you kidding? By myself? I'll have to pretend I'm out once my bingo friends start coming round to see me.'

'Yeah, that's true.' Jack smiled. 'You've always drawn 'em like a magnet. I was forgetting.'

'You was getting downhearted, Jack, I know that. I'm not daft. You're sitting in your best mate's front room, drinking a cup of tea, and he's not here and never will be.' Liz seemed to be drawing strength from her brother's weakness.

'Lizzie! You're one in a million, you know that?' He shook his head at her. 'And you can read me like a book.'

'Yeah. Who d'yer wanna give my old television set to, then?' she asked with a knowing smile.

'No one! I was thinking about you!'

'So you wasn't trying to kill two birds with one stone?' She pulled her little blue tin out of her pocket and sprinkled some snuff on to the back of her hand.

''Course I wasn't.' Jack looked away and wondered if Liz could see into his mind. It was true, he did have an ulterior motive, but the thought really had only just come to him.

'Anyway, if I do decide, I'll let you have first refusal,' Liz said, in a mock-posh voice.

'Don't do me any favours,' he grumbled and sipped his tea, wishing he hadn't mentioned it in the first place. Liz was a canny woman and probably had a hunch he was thinking of paying Patsy a visit.

As Kay gazed out of an upper window of the 253 bus into the city on her way to work, the idea of forging her father's name on a passport form became a real possibility. It seemed the only way, since Jack had repeated the night before that she would only be allowed to go abroad when she was twenty-one. Unable to contain herself, she flashed a smile at the plump West Indian lady sitting beside her. Kay blushed as she heard herself telling a complete stranger that she was going to Spain for a holiday. 'Any room in your suitcase for me?' The woman grinned, showing off gleaming white teeth. 'I could do with some sunshine in me bones.'

Standing up ready to get off at the next stop, Kay bent down and whispered into her travelling companion's ear, 'I'm gonna forge my passport form.'

The woman's eyes widened and before she could say anything, Kay shrugged. 'It's the only way. My dad won't let me go.' Making her way along the aisle, she grabbed the handrail as the bus pulled to a halt. 'Don't look so worried,' she called back, 'it might never happen!'

'I hope for your sake that it don't!' The woman shook her head at another traveller. 'Kids,' she said, and suddenly burst out laughing. Her peals rang through the bus and caused a fever of excitement to light Kay up as she jumped down on to the pavement. The woman was wishing her luck.

Making her way towards the building where she worked as typist and Girl Friday in the company secretary's office of Thompson's Windows, Kay began to make a mental list of the clothes she would take on holiday and the things she would need to buy. Her fortnightly salary amounted to just under fifteen pounds after stoppages, and she had hardly any savings. She would have to take the part-time job she had been offered in the tobacconist's the previous week, which would mean a ten-minute walk after work. It would also mean that her Saturdays and Sunday mornings would be spent serving customers instead of seeing her mates in the coffee bar.

'Day-dreaming again?' Jane from the typing pool grinned as she leaned across Kay and caught the far-away look in her eyes.

'Yeah,' she smiled, 'well, you know.'

Laughing, Jane looked up at the big round clock which hung below the company sign. 'We're ten minutes early. Fancy a frothy coffee?'

'Yeah, but that would make us ten minutes late, and you know what Mr Grieves is like for punctuality.' Kay pushed open the heavy glass-panelled door.

'I'm sorry to hear about your uncle,' Jane said, pressing her finger on the small brass lift button.

'Thanks.' Kay didn't want to think about it.

The sudden arrival of the lift, and the crash as Alf threw back the metal concertina doors, ended the conversation. Alf was thick with establishment.

'Makes a change for you girls to be early,' he said in his high-handed way. 'After a rise, are you?'

'No, Alf,' Kay smirked as she stepped into the lift, 'we just can't wait to see your welcoming face.'

Looking at his watch, the stern-faced man put it to his ear to check it hadn't stopped. 'We'll wait a few minutes,' he said, raising his chin defiantly. 'No point in wasting energy. There'll be more staff arriving soon.'

'Don't worry about it, Alfred, we'll walk.' Kay stepped out of the lift followed by her friend, and together they quickly stepped up the wide granite stairway, their stiletto sling-back shoes creating a clicking echo as they raised their voices so that Alf would hear them say how antiquated the lift was, and it was time the firm changed it for an automatic one. Then, slipping into one of the panelled boardrooms, they sat down on velvet-covered easy chairs and shared a filter-tip cigarette, keeping an eye on the frosted glass walls for anyone passing by.

Kay listened with keen interest as her friend related her crazy weekend adventure. She had met a gorgeous mod at the Tottenham Royal dance hall and was in love again. A feeling of envy flared briefly in Kay but soon died. She had had boyfriends and a fair share of dates, but none of them had made her feel the way she had about Zacchi, the gypsy she left behind on the hop fields in Kent, just over two years ago. One day he would appear on her doorstep – she felt sure of it.

'So what was you day-dreaming about earlier on?' her friend asked, hoping for a return love story.

'Nothing much.' Kay pushed back her chair ready to leave. 'Come on, we'd best get out of here before we're caught.' She had no intention of telling her about the plan, no matter how friendly they were. No one must know. They might just spill the beans and stop her doing something that now seemed the most important thing in her life – getting a passport.

Cautiously the girls crept out of the plush surroundings; if Kay had had any idea right then that she would feel like ending her misery in that very same boardroom, after being falsely accused of a crime she did not commit, her smiles and hopes would have been shattered. She had had a glimpse of prison life as a young child, when her dad had taken her to see her uncle Bert's brother, Frank, on the Isle of Sheppey – before she was taken for a paddle in the sea.

* * *

'Hallo, Thompson's,' said Kay in her poshest accent, learned from Marge on the switchboard. 'Thank you – putting you through now.' She pulled a plug on a black lead and pushed it into the correct extension number; pushed another key forward and told another caller she was sorry to keep him waiting. Answered another outside line, pulled at another plug and put the customer through; pushed another key forward and told someone else that the extension they wanted was now free, that she was connecting her. Reflexes on the switchboard had to be fast and concentration at peak level. Kay loved it. It was the highlight of her day when she relieved one of the telephonists for an hour, and was always surprised at how the time had flown by once the woman returned to take up her position.

'Come on, Kay, up you get,' Marge smiled at her apprentice. 'You'll be putting me out of a job soon.'

'Did you remember to buy my fruit?' June, the second telephonist asked. 'I've lost four pounds already. Hallo Thompson's. Thank you, you're through – I forgot to ask you to get me some cottage cheese for my dinner tonight. Sorry to keep you – line's still engaged. I've got to lose a stone in three weeks.'

Laughing, Marge said that one day June would say the wrong thing to the wrong person and upset a caller. Turning to Kay, who was removing the headphones, she gave her a studious look. 'You're looking a bit serious, lovey. Nothing wrong is there?'

'No, I was just thinking about my second job. I should be starting next week. I've never served in a shop before.'

'Second job?' Marge was grave.

'Maynard's, up by the Angel station.'

There was a heavy silence as both Marge and June looked from her to each other and back again. 'They don't allow you to have a second job here, lovey.' Marge spoke as if it were written in blood.

'Well, I won't tell them then.'

June covered her ears and chuckled. 'I never heard a word of that.'

'If they find out, Kay, they could give you the sack.'

'Oh, Marge . . . they wouldn't do that!'

'It's happened before, sweetheart. They don't like to think that your mind's not on the job they're paying you to do. And let's face it, Kay, you are a bit of a scatterbrain at times.'

'No I'm not! Well, not when it comes to my work.' The door suddenly flew open and Mr Grieves appeared, looking far from tranquil.

'Isn't it time you were back in the office, Kay?' He looked at his pocket watch. 'You should have been off the switchboard four minutes ago.' He let the door swing shut between them.

'See what I mean?' Marge said, half smiling.

'Yeah,' Kay was thoughtful. 'You two won't say anything, will yer?'

They shook their heads; they wouldn't dream of splitting on her, but they didn't think she should take the risk of losing her job.

'I need the money,' said Kay, walking towards the door, 'I'm saving up to go on holiday. To Spain.'

'I don't know,' Marge shook her head again. 'That kid seems to tempt providence at least once a month.'

Laura tried to keep the worry of Kay out of her mind while she was at work in the fashion department at Hammond's. She knew her daughter could be moody at times, but this business of going abroad seemed to have possessed her. She wasn't sure that, should Kay get a taste of travelling, she would want to settle down again.

'I can't see anything wrong with it.' The customer looked sideways at herself in the long mirror.

'I'm not sure . . .' Laura was trying tactfully to persuade a fifty-year-old woman away from the trapeze-line dress which stopped just above the knee, and was beginning to lose interest. When Liz came bustling in she was more than pleased to see her.

'Laura – I don't think I can go through with it.' Liz looked flushed and out of breath. Perspiration was trickling from her forehead down the side of her face. 'This bloody watch Jack got me to replace the bangle I lost is losing time, I swear it.'

Laura lifted Liz's hand and checked the time. 'It's fast, Liz, by ten minutes.'

'I'm sweating like a pig.' Liz wiped her forehead with a hanky, and then her armpits, feeling acutely embarrassed when the customer threw her a disgusted look.

Laura knew this woman was capable of finding a few select words to make her sister-in-law feel like dirt, so she took Liz by the arm and guided her away.

'I shan't keep you a moment.' Turning from the smirking face she winked at Liz. Then looking back at the woman Laura paused, and pretended to admire her from the short distance between them. 'You know I think you were right, that style and colour does suit you. I thought those pink roses were too much, but they bring out the colour of your eyes.'

'Oh really?' The woman lapped up the compliment like a cat with double cream.

'I'll leave you alone for a couple of minutes. Feel free to wheel the other mirror over so you can see how lovely you look from all sides.' Seeing the suppressed grin on Liz's face, Laura marched her away.

'She looks like a lampshade gone wrong,' Liz murmured, keeping a deadpan expression. 'How she couldn't tell you was giving her the old flannel, I'll never know.'

'It's what she wanted to hear,' Laura whispered.

'I didn't mean to be late, Laura. I didn't wanna let you down.'

'You're not late, Liz. Bang on time. Stop worrying – you're making *me* feel nervous.'

As they moved through the store and into the staff canteen, Laura felt Liz relax when she saw the other members of staff smiling and sharing a joke or two. Once they spotted Liz, they gathered round and made her welcome. Feeling comfortable about leaving her there, Laura went back to the ageing would-be Dior model in her own department.

After her first day at work, Liz was only too pleased to follow Laura through the green gate into Delamar Place to spend ten minutes with Kay's grandfather. Once inside that small haven with the old brick wall separating them from the busy Whitechapel Road, Liz sighed with relief and admired the tiny front gardens of the cottages which were full of daffodils, tulips and hyacinths. Laura's dad, known as Billy to Liz, looked up, smiled and stretched. He was proud of his front garden and even prouder of the lovely, weed-free old paved pathway.

'Well?' he grinned, showing off a new set of teeth. 'How'd you get on, Liz?'

'Piece of cake.'

He nodded and shrugged. 'And a nice cup of tea to go with it, I suppose?'

Laughing at his little joke, they waited while he finished the job in hand, easing a stubborn weed from between the stones.

'It's a wonder you don't do your back in, Billy, bending over like that,' said Liz with a touch of concern.

'My back's got more spring in it than a young chicken. And don't forget to wipe your feet.'

Following the old man into his small, cosy living room, Laura couldn't help feeling a touch of regret at the passing of the old gas mantles which she had loved to hear burning as a child. The gentle hiss was a familiar, comforting sound. Only five months ago electric light bulbs had taken their place. The cottage had finally been converted and brought in line with the very modern world of the sixties.

'Three sugars, innit, Liz?'

'Yes, Billy, and strong.' Liz sank back into the comfortable old leather armchair and kicked her shoes off, while Laura bent down beside the small Victorian fireplace and poked at the orange glow before adding a bit more coke.

'He'll never change, will he?' Laura chuckled.

'Let's 'ope not.'

'I think it's where our Kay gets her stubbornness from.'

'You reckon?' Liz chuckled knowingly.

Laura ignored that. She knew her sister-in-law well enough to take the meaning. 'Look at this, Liz. He's still putting crumbs out for that mouse.'

'Better than having a dog to feed. Cheaper.'

'Yeah, but what happens when the mouse has babies?'

'It won't!' her dad yelled from the scullery. 'She's a boy!'

'And how do you know that?'

'Mice 'ave been trying to set up 'ome in this cottage for years and I've managed to keep them down. I should know the difference by now!'

'That's put you in your place.' Liz closed her eyes.

'We'll see,' Laura said, settling herself in the other armchair. 'Mr Know-all's not always right.'

'Thought I'd 'ave a bit of liver and bacon for me dinner,' Billy said as he arrived with the small tray. 'You found yourself a chap yet, Liz, or what?'

'Dad!' Feeling acutely embarrassed, Laura eyed Liz for her reaction.

'Thought I might move in with you, Billy,' Liz teased, hiding the hurt. 'You can get a good tune from an old fiddle.'

Setting the tray down on a small wooden table, the old man laughed. 'Not me, girl. Too set in me ways. And Billy's willy's had it. I haven't had a bone in me dick for years.'

Liz roared with laughter while Laura could do nothing but shake her head, mildly disapproving. Leaving them to talk over old times, Laura went into the part-modernized scullery to peel some potatoes ready for her father to boil, and to toss the thick slice of lamb's liver in flour. Gazing round the scullery she felt a mixture of pride and sadness at the way the old man kept it. He still used the fuel-fired copper boiler to do his washing, and her mum's old mangle to squeeze the water from his clothes. She couldn't knock it though, his tea towels were sparkling white and the smell of washing powder, bleach and starch reminded her of the old days when she was a child and helped her mother with the Monday wash. She hoped he would never get rid of the old washboard propped in the corner.

'At least you can rest in peace, Mum. He takes good care of himself,' she murmured.

'I tell you, Liz!' her dad was shouting now, and laughing. 'When I woke up in that ditch the next morning . . .'

They were talking about Liz's favourite subject – hop-picking. At least they had their stories. Machines might have ripped away the future for hop-pickers but they couldn't snatch back the wonderful memories.

Folding a tea towel over a wooden rail, Laura's mind was filled again with Richard. She remembered having counted up the few weeks of each year they were together; it amounted to just five months. They had only ever seen each other during the hop-picking season, since both were married and committed to their families. The end of hop-picking had meant the end of their affair.

Richard often moved in and out of her thoughts. Apart from her husband, Jack, he had been her only love. And they had loved each other. Possibly still did. But their relationship had to be left to fade away, for everyone's sake. Especially Kay's. Guilt swept through Laura as her daughter's face now filled her mind. The time when she cried to Laura that she knew about the affair and how she didn't want her mum and dad to get divorced.

'Laura!' Liz's voice broke into her thoughts. 'Your dad wants me to take a trip over to France with 'im! Can I trust 'im, or what?'

Laura tried to smile, but it was impossible when her mind was on other things. Not that she didn't want to be with Jack – she did. They were all right now. Both had worked at getting back what they had before the marriage went on the rocks. But it wasn't the same as Richard, and she knew in her heart that it never would be. It seemed to Laura that emotions had a will of their own, and no matter how hard the fight, she couldn't change what happened by itself, inside.

'What's up now?' Liz took Laura by surprise as she stood in the doorway. 'You look as if you've lost two bob and found a penny.'

'I'm all right. Miles away.' She forced a smile. 'I'd best be getting on home. Jack'll be wanting his tea before he goes out to his meeting.'

'All right, Mog, you do that. I'll stop a bit longer, keep your dad company.'

Kissing her father lightly on the forehead, Laura squeezed his arm. 'Phone if you want anything, Dad, won't yer?'

'If I want anything, I'll walk round and ask you. I'm not using that contraption unless I 'ave to. Don't know why your Jack went to the expense of having it put in here in the first place. Just another bloody bill to think about.'

Laura folded her arms and stared him out until he finally gave in.

'All right, all right. If I don't feel well enough to come round, I'll use the bloody thing.' He looked up at his daughter's insistent face. 'Especially if I take bad in the night.'

'Good. That's what it's there for. I'll pop in after work tomorrow. Have your laundry ready for me to iron, OK?'

'Yeah, yeah, yeah. Go on, get going. You should be there when your old man gets in from work.'

'From where?' Laura asked pointedly.

'Oh, right, I forgot. The strike. What's new?'

'Don't ask, Dad. I'm sick of hearing about it. One thing I do know, it's spreading fast. See you at work, Liz.' With that Laura left, closing the door quietly behind her.

As she walked along Cleveland Way, Laura mulled over Liz's words. *Lost two bob and found a penny.* Little did her sister-in-law know how near to the mark she had been. Leaving Richard behind for Jack had felt a bit like that at the time. But the pennies were mounting up again, like the months that had passed. She half hoped that Richard would eventually fade from her mind altogether, leaving her free to love only those who were close to her.

Waves of guilt broke over her again. It wasn't fair on Jack that she should even be thinking about that time. He had done his utmost to make it up to her once they were back together. And he had turned out to be a good, caring husband. And loyal too.

* * *

Looking down from the makeshift platform at a meeting of dockers and speakers outside the gates of St Katharine's Dock, Jack was missing Bert's company and moral support. Some of the faces were familiar to him, but out of the hundreds of men there, he recognized only thirty or so from his own wharf. Blocking his emotions in order to deliver the rest of his speech, Jack tensed his body and clenched his fists.

'When they gave Bert's job to an outside man instead of a regular, they were doing no less than testing our strength! Over a dozen names were submitted and they chose one who just so happened to be a casual worker! Coincidence? I don't think so! And as we all know, his wasn't the first job to go that way!

'That firm has over three hundred men on the permanent labour force! And this isn't the first time it's drawn on the casual labour pool for work!' He stopped for a breather while the men, aroused, yelled their own opinions on the subject.

'And now we hear rumours that the National Dock Labour Board has taken the decision that firms *may* use unregistered labour. Well, if that turns out to be the case, brothers, I vote the men in our wharf stay out until the decision is revoked!'

A loud cheer went up and the men raised their hands to show they would remain on strike. Bringing his speech to an end, Jack dropped his tone and spoke gravely.

'And for those few misguided anti-strikers who have been heard to say that I'm using Bert's death to attack the London Board, they are very much mistaken. When this dispute is over – and please God, may it be soon – and the London Port Employers have realized how wrong they were, then maybe we can say that something good did come out of something tragic, and Bert's death hasn't been a complete waste.'

A hush fell on the crowd as one by one they removed their caps to show respect for a fellow docker.

Jack was pleased to see Kay as he strode along the Whitechapel Road on his way home from the meeting. She hadn't seen him, and he quickened his pace to catch her before she went into Lyon's coffee shop. He didn't dare call out for fear of embarrassing her, should there be a young man on the other side of the window she was peering into.

'All right, babe?' he playfully tapped her head with his folded newspaper.

'God, you scared the life out of me!'

Jack had been right; a quick glance into the shop and he could see young Pamela and a couple of boys inside. 'See you later,' he grinned, and walked on.

Checking her reflection, Kay pushed open the glass door and made her way towards the threesome.

'Coffee?' Tommy was quick off the mark.

'Please.' Kay remembered how she'd wished he was a bit taller when she first saw him.

'Cappuccino?'

'Prefer frothy coffee, if that's OK.'

Pamela started to giggle and tossed back her long, straight black hair. 'It's the same thing, Kay!'

Ray Charles's voice, on the juke box, broke through the embarrassing pause as he sang 'Hit the Road Jack'.

'Guess what I've got in my handbag?' Kay boasted.

'Can't be bothered.' Pamela pushed her fringe out of her eyes and made a point of not looking at Kay. She was irked about something, and Kay was in no doubt that she would let her know what it was once the boys had gone. She sat down and pushed her face up close to Pamela's.

'Think of a hot, sunny, sandy place – palm trees . . .'

'That's a lot to get in a little handbag!' Micky grinned.

'Two words: the first begins with "p" and the second with "f".'

Arriving with a steaming cup of coffee, Tommy started to laugh. 'A "p" and "f", eh?'

Before they started making crude guesses, Kay pulled a manila envelope out and waved it in Pamela's face. 'Passport form,' she grinned.

'It isn't!' she shrieked, shedding her sophistication. 'Honest?'

'Yep.'

'They said yes?'

'Not quite.'

'What d'yer mean, not quite? Either they did or they didn't!'

Kay shrugged. 'They didn't.'

Sitting back in her chair, Pamela pouted, sulking, and looked daggers at Kay. 'You're not funny.'

Leaning forward, Kay whispered to all three of them. 'I've got it down to a fine art now. I've been practising.' They waited. 'My dad's signature. I'm gonna forge it on to this very special visitor's passport form. And I went into the booth on Whitechapel station on my way here and got my snapshots done.'

'Let's 'ave a look then,' Tommy was making it clear just how keen he was on Kay.

Pulling them out of the pocket of her suede jacket, she passed them over without so much as a thought. Her mind was still on the passport form. 'So you can go ahead and book the tickets.' She sat back in her chair, sipped her coffee and winked at Pamela. 'Six weeks' time and we'll be sunning ourselves silly.'

'You can't do it, Kay,' Pamela shook her head.

'You watch me. This afternoon when Dad's at his strike meeting.'

'I mean it! You can't *do* it!'

'It doesn't matter what you say – it's as good as done.'

Looking at his watch, Tommy stood up. 'I'm gonna 'ave to go.' He passed the photographs back to Kay. 'Will you be in the Black Boy tonight?'

'No,' Pamela answered for her. 'The Beggar's. You get some good parties there.'

'Yeah. Good villains as well.' Tommy made it clear he wouldn't be going.

'How about the Prospect of Whitby?'

'Nar. Full of medical students.' He was having none of that.

'How about the Artichoke?'

'Sounds good to me,' Pamela chimed in.

'As long as we don't stay in there but go on to the Black Boy or the Two Puddings.'

'See you at eight,' Tommy said, smiling at Kay. The two boys strolled out as if they had all the time in the world.

'Thanks for flirting with Tommy.' Pamela was fuming.

'I never so much as showed a knee!' Pulling her mug shots out of the envelope, Kay was taken aback. 'Look at this! One's missing. Tommy must 'ave torn it off.'

There was a pause, and their eyes met, Pamela feeling jealous and Kay suddenly in the mood for love and romance.

'You're really gonna do it, then?'

'Yep. I've got my seven and six, my photographs and my form. I'm all set. Spain, here we come!'

Chapter Three

Liz was serving Bob, the fire officer, with a cup of tea and a cheese roll when Laura arrived looking flushed and unnerved.

'That'll be tenpence, love,' said Liz, giving Laura a quick once-over. 'What's up with you?' she asked, pressing a key on the till. 'Another snotty-nosed customer got under your skin?' She handed Bob the change and tut-tutted when he grabbed her hand playfully.

'Liz, ask one of the others to cover for you. I need to talk.'

'That bad?'

Laura couldn't answer; she was on the verge of tears. Dragging a chair out from under a table for two, she sat down and pulled a filter-tip cigarette from her packet and waited for Liz to join her.

'Try to hide your feelings a bit, Laura, for Christ's sake. The world and all its children can see you're fuming about something.'

Laura sipped her tea and tried to compose herself. It wasn't going to be easy, confronting Liz, but it had to be done. She had to know right away whether her sister-in-law knew about the devastating secret that Jack had been keeping from her.

'Come on then,' Liz sniffed, 'spit it out. Who's upset yer?'

'Can't you guess?' Laura couldn't keep the spite out of her voice. 'Who's usually responsible for turning me inside out?'

Liz sighed. It had to be her brother Jack. Who else could bring out the worst in Laura? 'What's he done now?'

'*You* tell *me*.' She looked into Liz's eyes and waited.

'Tell you what?'

Laura drew a letter from the pocket of her red and navy blue dress and pushed it towards Liz. 'If you know about this, Liz, I would rather you said so. Please don't lie to me.'

While Liz slowly read through the letter, Laura talked quietly. 'I can't believe he's been keeping in touch with her all this time. I never made any demands. I just presumed he would put that part of his life out of his mind. Now I can't stop wondering if he's been up there to see her; see their baby. Maybe he's waiting for the right time to tell me he wants to leave. Perhaps he's just been pretending he's happy with me, when all the time he's been making plans to leave once Kay's left the nest.'

'No, Laura! That's rubbish and you know it. He idolizes you. This was a serious mistake that he's still having to pay for.' Liz folded the letter and slipped it back into the envelope. 'How would you feel if he *had* wiped her and the boy out of his life?'

'How did you know it was a boy? It doesn't say so in that letter.'

'Jack told me.'

Covering her face with both hands, Laura took a deep breath and willed herself not to cry. She hoped Liz wouldn't try to get her to speak. She needn't have worried, they had known each other long enough to realize when silence was sacred.

Laura finally came out from behind her hands and managed a weak smile. 'It hurts,' she said with a touch of bitterness.

'If I talk,' Liz said, 'are you up to listening, or shall we wait till the day's done and we can be private?'

'Wait. I'll come round to you after work. I'll leave cold ham and salad for Kay and a note to say where I am.'

'And Jack?'

Laura turned away, swallowed hard. 'I'll leave enough for him as well.'

'Good girl.' Liz squeezed Laura's hand. 'It'll all come out right, you'll see.'

Laura raised her eyes and looked into Liz's face. 'Two years he's kept this from me. Sharing something as important as a child with someone else. There's a lot to be put right, Liz. I thought that like me, Jack had stopped living lies.'

'This is a lie left over from the past, Laura. That's different. Just remember that the little boy didn't ask to be part of this. He's innocent. Probably the only innocent one in this drama. You played your part in it as well. While Jack was happy somewhere else it gave you a clearer conscience to, well, you know . . . Richard Wright?'

'I might have known I'd be held responsible!'

Chuckling, Liz picked up the empty cups and saucers. 'That's more like it. Anger's better than sorrow any day. See you later.'

Once Laura was back in her own department, with no customers to attend to, she pulled out the letter and read it again.

Dear Jack,

Just a line to say that the chickenpox has finally gone and we are having peaceful nights again. Thank you for the postal order, it's a weight off of my mind to know that I can pay a month's rent in advance. My mother is still asking me to move in with her but I know it would never work; not while I have little Jac with me. Only last week she dropped hints about my having him adopted. She means well.

I have managed to get some piece-work, machining zips into men's trousers. At least it means I can work and look after the sprat at the same time, and it puts bread on the table. No other news. I don't get out much, but my mother's making inquiries about a second-hand television she knows will be coming up for sale. Some lucky sod will be buying an eighteen-inch set, no doubt.

There seems to be more work up here, for the men that is. Especially skilled builders and decorators. Everyone seems to be having small extensions built. All right for some. Tom will be coming to sit with me tonight. He's been very kind and I'm growing fond of him.

Try to get up here soon. We don't want you to lose touch with your boy, do we?

Write soon,

Patsy.

Laura shivered, thinking back to the time she first discovered that Patsy was carrying Jack's child. She couldn't help wondering if she should have kicked him out then. She wondered what her present life might have been like now, had she done so. At the time her main concern had been Kay. She hadn't wanted to put her through the trauma of her parents splitting up, filing for divorce. Maybe she had been wrong. Maybe Jack had spent the past two years wishing he was with this other woman.

'Mum?' Kay's voice echoed around Laura's thoughts as she sat hunched over the letter, choked, with tears in her eyes. 'You OK?'

Snapping out of her melancholy, Laura looked up and blinked. 'Kay! It *is* you. I thought I heard your voice.'

'Of course it's me.' She eyed the letter in Laura's trembling hands. 'Bad news?'

'No, not really. A letter from an old friend. I was swept away with nostalgia for a minute.' She slipped the letter back into her pocket. 'What're you doing here? Shouldn't you be at work?'

'I pretended I didn't feel well this morning. Mr Grieves finally condescended to let me go after lunch-time.'

'You did what?' Laura felt herself tense, gazing at her one and only child who seemed to be maturing by the day. She found herself wishing she could turn back the clock and relive those times when chubby little Kay with blue eyes and blonde hair would nuzzle up to her and fall asleep on her breast.

'I had somewhere to go, Mum. And I've got something to tell yer.'

Kay's voice hadn't really changed that much, she just said things differently now. Informed Laura of things instead of asking permission.

'Promise you won't shout at me?'

'I promise, babe,' Laura said, knowing she didn't have it in her at that moment to shout at anyone. She pulled another chair up close to hers and motioned for Kay to sit down, hoping a customer wouldn't suddenly appear. Cupping Kay's face, Laura leaned forward and kissed her soft, flushed cheek and gave her a reassuring smile. Her daughter looked as if she had all the troubles of the world on her shoulders.

'I've done something that's, well, criminal, I s'pose,' Kay chewed the inside of her cheek and studied her mother's face for a reaction.

'Criminal, eh?' Laura stopped herself laughing.

'I had to do it, Mum. It was the only way. I've got to get out of this country.'

Laura felt herself go cold. 'You've got to what?'

'Oh, no, I don't mean . . . I haven't done anything that means I've *got* to get out. I've done something so that I *can* get out.'

Laura sank back in her chair. 'Oh, I wish you wouldn't do that to me, you little cow,' she murmured feeling somewhat relieved. 'I know what you've done. You've gone and got yourself a passport.'

Kay nodded slowly and swallowed hard. 'I had to do it. I feel like I'm suffocating. I need to get away. I need to feel some space around me.'

Laura stood up and paced the floor, one hand on her forehead. 'Kay, am I getting this right?' She looked her daughter straight in the eye. 'Did you sign your father's name on a passport form?'

Kay looked back sheepishly. There was no need for her to say anything.

'Terrific! And what do you think he's going to say about that?'

'Oh, we mustn't tell him! Not until I'm on the way and it's too late for him to stop me. I'm trusting you not to tell him!'

'Thanks. That's very good of you.' Laura sat down again. 'I wonder what else is in my stars today?'

'I won't ever tell Dad that you knew.'

'Oh, right.' Laura could hardly believe her ears. Kay was becoming an independent young lady. Laura's thoughts went back to Jack's two-year-old son and her heart sank. She felt suddenly alone.

'I wouldn't have done it if it didn't mean so much to me, honest.'

'No, love,' Laura sighed, 'I can see that. When do you go?'

'In five weeks' time.'

'And where's the money coming from? Or am I supposed to pay for you to give me all this aggravation?'

'No. I've got a part-time job. Working in a sweet shop after work and at weekends.'

'And when did that come about?' Laura wondered what else had been going on while she had been day-dreaming.

'I've been looking for a job for ages.'

'And where is this sweet shop?'

'Islington.'

'Islington. You couldn't have got one locally, of course. That would have been too straightforward.'

'What's wrong with it? I work in Clerkenwell – it's just up the road!' Kay was beginning to lose her cool.

'Which will mean you catching a train late at night and at weekends!'

'It won't be late at night. I finish at half past eight and will be home before nine.'

'And what time does it get dark in April?'

'Oh, Mum, this is ridiculous! I'll be eighteen this summer!'

'It's north London, Kay. The Angel Islington's not the sort of place to be hanging around stations.'

'I won't be hanging around anywhere. I'll go to work, catch a train, come home. Simple.'

Laura felt much older than her thirty-nine years. 'OK,' she shrugged, hoping Kay would pick up on the note of weariness in her voice and lift her from the depths she was reaching.

'And you won't say anything to Dad about the passport?'

'No, I won't say anything,' she said, realizing she was hoping for too much. Kay was on a different plane.

'Good.' Kissing her mother on the cheek, Kay gave her a hug. 'Love you,' she said and hurried off.

Laura watched her go and wondered why she felt so depressed. Nothing terrible had happened. Not really.

'Do you have any Mary Quant dresses?' A girl, Welsh, probably a student, appeared before Laura.

'No, love, this store is a bit more conservative than that.'

'Don't you mean boring?'

'Yeah, boring. That's right. It does need to move with the times.'

The student agreed and left, as if an emotional, watery-eyed saleslady were part of everyday life.

'We all need to move with the times,' Laura murmured to herself. 'Things are on a roll all right. It's enough just keeping up.' She pulled the letter out of her pocket again and quickly put it back as a bubbly blonde approached, grinning from ear to ear. Not really paying much attention to the customer, Laura took a comb from her handbag and checked her appearance in a tiny mirror.

'I didn't know you worked in 'ere, Laura.' It was Milly, a friend she hadn't seen in months, years in fact.

Laughing, Laura put her comb and mirror away. 'You're marvellous, Milly, you know that?'

'Am I?'

'Yes. I was feeling a bit low to tell you the truth, and seeing you dressed up to the nines and looking as lively as ever is a real tonic.'

'Yeah? That's good. I was a bit naughty down 'opping, wasn't I? Trying to tease your Jack away.' She looked pensive. 'Never did work though, did it?'

'How's Georgie?' Laura was feeling better by the second.

'Gets out next week. That's why I came in. Thought I'd buy a nice new coat to pick 'im up in.'

'Is that how long they gave him?'

'Yeah. Bleeders. And all for what? A few bangle watches and a coupl'a dozen bottles of whisky. Still. I think it's taught 'im a lesson. He thought he was too clever to get caught. He had a good run before they did nab 'im, mind. He swears blind he's gonna go straight from now on.'

'Well, perhaps it was blessing, eh?'

'Yeah. Now, then, I fancy a nice camel coat with a bit of fox on the collar. Something like the one in the window. What d'yer reckon?'

'I've got just the thing. Expensive though.'

'That's all right. George 'ad a bit put by, if you know what I mean.' She grinned and winked at Laura.

'Oh, Milly,' Laura let out a throaty laugh, 'I am pleased to see you. You're one in a million.'

'Funny you should say that! It's what I used to think about you. Always wished I could be as classy. Where d'yer get it from, eh? You're just a common old East Ender, after all's said and done.'

Laura dropped her mirror back into her handbag and shrugged. 'That's me, all right.'

'Come on, then. Bring me a coat I can be proud to walk down the Whitechapel Road in. I'll show some of them women out there that I can afford to shop in 'ammond's!'

Walking away from the store after closing time, Laura did her utmost to persuade Liz that she felt much better about the letter, that she didn't need to talk about it any more. But Liz in her wisdom thought Laura was just shelving it. 'If you don't talk to me about it, Laura, you'll bottle it up and explode at Jack at the wrong time.'

'No, Liz. I won't. I know what I'm doing, believe me. I'm gonna handle this my way.'

'Oh yeah?' Liz looked worried. 'And what way's that when it's at home?'

'Never you mind. Now then, you coming in to have a cuppa with Dad, or not?'

''Course I am. I need old Billy-boy to keep up my sense of humour.'

'All he ever does when *I* go in is moan.'

'Ah, well, you've either got the gift or you 'aven't. I bring out the devil in 'im.'

Unlatching the green gate into the tiny cul-de-sac, Laura smiled to herself. It was the effect Milly had had on her. She couldn't think why, but what did that matter as long as it worked and she felt lighter.

'What are you gonna do about the letter, then?'

'I'll tell you – once I've done it. Fair enough?'

'No. But I can see it's all I'm gonna get.'

'Spot on, Liz, spot on.' Laura knocked loudly on the cottage door and then used her own key to let them in.

'I'm not deaf!' yelled her dad from his place by the fire.

'See what I mean?' Laura shrugged and closed the door behind them. 'You got that kettle on yet, Billy, or what?'

'I have. And what's more, I've been out specially to get a bit of angel cake. And it wasn't cheap!'

As Liz pulled her coat off, Laura collected Billy's ironing, kissed her dad hallo and goodbye.

'Save me a bit of that cake!' she called over her shoulder as she made to leave.

'I dunno why you can't sit down for five minutes,' Billy called back. 'Always on the bloody go!'

'When they invent irons that work by themselves I will!' Laura shut the door behind her, pleased that each of them was filling a tiny gap in the other's life.

'The London Port Employers can urge all they like. It's like whistling in the wind as far as I'm concerned.' Jack was on his high horse again. 'We're in a strong position all right – and they know it. You wait and see the turnout on Sunday. This'll be a mass march to remember.'

'I'm pleased it's going well.' Laura sounded sincere as she dished up some shepherd's pie and handed a plate to Jack.

'Are yer? Makes a nice change. So far you've done nothing but tell me how we shouldn't be making all this trouble for the country. What's changed your mind?'

'If that many men are willing to come out it must be for a good reason.' She piled processed peas on to his plate. 'I hate to think of those oranges and bananas rotting in the ships, though.'

'You think we don't? There has to be some losses. Stands to reason. Better a bit of fruit than a whole bloody industry.'

'I suppose the march on Sunday'll take up most of the day?' Laura asked, trying to sound casual.

'Oh, yeah. Bound to. Why?'

'Oh, nothing really. I was just thinking I might go and visit Fran. I've been promising to go ever since she moved out.'

'Harlow?' Kay said, getting herself a glass of water. 'That's miles away.'

''Course it's not. Anyway there's an early train. We'd have most of the day together, then I could catch one back somewhere around seven.'

'Wouldn't catch me going all that way for just a day's visit.'

Laura was sorely tempted to ask Jack why not, since Leicester was much further, but she bit her tongue and bided her time. 'It was just an idea. If you'd rather I didn't go—'

'Tch. 'Course you can go. I'll treat you to the fare as well. I was only thinking of you tiring yourself out. You're bound to wanna cook me something hot when you get in.'

'Always thinking of your stomach, eh, Dad?' Kay teased.

'Have some carrots,' Laura grinned, approaching him with a large spoon.

'Careful! Don't wanna get gravy over me clean shirt. I'm seeing the lads tonight in the Grave Maurice.'

'You're what?'

Jack wiped some gravy from the corner of his mouth. 'The Grave Maurice. What's wrong with that?'

'You never use that pub.' Laura felt her heart sink.

'Bert's brothers do. And they suggested we meet some of the other union leaders there. It's not a problem.'

'Bert always said he wouldn't step inside that place. It's where the villains meet up, you know it is.'

'Oh shut up, Laura, you're talking about men we know. Frank and Freddie? What d'yer think they're gonna do, pull a gun? Tch. Villains!' He eyed her carefully. 'It's only a pub.'

Letting out a worried sigh, Laura began to eat her dinner. 'Haven't seen Bert's brothers for a couple of years, other than at the funeral. Right couple of spivs they looked as well.'

'You haven't dished any up for Kay.' Jack looked questioningly at his daughter.

'Me and Pamela's having pie and mash.' She pinched a carrot from his plate as she left the kitchen.

'Good. More shepherd's pie for us.' He winked at Laura, waiting for her to reach out and pick up the dish from the top of the gas oven. But she ignored him, and felt a wave of satisfaction when he finally got up without saying a word and got it himself. There was hope yet for her changing his Victorian attitude towards a woman and her work in the kitchen.

Spooning more hot food on to his plate, Jack looked suddenly pensive, and Laura wondered if he was thinking about his small son. She could feel herself sinking again.

'They're gonna be debating this strike in the 'Ouse of Commons, you know.'

Relieved that she was wrong about his thoughts, Laura poured herself some water from the pink glass jug. 'You have to expect that, Jack. It's turning into a serious unofficial strike now. Everyone's talking about it. I heard a couple of blokes in the canteen saying that you'll never get the government behind you on this one.'

'We'll see. The longer we stay out, the deeper in trouble this government'll be. They know that. They're testing us, see how far we're prepared to go.'

'And?'

'How far? Until they give in. We're not just talking about a little dispute, Laura. We're talking about the future of dockers and the docks.' He sat down, picked up his fork, then pushed his plate away. 'I've lost me appetite thinkin' about it.'

Laura had never seen him like this before, and had a nagging feeling it was because he and the men were in a no-win situation. They might even have walked straight into a political plot to weaken the union. And if Laura's mind was working that way, she knew for sure that Jack's would be too.

'Bert's brothers aren't gonna get involved in this dispute, are they?'

Jack looked back at her, a reassuring smile on his face. 'They're probably already involved, Laura. People like me and the other union leaders are just spokesmen, if the truth be known. This country's run by villains and corrupt politicians.'

'You are joking?'

'Yeah. 'Course I'm bloody joking.' He winked at her. 'Don't suppose you fancy a cuddle on the sofa before I go out?'

'Too early in the day. You can wake me up when you get in tonight though.' She was surprised to find herself flirting with him. She thought they had been married too long for all that. There was no doubt in her mind that the letter she had found in his jacket pocket, before she sent it to the cleaners, had aroused a bit of jealousy.

Leaning forward in his chair, Jack reached out and caught her as she passed and landed a big kiss on her small round buttock. 'I fancy you rotten,' he grinned.

'Make sure you're home early then.' She tweaked his ear and made a sharp exit.

* * *

Standing in a short queue at the ticket office on Sunday morning, Laura began to have doubts about the trip she was embarking on. Up to now she had had her sights firmly fixed on seeing the woman and Jack's illegitimate son; to find out for herself what she was like and just how deep the relationship was. Had she confronted Jack, she felt sure he would have lied to get himself off the hook.

She pushed her left foot further into the new shoe, trying to ease the blister that was developing on her heel. Pointed toes might look good but they were murder to get used to. Brushing a dust mark from her bottle green skirt, she wondered if the costume she had chosen was a bit too smart. Maybe she should have worn something a bit more casual. Slacks even.

She started to wonder about her dark auburn hair that tumbled down around her shoulders. Shouldn't she have swept it up into a topknot?

'A day return to Leicester please,' she heard herself say, as if part of her had decided to take the lead. Another part wanted to run back home and forget the whole business. In her heart, though, she knew that this was not something to be put off. She had found herself thinking about it every spare minute, and a night hadn't passed since she found the letter when it hadn't crept into her sleep, giving her nightmares.

Sitting on the platform waiting for the train, Laura glimpsed the headlines on someone's newspaper, *Docker's Strike Halts Exports!*

Even though it was a national issue, she felt sure it wouldn't be long before the newspapers would home in on the human interest stories. Bert's name would be spread across the front pages of the local rags, at least. She dreaded to think what it would do to Liz.

'Who'd 'ave thought it, eh?' The elderly woman sitting on the bench next to Laura grinned at her. 'Working classes holding the country to ransom. About bloody time as well. Good luck to them boys, that's what I say!'

Laura found herself smiling back at the stranger and wondering what she *would* say if she knew just how involved her family were. 'Is your husband a docker?' she asked instead.

'No, love. He's six foot under. Used to be a coalman. He was good an' all. A grafter. More's the pity. The pay was lousy and the work was hard. Humping coal on his back non-stop, and for what? To end up with 'is lungs full of black dust.' She folded her newspaper and placed it on her lap. 'I wouldn't mind if he got a bit of respect for the hard work and hours he put in. Still, there you are. That's a working man's lot, innit?'

Laura shrugged and sighed. What could she say? Pushing open the gold-coloured clasp of her handbag, she pulled out a bar of Fry's chocolate cream and an Aero. 'Which one d'yer fancy?'

The woman's face lit up. 'Wouldn't mind a small section of that Aero. It's my favourite.'

'Here, take it. I'm watching my weight.'

'Ta, love. I won't say no in that case. Mind you, lovely figure like yours.'

'Ah, but, it wouldn't be if I ate as much chocolate as I would like!'

'True.'

Feeling lighter inside, Laura watched as other trains pulled into other platforms, enjoying the hustle and bustle of King's Cross.

'Where you off to, then?' the woman carefully peeled back the wrapper and then the gold paper.

'Visiting an old school friend who's moved up to Leicester,' Laura lied. 'You?'

'Oh, I'm not going nowhere, love. Waiting for my daughter and grandchildren. They come every Sunday. We go over the park and 'ave a picnic. Her old man left 'er for someone else.'

Laura popped a piece of chocolate into her mouth and imagined herself being a grandmother. She tried to visualize Kay with a baby in her arms and maybe a little one pulling on her skirt. Then she remembered why she was there waiting for a train. There seemed to be no let-up to the constant reminder of her personal anxieties.

Stepping out of Leicester railway station, Laura found herself face to face with two placards on either side of the newspaper seller. The scrawled headline on one was *Gunfire As East Germans Attempt Escape Over Berlin Wall*, and on the other, *More London Dockers Out!* There seemed to be no escape. Approaching the smiling face of a flower seller, Laura asked for directions to St David's Road.

'Taxi or walking?' The woman wrapped a bunch of daffodils and handed them to a customer.

'Walking,' Laura wondered why she had asked. If she had intended to go by taxi, surely the driver would know the way. 'If it is walking distance, that is,' she asked carefully.

'Along London Road, left into Evington Road, left into East Park, about half a mile on, past Spinney Park, left into St Saviour's, up the hill, past the Imperial Hotel and then,' she looked up at the sky thoughtfully. 'Then you'd best ask again. It's somewhere around that way. Big houses. Split into flats.'

'Thanks. I'll take a mixed bunch, please.'

'You can remember all that, can you?' The woman sounded surprised.

'Left, left and left; Evington, East Park and St Saviour's,' Laura confirmed.

'That's one way of looking at it. Two bob, love.'

Laura passed over the coin and thanked the woman again.

'Taxi won't cost you much, love. Otherwise it's gonna take you a good half an hour.'

'That's OK. I'm in no rush.' Turning away Laura found herself smiling. She suddenly realized what it was about the woman that had attracted her attention. 'You're a Londoner!' she called back.

'Too right. I was evacuated up here and never bothered to go back. Married a taxi driver!' She nodded towards the black cab parked a few yards away. Her husband was in the driving seat, sound asleep. A certain smile flickered between the two women.

'Business is quiet,' she shrugged.

Showing a hand, Laura walked away feeling more comfortable about being in a strange town. Leicester wasn't a bit like she had imagined. It reminded her very much of London south of the river. For some reason she had pictured it being a small grey town instead of the lively place it was.

Deep in thought, rehearsing over and over what she would say to Patsy when she opened the door, Laura almost missed her third left turning and was halfway across the road when she realized, stopping suddenly and causing a young man behind to bump into her. Feeling like an idiot, she quickly made her way towards St Saviour's Road and stepped up her pace as she walked uphill towards the beautiful Victorian Imperial Hotel, but slowed down again when the three-faced clock on the bell tower struck the hour. Again she was reminded of London, and Big Ben.

On a wild impulse, she stepped into the hotel entrance, her heart beating nineteen to the dozen, and followed the sign to the lounge bar. Once inside she felt like turning away. It was mostly men, and the women there all had male partners. Bracing herself, she walked with her head held high to the bar, a confident, serene smile fixed on her face, and asked for two gin and tonics.

'My husband will be joining me in a minute,' she said, taking her purse from her handbag.

'That's quite all right, madam.' The barman took her by surprise as he made it clear that money need not pass between them. 'If you'd care to tell me your room number and name, I'll put it on your bill.'

'But we haven't registered yet,' Laura smiled, wondering how she would get out of this one. 'Just in from London. My husband's parking the car.'

'The name will be fine, madam.'

'Thank you. It's Mr and Mrs Smyth-Winter.' Where that fictitious name came from she had no idea, but she liked the sound of it, and surprised herself at how easily she slipped into the part.

'If madam would like to take a seat.'

'Thank you, yes.' Laura looked around her and spotted a small round table in a corner not far from the door. She could make a quick escape when he wasn't looking.

With a mixture of excitement and trepidation, Laura settled herself and idly turned the pages of the complimentary copy of *The Times* which had been left neatly folded on the table. Again a headline hit her: *Unofficial Dock Strike: Minister Against Intervention*.

Reading with interest, she hardly noticed the two gin and tonics being placed carefully before her. 'Would madam care for ice and lemon?'

'Thank you.' She stopped herself laughing as the waiter gracefully tonged ice cubes into each glass.

'I hope you enjoy your stay.' He smiled and walked away, balancing the small silver tray on fingers and thumb.

Gazing at the drinks, Laura wondered whether to finish one and leave, making it look as if she were on her way to the Ladies', or go for the kill and drink both. She took out a cigarette and decided to see how it went. If the lounge bar continued to fill up, she could easily go unnoticed and enjoy what would amount to a double. She certainly needed it. Not caring whether it was correct for women to smoke in that part of the country, she lit a cigarette, thankful for the mock tortoiseshell lighter that Liz had given her. The usual box of matches would never do. Not in these smart surroundings.

'I say, is this seat taken?'

Laura looked up from her newspaper into the bleary eyes of a grey-haired man with a huge handlebar moustache. 'Not at the moment, but it will be.' She tried to sound polite in case his intentions were honourable.

'I was about to join you.' He spoke as if he were doing her a favour.

Having finished one gin and tonic and not really in the mood for another, she was relieved that the intoxicated gentleman swaying before her had given her the best possible excuse to leave.

Dropping her cigarettes and lighter into her handbag, she threw the man a look and walked with dignity out of the bar. Once in the street she quickened her pace, terrified in case someone came after her.

Pushing one hand into the pocket of her costume jacket, she withdrew a crumpled piece of paper with Patsy's address scrawled on it. Having come from one embarrassing situation in the hotel she felt easier, somehow, at going into another. Not that her stomach wasn't churning, but at least the palpitations that kept coming and going on the train had eased off.

When she finally arrived at Patsy's door, Laura felt her heart lurch. She stood for a moment, wondering whether she should turn back, when the sound of a child's cry weakened her. Before she knew it, her finger was on the bell-push clearly marked Flat 1.

Standing in the doorway with the young boy in her arms, Patsy's face was full of surprise as she gazed into Laura's. Neither of them said anything until the child grinned and pointed a chubby finger at Laura's black and gold brooch.

'Mummy's,' he said. There were still tears on his cheeks.

Unable to think of anything to say, Laura turned her attention to Jack's son. 'Why was he crying?' she said, feeling self-conscious.

'Fell over. Bump!' The child answered for Patsy.

'You'd best come in,' she said quietly, standing aside. 'In there.' She nodded towards a cream-coloured door.

Lifting the little boy into his play-pen, Patsy gave him a biscuit, which brought a smile to his face. Then she added a few toys which were spread around the floor. 'You can take your jacket off. I won't steal it,' Patsy joked.

'I'm not stopping.' Laura felt a pang of jealousy as the two-year-old looked up at her with Jack's blue eyes.

'No mistaking whose boy he is,' Laura smiled weakly. Then turning away to hide the pain, she stared out of a large Victorian window. 'You knew who I was the moment you saw me.'

'Oh, Jack's very proud of his family. He's shown me photographs. A reminder, I suppose, that he's not free to come and go as he might like.'

'Jack is free to do what he wants, and don't kid yourself otherwise,' Laura hit back. Any compassion she felt when Patsy first opened the door was slipping away, and there was nothing she could do to stop her anger rising again, or unwelcome tears welling up in her eyes.

'So what brings you here, then, after all this time?'

'I don't know,' Laura said, turning to face her rival, not caring that the tears were now trickling down her cheeks. 'I wish I could say something sensible.' She wiped her face with the back of her hand. 'I hadn't bargained on the waterworks.'

'Here.' Patsy took a clean white handkerchief from a pile of ironing on the sideboard and pushed it into Laura's hand. 'You've got some pluck, I'll give you that. Many's the time I've wanted to knock on your door.'

'Why?' Laura composed herself, determined to maintain a level of dignity.

'Tell you about me and Jack.'

'You didn't have to. I already knew. I was waiting for it to blow over.'

Patsy gave a burst of mock laughter. 'And look what blew in before it "blew over".' She half turned so that Laura could have a full view of the small boy.

While Patsy was in the adjoining tiny kitchen, Laura looked around at her spotless, simply furnished room. It was obvious that she wasn't too strapped for cash. Little Jac was dressed in a clean, pale blue knitted suit and it was obvious from the pile of ironing on the sideboard that he had plenty of clothes and a grandmother, probably, who was very good at knitting.

'Does Jack often send you money?' Laura felt like biting her tongue. She hadn't meant it to come out quite like that.

Arriving with two cups of tea, Patsy shrugged. 'He does what he can. If I had my way I wouldn't take anything.'

'He should send you money. It's only right.'

'Are you going to sit down, then?' Patsy had a way of making an invitation sound like an order.

Laura peeled off her jacket, threw it on to the back of an armchair, and sat on the edge of the cushion. 'I found a letter in Jack's pocket. I was getting some clothes ready for the cleaner's. I wasn't looking for it. It came as quite a shock.'

'Why? You knew Jack had got me pregnant: at least he said he'd told you, when you were in Kent.'

'He did, I just didn't think.' Laura sighed and hung her head. 'I suppose I just buried my head in the sand. It stands to reason he wouldn't have just left you to . . .' Laura's voice trailed off.

'So what's your problem, then? I'm sure you didn't come all this way just to spend five minutes with Jack's little bastard.'

'I didn't come to make trouble.' She looked into Patsy's big brown eyes and felt a wave of guilt. 'I'm not angry any more, and I don't blame you.'

'Maybe you should. I knew what I was doing. I wanted his child.' She looked down at little Jac playing happily. 'Funny little bugger, isn't he?'

'And what about your feelings towards Jack?' Laura dreaded the answer, fearing the worst.

'I still admire him – got great shoulders.' She sipped her tea. 'I do have a boyfriend. My love for Jack soon faded. I would like my son to know his father. But that's asking too much, I suppose?' She eyed Laura carefully.

'Yes. I think it is.' There was a pause. 'It has to be all or nothing with me, none of this family sharing. It's not right.'

'Well, I don't want Jack any more, and he never did want me, not for a wife, that is.'

They sat there, quietly drinking their tea, eyes down. The only sounds came from Jac, content to sit and pick the chocolate chips out of his biscuit.

'My mother lives just around the corner,' said Patsy finally. 'I was about to get Jac ready to go round there for Sunday dinner. She always feeds us Sundays.'

'I'd best be going then. She'll be expecting you.'

'Yes, she will. I'm sorry you've had a wasted journey.' Patsy's tone was very cool. 'Waste of a train ticket.'

'No, I don't think it was.' Laura stood up and reached out for her jacket. 'I'll see that Jack sends you a regular amount of money.'

'That's very charitable. I must say I wouldn't be as soft. But then Jack's not the sort who needs his wife's permission to feed and clothe his own son, is he?'

'Of course it's a bit difficult at the moment, with the strike. But once it's over, he'll make up for the months.'

'That's a very nice costume. Looks classy. Expensive. And that brooch, by the way, is identical to one he gave me three years ago. Must have been a job lot.'

Laura felt the tears well up again. She pressed her lips together and composed herself. 'Look, I'm sorry if you've had a rough time.'

'Like I said, I've got a boyfriend. But he refuses to take on someone else's kid. Especially a southerner's. Can't blame him. So there we are. That's the fine mess your husband's got me into.'

'But you said it was your doing,' Laura whispered, realizing she had pushed Patsy too far when she saw her cheeks redden with anger.

'Oh, yeah,' she grinned, 'I forced him to have sex with me, if you can believe that.' She shook her head. 'Jack made love to me more times than you've given him a hot dinner! The fact that he was too drunk to care one night, when he didn't have something with him, is neither here nor there.'

'I've made things worse by coming.' Laura's stomach turned over.

'No. I don't think so. Hasn't affected *me* one way or the other, to be perfectly honest.'

'You seemed relieved to meet me when I first came.'

'I was.' She smiled serenely. 'I used to dread you coming after me, when I was in London having the affair with Jack. I was terrified of you. We can blame Jack for that.' She tossed her ginger curls off her face. 'And now I'm not. And you know why? Because I've got his son – and you haven't.' She was still smiling.

Laura could do nothing but look at Patsy's face, waiting for some sign of remorse, regret, maybe a little shame?

'That's right,' Patsy grinned spitefully, 'I've got a son and you haven't.' She spoke the words slowly, deliberately.

'Please don't say that.' Laura could feel the old hurt moving back into her chest. 'You don't know what you're saying.'

'I do, actually. I heard nothing else for bloody years! That sacred child you lost. Well my boy is alive and kicking and needs clothes on his back. So it's useless coming at me with all that self-pity.'

'God, you are one strange woman.' Laura managed to regain her self-respect.

'I don't want to seem rude, but . . .' Patsy looked at her watch, 'especially after you've come all this way.'

Grabbing her handbag, Laura made for the door, and turned to Patsy.

'Your son is the image of my daughter. Except for the ginger hair. But still, maybe that will lighten as he gets older.'

'Maybe. I'll get Jack to keep you informed.'

Jack settled himself in a quiet corner of the Grave Maurice and wondered what he would be having for dinner that day. He had got it wrong about the strike meeting, it was a three o'clock start, so he had time to spare. Maybe he and the boys would go off for something to eat once they'd had a couple of beers and a chat.

Not much had been said the night before, not by Bert's brothers in any case. They had been content to sit back and listen to Jack's opinions about the strike and his plans, throwing the occasional question his way. He undid a small knot of blue paper and shook salt into his bag of potato crisps.

'What you drinking, Jack?'

'Hallo, mate, I didn't see you come in. A pint'll do me.' Jack swallowed the remains of a beer in one go.

'Laura get off all right?' The immaculately dressed Frank sat down opposite Jack and motioned to his brother, who was standing at the bar, that both he and Jack would have a pint and a chaser.

'Yeah. Though why she wants to travel all that way to spend a few hours chin-wagging, beats me.'

'Nice part of the world, Suffolk.'

'Essex,' Jack corrected.

'What's the difference? Coupl'a miles?'

'Think so, yeah.'

'Well we won't argue about that, then.'

Jack had no intention of arguing about anything, not with either of Bert's younger brothers. They had changed quite a bit since the time when Jack taught them to make paper aeroplanes, way back in 1938 when he was nineteen and they were seven and nine. He suddenly found himself wondering what kind of a mood Frank was in. He felt distinctly uncomfortable and wasn't sure why.

'How's Liz coping?' Frank asked, trying to sound interested.

'Seems OK, Frank. Likes her job in the canteen.'

'Good.' Slipping a hand inside his jacket, he pulled out a thick white envelope. 'Give this to 'er for me, will yer? Say it's from me and Freddie.'

'Oh, right.' Jack tucked the envelope into his pocket.

'That should see her right for a while.' Frank sat back in his chair with an air of pride and satisfaction.

Setting the drinks down on the table, the second brother nodded at Jack. 'All right, mate?'

'Yeah. Not bad.' He swallowed some of the beer and had a strange feeling he was going to need the chaser.

Moving along the bench so that Freddie could sit next to him, Frank began to stroke one of his thick black eyebrows. 'So, Jack . . . another meeting this afternoon, eh?'

'Yep. Should be quite a turnout.'

'Mmmm.' Frank sniffed and drank some of his beer, leaving a silence.

'There are some people, Jack,' Frank said, his face expressive, 'top-notch people, that is, who are not very happy about this strike. They seem to think it's all getting a bit out of hand.'

'Nothing wrong with that, is there? Should be good publicity.'

The brothers looked at each other, showing their mutual disapproval in the nicest way possible, with a half-smile.

'It's getting a little bit embarrassing – for us, that is. A couple of Members of Parliament are a bit put out as well.'

'Oh yeah?' Jack waited to hear what was on their minds.

'Letters and parcels bound for places like Argentina, East Africa, they're stuck in sorting offices. Not to mention other exports and imports, come to that. The Dock Labour Board ain't backing yer; and I hear that other unions think it's all a bit out of order.'

'Come to the meeting this afternoon and you'll see. Hear what the men 'ave got to say.'

'Yeah, but that's not really the point, is it, Jack?' Frank said, trying to keep a friendly tone. 'You've got the warehouse keepers up in arms. They've invested a lot of money increasing exports.'

'Ah, now we're getting there,' Jack said knowingly. 'Some of them warehouse keepers are friends of yours, I take it?'

'Colleagues. And not so much mates of ours, as Management.'

'I thought you boys were freelance?' Jack smiled, trying to lighten the atmosphere.

'Everyone has to answer to someone.' Freddie downed half his glass of beer. 'Can't have too many chiefs.'

'And us red indians don't do so bad,' Frank chimed in.

Suppressing his anger, Jack leaned his head to one side and looked the thirty-year-old in the eye. 'What's this about, Frank?'

'Don't ask,' he said, slowly shaking his head and smiling. 'It's far too complicated.'

'The thing is,' Freddie the fair-haired brother added, 'we definitely don't want our Bert's name spread across the newspapers. And we don't want him used any more for other people's ends.'

'That's never been the case!' Jack snarled. 'And you fucking well know it!'

'Come on, Jack boy, don't be like that,' Freddie said, lighting a cigar.

'I'll be any way I like! And not so much of the boy. I gave you a cuff round the ear sixteen years ago when you was a small fry. Don't think I wouldn't do it again.'

The two brothers looked at each other and raised an eyebrow, hoping to undermine Jack.

'Do you two realize how important this dispute is? Have you any idea what could happen to the docks if we sit back and let them bastards do what they want?'

'Jack, Jack, Jack.' Freddie paused and blew smoke rings towards the ceiling. 'You can't stop progress. This is the sixties, not the thirties. New roads are planned. Containerization's on the cards. Bringing stuff in and out of the country through the docks'll be history. Another decade and they'll be flying it all in and out by aircraft as big as your smaller ships. And that'll only be the start.' He drew on his cigar again. 'You're bashing your 'ead against a brick wall, mate.'

'I can't believe I'm hearing this.' Jack felt choked and angry. Downing his whisky in one go, he stood up without saying a word. As he turned to leave, Freddie grabbed his arm. 'Keep Bert's name out of it, eh?'

'I think it might be a bit late for that.'

'It's never too late, Jack boy.' His smile was full of threat. 'Not if you've got a brain, that is.'

Jack scowled and pulled his arm away. He stormed out of the pub, full of revulsion. As he marched along the Whitechapel Road he realized that Bert's brothers had changed quite a bit in the last seven or eight years since he used to drink with them regularly. He had often wondered why they had slipped out of the local social scene. Now he knew. The mohair suits, the thick gold bracelets, the new Jaguar, it added up. They moved in the world of hardened criminals now, and he had to admit that he might regret it if Bert's brothers became his enemies.

Passing the Blind Beggar, where some of his docker friends drank, Jack felt a strong desire to go in and let off steam. He walked straight past instead, and turned left into Cambridge Heath Road on his way to Liz's small terraced house in Bethnal Green. She would give him dinner and he could get rid of the envelope in his pocket. He felt like hurling it over a wall, but guessed that it might be more than his life was worth. And besides, why shouldn't Liz have some of their ill-gotten gains?

Nodding to a passing neighbour, Jack realized he was shivering, not from the crisp April day, but with the mild shock of knowing that he could be under threat from people more powerful than Bert's two flashy younger brothers.

Turning into Columbia Road he considered the idea of emigrating. Maybe that would satisfy Kay's wanderlust! Arriving at Liz's door, he braced himself to face that living room with the brown fireside chair empty, where Bert should have been.

''Course I was expecting you!' Liz made her way along the narrow passage, Jack closing the door behind him. 'I heard the meeting wasn't till this afternoon and what with Laura goin' off to Harlow, I guessed you'd be round for a bit of Sunday dinner.'

Sitting down by the glowing gas fire, Jack warmed his hands and felt distinctly better now that he was in familiar surroundings, with the sound of the wireless in the background and the smell of roast beef drifting through from the kitchen.

'Where's the Sunday paper?'

'On my bed! I went back with it and a cup of tea this morning. It was bliss, I tell yer. A bit of luxury I should have allowed myself before now!'

'Why didn't yer? Bert wouldn't 'ave minded.'

'I know that. I just didn't, that's all. Wouldn't 'ave dreamed of it. Had to get the worker's breakfast, didn't I?'

'Leave off, Lizzie. Had to? You loved running round 'im and you know it.'

'I'm glad to see those two little sods didn't worry you too much.' Liz sat in the other armchair and slowly shook her head. 'Bert used to love them boys. His baby brothers. Then they grew up into what they are now.'

'I'm not with you.' Jack couldn't see how she could possibly know about their little meeting.

'Wheels travel faster than legs, Jack.'

'Are you telling me those bastards came round here?'

'As soon as you left the pub.'

Jack sipped the tea Liz had put down in front of him. 'They're way out of order. Who do they think they're dealing with, eh? Don't they think I've got contacts? One phone call is all it'd take and they'd get a bloody good 'iding.'

'I think you're gonna 'ave to drop it, you know.'

'Oh yeah?'

'Take a back seat. Let someone else take the lead. You don't know the sort of people Bert's brothers mix with now.'

'The people they'd like to mix with, you mean! They're all mouth.'

Liz put her cup and saucer on the radiogram next to her and stood up. 'I'd best turn that meat over,' she murmured. She couldn't bring herself to tell her brother just how serious the situation was, and how important the message delivered by the two men.

'So they came to see you 'oping you'd talk me round?'

'Something like that, yeah.' Liz walked back into the kitchen.

Jack remembered the white envelope in his pocket and it made him feel confused. Maybe it wasn't out of the goodness of their hearts that they were treating Liz, nor out of respect for Bert. Looking down at the envelope he could see it hadn't been sealed and, as he pushed it open with his thumb, that it was crammed full with grubby five- and ten-pound notes. He reckoned there had to be three hundred quid in total. It was becoming very clear that while the boys held an invisible gun in one hand, aimed at Jack's head, the other was offering a financial settlement.

While Liz busied herself in the kitchen throwing vegetables into boiling water, Jack stared into the fire, working out the best way to handle the situation. He could, without too much loss of face, slip into the background and let the other union leaders rule the waves, or try to. He had a perfect excuse. He could say the constant reminder of losing Bert so suddenly, and his name being thrown about the way it had been, was proving too much for his family. Or that his sister was living in fear of the press knocking on her door. Or, better still, he could say she was scared that her innocent Bert had become the cause of a widespread national strike.

A loud ring at the door startled Jack and for a second or two he felt genuinely scared. Shaking himself, he called to Liz that he would answer it.

'It'll be our Kay!' she called out.

'Will it?' Jack felt relieved and pleased. He hadn't seen much of his daughter since the strike had started and he was missing her. What he hadn't expected was to see Kay in tears and looking angry.

Settling her on the sofa, Jack took the small glass of brandy Liz offered and swallowed it in one go.

'That was meant for Kay!' Sometimes Liz couldn't believe her brother. 'That's typical, Jack, that really is.' She could see Kay found it amusing.

'It's all right, Aunt Liz. I don't need a drink. I'm probably overreacting.'

'What d'yer mean, Kay, overreacting? About what?' It pained Jack to see his girl in tears, even if they were from frustration rather than grief.

'You'll only get annoyed if I tell yer.'

Sighing, Jack pushed his hand through his thick blond hair. 'I won't get annoyed, all right?'

Kay blew her nose and took a deep breath. 'Someone just shouted abuse at me.'

Liz and Jack waited patiently while she composed herself. 'You didn't walk out in front of a car again, did yer?' Liz asked.

'No. 'Course not. I only did that once before, Aunt Liz, and I was nine!'

'You frightened the life out of everyone around yer, including the poor driver,' Liz said, remembering.

'Yeah. And everyone screamed at me for being careless.'

'Never mind all that now,' Jack put his arm around Kay's shoulder, 'who's upset yer?'

'Promise you won't ask who she was?'

'I know 'er then, do I?' Jack spoke before he thought.

'See! You're interrogating me already!'

Liz caught his eye, her expression daring Jack to lose his rag. He shrugged and said he was sorry.

'That's all right,' Kay murmured. 'Just give me a minute.'

They sat waiting for the silence to end, having no idea what was coming next. Liz looked as if she were trying to suppress a giggle, and Jack noticed. He kept his eyes firmly fixed on the floor to avoid looking at his sister, knowing how easily they could both lose control at the amusing side of this scene.

'Someone just yelled and swore at me. Said it was my family's fault that she wouldn't be roasting a joint today but making do with vegetables and Yorkshire. She said that Mum should try living on strike pay with six mouths to feed.' Kay lowered her voice, her head bent. 'She said you was happy to see the strike go on, so long as Mum and me kept you.'

'Did she now?' Jack spoke quietly, turning his head away so that neither she nor Liz could see his shame-filled face. He felt as if the mud was being hurled from all directions. He couldn't understand it. If he was doing something underhand, that would be different – but fighting for rights? He inhaled slowly as it dawned on him that when it came down to it, all he really wanted now was a quiet, uncomplicated life.

'Sorry, Dad. I should 'ave kept it to myself.'

'No,' Jack shook his head, 'you did the right thing. Next thing we know, they'll be cursing Bert's name.'

Taking Jack and Kay by surprise, Liz's sudden cry filled the room and she trembled from head to toe. Unable to control herself, she cried out, over and over, for Bert. Jack and Kay could do nothing but watch helplessly as she sobbed and rocked to and fro, grieving for the man they loved and missed, and the situation that had developed after his death. It seemed to be affecting all their lives.

After eating Sunday lunch in a less than happy mood, Liz, Jack and Kay curled up by the gas fire, watching television, and one by one fell asleep.

There had been a debate which almost turned into an argument over which programme they would have on. The FA Cup special, Burnley versus Tottenham, was on at ten minutes past two, and ran through Liz's favourite programme on the other side, *Interpol Calling*. Liz had argued that since the football was a repeat from the day before and she knew full well that Jack wouldn't have missed it, they should switch over for *Interpol Calling*, switch back to football once that was over, and then see her favourite actor in *The Big Steal*. There wasn't much Jack could say; she had laid down the law, arguing that since it was her house she would watch what she wanted. As it happened, it was exactly what Jack wanted too. He was astute when it came to his elder sister, who had been more like a mother to him since their parents died when he was a boy.

Stretched out on the sofa, Jack's low snoring drifted through the room, and it was a miracle that the vibrations hadn't woken either Kay or Liz who were fast asleep in the worn, feather-cushion armchairs. None of them had intended to sleep for so long, and when the doorbell pierced their slumber, they were surprised to see that it was nearly seven o'clock and the sun was going down.

Easing herself out of her armchair, Liz steadied herself before walking along the narrow passageway. She knew that at her age it was unwise to rush about after a doze.

'Just woke up, Liz?' Laura could see she had.

'Bloody blimey,' Liz said, 'you're all here now. Shut the door behind yer.'

Laura followed Liz into the sitting room and could see at a glance that they had all been sleeping. 'Looks like I'm the only one awake enough to put the kettle on,' she joked.

Dropping back into her chair, Liz nodded. 'Couldn't agree more.'

'How did the meeting go then, Jack?' Laura called from the kitchen.

'Dunno. I missed it.' He pulled out his tobacco tin and pushed the lid off with his thumb.

'You did what?' She stood in the doorway, kettle in hand.

'I got it wrong. It wasn't this morning. It was this afternoon, and I fell asleep after my dinner.'

Liz knew why Jack hadn't gone to the meeting, but Kay looked puzzled. Her dad was lying and she knew it. He hadn't fallen asleep when he said he had.

'How's Fran settling down in Harlow, then?'

'She's OK, Jack. D'yer mind if I make myself a cold meat sandwich, Liz? I'm starving.'

''Course not. Help yourself. Do you want one, Kay?'

'No thanks, Aunt Liz. Wouldn't mind another piece of that apple pie, though, with cream.'

'Well go and help yourself then. Don't leave it all to your mother.'

Once Kay was safely out of earshot, Liz leaned forward and spoke to Jack in a low voice. 'Why don't you sit down quietly tonight and tell Laura about Frank and Freddie? You won't be able to hide the fact that you're pulling out of the fight.'

'I'm not gonna pull out, Lizzie. I'll step down as spokesman, that's all.' He stood up and stretched. 'That sleep's done me good. I've got a clear head about it now.' He pulled his braces up over his shoulders. 'Anyway, I've said all I've got to say. Won't be a bad thing to let someone else have a go. Be all right if I 'ave a wash and shave?'

Liz looked up at her brother and shrugged. 'I suppose so,' she said thoughtfully. 'You'll 'ave to use Bert's razor.'

''Course I will. What's wrong with that?'

'I dunno.' Her face suddenly lit up. 'He might 'ave something to say about it though, if he can see down here.'

Jack looked up, cocked his head to one side and raised his voice. 'You don't care if I use your razor, do you, Bert?'

'Turn it in, Jack.' Liz tried not to laugh.

'Shhh . . . he's trying to tell me something.' Jack pretended to be listening. 'You know I wouldn't do a thing like that!' he said to the ceiling. 'Anyway, I don't like Imperial Leather, you know that!'

'You're bloody mad, Jack,' said Liz, wiping a tear from her eye.

Jack leaned forward and put his face close to Liz's. 'Yeah. And don't you forget it.'

'What's that supposed to mean?'

'It means, Lizzie, anyone who talks to the ceiling, or a chair, or the air, might be on course for losing some of their marbles.'

'You'll find some mustard made up in a little white eggcup, Laura! It's on the shelf above the green cupboard!' Liz called out, changing the subject and keeping her flushed face away from Jack.

'The next time that bubbly widower invites you to a seance, tell him to pick up the blower and talk to me. I'll give him a message or two!'

'I only went the once, Jack. Gawd knows how you got to know about it.'

Jack tapped the side of his nose. 'The East End's not all that big a place.' He gave her a wink. 'If he wants to date you, there's nothing wrong with that. But tell him you'd rather go to the pictures.'

'Leave off, Jack. Dates at my age?'

'You can bet on it. There's a lot of lonely men out there, Liz. Just make sure you don't pick the wrong one.'

'Honestly, Jack! Bert's not been gone five minutes—'

'I'm not talking about a bit of the other. I'm talking about companionship.'

'Oh right,' she said, embarrassed, 'I'll remember that when a bloke struggles to undo my Cross-Your-Heart brassiere.'

Jack left the room, laughing to himself. 'All right if I put one of Bert's shirts on?'

'Yeah, go on then.' Liz knew exactly what Jack was up to. He was bringing the memory of her Bert out into the open, and it made her feel good.

Walking arm in arm with Laura along Cambridge Heath Road, Jack was suddenly aware that Kay had dropped behind. Turning his head to call her, he realized that the last thing his teenage daughter wanted was to be seen out with her mum and dad. 'You all right, Kay?' he called, more out of habit than concern.

'Yeah. I'm gonna cut through Barmy park.'

'You'll 'ave to be quick then. The park keeper'll be locking them gates soon!'

With the experience of a townie, Kay zigzagged expertly between the traffic and disappeared into the wide gateway next to Bethnal Green tube station.

'Jack . . . there's something I want to tell you,' Laura pulled her arm away from his and pushed both hands into the pockets of her jacket.

'Fire away.'

'I didn't go to Harlow today.' She held her breath, ready to deliver the next crashing blow.

'I know that.' He sounded very matter-of-fact.

Laura stopped dead in her tracks and threw her shoulders back with an air of indignation. 'You what?'

He slipped his arm around her waist and walked her along the pavement, smiling into her mystified eyes.

'You found Patsy's letter, right?'

'Liz!' Laura couldn't believe her sister-in-law would go behind her back.

'Oh, charming. Liz knows about it as well. Why not tell the whole bloody world!'

'Well, if it wasn't Liz?'

'Oh, Laura! One day it was in my jacket pocket, the next day it was gone, then it was back again.'

'I don't know what to say.' Laura allowed him to walk her under the railway arch instead of turning left for home.

'Wait till we get to the Carpenter's. I'll buy you a rum and black and we can talk about it.' He squeezed her arm. 'That sound all right?'

'I don't know. Do what you want. Let's not change the habit of a lifetime.' They walked on in silence, each wondering what the outcome of the evening would be.

Pushing open the door of the pub, Jack showed a hand to a few dockers who were drinking at the bar. He quickly looked round for a quiet table and pointed at one in the corner. Laura settled herself down while he had a word with his friends and ordered a round.

'Bit out of order, wasn't it, Jack? You not turning up this afternoon?' The man was a large docker and not someone to fall out with.

'Sometimes, Jim, problems at home are more important than anything.' He looked him straight in the eye and hoped for the best. 'We've just come from Liz's as well. Poor mare. Wouldn't stop crying over Bert.'

The man squeezed Jack's shoulder. 'Give Jack a whisky, will you, Dave.' The barman stopped what he was doing and pushed a glass under the optic.

Downing the whisky in one go, Jack shuddered. 'That's better,' he said, and forced a sigh. 'I think I'm gonna 'ave to take a back seat for a while.'

'Understandable, mate, understandable. We'll pass the word. Just show your face now and then though, eh? The men 'ave got a lot of respect for you, Jack.'

Feeling lighter, Jack paid for his round and carried the drinks to the table in the corner and sat down.

'I take it you saw Patsy?' Jack drew a deep breath and pulled his tobacco tin out of his pocket.

'And the little boy.'

'I'm sorry, Laura. It was the last thing I wanted, you seeing that letter.' He sighed. 'You had to find out sometime, I s'pose.'

'It's my own fault. I knew when she was pregnant. I should have worked it out for myself. But I wish you'd told me you were writing to her, Jack.' She sipped her rum and blackcurrant. 'I feel as if we've been living a lie.'

'Don't be daft, 'course we haven't. And look how you reacted once you did know! You was on the next train up there.'

'She's more attractive than I thought she'd be.' Laura felt the jealousy rise again. 'I'm surprised you're not living with her instead of me.' She tried to keep the anger out of her voice.

'Well that proves something, surely?'

'Does it?'

'Yes, it does. It proves I love you and not her.' He drank some of his beer and wiped the froth away from his mouth with the back of his hand. 'Always have done.'

'He looks so much like you and Kay . . .'

'Yeah?' Jack sounded pleased. 'I've only been the once. Just after he was born. Since then I've sent 'er a letter each month with a bit of cash in it for the rent.'

'Don't you think we should have done a bit more than that?' Laura could hardly believe she was saying it. 'He is Kay's brother, after all.'

'She didn't want any more than that. Only the rent. I wanted to see him, but . . .'

Laura pulled a packet of cigarettes out of her handbag. 'That's not the impression I got. I think she'd like some money for clothing. Not that Jac looked hard done by. I saw a pile of his things on the sideboard. I expect her parents and her boyfriend help out.'

'So.' Jack had had enough of this. 'Where does that leave us? Am I gonna be sent to Coventry or what?' He looked at her sheepishly.

'No. But you might find yourself on a train to Leicester if you're not careful.'

'Gimme a break, Laura.' Jack avoided her eyes for fear he might see something he didn't care to. 'D'you want another drink, or what?'

'You should have told me you were writing to her, Jack. It opened up a very sore wound when I found that letter.'

'OK. I was in the wrong! I should 'ave told yer. What d'you want me to do, beg forgiveness?'

'I'll think of something.' Part of her wanted to say it was all right, but in her heart she knew she would be lying. 'Let it lie for now.'

Chapter Four

Standing behind the counter of Maynard's tobacconist's, Kay felt very nervous as she watched Gladys turn the *Open* sign around and unlock the front door. She was beginning to regret taking on the work and wondered if she would be able to cope. Arithmetic had never been her strongest subject at school, and she dreaded the thought of giving someone the wrong change.

'You'll be all right, luv,' Gladys winked at her. 'They won't bite your head off. Just watch me at first, you'll soon get the hang of it.'

Forcing a smile, Kay tried to ignore her rumbling stomach. 'My hands are sweating.'

Smiling, Gladys brushed her grey curls back off her face and peered into a small square mirror. 'That's why I took you on. I prefer to have sensitive people around me instead of some of the flashy women we've had in here from time to time.' She squeezed Kay's arm. 'Why don't you put the kettle on? Only three sugars for me. I'm slimming.'

'Everyone seems to be on a diet in our firm,' Kay said, spooning sugar into both their mugs. 'They all wanna look like Jean Shrimpton.'

'You mean they all want to look like you! Seventeen . . . I wish I was your age again. Best time of your life. Or should be.' She looked sideways at Kay. 'Pity you 'ave to spend so much of your life working. Should be out there having fun. Money's not everything, you know.'

'It is when you need it. I'm saving to go abroad.'

'Ah . . . that's different. Money for fun – I'm all for that.'

'And my dad's on strike, otherwise my mum would have been able to help pay for the holiday.'

'Your *mum* would?'

'Dad doesn't want me to go.'

Gladys raised a hand, 'Say no more.'

Snapping two fingers off her Kit-Kat, she narrowed her eyes. 'What you wanna remember is this: don't go getting yourself locked into a courtship before you've turned twenty.' She dipped the chocolate biscuit into her coffee. 'I've seen more girls 'aving to get married before they've got the key to the front door than I've had baked beans. And I was one of the silly cows as well! It's the eyes. They get you with their eyes. My Tom did. One look from him and the bit between my legs was throbbing.'

Kay liked her new boss, they got on like a house on fire, but as soon as it was time to get down to business, Gladys's personality changed. She was very efficient, and made it clear that she took pride in the shop; how it looked, how good the takings were and how long she had been manageress. Eight years sounded like a lifetime to Kay, but it made her feel comfortable knowing that Gladys knew exactly how to handle the awkward customers.

'You're a bit on the naïve side, Kay,' she said as they locked up at closing time, 'but there's no better way to learn about the human race than when they're parting with their money. They'll catch you if they can. You're gonna 'ave to learn how to read people's faces.'

When Kay walked into the kitchen later that evening, Laura and Jack were sitting waiting to see how she had got on. 'I've kept your dinner on steam. I don't think it will have spoiled,' Laura fussed around her.

'I don't care if it is. I'm starving!' Kay dropped on to a kitchen chair and smiled into Jack's grinning face. 'It was good, Dad! I liked it. And the extra cash'll come in handy.'

'For what?'

'New clothes, that sort of thing.' She hated lying to her dad but it was necessary.

'We're not on poor street, you know.'

'I know that. It's just that, you know, I wanna be independent.'

'Just like your mother, eh?'

Placing the hot plate in front of Kay, Laura tossed her hair back, proud. 'Nothing wrong with that.'

'True. So long as I don't end up being a spare part around here.'

They couldn't help smiling at the way he always put on the hangdog expression when he wanted a bit of attention and sympathy. Leaving the kitchen, he called back over his shoulder, 'Wouldn't mind a cup of tea by the telly!'

'Thanks for not telling Dad about my going to Spain, Mum.' Kay pushed a forkful of meat pudding into her mouth.

Laura looked at Kay, her eyes wide. 'God help me when you've gone and I do have to tell him. He'll hit the roof.'

There was a ring on the doorbell. 'That'll be Pamela,' Kay smiled, 'I knew she'd 'ave to come round to see how I got on. Anyone'd think this was my first job. Open the door for 'er, Mum.'

'What did your last slave die of?'

Kay laid down her cutlery. 'Sorry, I didn't mean to—'

'I'm only kidding. Don't be so sensitive!'

'Hallo!' Pamela's singsong voice reverberated along the passage and into the kitchen. 'Where is she?'

Looking up at her friend's sparkling face, Kay knew by her expression that she had something she couldn't wait to tell her.

'That looks nice.' She studied Kay's dinner.

'There's some left,' Laura said, following Pamela in. 'Have you eaten?'

'No, I'm on a diet.'

'You *are* joking?' Laura eyed the skinny form in front of her.

'I'm not. The girls at work say I've got enormous thighs. How can I wear a bikini with enormous thighs?'

'Keep your voice down!' Kay snapped. 'Dad's in the front room.'

'Sorry,' she mouthed. Turning to Laura, Pamela pulled her short skirt up above her knickers. 'See,' she said, looking as if she were about to cry. 'Look how thick they are.'

'But look how skinny the rest of your body is, love! You won't necessarily change your legs by not eating. That's your natural shape. Family genes coming through.'

'You mean I'm always gonna have tree-trunks for legs?'

'That's right,' Kay said, 'just keep 'em covered up while you're out with me.'

Laura watched, bemused, as Pamela dropped on to a chair and wept.

'Take no notice, she's always doing that. It's not real crying. She only does it to get attention.'

'I do not!' Pamela sat up straight and the waterfall ceased instantly. 'I'll have some of that meat, Mrs Armstrong, but no pudding, thank you. I never eat stodge.'

'Help yourself.' Laura left them to it and joined Jack in the front room.

'You insult people all the time, Pamela.'

'Now what 'ave I said?'

Kay nodded towards the steak and kidney pudding in the steamer. '*I never eat stodge*,' she mimicked.

Pamela looked puzzled. 'What's insulting about that?'

'Just help yourself to what you want and shut up,' Kay grumbled, 'it's been a long day.'

Peering into the saucepan, Pamela turned up her nose. 'I don't think I'll bother. Can I make myself some toast instead?'

'Did you bring the holiday brochure?' Kay spoke quietly, coming straight to the point.

'Er . . . no.' There was a touch of worry in her voice.

'Why not?'

'Because there isn't one. Not for where we're going. Well there is, there's lots actually, but not for us.'

Kay narrowed her eyes and drew breath. 'What's that supposed to mean?'

'Well . . . the man who's arranging all this knows the hotel owner in the resort where we're going, on the Costa Brava and—'

'Which resort? You said you'd find out which one today!'

'I forgot. Anyway,' she grinned broadly, 'I've paid our deposits so we're definitely booked in. And we won't have to share a room with anyone else but each other. I saw a photograph of the hotel. It's very nice.'

'Where do we fly from?' Kay was losing her patience.

'We don't.' Pamela popped two slices of bread under the grill. 'How d'yer turn this thing on?'

'You're not telling me we go by boat and coach?'

'Oh no! Train, boat, then an overnight sleeper train, then a coach, then another train and then a Spanish bus. That way we'll get to see more of France and Spain. And it keeps the price down.'

'You mean it's not gonna cost forty pounds, then?'

'Oh yeah. But the man who's arranging it said that was very cheap.'

'Only by three pounds! I checked in the other brochures. And that's flying!'

'Is it?'

Sighing, Kay pushed her plate away. 'I take it you *have* found out the date we go?'

'Yeah. In two weeks' time.'

'You said it would be four or five weeks, at least!'

Pamela looked thoughtful. 'Did I?'

Closing her eyes, Kay imagined herself strangling her best friend. 'It's all right for you,' she grumbled, 'you've already saved up for it.'

'No I haven't. I'm skint.'

Eyeing her carefully, Kay waited for a grin to appear on Pamela's face. She hoped it was a joke.

'I'm gonna have to borrow it.'

Pushing one hand through her hair, exasperated, Kay began to regret they had ever made plans to go away together.

'Who from?' she asked, not thinking for one second that she would get a sensible answer.

'My mum and dad of course.'

'How do you know they'll lend it to you?'

'Because they said they would.' Pamela eased the lid off the biscuit tin and helped herself to a chocolate finger. 'They'll lend you some as well if you want. They're loaded.'

'No.' Kay clenched her teeth. 'I'll manage,' she said, suddenly feeling low. There she was, working all hours to get the cash together, and Pamela could get it from her parents simply by asking. It didn't seem fair.

Kay scraped the remains of her dinner into the waste bin and washed her plate. 'I think I'll have a bath and an early night.'

'Right-ho. I only came to tell you that I've booked.' She helped herself to another biscuit. 'You could say thank you,' Pamela said, a hurt look on her face.

'Yeah. Thanks a bundle. You're a really good organizer.'

'At least I'm good at something, then,' she said, pleased with herself, taking Kay's sarcasm for real. 'I'll see if I can get the man who's arranging all this to let me borrow the photograph for you. The other girls think it's great.'

'Is it an all-girl party then?' Disillusionment was setting in with every passing second.

'Oh no. Four blokes, I think. And if they're all like the two I saw today,' she grimaced, 'they're about as exciting as boiled sausages.'

On the Friday morning before departure day, Laura smiled into Kay's worried face. 'You don't look very excited.'

'Scared more like. At what Dad'll say.'

'He won't find out.' Laura smiled. 'We've done a good job on him.

He really believes you're off to the Isle of Sheppey to stay in Aunt Liz's caravan. What the eye doesn't see.' Laura winked at Kay. 'We'll tell him once you're back. Won't have any choice then, will he? You'll be as brown as a berry.'

'Hope so.' Kay looked at the kitchen clock and quickly swallowed the remains of her tea. 'Thanks for the fiver. I'll bring you back a souvenir.'

'Don't be silly. You spend it on yourself. That's why I gave it to you. And if you run out—'

'I know, I know. Borrow it off of Moneybags.' She made for the door. 'Stop worrying, I'll have plenty. See you tonight.'

Arriving five minutes early at the bus stop, Kay let her mind wander, thinking of the next day. She tried to imagine herself lying on a long stretch of golden sand and swimming in a clear turquoise sea. She made a mental list of the few incidentals she would have to buy during her lunch-break. Her aunt Liz had been round the day before and slipped five pounds in an envelope between her eiderdown and pillow. *A little treat* was scribbled on it in green biro.

When the bus arrived, Kay climbed aboard and looked for her West Indian friend.

'Over here, darlin'!' Juanita called out, her beautiful smile sending a surge of excitement through Kay. Sitting down next to her, Kay squeezed the woman's arm. 'I can't believe it's come round at last.'

'Have you told your father yet?'

'No.'

Juanita sucked her teeth and slowly shook her head. 'You're one hell of a brave girl, or somethin'.'

'What do you want me to bring you back?' Kay said, wanting to change the subject.

Juanita thought about it. 'A nice big Spanish señor!' She roared with laughter and her warm, sweet-smelling body shook.

Taking her arm, Kay moved closer and rested her head on Juanita's solid shoulder. 'I'm really looking forward to it, Juanita,' she sighed.

'I know, I know.' Juanita turned away and stared out of the window. 'Just be careful, eh? I want to see you back on this bus as happy as you are now.'

'I will be. The only difference'll be that I'll be blacker than you are.'

'You think so?' she tried not to laugh. 'With that skin?'

'Two weeks of non-stop sunshine.'

'And you'll look like a lobster.'

'I'm not stupid, you know. I have bought some protection cream. I'll wear that for the first few days, then I'll put oil on.'

Juanita looked at Kay with half-closed eyes. 'Oil?'

'Why not?'

'Listen. You don't put oil on, y'hear?' She raised her voice as if she were scolding a child. 'You put oil on that paper-thin white skin and you'll be covered in blisters!'

'All right, all right!' Kay felt her cheeks flush with embarrassment as other people on the bus looked at the two of them shouting at each other. 'No oil – OK?' Kay pulled away and folded her arms defiantly. 'Not until the end of the second week.'

'I don't know! As if I haven't got enough with three grown-up children to worry about, I have to get lumbered wit' you.'

'Perhaps I can meet these grown-up sons of yours when I get back, when I'm brown, when I won't stand out like a sore thumb.'

'Maybe. We'll see. You could do with some spice in your bones, that's for sure.'

For the rest of the short journey into the city, both Kay and Juanita were wrapped in their own thoughts as the bus crawled along through the rush-hour traffic.

'Show me the palm of your hand,' Juanita broke in.

Kay did as she was asked, making sure the bus conductor had seen that she wanted to get off at the next stop. With her eyes on him and her palm spread, Kay waited for Juanita to tell her fortune, assuming that was her intention. Instead of words of wisdom, Kay felt two coins being pressed into her palm, the size of half- crowns.

'I can't take that.'

'Why not? My money not good enough?' Juanita's big brown eyes widened.

Kay bent down and kissed her on the cheek. 'Thanks. I'll send you a postcard!' she said, as she ran along the aisle towards the exit.

'You don't have my address!'

'I'll send it to the bus!' Kay yelled and then jumped down on to the kerb. Waving through the window, she felt a lump in her own throat as she saw tears rolling down Juanita's brown cheeks. 'I'll be all right!' Kay called out, as the bus pulled away.

Using every bit of concentration she made a mental note of the bus's number-plate, and as she crossed the road and walked along St John's Street, she repeated it over and over again.

'Six minutes early again?' Alf dragged the gates shut and pressed the button to ascend. 'You're getting a bit keen, ain't yer?' he accused.

Kay wouldn't answer him; she was still repeating the bus number-plate and didn't want to lose it.

'And no nipping into that boardroom! I've seen yer! Sneaking in like a cat burglar!' he called after her.

'Don't waste your breath on her, Alf,' the stocky canteen manageress called out. 'Lazy little cow's not worth it. None of 'em are. You should see them in the Ladies' at tea-break. Only supposed to take ten minutes. Ha! Fifteen, more like. Fill the place up with smoke and giggling and all.'

Alf crashed the gates closed. 'They should go in the army, the lot of 'em; boys and girls alike.'

Grabbing her notepad from her desktop, Kay jotted down the number-plate. When the door suddenly flew open and Mr Grieves marched in whistling a little tune Kay stiffened, knowing he would be embarrassed when he realized he had an audience, and a junior at that. She had never heard him whistling before.

'Morning Mr Grieves!' she said boldly, letting him know she was there before he did anything else out of character.

'Eh? Oh, it's you, Kay. Yes, well, it's good to see you in early for a change.' He peered suspiciously at her. 'You're looking a bit flushed.' He instinctively looked around the office as if someone else might be there. Someone who shouldn't be.

'I arrive at the stop in good time every morning to catch my bus,' Kay was beginning to get annoyed, 'and I always catch it. If the traffic's bad, I'm a couple of minutes late; if it's good, I'm early.'

'Fetch me the P. R. Marshall file, would you please, Kay. We may as well make an early start.'

'I haven't taken my coat off yet.'

Mr Grieves looked at her over the top of his bifocals. 'So I see.'

Pulling her coat off, Kay threw it on to her typist's chair, dragged the file he wanted from a small grey cabinet and put it down on his desk.

'I'll take my coat to the cloakroom now, if that's all right.'

Mr Grieves said nothing. He gave her a look instead, which spoke for itself. She had better watch her manners.

Slipping her coat on to a hanger in the ladies' powder room, Kay turned to the other girls who were busy studying their faces in the large wall mirrors, and applying make-up.

'What you looking so chuffed about?' said June from the switchboard, slipping a gold-cased lipstick into a white make-up bag.

'If you don't know now, you never will.' Kay grinned back at June's reflection.

'Oh, of course! It's tomorrow you're going away.'

'All right for some,' one of the girls from the typing pool said coldly. 'Must be nice to be an only child. Having your parents pay for you to go abroad.'

'That's where you're wrong!' Kay rejoined. 'It's coming out of my own purse, actually!'

'Yeah?' The girl flicked more mascara on to her upper lashes. 'Your purse must be like the magic porridge-pot then, the salary this tight-fisted firm pays.'

June threw Kay a look, warning her not to say too much. Kay was quick to pick up on it. 'I've been saving up for a year,' she said quietly. Wanting to end it before she was asked any more questions, Kay left the cloakroom without combing her hair.

'We've got a lot to get through today, Kay.' Mr Grieves spoke to her through the frosted glass partition that separated Kay's desk from his.

'You'll need to tie things up so that Doreen knows where everything is while you're away.'

Kay looked across at Doreen and they simultaneously rolled their eyes. Doreen was Kay's senior and had taught her everything she knew, efficiency being top of the list. Between them they had everything tied up, and each knew that Doreen could handle the responsibility for two weeks without too much difficulty.

'I want you to finish my letters before you start sorting the pay packets.' Mr Grieves sounded as if he begrudged her going away. In truth, he was probably feeling a bit peeved because he had never been abroad himself, and was Kay's senior by twenty years. He was in a rut.

'I'll start typing the registered envelopes as soon as you're ready.' She spoke quietly and with respect. Despite his sometimes austere manner, she knew he was an old softie at heart. It was the same every Friday fortnight on pay-day. The busiest day for the chief accounts clerk.

'I can always stop when you're ready to dictate,' she added, trying to ease the feeling of tension in the office.

'Good girl.' He went back to his figure work.

Pulling her typewriter forward, Kay caught Doreen's eye again and a smile passed between them. Doreen often teased Kay that when she turned on the charm, Mr Grieves was like putty in her hands.

'Now then . . .' Kay started to talk to herself, a habit which could be irritating to others. Mr Grieves, James the junior and Doreen often complained about her mumbling.

'Where did I put the registered envelope list?' She pulled at each of the four drawers in her desk, and still couldn't find it. She tried them all again. No luck.

'Kay!' Grieves sighed loudly. 'If you open another drawer . . .' His voice was tinged with threat. 'I'm trying to concentrate!'

Kay apologized, and made an effort to make less noise. Searching through some papers in a wire tray on her desk, she finally found the list she needed.

'Seems I'm not the only one who chose this month to go away.' She was talking to herself again. 'One, two, three, four, five,' she quickly counted aloud, 'six, seven—'

'Shhh!' Grieves made his feelings known for the second time. Reprimanding herself, Kay settled down to work and tried not to be distracted. She was excited, and as much as she tried to act as if it were a normal busy pay-day, she couldn't stop the surge of excitement that swept over her from time to time.

Doing her utmost to concentrate on her work and not think about the packed suitcase in her bedroom, Kay began to type addresses on the registered envelopes which were to be posted to members of staff who were away that week, either on holiday or off sick.

There were over six hundred people on the staff and it was Kay's responsibility to separate and put into bundles the departmental salaries, ready for collection.

Later that day, just as she was about to slip a pay packet into a registered envelope, the bell went for tea-break. Pushing her typewriter back, Kay had no idea that an empty registered envelope addressed to Mr Woods had also been forced to the back of her desk and had fallen behind it, hidden from view.

By late afternoon, several staff from various departments had been in to collect the salaries, and the filled registered envelopes had already gone to the post room.

'Afternoon.' The soft voice of Stephen Drake drifted into Kay's thoughts as she sat staring at nothing.

'Oh, sorry,' Kay said, 'I was miles away.' She looked up into the drawn face of the eighteen-year-old and grinned. 'Hope you haven't been standing there too long?'

'No, I've just arrived.'

Kay took the bundle of salaries from the tray, put them to one side and began to write in the receipt book. *Salaries – 8 M*, before realizing her mistake. 'You're not from the Mail Sales department, are you?'

'No. Bought Ledger,' said Drake quietly.

'I'm going mad.' She smiled, crossed out the M and wrote *Bought Ledger* instead.

The young man signed, flicked through the salaries, counting them under his breath, then turned to leave. As he reached the door he asked Kay what he should do about the head of department's salary, Mr Woods, who was away on holiday.

'Oh, his will be sent on by registered post,' she smiled, thinking that Wood's wasn't the only one to be escaping Thompson's for a while.

'You're sure about that?' Drake asked.

'Oh yeah,' Kay wondered why he was blushing. She showed him the list on her desk and pointed out Mr Woods's name.

'Ah, right. Thanks.' A little awkward, the young man left the office. Something didn't feel right, but Kay couldn't decide what it was.

Once outside, Stephen Drake leaned by the door, looked through the salaries again, pulled out the one marked for Mr Woods and slipped it into his inside pocket.

As he walked along the corridor a broad grin swept across his red face. The stupid little tart had made a mistake and made his day. It was a fat pay packet, and Mr Woods being the head of department probably earned more in a week than he did in a month. And since he was on holiday leave, it meant that instead of a fortnight's salary in that packet, there would be four weeks' worth of cash.

It was true he had signed for eight salaries and would only be handing in seven, but the dizzy blonde had messed up the receipt book in any case, making another mistake over the name of his department. He was home and dry, and didn't give a toss as to how she would explain the missing salary. After all she was common as muck, from the worst part of London – probably came from a family of thieves. Whereas he, Stephen Drake, was the son of a Detective Superintendent at the Met.

Feeling pleased with himself, he pushed his finger on the lift bell for a few seconds longer than necessary.

'You're young enough to walk down!' Alf was far from pleased at being called up to the third floor by a junior.

'Sorry, I wasn't thinking.' Drake had taken on his innocent, shy look again, but there was no fooling Alf. He had seen dozens of people come and go at Thompson's and prided himself on his perception of character.

Slamming the gates shut, Alf stared into Drake's face. 'Someone filed a complaint against me five weeks ago, he said I was a bit on the slow side. Said he had to wait five minutes for the lift.'

Drake shook his head. 'Some people have no respect for their elders. Whoever it was should have had a good dressing-down.'

Throwing the gates back on the ground floor, Alf felt a pang of concern. This young man was very smart, both in dress and thinking. The type to go far. The sort who could easily rise to a managerial position.

'I can assure you it wasn't me.' Drake looked straight into Alf's face, daring him to answer back.

'No. I just thought I would mention it, in case you knew.'

'If I hear anything.' Drake gave the worried lift man a friendly punch on the upper arm and walked with his head high out of the building to the annexe, where he worked as a junior office clerk.

Alf inhaled slowly, pursed his lips and wondered why that young man made him feel uncomfortable.

He wasn't the only one. There was no way Kay could have known that Drake was going to be the cause of a nightmare she would have to face after her holiday, but somehow she felt uneasy about him and couldn't think why. Looking up at the clock on the wall above Doreen's desk, she was relieved to see it was ten minutes past five.

After a hectic day, the office now had a calm air about it. 'You, er, you can knock off now, Kay.' Mr Grieves looked over the glass partition. 'I expect you've some packing to do?'

'I've been packed for a week,' she grinned.

'And don't get oil on my bikini!' Doreen placed the cover on her adding machine. 'Or my sun-dress!'

'Oil? You'll burn to a cinder.' Grieves pulled on his trilby. 'Now then.'

He moved closer to Doreen and whispered something in her ear, causing her to turn around and smile at Kay. They both stood there, smiling at her.

'This is for you, love.' Doreen held out a white envelope. 'It's from me, the girls on the switchboard, and Mr Grieves.'

Moving slowly forward, Kay felt tears welling up in her eyes. They were giving her a card, wishing her *bon voyage*. Tearing it open, she kept her eyes down, determined not to cry like a baby but to accept the gesture like an adult.

As she drew the card out and opened it her eyes nearly popped out of her head. Three crisp new ten-shilling notes were inside. Swallowing the lump in her throat, she pressed her lips together and nodded.

'It couldn't have been easy, love. What with your dad on strike.'

'Everyone's being so kind . . .'

'Compassion is only shown to those who deserve it, Kay.' Mr Grieves tipped his trilby and wished her a safe journey and Doreen a good weekend, and as the door swung shut behind him, Kay felt a certain sympathy for him.

'He's not a such bad bloke, is he?' she said.

'Not when you get to know him.' Doreen tied her silk Paisley scarf under her chin.

Standing by the door, Kay looked back at her tidy desk and felt a nagging worry, as if she had forgotten to do something important.

Turning the lights off, Doreen placed a hand on Kay's shoulder. 'It'll be there when you come back,' she smiled.

Tired at the end of a busy day, they left the silent office, the empty registered envelope addressed to Mr Woods still wedged between the back of Kay's desk and the partition.

On her return from Spain, she would have to face the consequences of that small accident, which would thrust her into the adult world more quickly than she could anticipate.

Chapter Five

Standing in the tiny sleeping compartment of the French train, heading for the Spanish border, Kay stared bleakly at the small top bunk. 'I can't sleep up there, Pamela, I just can't. I'll be sick again, I know I will.'

'No you won't. You've had your travel pills.' Pamela was beginning to lose her patience.

'They didn't work on the boat, did they!'

'Only because you didn't take them early enough. Now climb up there and try the bed out.'

'Call that a bed? If I'd 'ave known we'd be travelling for this long, I would never have come.'

'Stop moaning.'

'What if I need to be sick again?' She turned to one of the other women who was sharing the sleeping compartment with them. They had been doing their best to ignore her.

'Please let me sleep below.'

'I'm very sorry, but no!' One of the women cut in. 'I said all along that I wanted to be below. And we were here first!' She looked fiercely back at Kay. 'And please take something up there with you to be sick in. Should the occasion arise.'

'And if you are sick,' the woman's companion added, 'make sure you take the vessel away and wash it.'

'If you stop thinking about it, it probably won't happen,' her friend chimed in.

Kay gazed at the women and wished she had the energy to tell them what she thought, but she felt like death. And the prospect of sleeping on the train didn't help, with hours to go and still suffering from the after-effects of the rough crossing from Dover. She looked up at the bunk again and thought about her bedroom at home, where all would be so very still and quiet. Then she thought about her mum and dad, and two weeks suddenly seemed like a lifetime.

'Now, if you don't mind, my friend and I would like to eat our sandwiches without a running commentary on your stomach!' The women sat on the edge of their bunks and peeled greaseproof paper from their sandwiches. The smell of hard-boiled eggs filled the compartment.

After another visit to the lavatory, Kay opened a window and sucked in fresh air which tasted wonderful. Feeling slightly better, she turned to Pamela. 'I'll be all right soon. Those bloody bitches don't help much.'

Pamela poured some lemonade into a paper cup. 'Here, get this down you.'

'When this train stops, I'm getting off.' Kay drank the lemonade down in one go.

'We'll all be getting off.'

'And I'm turning round and going back.' She let out a long, loud belch, and didn't care who heard her.

'Good. Can I borrow some of your clothes then?' Pamela knew how to handle Kay. They had, after all, been friends since nursery school.

'What 'appens after this train, anyway?'

'A nice long coach trip over the Pyrenees mountains which rise to . . .' Pamela closed her eyes, remembering what she had been told that day, 'over eleven thousand feet. That's high.'

'I hope you enjoy the view.'

''Course I will. We both will. No choice really. The roads are very narrow and winding.'

'At least you read up on it. I suppose that's something.'

'No I never. This woman at work told me all about it. She went last year. Never again, though.'

Kay stared into Pamela's face. 'Why not?'

'I don't know. I didn't ask. She just said never again.'

The biggest mistake of their arduous journey to Spain was that Kay allowed Pamela to talk her into sitting on the back seat of the coach. She said she would be better off away from the engine. Kay could see the sense in that, until she learned where the engine actually was. Then it was too late to change seats.

The Spanish coach driver was obviously used to the route across the mountains. It seemed as though he knew every hairpin bend. When the rear end of the coach tipped over the edge of a road, the madman would roar with laughter at the screams coming from Kay and Pamela. The higher the coach climbed, the faster the driver seemed to go. Kay wanted to be like the others and enjoy the view, but she couldn't bring herself to take her hands away from her eyes.

'You know what's worse than this?' Pamela murmured. 'We've got to go through it all again on the way back.'

When the nightmare ride finally came to an end and the mountains were behind them, Kay and Pamela fell asleep on each other's shoulders and didn't wake until the coach pulled up outside Hotel Ruiz, in the tiny resort of Costa Lana, four hours later.

Half asleep and exhausted, the girls struggled with their suitcases, following a porter who led them and a few others out of the small hotel and up a side-street. Neither of them could be bothered to ask where they were going. All they wanted were their beds. It was ten o'clock at night.

They were guided through the living room of a Spanish family, up a narrow staircase and into a small but clean twin-bedded room. Once the young Spanish porter left them, Kay dropped on to her bed and stayed there. She was almost asleep when she felt Pamela pulling at her arm.

'Kay, I'm starving. Let's go and get something to eat.'

Forcing her eyelids open Kay slowly shook her head. 'I'm too tired.'

'No you're not. It's all in the mind. Come on, we're in Spain now. It's early. People don't go out until now.' She poured the remains of the lemonade into a glass she found in the bathroom.

'Drink this and you'll feel better.'

Kay did as she was told but didn't feel better. The lemonade was warm. 'Can I go back to sleep now?'

'No. We're going out to explore the nightclubs.'

'You go. You're bound to see some of the people we travelled with. Talk to them.'

Leaning back on fat pillows, Pamela sipped her lemonade. 'Did you clock that dishy bloke in Reception? He was gorgeous.'

'Go and talk to him, then.'

'He touched my hand deliberately when he handed me our key.'

Pulling herself up into a sitting position, Kay stared at her feet. 'I need a bath,' she yawned.

'No. A shower.'

'A nice long soak—' Kay stopped in her tracks. 'Why did you say no?'

'It's a lovely shower.'

'There isn't a bath, is there?'

'Spanish people must take showers,' she shrugged. 'I s'pose it's because there's a water shortage out here,' Pamela commented thoughtfully. 'Daft really, 'cos there's a lot of sea. What you wearing then?'

Kay peered at her through half-open eyes. 'What?'

'Tonight. When we go out to the nightclub. What you wearing?'

'You mean it. You really expect me to go dancing after all that travelling?'

'After your shower.' She grinned again. 'I'll unpack while you're in there. I'll hang everything up properly, in the ward—' she gazed around the room until her eyes settled on a painted cupboard. 'In the cupboard. You can have the best hangers.'

Kay felt a pang of guilt. Poor Pamela was trying so hard, and all she had done was complain. 'Share the hangers out fair and square. But you don't have to unpack for me.'

'I want to.'

'You want to see what I've brought with me, you mean?'

''Course. I might wanna borrow something.'

Kay let herself be persuaded into the shower, and with warm water cascading down, she gently rubbed the spicy Spanish soap over her body until she was covered in suds. The water was much softer than at home, and she began to feel better than she had in a long time.

'Can I borrow your mini-dress? The black Mary Quant-style dress with the white thingumabobs down the front and back!' Pamela yelled from the other side of the door.

'Yeah, but not until I've worn it first. You can 'ave it tomorrow night.'

'But he'll 'ave seen you in it!'

'Exactly!' Kay laughed to herself. This felt more like it. This felt like being on holiday. She was beginning to relish the thought of nightclubs and fun.

'I heard someone say it's been really sunny!' Pamela couldn't keep the excitement out of her voice. 'We'll dance until the sun comes up and then sleep all day on the beach.'

Wrapping herself in a big white towel, Kay stepped out of the bathroom. 'I can't get over how warm the air is.'

'I can't get over those Spanish eyes,' Pamela said dreamily.

Dropping down on her bed, Kay drew her knees up and stretched her arms. 'I feel brilliant!'

'Thank God for that. I thought you was gonna die on that boat.'

'Don't! No more, Pamela. And I mean it. I want to forget that trip. OK?' She glared at her friend.

'I don't know whether to 'ave a shower or not.' Pamela turned away. 'And if you ever talk to me like that in front of anyone else,' she pulled a dress out of the cupboard, put it up to her and admired her reflection in the wall mirror, 'I'll talk about small cubes of pork fat on a piece of string.'

'Enough!' Kay screamed. 'It's not funny!'

'I know it's not bloody funny! The way you *talk* to me!' Pamela's face was white, her dark blue eyes alive with anger. 'You're always so bossy!' She turned her back on Kay and lowered her voice. 'Or putting me down, and sometimes in front of other people.'

Kay inhaled slowly and thought about it for a minute. 'It never occurred to me I was doing that.'

'Oh, it's not *you*! I don't even know why I said it.'

Seeing that Pamela was keeping her face turned away, Kay slowly circled her. 'Pamela? You OK? You're not crying are yer?'

'No, I'm not,' she sniffed, trying to control her face.

'Hey,' Kay put her arms around her best friend's shoulders. 'I'm sorry. I didn't realize I was being a cow.'

'It's not you.' Another pained expression suddenly spread across her face.

Guiding Pamela towards her bed, Kay sat down next to her and stroked her back. 'What is it, Pamela? You can tell me, surely?'

'It doesn't matter.'

'Of course it does.' Kay tried not to be upset. One of them had to be strong. They were, after all, in a strange country.

'It's my mum,' Pamela covered her face with her hands.

Kay was beginning to fear the worst. 'She's not ill, is she?'

'No.' There was a pause. 'I miss her.'

'You miss her?'

'And my dad.'

'You miss your dad as well?' Kay bit the inside of her cheek and didn't even smile.

'And my cat!' Pamela threw herself on to the bed, buried her face in a pillow and howled. 'My cat'll be looking for me, I know he will! He'll be sitting outside my bedroom and he'll be crying and my mum'll start and so will my dad. They'll all be crying, and it's Sunday night!'

Kay wanted to ask what was significant about Sunday night but she didn't dare speak. She stuffed the corner of her pillow in her mouth and kept her back to Pamela as she lay on her own bed. Her body shook, and all she could hope was that should Pamela come out from under the pillow, she would think that Kay was crying, not laughing.

'My grandma and grandpa always pop in of a Sunday night,' Pamela sobbed, 'they'll be in a state as well. And that's bound to start Joey off!'

That was it. That was more than Kay could stand. She shrieked with laughter and couldn't stop. It was Joey that did it. Joey, the half-dead blackbird that the family were nursing back to life. The bird had been with them for four months. They had even bought it a cage, swing, small mirror and every other comfort available for the feathered pet.

Sitting bolt upright, Pamela stared disbelievingly at Kay. 'You're laughing!'

'And so would you be, if I was going on about a half-dead bird missing me!' Kay buried her head in her pillow again. The next thing she knew, Pamela was thumping her with something soft, and she was happy to retaliate. The pair of them were enjoying a really good pillow fight.

Thirty minutes later they stood by the door of their room, admiring each other. Kay had given in over the Mary Quant-style dress and thought it looked better on Pamela in any case.

'Maybe I should have worn my denims . . .' Pamela stood awkwardly, checking her reflection in the mirror. 'I'm overdressed next to you.'

'I'll 'ave my frock back, in that case.'

'You think I look all right then?' Pamela was begging for a compliment.

'You look great. And the only reason I'm in jeans is because I . . . feel in that kind of a mood,' she shrugged. 'Come on! We've washed our hair, polished our shoes – now let's see what this place has to offer.'

Ten minutes later, they were handing in their key to Reception in order to let Pepe, the handsome receptionist, know that they were going out on the town.

'The Cellar!' he called after them as they waltzed out of the hotel. 'It's very best!'

'You have beautiful eyes!' Pepe shouted into Pamela's ear as he held her close. 'They are like sky before night. Beautiful hair. It is like—'

'I love this song!' Pamela yelled back. She had to shout to make herself heard above the noise in the Cellar. Forgetting that she had always been singled out as a growler at school, she began to sing along to 'Rambling Rose' as she eased herself out of the tight grip that Pepe had on her.

'Why?' Pepe asked, gazing into her face, trying to win her over with his big brown cow-eyes.

'Why what?' she asked, irritated that he was interrupting the song.

'Why you no come close?' He tried his best to sound offended.

Even though Pamela had had quite a few Martinis she still had her wits about her. 'You're too hot, Pepe!' she laughed.

'Pamela!' Kay shouted, trying to be heard above the din. 'I'm going back to the hotel!'

'Why? This is great!'

'I'll see you later.' Weaving her way through the mass of bodies, Kay made for the exit, keeping her eyes down so she didn't have to acknowledge the smiles of local boys reaching out to stroke her long blonde hair.

Once outside Kay was grateful for the fresh air, which although warm was a lot cooler than the tiny nightclub. Making her way back to the hotel she wondered how Pamela could be so full of energy after two days of travelling. She was ready for her bed. The bright white spotlights of the Cellar and the smoky atmosphere had made her eyes smart, and there was a dull ache spreading across her forehead.

Ignoring complimentary remarks from a group of Spanish boys, she walked quickly along the narrow pavement and turned left, believing that was the way back to the hotel. She couldn't stop the niggling feeling inside reminding her about Pamela's well-being. After all, it was only the first night. Remembering that her friend's dancing-partner worked at the hotel she felt easier, telling herself that Pamela was probably in less danger with a local than with one of the gorgeous French students they'd met at the Cellar. It was the delicious aroma of freshly baked bread that caused Kay to stop and take in her surroundings. At first she was interested to know where the smell was coming from, but when she realized that she had no idea where she was, a surge of panic shot through her. Had she taken the wrong turning? Or was it left out of the club and then the third on the right?

The narrow cobbled street was practically in darkness, only a glow coming from the windows of one or two of the old terraced houses. Looking further along the street she could see that the bakery was lit up and the door was open. She quickly made her way towards it, praying that someone inside could speak English. Maybe he or she could direct her to her hotel.

Fear gripped Kay and she suddenly stopped in her tracks. She had forgotten the name of the hotel. Looking backwards, she wondered if she should retrace her steps to the nightclub. Knowing she would have to pass the local boys who were hanging around, she decided to go forward. Bracing herself and trying desperately to remember something about the hotel as a reference, she made for the bakery.

Standing in the doorway, Kay found herself face to face with a man, whom she imagined to be the baker's assistant, kneading dough on a large wooden table. She stood for a few seconds staring at him, wondering if her eyes were playing tricks. Was that Zacchi, her first love whom she'd met in Kent, on the hop fields?

'We're not open, but you are welcome to try some hot bread,' the young man smiled. 'Or a cake?' He pinched three strands of dough together at one end and began to plait with expertise.

It must have been the Martinis, thought Kay. Of course it isn't Zacchi. He's taller, his eyes are a lighter brown, but his black hair and eyebrows and long lashes, they're nearly the same . . .

'You look as if you've lost your way.' He was laughing at her, and Kay could feel herself go weak at the knees. He had the most wonderful smile she had ever seen, and his golden skin showed off his pearly-white teeth.

'I have,' she said, unable to keep anxiety out of her voice. 'And I can't remember the name of my hotel.'

Smiling, he pulled some dough from a larger piece and threw it on to the floured surface. 'Can you remember your own name? Or do you wear a label around your neck?' He was flirting with her and she loved it.

'You've got flour on your hair and nose. And it's Kay.'

'You've got a very pretty face, and it's Chris.' He blew a loose strand of hair from his face and suddenly looked shy. 'I'm supposed to wear that hat.' He nodded to a sparkling white baseball cap.

'Well wear it, then!' Kay reached out and grabbed it, then placed it firmly on his head. 'Shall I tuck the loose curls in?'

He took a slow, deep breath. 'You want me to explode?' He shook his head. 'Those lovely slim hands touching a man's neck would send sparks flying up and down his spine.'

'I'm sure.' Kay backed away from him, wondering if her mascara had run as her eyes had watered from the smoke at the nightclub.

'You arrived today, I take it?' He looked at her sideways.

Was he psychic too? 'How can you tell?'

'Lily-white skin,' he grinned, looking from her face to her hair and making it obvious he was impressed. 'It's very blonde. Do you bleach it?'

'No I don't!' How dare he suggest she used peroxide? 'I occasionally put lemon juice on it, but that's all.'

Carefully placing a second plaited loaf on a proving-tray, he nodded towards a wooden stool. 'If you want to sit down and wait for ten minutes, I'll help you find your hotel.'

Watching him work on another piece of dough, Kay studied his face to see what it was that made him so attractive.

Chris's eyes were almond-shaped; his nose straight; his jaw square, and his smooth skin had a deep golden tan. He had high cheek-bones and thick, dark eyebrows. He was very handsome and try as she might, Kay could not find any fault with his looks. And he had charisma.

He's probably the most conceited man on this earth, Kay told herself, turning her attention to the next best thing – hot crusty bread on the cooling-rack.

'If you look in that blue and white dish, you'll find some butter. Knife in the top drawer,' he nodded towards a small scrubbed pine table in the corner of the bakery. 'If you think we need plates, they're in the cupboard underneath.'

Was he a mind reader too? 'How come you speak such good English?' Kay said with a touch of suspicion in her voice. She couldn't help herself. This bloke was too good to be true.

'I lived in England from the ripe old age of two,' he said.

Kay smiled inwardly. That's what it was about him. 'You do look like a Londoner, as it 'appens.'

'Disappointed?'

'Why should I be?' She was noncommittal.

'I could be the first Spanish bloke you've spoken to, and I turn out to be regular old townie from back home.'

Pushing the last loaf of bread into shape, he slapped it down with the others and lifted the large metal tray with one hand, raising it level with his broad shoulders. 'Don't go away, I won't be a minute.'

Hearing him speak fluent Spanish to someone in the back room, she felt herself melt inside. Watch yourself, Kay . . .

Taking a small loaf of bread from the tray, she broke off two pieces and split them in half. Spreading unsalted butter thickly over each piece, she felt her mouth watering.

'This is delicious,' she told Chris as he strolled back in. He pulled off his white apron and proceeded to wash his hands under a tiny brass tap over a minute sink in a far corner of the room.

'I didn't realize how hungry I was.'

'Come on,' he said, pulling off his cap, 'we'll eat it going along, while you try and remember the name of your hotel.'

'I have remembered. It's Ruiz.'

'Oh, so you're only as thick as one plank, then?'

Ignoring the remark, Kay walked by his side, wishing Pamela could see her with this tall, handsome hunk of a bloke. She thought he must be twenty-two or twenty-three.

'So how long are you gonna be working over here for?' Kay asked as she tucked into the warm buttered bread.

Taking her hand and guiding her round a small group of Spanish boys, Chris smiled at her. 'For good. Or for bad; depends which way you look at it.'

Once they were safely past the noisy gang, instead of letting go of Kay's hand, Chris locked their fingers. 'I didn't want to go into my father's restaurant business, so we decided to leave home and set up here, in our family's village. Not that it's much like a fishing village any more,' he said, looking into her face.

'We?' Kay wondered if he was married.

'My brother bought a small bicycle shop – we'll pass it soon – and I took over the bakery. Neither of us are married. We've been here for just over a year.'

'Sounds perfect.'

'It could be,' he said, giving her a studious look. 'You know what I'm going to tell my brother tonight?'

'No.' She felt his eyes on her face and prayed she wasn't blushing.

'I'm going to tell him that tonight a star fell from the sky and landed in my bakery.'

Kay raised her eyebrows and gave a slow smile. 'Not a poet as well, are you?'

'No. I mean what I say.' He squeezed her hand.

'Yeah, I'm sure.' She wasn't going to fall for that one.

'Come on.' His face was full of fun. 'I'll introduce you to him. I know exactly which bar he'll be in. He's in love with the blonde German waitress.'

Before Kay could object, Chris was running and pulling her along with him. His laughter filled the air, and it was contagious. She was laughing too, and feeling very happy.

'Do you believe in love at first sight?' he yelled.

'Yes, I do, as a matter of fact!' She remembered Zacchi.

'So do I,' he said. Then without warning, he suddenly swept her up into the air and swung her round.

Shrieking and laughing, she begged him to stop. People were looking. He brought her gently back down to earth and cupped her face in his hands. 'I don't care who's staring at us,' he murmured.

'Neither do I.' Kay was surprised at her own words, and even more surprised when she stood on tiptoe and kissed him lightly on his full lips.

'Come on. I want my brother to meet you.' He tousled her hair and then put his arm around her shoulder, leading her into the small bar.

Chris introduced Kay to his brother Charles and a few friends who were there. 'She . . . is only sixteen, only sixteen . . .' Charles began to sing.

'Seventeen, actually,' said Kay, playfully indignant. She liked Charles instantly; the eighteen-year-old was full of himself, and she could imagine Pamela would go for him in a big way.

'Oh, well then.' He folded his arms and smiled at her and Chris. 'I expect you'll want me to stay out of the apartment tonight?' Before either of them could say anything he leaned forward, pushing his face up close to Kay's. 'But only if I get a turn tomorrow.'

Chris and the rest of them began to laugh as Kay became suddenly aware that she was a stranger, and fearful of what she had walked into. Stepping back, nearer the door, she looked at Chris and saw him in a different light. Maybe the instincts she'd had in his shop were right. He was too good to be true. Remembering how she had allowed herself to get into a dangerous situation with Zacchi, she felt herself go numb. Turning quickly, she ran out of the bar, angry as much with herself as with them.

She ran a short distance, then stopped and looked back. No one was following her. Composing herself she asked an English couple if they could direct her to the Hotel Ruiz.

'Turn around,' the man gave her a relaxed smile. 'It's behind you!' he said, in true pantomine style.

Kay was so relieved she felt like hugging the couple. She thanked them and went through Reception to the hotel bar, and was even more relieved to see Pamela.

'Where 'ave *you* been?' Pamela was beside herself. 'I was just about to get the manager to phone the police!'

Kay sat on a stool at the bar and slowly shook her head. 'I'll tell you later, when we're in bed. Where's Romeo?'

'Sitting at the hotel switchboard, can you believe? Talk about Jack of all trades and working all hours.' Pamela looked at her watch. 'He'll be finished in just over an hour. I'm waiting for him.'

'It's nearly three in the morning, for God's sake. Can't we go to bed?'

'You can. I'm not stopping yer.' Pamela looked as if she really had had one drink too many.

'Please come with me. I don't want to go to the annexe by myself. I'm scared.'

'What of?' Pamela studied Kay's pale, frightened face and nodded slowly. 'Tell Pepe I'll see him tomorrow, will yer, Juan?'

Juan, the barman, pushed his thumb forward. 'OK! Swinging!' Norman Vaughan's catch-phrase had obviously reached Spain.

Slipping down from the bar stool, Pamela looked sideways at her friend. 'You OK?'

'More or less.' Linking arms, the girls left the main hotel building and made their way to the annexe.

'Where did you get to, then?'

'I found a bakery.'

'You what?' Pamela cut in. 'I'm starving!'

Laughing quietly, Kay took an elastic band from her pocket and pulled her hair back into a pony-tail. 'I met the baker as well.'

'Did they have any cakes?' Pamela stopped in her tracks.

'Warm cakes, yeah, and hot bread.'

'What are we waiting for then?'

'You wouldn't catch me going back. Not in a million years.' Kay carried on walking.

'Where is it? I'll go.' Pamela stood her ground.

Turning back to look at her friend, Kay thought about it. 'OK,' she said, 'we'll go, but there's somewhere else I want to go first. A bar. I've got something to settle. Come on, I'll tell you about it on the way.'

Surprised but pleased with Kay's sudden change of heart, Pamela slipped her arm through Kay's. 'I had a great time in the Cellar after you left. A gorgeous Frenchie asked me to dance. We're meeting him on the beach in the morning.'

'Oh *are* we?'

'We don't have to stay with them. It's very casual. It's not a date or anything.'

'You said *them*?' Kay looked suspiciously at her.

'Yeah. A whole load of French students. Staying on a camp site. It's party night every night by the sound of it.' Pamela looked as if she had already been in the sun. She was positively glowing.

'Anyway, enough about me – your turn! What's so special about this old baker man?'

Kay shrugged nonchalantly, tucking her red blouse into her denims. 'He's just a kindly old man, that's all.' She smiled to herself and suddenly felt in the mood for a bit of fun.

'I said she would be back!' Charles looked happy to see Kay.

'Don't fall off your ego,' Kay snapped, a sulky expression on her face. 'I came to set the record straight.' She turned to Chris who was sitting by himself at a small table. 'You insulted me.'

'Kay!' Pamela spoke in a low whisper. 'You don't talk like that to a *god*.' She couldn't believe her own eyes.

'He never said a word!' Charles looked pleadingly at Kay, 'It was me. *I* owe you an apology.'

Kay looked from Charles back to Chris and waited. Chris said nothing, just looked back at her. With a cool expression on his face he slowly raised his legs and stretched them out on top of the table in front of him.

'What's going on, Kay?' Pamela whispered in her ear.

'This lot had a good laugh at my expense!' she deliberately raised her voice.

Charles made a display of innocent frustration. 'It was a joke!' He glared at Chris. 'Tell her then!'

Chris folded his arms defiantly and chewed on the wooden toothpick stuck in the corner of his mouth.

'Well, I dunno what's going on,' Pamela said, 'but I fancy a cappuccino.' She perched herself on a bar stool and smiled at the blonde barmaid, Sieglinde. 'Make that two,' she said. 'One for Kay.'

Sieglinde gave Pamela a thumbs-up sign and smiled. 'That's good,' she said, 'a good move.'

Leaving Sieglinde to it, Pamela swung around and looked from Kay to Chris. They were glaring at each other.

'It must be love,' Charles whispered in Pamela's ear. They both enjoyed the scene and within seconds were chatting away.

The other Spanish lads looked at each other and waited to see which of them would give in first and speak. They knew it would be a mistake for any one of *them* to start flirting with Kay.

Suddenly swinging his legs off the table, Chris sauntered over to the jukebox and studied the labels. Making his choice, he then turned away and took up his earlier pose, keeping himself to himself. Charles and the other lads looked at each other, wondering which record Chris had chosen. It could make or break a possible romance.

Kay joined Pamela at the bar and sipped her coffee, keeping her back to the vain, loathsome man she had foolishly allowed herself to kiss. She hated him for the way he was behaving, and wondered how she was going to leave the bar with dignity. As the record started to play she felt Pamela's eyes on her face and resisted the urge to smile. They all listened with interest as the music drifted through the bar. Recognizing the record, Sieglinde reached up to the controls above the counter and turned up the sound, giving Kay a cheeky wink as the lyrics of 'Venus in Blue Jeans' filled the room.

> She's Venus in blue jeans,
> Mona Lisa with a pony-tail
> She's a walking, talking work of art
> She's the girl who's stole my heart . . .
> My Venus in blue jeans, is the Cinderella I adore . . .
> She's my very special angel too
> A fairy tale come true . . .

Resisting the urge to join in with the others, who had begun to pick up on the lyrics, Kay slowly swung around and smiled back at Chris, who had his eyes fixed on her. His legs were no longer stretched out on the table.

* * *

They say there's seven wonders in the world,
But what they say is out of date.
There's more than seven wonders in this world . . .
I just met number eight . . .

Smiling, she walked towards Chris and took his outstretched hand. He pulled her down into the chair next to his.

'I suppose I'll have to walk you back to your hotel?' Charles grinned at Pamela.

'But no funny business!' She tossed back her long dark hair.

'Would that I dare?' he laughed. 'Don't want you setting Kay on me.'

'Never mind Kay,' Pamela stepped down from the bar stool. 'I can throw a good punch, you know.' She looked up into his cheeky face. 'Come on then, Goldilocks. I'm dead tired.'

'Tonight . . . they will make love on the beach.' A Spanish boy grinned.

'I think not,' said Sieglinde, drying glasses. 'Those girls are good.'

'You hope so, eh?'

'I am not worried. Ten days, and the girl will be gone. I am here for a long time,' she shrugged.

It was almost four a.m. when Kay and Chris strolled hand in hand along the calm shore of the Mediterranean. 'You know what would be nice?' Gently he pulled Kay down on to the soft sand. 'If we could stay here and watch the sun come up.'

Kay curled herself into his strong, tanned arms. It was exactly what she had been thinking. 'Wake me up if I fall asleep,' she murmured.

'You won't fall asleep.' Chris kissed her gently on the mouth and she responded, her entire body beginning to throb with longing.

This was a new experience for Kay. Lying on a soft golden beach, waiting for dawn to break and listening to the sound of the sea lapping the shore. It was like a dream come true.

For Chris, it was just another holiday romance. Except that the girl lying next to him seemed different to all the others. She was natural and relaxing, comfortable to be with. It made him feel uneasy.

Chapter Six

Settling themselves in the living room by the gas fire, Laura and Jack tucked into their fish-and-chip supper and were enjoying an episode of *Coronation Street* on television. It had been a drizzling, grey day and Jack had stood for several hours outside the gates of the Royal Albert Dock. The mass meeting of dockers included men from Tilbury, Surrey and East India Docks.

Jack Dash, the union leader, had been there and spoken well. He had told the men that the situation in the Port of London was critical. He also confirmed that unregistered labour was being used at one of the wharves, while elsewhere, two thousand dockers could not obtain work.

'They're planning to fetch meat in by air, y'know?' Jack said, breaking off a small chunk of steaming hot crispy cod. 'Flying it in to Southend.'

'Oh yeah?' Laura tried to sound interested, but she was involved in an argument going on between Ena Sharples and Annie Walker.

'Tilbury hasn't come out yet, but some of the Surrey men are with us. Bloody Joint Import Trades Committee sent a telegram to the Prime Minister requesting that importers get permission to unload their own cargoes! They want their bloody brains looked at.'

Making himself a chip sandwich, Jack tried to get interested in the weekly serial, but his mind was still full of the strike.

'Mead's going on about letting fleets of lorries into the docks to collect cargoes. I tell you, Laura, this country's gonna be in a sorry state if it goes on the way it is.'

'Try not to worry about it, Jack, eh?' Laura was bored with hearing about it.

A long ring on the doorbell broke into their thoughts. 'Who the hell's that?' Jack moaned.

'Might be Liz.' Laura hoped it was. Jack never went on about the strike when she was around. 'You get it, eh? I can't miss any of this. I think Annie Walker's gonna win.'

'It'd better be Liz,' Jack said, standing up. 'Anyone else can go for a quick walk. Especially if it's another Bible-basher.'

Pouring herself a glass of Tizer, expecting Liz to walk in any minute, Laura focused on the row going on between her two favourite characters, ready to fill her sister-in-law in on the affairs of the Street.

Instead of coming back into the living room, Laura heard Jack go into the kitchen. She could hear men's voices and thought she recognized them. Opening the small serving-hatch between the rooms her heart sank when she saw Bert's two brothers, Frank and Freddie, sitting at the kitchen table.

'I'm just making a cup of tea, Laura. D'yer want one?' Jack looked far from happy.

'No, I'll wait till later. Don't forget your fish and chips,' she added, eyeing the brothers.

'All right, Laura?' Frank smiled.

'Fine thanks. You?'

'Could be better, but there you are. Heard from Kay yet?'

'Not yet, no, but I expect we will.' Laura managed a smile and nodded to Freddie before closing the hatch doors. Settling herself down again, she couldn't help wondering what the two villains wanted with Jack. She hoped he wasn't mixed up in anything that involved them.

'It's like old times, eh, Jack, us being 'ere in your flat.' Freddie said. 'I know we was here for the funeral, but that was different.'

'Last time before that was one Christmas a few years ago. Bloody good party it was an' all. Bert sang 'is favourite song, naturally.'

All three men laughed at the memory. 'He didn't have a bad voice as it happens,' Jack said, pouring boiling water into the chrome teapot.

'No, you're right,' Frank lowered his head. 'I s'pose you're wondering why we're here?'

'If it's the envelope that's worrying yer?'

''Course not,' Frank cut in.

'I 'aven't given it to Liz yet, for a reason.'

'We didn't know you hadn't, Jack. That's not why we're 'ere.' Freddie rubbed his eyebrow. 'We 'aven't really felt right since we saw you in the Maurice. You looked a bit choked when you left.'

Jack felt like telling him that he wasn't upset, but angry. He thought better of it. 'I don't know if Liz'll take the cash, to tell you the truth. She can be a funny cow at times.' Jack poured milk into each cup.

'Beer money, Jack, that's all.'

Jack looked into Frank's suntanned face. 'Yeah?'

'Now that it's really sunk in about Bert,' Freddie began, quick to change the subject away from backhanders. 'He was a good bloke. We thought a lot of 'im.'

Frank covered his face with one hand. 'A fucking good brother as well.'

Freddie's eyes were filling with tears. 'We never saw much of 'im during the last couple of years. You know 'ow these things go. Families lose touch.'

Pouring the tea, Jack wondered what Frank and Freddie really wanted. They were upsetting him talking about Bert, and he wasn't sure how he would handle it if they had something else on their minds and were using his late best friend as a smokescreen.

'Bert was one of the best, Freddie. You only have to think back to the turnout at his funeral to see that. Anyway, what d'yer want with me?' He placed their tea in front of them and folded his arms, ready to stare them out if necessary.

'What you've just given us, Jack. A cup of tea and a chair.'

'If you two are winding me up, you can piss off now.' Jack could feel the blood pumping through his veins.

'We're not 'ere to wind you up,' Frank sighed. 'We miss Bert!'

'Fair enough . . . fair enough.' Jack sat down at the table and pulled his tobacco tin from his trouser pocket.

'You saw a lot of 'im, didn't yer?' Freddie said, wiping away a tear.

Jack sucked on his bottom lip and nodded, giving them the benefit of the doubt.

'He was happy enough, wasn't he? I mean, he didn't want for anything.'

'Drink your tea, Freddie. You're letting your emotions get the better of you.' Jack didn't need these two pouring their hearts out to him.

'How's Liz?' Frank blew his nose. 'She's all right, ain't she?'

'Doing 'er best. You know Lizzie.' He looked sideways at Frank. 'Well, you used to.'

'Don't be like that, Jack.' Freddie pulled a white envelope from his inside pocket. 'Don't you think we wished we'd 'ave visited them more often?' He dropped the envelope on the table. 'There's a bit more cash for Liz, and for you.' Freddie eyed Jack with caution.

Standing up, Freddie swallowed the remains of his tea. 'You ready, Frank?' He looked at his gold wrist-watch.

'Yep. We've got a little bit of business to see to, Jack. Otherwise we'd stay longer.'

With one hand on the kitchen door, Freddie turned and looked Jack in the eye. 'Sounds like the strike'll be over soon. You did the right thing.'

'Oh yeah?' Jack could feel his heart sink. 'What makes you say that?'

'Stands to reason. The attention's off of Bert. You've made things a lot more comfortable for us.' He held his hand out to shake Jack's.

'If you wanna use them notes to take Liz and Laura on a nice holiday abroad, that's fine by us.'

Before Jack could tell them to take their filthy money, the two brothers were out of the kitchen, heading for the front door.

'See yer, Jack!' Freddie called over his shoulder.

'Say hallo to Liz for us!' Frank added.

The street door slammed shut behind them. Jack shuddered. He stared at the white envelope in his hand. *Beer money*. That's what they had called it. Beer money.

Laura leaned in the kitchen doorway and folded her arms. 'Forget it, Jack. They're not worth losing sleep over.'

Jack looked up at her. His white face said it all. He was too bitter to speak. The only reason for Bert's brothers to call round was in the envelope. The second payment. The other half of the bribe.

'I feel like burning it, Laura.'

Snatching it up, Laura pushed it into her cardigan pocket. 'We'll tell Liz about it and let her decide. If we don't want this, Jack, there are a lot of people who will. People who won't know or care where it comes from so long as it puts clothing on their kids' backs.'

Jack laughed at her quietly. 'You gonna stand on the corner of Brick Lane Sunday morning and give it away, I s'pose?'

'All we 'ave to do is split it up and pop envelopes through doors. I know a lot of families on this estate who'd appreciate hard cash.'

Jack sighed heavily. 'It's filth money, Laura. From London scum.'

'Oh come on, Jack! *You're* so innocent?'

'No I'm not! I've nicked stuff from the docks and no doubt I'll do it again, but that's different! A box of Jersey spuds? A crate of oranges? Perks! They expect it!'

Laura knew it wasn't just the history of the money that was tormenting Jack, it was the reason it had been given that was tearing him apart. He believed in the strike, and wanted to be on his soapbox urging the men not to give in. And then there was his pride. Bert's two flash brothers had kicked it about as if it were an old tin can, and then crushed it flat.

'Come on. Come and cuddle up on the sofa.' She stroked his thick blonde hair and pushed her slim fingers into his neck, gently massaging away his troubles.

Looking up at her with his light blue eyes, Jack reminded Laura of Kay and another worry swept through her. She prayed she would be all right abroad, with all those foreigners.

Wrapped in each other's arms on the sofa, later that night, Jack and Laura were quiet. They had turned off the television, the lights were down low and they were listening to their favourite record, Nat King Cole singing 'Unforgettable'.

'I don't really understand why they gave you that money, Jack,' Laura said, after a while. 'Why don't they want the strike to go on? What's it to them?'

'It's probably all down to one warehouse keeper. Frank and Freddie are members of a certain firm, and that firm is probably involved in importing tea . . . sugar.'

'Yeah? So?'

'The tea and sugar doesn't come over in little bags.'

'I know that. Get to the point!'

'Well, hidden amongst all those billions of tea leaves and grains of sugar there'll be something else far more valuable.'

Laura sat up and stared, disbelievingly, into Jack's face. 'Drugs?'

'Now you know why it's scum money.' Jack reached for his tobacco tin.

'Blimey, Jack. It never occurred to me.' She shook her head slowly. 'Are you sure?'

'Why d'yer think some of them use casual labour when it suits 'em?'

'And you know this for a fact, do yer?'

'Common sense.'

'Are you saying that's the reason why this strike started up? That the wharf manager took a man on because they were running drugs and he was part of it?'

'No, of course not. That company's got nothing to do with it. It's the other one or two warehouses, here and there, who discourage the dockers from striking in their own sweet way. They wouldn't want anything to hold up the trafficking.'

'Bloody hell. I'm glad you've taken a back seat, Jack. You could 'ave ended up with your face slit.' Laura dropped her head back on to a cushion.

'Don't be silly. They don't do things like that. I would 'ave just disappeared, that's all. Man Missing Presumed to have Run Off with his Mistress.' Jack was trying to turn it into a joke.

'You could still 'ave 'ad your throat cut.' She felt a shiver run down her spine.

'Nar. A bullet through the 'ead, maybe,' he chuckled, lighting a roll-up.

'It's not funny, Jack.'

'You're telling me.' Jack didn't think any of it was funny. The East End had always had its thieves, its gangs, but the past decade had seen America filtering through. Mafia-style firms were becoming more established.

'You know, I wouldn't mind getting out of this country. Emigrate to Australia.'

'Oh leave off, Jack,' Laura laughed, 'you? Emigrate? You nearly threw a fit when I suggested we all went to Spain for a holiday! If ever there was a home-bird, it's you.'

'Yeah well, I do love this country and I think it's worth working and fighting for.' He sighed and shook his head. 'It's corrupt, Laura. Corruption runs through every establishment you can think of. Even the law.'

'Maybe it's the same in other countries?'

'Maybe. Don't make it right though, does it?'

'I dunno, Jack. Right pair we are. How often do we sit here like this without having to worry about Kay crashing in any second?'

He grinned at her. 'Funny you should say that.'

'I thought you'd never ask.' Easing herself further down the sofa, Laura stretched out one leg, allowing her silky green skirt to rise above the top of her black suspender. 'Not bad for thirty-nine,' she teased.

Jack ran one finger from her knee upward and moved his hand across her flat stomach. 'You know what I'm gonna do tonight?'

'Tell me,' she kissed his neck and let her legs fall slightly apart.

'I'm gonna kiss every inch.' He began to unbutton her dress. 'Yep, every inch, if it takes all night.' He lowered his head and filled his mouth with her erect nipple, sucking and licking, sending a wave of delicious craving through her body.

Looking into her soft green eyes, Jack pushed his hand under her, cupping and squeezing, gently playing with the soft, dark curls between her legs. Then, easing her off the sofa and on to the rug in front of the gas fire, he began slowly to take off her clothes.

Chapter Seven

Liz had taken to Joe on her first day working in the canteen at Hammond's. He was the only one, it seemed, who could make her laugh and bring her out of a blue mood. Joe from maintenance, as he was known, was also on his own. His wife had died three years previously and to fill the gap he had joined a spiritualist group.

That evening the meeting was taking place in Rose Davenport's living room, and from the moment Liz entered the clean and polished two up two down, she wished she hadn't. Telling herself that this would be her last session, she sat at the round dining table feeling easier, knowing she would not have to put up with Rose's snobby ways after tonight. She was worse than some of the women who worked in Hammond's.

'We don't seem to understand who the message is for. Could you please spell out the name of the person you wish to contact?' Rose's shrill voice broke the silence.

'I think someone else should be the contact,' Joe said quietly.

'Don't be silly, Joe. It just needs a bit more time, that's all. Come on.' Rose urged the spirit; 'Stop wasting our time!'

'You'll make it angry, Rosie. You've got to coax, not demand.' Joe took his finger off the glass.

'Oh, no that *won't* do, Joe! You've broken the link now.' Rose was beginning to lose her patience.

'I don't think it's going to work this evening,' Mary, the eighty-year-old, had had enough. 'I'm desperate for a pee and a cup of cocoa.' They always had hot chocolate after a chat with the spirits. 'Why don't we stop, eh?' She looked at Liz for support.

'Well, let's see if we can decipher what I've written first.' Rose was in before Liz had a chance. Pushing the paper towards Joe, she crossed her arms defiantly and eyed Liz. 'I think we have a non-believer in the room.'

Liz was only too pleased to make her escape into the kitchen. 'I'll make the cocoa if you like. Then you can get on with it.'

'Sit down, Lizzie. We're not finished yet. And anyway, it's Rosie's night to make the drinks.'

'You were going too bloody fast, Rose. There's not one space in between these letters.' Joe tried to break and separate words from the continuous lines of scribble.

'If I'm not back in five minutes,' old Mary said, switching the lights on, 'start without me. I think that chocolate Ex-Lax is beginning to work, Liz.'

Liz smiled inwardly at Rose's loud sigh of disgust and wondered if she might come to just one more meeting after all. Lovely old Mary crossing swords with this woman was worth coming out in the rain for. She knew the old girl did it on purpose, slipping in what Rose would refer to as a *vulgarism* here and there.

'*YaK K hctaw*? It must mean something, it's repeated that three times.' Joe said.

'Let me see that!' Rose snatched the paper away. 'Well it's obvious what's happened! I sometimes do mirror writing when I'm in touch.'

'Well,' Joe looked thoughtful, 'if you have been writing backwards, Rosie, and nothing would surprise me, this message could be for you, Liz. *Watch K Kay*.'

Liz took the piece of paper from Joe. 'You could be right, you know. Let's give it another go.'

Enthusiasm was never far away with this group; within seconds they had their fingers poised over the glass.

'We'll wait for Mary,' Liz said. 'And I'll take down the message this time, as it's for me.'

No one could argue with that, not even Rose, who hid her feelings of rejection quite well. 'Someone should call up to that woman and ask if she's going to be there all night!'

Without wasting a moment, Liz was up and in the doorway. 'Is the chocolate working, Mary?'

'Yes! It's wonderful! I don't want to come down, start without me!'

Back in her place, eyes closed, head bowed, finger on the glass at the centre of the table, Liz took a deep breath and began. 'I'm sorry we broke away when you were trying—'

'Ask it if there's a message for anyone in the room!' Rose cut in.

Containing her impatience, Liz took another deep breath. 'If you do have a message for any one of us, please spell it out and I'll do my best to write it down.'

The glass moved quickly around the edge of the mirror, stopping at letters of the alphabet which had been marked on with Rose's black eyebrow pencil. Keeping her index finger in contact with the sherry glass, Liz carefully wrote down the message until the glass came to a pause.

'Lights!' ordered Rose.

'There's enough light.' Liz stared down at the notebook. 'Give me a minute,' she murmured.

'If this is a message from my Bert about our Kay, it's a bit muddled.' She slowly began to read. *Watch K K Watch her Trouble K Watch her.*

'I think I've had enough for one night.' Liz stood up and looked at her new friend. 'You don't have to leave yet, Joe, if you don't want to.'

Easing back into his chair, Joe looked at the others. 'As if I'd let you go through the backstreets by yourself.' Pulling his cap on and rising from the table, he turned to the others. 'See you in a fortnight. Keep smiling.'

Making their way along Vallance Road, stepping around small puddles, Liz and Joe enjoyed the warm evening air after rain. The smell of baking bread wafting along the narrow cobbled street made Liz feel hungry. 'I could eat a nice hot bagel, Joe. I'm—' Before she could finish the sentence, he was guiding her into the Blue and White all-night Jewish baker's.

Thankfully the little corner shop wasn't too busy. Just a couple of taxi-drivers enjoying a chat. 'This your new girlfriend, Joe?' one of them joked.

'I'm old enough to be your mother and you're young enough to go across my knee,' Liz returned, eyeing the cheesecake behind the glass counter.

'Well, let's hope you've got plenty of money.'

'Wouldn't mind a piece of that apple strudel, Becky,' Liz asked, wondering at the taxi-driver's last remark.

'I s'pose she's the reason we haven't seen you at the last two card games, eh, Joe?' The man wasn't going to leave it be.

'Nar,' Joe slowly shook his head. 'My prostate's been on the blink again.'

'Go on! Funny that. You've always seemed fit as a fiddle and twice as sharp. Still, I always did think you was a bit deep.'

Paying for her bagels and apple strudel, Liz bade them goodnight and she and Joe left the shop, a nagging doubt at the back of her mind. Was the taxi-driver trying to tell her something?

Turning on the fire in the small living room, Liz told Joe to pull the armchair up close to the heat while she put the kettle on. 'There's some rum in the sideboard if you fancy a drop.'

'I've been thinking,' he said, following her into the kitchen. 'I've got no money, Liz, and no sex to offer yer, but . . .' he took a deep breath, 'I'm yours if you want me.'

Smiling, Liz turned to face him. 'That's a lovely offer, Joe love, but it's a bit too soon.'

'Oh, I don't mean yet. Gawd, no. In time. If you fancy a bit of company in the evenings. Someone there in the mornings.'

'Ask me again in a year, eh?' She kissed him lightly on the side of his face.

'So you don't mind, then? You know, about the . . .'

'Sex? 'Course I don't. I've got no interest in all that now. And as for the money, well, I've got none either and never have had. So what I haven't had I can't miss, can I?'

'That's true, Liz, that's true.'

'But to be honest, the pictures would suit me better than them bloody seances you keep taking me to.' She placed two mugs on a tray. 'Bert wouldn't really have approved and, well, it does upset me a bit, to tell you the truth.'

'Ah, you're just a bit upset over that message about Kay, that's all.'

'No,' she chuckled, 'I was pushing it with my finger the second time round. I'd had enough of that bloody Rose woman.'

Later that night, as Liz lay in her darkened bedroom, she couldn't help thinking about the taxi-driver. There was a look on his face, and she couldn't fathom what had been behind it. Sighing, she turned over and eased her shoulder under the soft feather pillow and tried not to worry about her Kay in a foreign land. She had only told Joe a half-truth about pushing the glass. She had started to force it towards the letters but then it seemed to have a life of its own, moving by itself, regardless of Liz's fingers.

For the next two days, until her niece was home, safe and sound, Liz knew that the feeling of dread inside her would stay right where it was.

Chapter Eight

'It's me, Kay!' the voice screeched over the telephone. 'We're at Dover!'

'It's all right, Kay,' Laura laughed, 'you don't have to shout.' Laura was choked at hearing her daughter's voice again. 'What time will you be arriving at Victoria?'

'I dunno! There's trouble with the trains so I'm gonna be late whatever happens. You won't have to meet me. We've been offered a ride in a taxi.'

'What d'yer mean, offered a ride? Who with?'

'This man and woman we met on the boat. They live near Aunt Liz. They know her. Alf and Sarah. I'll have to go, Mum. Wait up for me, won't you?'

''Course we'll wait up for you,' Laura swallowed tears, 'I can't wait to see your silly freckled face.'

That Friday evening seemed the longest in Laura's life. Sitting beside Jack on the sofa, she tried to get absorbed in the television; *Take Your Pick*.

Lighting her second cigarette, she rehearsed to herself how she would deliver the news to Jack about Kay's holiday and where she had actually been. Time was running out and she would have to speak up soon. Kay might knock on the door any minute.

'What's with the chain-smoking?' Jack said casually, his eyes on the screen. 'What's on your mind?'

There was a moment's silence as Laura plucked up courage and searched for the right words. Jack was a placid man most of the time but experience had seen him flare up within seconds and take days to calm down.

'I'll tell you after this show,' she said, giving herself breathing space.

'That bad, eh?'

Loud banging on the front door startled them both. Jack peered across at Laura, his eyes narrowed. 'If that's not the copper's knock I don't know what is.' He pulled himself out of his armchair.

'Don't be daft,' Laura's face lit up, 'it's Kay!'

'No, that's not her.' Jack pulled his braces over his shoulders, sucking on his bottom lip. 'There's nothing I should know before I open that door, is there?' he asked, with more than a touch of worry in his voice. 'You've been on edge for a couple of days now.'

'No, of course not.' Jumping up quickly, Laura's hand flew to her face. 'Oh Christ! There's still a carton of cigarettes in the wardrobe!'

'No there's not. I got rid of 'em this afternoon.'

While Jack made for the street door, Laura stood in the darkened passageway, listening.

'Mr Armstrong?' she heard one of two uniformed officers ask.

'May we come in, sir?'

'I hope you're not the bringer of bad news? We've had more than our fair share lately.' Jack spoke in a low voice.

'There hasn't been an accident, sir. Nothing like that. We'd just like a few words with your daughter, Kay.'

'Oh yeah?'

Laura felt her heart sink as she recognized dread in Jack's voice. Something was wrong. Something bad had happened.

'If we could come in, sir? It shouldn't take long.'

Closing the door behind them, Jack led the way into the front room. Laura's brain worked nineteen to the dozen. She couldn't imagine Kay getting up to anything, not on holiday.

'I take it she has arrived back from her holiday, sir?'

'No, as a matter of fact she's late.'

Laura silently prayed that they hadn't found out about Kay forging Jack's signature on her passport form. Staring into their solemn faces, she heard herself telling them to sit down as she switched off the television.

'So what's my seventeen-year-old been up to, then?' Jack smiled. Trying to hide his concern, he dropped into his armchair and picked up his tobacco tin from the coffee table.

'We believe she's involved in something quite serious.'

Laura turned icy cold, unable to do anything but stare at the policeman who seemed at ease with the silence that hung heavy in the room.

'According to information given by her colleagues at work, your daughter was due home today?'

'That's right,' Jack lit a roll-up. 'Should be in any minute. We was getting a bit worried, as it happens. She is on the late side.' He drew on his cigarette. 'What's she been up to at work then?'

'What makes you ask that, sir?' asked the younger police officer.

'Stands to reason. You went there before you came 'ere.'

'She's under suspicion of theft,' the second officer added.

Jack roared with nervous laughter, then looked at Laura and winked. Kay stealing? It was out of the question. 'What she s'posed to 'ave pinched then?'

'A pay packet's gone missing from the office where your daughter works. So far our inquiries lead us to believe that she might've taken it.' The officer shrugged and gave Jack a half-smile. 'Maybe she was a bit short of pesetas?'

Jack shook his head and grinned. 'You're barking up the wrong tree, mate. Kay's no thief. And she would hardly need pesetas on Sheppey.'

'You mean the Isle of Sheppey?' The officer looked across at his colleague. 'We were told she'd gone to Spain.'

'Do me a favour – Spain. She'd need a passport for that.'

Laura studied Jack's face, and when he smiled reassuringly back at her she was filled with remorse, knowing that at any second it would have to come out that she and Kay had gone behind his back. It would be devastating.

'You're confusing our Kay with someone else,' he said.

'I don't think we are.' The officer caught Laura's eye and waited. It was obvious from his expression that he knew she had something on her mind.

'She did go to Spain, Jack,' Laura murmured, keeping her eyes fixed on the floor.

Looking at his watch, the police officer sighed. 'Perhaps we'll call back tomorrow. I expect her plane was late in.'

'What you talking about? How could she go abroad without a passport?' Then, as it dawned on him, Jack threw his head back as if he'd been struck by lightning, and swore. He shook his head slowly. 'Stone me. I never thought you'd go behind my back and sign that form.'

There was a tense silence and the officers looked from one to the other.

'What right did you 'ave to undermine me like that?' Full of anger, Jack couldn't see the warning looks Laura was giving him. She wanted to scream at him, tell him to keep quiet. Tell him to think before he spoke. But knowing that was one of Jack's weaker points, she began to get angry herself. He was playing his usual game of turning things around so that she was at fault. She had seen it before, many times. Now he was pushing it too far.

'You can be a silly bitch at times. D'yer think I didn't 'ave my reasons for not wanting her to go out there? She could 'ave got dragged off by some sodding—'

'I never undermined yer! She did! And all because you wouldn't let her go! She signed your name on the form!' Laura screamed at him. 'It's *your* bloody fault! If you wasn't so stubborn.'

'She forged her father's signature? On a passport form?' The officer spoke slowly, emphasizing each word. 'And you don't think she's capable of taking a bit of spending money?' He turned to his colleague and a look passed between them.

'I think we'll wait for her to come in.' He sank back on the settee and folded his arms. 'Let's hope she's not too long.'

Clutching the handle of her suitcase, Kay waved goodbye to Alf and Sarah as the taxi pulled away from the grounds of the flats. It had just gone nine p.m. and as tired as she was, she couldn't wait to show off the presents she had brought back.

Pressing the lift button she felt excited at being back home in Stepney. The *No spitting* sign on the brick wall was like a welcome-home plaque, and the familiar smell of flowers from the cottage gardens opposite brought a smile to her face. The holiday had been wonderful. A dream come true. But it was good to be back, even if it did feel chilly. Almost as exciting as leaving in the first place. And Spain would always be there. Spain with its night life and eternal sun. Spain with its promise of a lifetime for her and Chris – running a small chain of bakeries.

Pulling the lift door open, she dragged her suitcase out and carried it to the front door. Finding the bell in the dark she held her finger on it for longer than she would normally, to announce her arrival.

It was a grim-faced Laura who opened the door. 'Hallo, Kay. I'm afraid we've . . .' unable to say any more, Laura reached out and drew her in. 'Oh, Kay. What have you done?'

'Mum?' Kay pulled back and looked into the haunted face. 'Dad's not that angry with me, is he?'

'No, love. He's not angry with yer.' She wiped her eyes with the back of her hand. 'Push your suitcase up against the passage wall.'

'But the presents. Can't I give 'em to you now?'

'Later, Kay. We've got visitors.'

When Kay saw the policemen, her heart sank. Had someone else died? Were they there to break the news?

'Kay, there's been some trouble at Thompson's. A wage packet's been stolen.'

A broad grin swept across Kay's face. 'At Thompson's? God. Trust me to miss all the drama.' She smiled at the two policemen. 'I don't know how I can help. I've been away. I've just got back from Spain.' Glancing at her dad, she lowered her eyes.

'So we gather. It came as a surprise to your father.' The officer's tone and dour expression made it clear that they were not amused. 'We understand from your parents that your passport was obtained by a forged application form?'

Kay looked from Laura to Jack. Surely they hadn't betrayed her?

'They found out from your mates at work, Kay,' Laura murmured.

The senior officer looked from his watch to his assistant who seemed to read his mind. A brief nod passed between them. 'Kay Armstrong—'

'*No!*' Laura's green eyes were wide and full of fear. 'You can't do this!'

Grabbing Laura's arm, Jack swallowed hard. 'Leave it, Laura.' His instincts were to the fore. He had read the expression on the officers' faces and knew what was coming. Furious as he was, his only thoughts now were for Kay and how best to support her through the next few hours.

Pulling Kay in close, Jack felt a sudden surge of emotion, as though an electric current was passing through his body. They were going to arrest Kay. They were going to take his girl in for questioning.

'What's going on? Dad? What's happening?'

'Kay Armstrong, I am arresting you on suspicion of theft and forgery. You are not obliged to say anything unless you wish to do so. But what you do say may be put in writing and given in evidence.'

'You can't do that,' Laura cut in, defying them to argue with her. 'You dare take my child away!'

'We'll be taking your daughter to King's Cross police station where she'll be questioned properly.'

Trembling, Jack nodded. 'I'll get my coat,' he managed to say, throwing a sheepish glance at Laura.

'I don't understand!' Kay's face became distorted and she burst into tears. 'I haven't done anything, I don't know what you're talking about.' She backed away and began to sob. 'You can't take me away! Dad, tell them! Tell them I'm not a thief!'

'It's all right, Kay, it's all right.' Jack moved towards Kay as her hand went for the veranda door. With one quick movement he reached out and grabbed her, pulling her in close. 'It's a mistake, babe. We'll get it sorted.'

'But they're arresting me! They're gonna put me in prison! You've got to stop it!' She was still gripping the handle of the glass doors. Dropping from the back balcony was one way of escape and Kay's mind was racing.

'No they're not, silly.' Jack stroked her hair. 'They just need to ask you a few questions, that's all.'

'Well let them ask me then.' She turned to the police officers. 'Ask me anything you like. You don't need to take me with you.' She looked at each of the solemn faces. 'What am I supposed to have done?'

Jack knew it would be useless trying to soft-soap these two. They had their job to do and as far as he could tell, little scenarios like this left them cold. He silently prayed to God that Kay hadn't been silly enough to steal that money. He would rather die than see her cross-examined in a court of law.

A stream of words poured from Kay as they journeyed from Stepney to north London in the back of the squad car. As she sat between Laura and Jack, she turned from one to the other for reassurance.

'But you must know something, Dad? Whose salary went missing? What does Mr Grieves think? He knows I'm honest. I handle loads of money every fortnight. I've never taken a penny, they know that.' She had stopped crying but her voice was shaky and she was trembling from top to toe.

'They wouldn't trust me with all that cash if they thought I was a thief.'

'Never mind trust! They shouldn't 'ave given a seventeen-year-old that kind of responsibility. You wait till this is over. I'll have something to say to that company!' Jack looked as if he might put his fist through a window.

The interview room at King's Cross was small, with just a few chairs and a small wooden table, a far cry from Laura and Jack's front room where they should have been at that moment.

Carrying a tray of hot tea, a uniformed officer arrived and his comforting smile eased the atmosphere. 'Would you like a biscuit? They're not very exciting.'

'No thank you,' Kay murmured, and started to cry again. The well-meant kindness was all it had taken to trigger her off.

Setting the tray down, the officer left the room and was instantly replaced by the arresting officer and the station sergeant.

While Laura looked as though she might pass out any minute, Jack's fists were clenched with anger. The officer was reporting to the sergeant his grounds for arresting Kay, and making it sound worse than it was. They were talking about her as if she were a criminal.

Once that was over, Laura and Jack were asked to leave the interview room and wait in the foyer while the female officer searched Kay and recorded her details.

'Your daughter will be interviewed by the detective constable and should he feel there is enough evidence against her, she will be charged and released on bail. If she's cooperative, it shouldn't take too long.' The constable threw Jack a look, advising him to leave him to it.

Taking Laura by the arm and avoiding his daughter's searching eyes, Jack led his wife out of the room.

The silence weighed heavily in the small room while the detective constable sat on the other side of the table and placed the red receipt book down, watching Kay for her reaction.

'How did that get here?' She stared down at the book. 'That's the salary receipt. I keep that in my top drawer, in my desk.'

Looking into Kay's face, DC McCormack sipped his tea. 'You do understand why you're here?'

'No, I don't, actually. I thought that you were only allowed to drag criminals into a place like this!' Knowing she was overstepping the mark, she added quickly, 'I s'pose for all you know I *am* a criminal.'

'You were brought in under suspicion of theft of a wage packet, and forging an official document.' Before she could interrupt, he quickly reminded her that she was still under caution. His stern voice and strong presence caused Kay to cower in her chair.

Keeping his eyes lowered, the DC thumbed through the pages and then stopped. 'Can you tell me why you made this alteration, Kay?' He looked straight into her face.

Through watery eyes, she focused on the line written in the book and suddenly blushed as she remembered making the mistake. She leaned forward in her chair as the scene came flooding back. 'Mr Woods's salary?' Her voice was tinny. There was a pause while they waited for her to continue, but her mind was racing as she slipped back in time. There had been something about that moment. Something about the expression on the face of Stephen Drake when he asked her what she would do about Mr Woods's salary, since he was on holiday.

'It went by registered post.'

'That doesn't answer my question.'

'What question?' Kay had lost touch with the present; she was still back there in the office on that Friday afternoon.

'Why did you alter this entry?' He pointed to the line in question.

'It was a mistake.' She was remembering clearly now. 'I thought Mr Drake was from Mail Service but he wasn't. He was from Bought Ledger.' She smiled. It had been a silly mistake after all. Soon she would be home and in her bed.

'Go on.'

'I wrote down eight salaries, then I was going to put Mail Service but I remembered where he was from, crossed out the M, and put Bought Ledger.' She was even beginning to enjoy the fact that she could throw light on the mystery.

'I see.' He sat back in his chair and rubbed his chin. 'So what happened to Mr Woods's salary, Kay?'

'He was on holiday. So it went by registered post.' She sipped her tea and began to enjoy the feeling of relief which was taking over from the turmoil inside.

'But Mr Woods never received it.'

Kay shrugged. 'Must 'ave got lost in the post, then.'

'Registered envelopes don't get lost. That's the point of having them registered in the first place.' He was taking on a more serious tone. 'And when your boss, Mr Grieves, checked with the post room, there was no sign of his name in the book. And the girl in the office couldn't remember seeing an envelope for him.'

'Well there was one. I remember typing it. And I remember pointing it out to Mr Drake when he asked about it.'

'You showed him the envelope?'

'No, I showed him my list of names of the staff whose salaries had to go by registered post.'

'Why didn't you show him the registered envelope?'

'I don't know!' He was beginning to irritate her. 'The list was there, right in front of me.'

'So you're saying that you definitely remember typing the envelope, putting the salary in and taking that, with the others, into the post room and giving all of them to Sylvia?'

'Yeah.' Kay smiled again. 'Ask Sylvia, she'll tell yer.'

'We did, and like I said, she doesn't remember it.'

There was another pause while Kay racked her brain. She didn't want to get her friend in trouble. Maybe Sylvia had taken the salary?

'Your father tells us you're not averse to a little forgery now and again?'

Kay bent her head, realizing that her foolish idea had turned out to be more serious than she had dreamed possible.

'Did you or did you not forge your father's name on an official document? An application form for a passport!' He was angry now. Angry, demanding and impatient.

Kay could feel the blood rushing to her face again. 'Yes,' she murmured.

'I'm sorry,' he said, cocking one ear, 'I didn't hear that.'

'I did!'

'You must have known that was a serious criminal act.' He leaned back in his chair and grinned. 'You've got some nerve, I'll say that. It takes a brazen face to pull off something like that.'

'It was the only way.'

'Mmmmm . . . and there's not much point being in a place like Spain if you've no pocket money.'

'I had pocket money. We're not exactly on poor street, you know.'

Giving her a warning look, the officer continued. 'Did you take Mr Woods's salary, Kay?'

'No. I'm not a thief.'

'But you are a forger? And some would say that's even more serious than stealing. What did you do with the empty registered envelope?'

'I took it to the post room with the salary in it.'

'But we've questioned three people in the post room. None of them can remember seeing it. Where did you get the money from to pay for this holiday abroad?'

'I worked for it.'

'But Thompson's only pay you seven pounds ten shillings a week.'

'I got another job. In the evenings. In the sweet shop.'

'Your boss doesn't seem to know anything about that. No one that we spoke to mentioned it. Seems a bit strange.'

'We're not meant to have a second job. Company policy.'

'So you're a liar too.'

'I am not!' Kay's voice was cracking, but she willed herself to stay calm. She wasn't going to let him beat her down.

'You told them you were breaking the rules, did you?'

'No. I didn't tell them anything. I would have got the sack if they'd found out.'

'You know what I think?' He leaned forward, pushed the red receipt book under her nose and slowly tapped the altered entry with his finger. 'I think you wrote *Salaries seven. Bought Ledger*. And that's what the young man signed for. Once he had left the office, you made the seven look like an M and wrote *eight* down next to it.'

Kay only took in half of that. She was more concerned with him saying that Stephen Drake had signed for eight. 'I remember now!' She sat up, a smile on her face. 'I remember! He stood there and counted the salaries, they all do. They have to, before they sign. Then he asked me again what was gonna happen to Mr Woods's. He must have seen it there! I must have put it in the collection group instead of the registered envelope batch.'

'But you said you also remember typing the registered envelope. And putting the salary in. And taking it to the post room!'

'Well I got confused! You keep confusing me! I remember filling the envelopes. I can't be expected to remember every name! I don't know, I must have made a mistake!'

'So that leaves the empty registered envelope that you typed. Where do you think that is?'

'I don't know. Maybe I never typed one out for him! Maybe I forgot! Why don't you talk to Mr Drake?'

'We have. He flatly denies seeing a pay packet for Mr Woods. And I believe him. He also swears you didn't alter that entry while he was there.' The inspector raised one eyebrow and stared into Kay's flushed face. There was a long pause.

'Kay Armstrong, I am now going to have to charge you.'

'No!' Kay cried, 'No! I didn't do it! It's not fair!' As Kay stood up, moved behind her chair and picked it up, McCormack's colleague was in like a flash, seizing her by the arms. The stream of words seemed to strike out and hit the centre of her stomach, sending flashes of white light and a million sparks up through her head.

Kay remembered little of the journey back to Stepney in the taxi. Sitting in the armchair in front of the gas fire at home, she didn't want to think about King's Cross police station. She would try to wipe it out for ever.

'D'yer want me to unpack for you, Kay? Or would you rather wait till the morning?'

'I'll wait.'

'You sure you don't want to show me your gifts?' Laura was doing her best to cheer Kay up.

'Give it a rest, Laura,' Jack said, 'it'll soon be bloody morning.'

'Yeah, don't feel like it though, does it? I don't know about you, but I can't see myself sleeping yet.'

'I'm gonna have to go through all that again.' Kay stared into the glow of the gas fire.

'Oh, no you're not!' snapped Jack. 'There'll be a solicitor present next time.'

'What good will that do? I'm a forger. I even admitted it.' She gazed up at him, almost trancelike. 'What does bail mean, Dad? I don't really understand.'

Jack rubbed his forehead and sighed. 'I dunno. They need time to investigate. Make more inquiries. It's all down to form-filling, I s'pose. Anyway, you're here and not locked up in a cell, that's something.'

The room fell quiet as the three of them gazed into the blue and yellow flames of the fire.

'How's Aunt Liz?' Kay rubbed her swollen eyes, which were puffy from crying.

'She's all right. Been talking to your uncle Bert again,' he laughed. Catching Laura's eye and her scowl, he tried to keep a straight face. 'She's gonna drive us mad now, you wait and see.'

'Why?' Kay asked.

'Saw it all coming, didn't she? Reckons Bert sent her a message a couple of days ago. "Kay, watch Kay, trouble".'

'Dad!' Taking a sudden interest, Kay cupped her mug. 'You're kidding me?'

'Does seem strange, I must admit,' Jack conceded.

'Strange, nothing! She was worried about Kay being abroad, that's all. It was on her mind.'

'Yeah, I s'pose you're right.' Lying back in the armchair, Jack stared out. 'I might go with 'er one night. Wouldn't mind a word with Bert.' He ignored Laura's sigh. 'I wonder if Mum and Dad are with him? Or our dog, even? Do dogs bark in heaven? That's the question.'

That was too much for Kay. She started to laugh. 'Be a noisy bloody place if they did.'

'Come on then. Let's see what you've dragged back from half way across the world.' Jack had achieved his goal, seeing the smile back on his daughter's pinched face.

'I haven't got the energy.' Kay said, hoping he would get the suitcase for her.

'We'll 'ave to wait till tomorrow then, won't we.' He sniffed and stretched his long legs.

'No you will not!' Kay jumped up from her armchair and marched out of the room. 'You'll look at everything now.'

'That was mean, Jack. You could have got it for her.'

'I know that, Laura.' He grinned and winked at her.

'Oh, right. Yeah. It worked too.' She chuckled then drew a deep breath. 'Talk about two peas in a pod.' She sipped her tea. 'What a life, eh?'

'It's only what you make it, Laura,' he said, looking up at the ceiling, wondering if she would remember her telling him that once.

She managed not to smile. 'It's not very nice when it crumbles before you though, is it?' She repeated the answer he had made two years ago when they were going through a crisis in their marriage.

It amused Jack that she had remembered, and surprised him. Laura was just as deep as he was, then?

Chapter Nine

The following Monday morning before Kay left for Thompson's, she and Laura shared a gloomy breakfast, sitting in the kitchen.

'I don't want to go.' Kay broke off a piece of toast. 'They probably all think I did it.' Feeling sick inside, she sipped some water, hoping it would ease the nausea.

'You don't have any choice, Kay. If you don't go to work as normal it'll make you look guilty.' Laura tipped cold tea from the teapot into the sink. 'Try and eat a bit of that toast, love. You've hardly touched anything all weekend.'

'I can't. It'll get stuck in my throat again.' She dropped the toast on to her plate.

'My gut feeling is to go with you. Take a day off work. Mondays are always quiet. They'd give me the time off, I'm sure of it.'

'No. If I have to go, I'll go by myself.' Kay dragged herself from the kitchen chair. 'I've got nothing to hide.'

'No. Someone has though, Kay, and wouldn't it be great if you found out who took that money?'

'Yeah. I s'pose it would.'

'You don't have to tell them you've been charged.'

'Oh yes I do!' A surge of defiance rose inside her. 'I'm gonna make sure everyone knows before they find out and whisper behind my back. Yeah, I'll go in. I'll show them. Don't you worry, Mum. They're not gonna get away with this, the bastards.'

'Kay! You're above that kind of language!'

'Am I? I don't feel it. Not any more.' Collecting her handbag and suede jacket, she swept her long blonde hair back off her face. 'I'm a hardened criminal now,' she half joked.

'Well, if you ain't a sight for sore eyes,' Juanita chuckled as Kay sat down beside her on the bus. 'I expected a little more colour in your cheeks. You look as if you've been dragged through hell.'

'I have,' Kay quietly said. 'Trouble is, I'm still there trying to crawl out.'

Juanita sucked her teeth and slowly shook her head. 'What happened to you out there, eh?' The smile had gone from her face.

'Out there was great. I fell in love. It's back here that's the problem.' Kay turned away, willing herself to be strong. She mustn't cry. She would walk into Thompson's with her head held high.

'Are you ready for it?' Kay gave Juanita a wry smile.

'No, but you had better get it off your chest.'

Kay started at the very beginning when she made the crucial mistake and altered the receipt book. She gave a methodical account of the whole drama almost as if she were recounting it to herself. Remembering, conveying, in a detached voice, what had gone on since they had last spoke.

Before either of them realized, the bus was pulling up at Kay's stop. Taking a piece of paper from her pocket, Juanita quickly wrote down her telephone number. 'Phone me this evening or earlier if you want to talk. I'm usually home by four-thirty.'

Slipping the piece of paper into her pocket, Kay thanked her friend and jumped down from the bus feeling much better than when she got on. Her stomach was still in a turmoil, threatening to throw everything out one minute and striking her with pain the next. But not her mind. Her mind was clear. Her conscience was clear. And her determination strong.

From the minute she stepped into the lift, the atmosphere could have been cut with a knife. Alf the lift man gave her a sympathetic smile while two of the women from the canteen threw her a knowing look. Their expression said it all. They thought she was guilty.

'I suppose the whole bloody building knows about it?' Kay said, firing the question at Alf.

'It's been the talk of the town,' he smiled. 'And a lot of people are very angry. We know you're a cheeky cow at times but we don't think you're a thief. So keep your chin up and don't let anyone put you down. If they do, come and see me for a pep talk.' Alf spoke in a fatherly fashion, which touched Kay.

'Thanks Alf.' She gave him a wink and walked away, pushing the swing doors with more vengeance then she meant to. Her plan was to remain cool. Cool and clever. Listening out for any remarks that were derogatory, any looks of suspicion. She needed to know who her friends were before she could attack the enemy. And she would attack. Verbal abuse or otherwise. Her bottled-up anger was bursting to escape.

Making a grand entrance into the Accounts office, Kay stood her ground, smiling defiantly at her colleagues. There was a deathly hush as each one turned to her. First it was Doreen, doing her best to smile. Then James, the junior clerk who, though she couldn't swear to it, seemed to be sneering.

'Morning, Kay,' Mr Grieves finally said. 'I'd like a word in private.' He looked embarrassed.

'No need for that. Anything you've got to say can be said in public. My washing is already on the line,' She smiled back at him. 'And before you ask, no. I didn't do it. I've been charged, but I'm innocent. OK?'

There was a look of surprise from both Doreen and Mr Grieves. Even James looked as if he might fall off his chair.

'The question is,' Kay spoke as if she were in court, the prosecutor rather than the accused. 'Where *is* the missing registered envelope with its fat contents?'

They stared at her in disbelief. How could she joke at a time like this? 'Would you like me to arrange some coffee?' Doreen looked sick with worry.

'No thanks, Doreen. I'll wait for the break. I've got too much to do.' Charged with a new-found courage, Kay stepped towards her desk, pulled out the top drawer and tipped the contents into the middle of the office floor. She did the same with every drawer and container on her desk until there was nothing left. The others sat rooted to the spot, staring down at the heap of office sundries, paper, notebooks and files.

'It's all right, I'm not gonna put a match to anything. Not yet.' Falling to her knees she began to search through the tip.

'Kay, we've already looked. Mr Grieves and I went through everything. That's why we came in early.'

'After this, it's your desk, James. And then Doreen's, and then yours, Mr Grieves. We must leave no stone unturned!'

Fearing for her state of mind, Mr Grieves stepped forward and offered his hand. 'Come on, Kay. There's no need for that.'

'No? Well you try being dragged off to a police station the minute you walk back from your holiday and see how it feels! You try being arrested!

Being questioned and charged for a crime you didn't commit. Then come and tell me that!'

The opening of the office door broke the tension. 'Ah, Mr Grieves, the Chairman would like a word with both you and Kay.' Miss Jamieson, the Managing Director's secretary, stared down at the floor, at Kay and at the mess.

'Ah, Miss Jamieson!' Kay made no move to get up, but leaned back on her hands and tossed her silky blonde hair. 'That's a very smart outfit you're wearing today. Straight from Harrods, no doubt?'

Ignoring the remark, Rebecca Jamieson turned to Mr Grieves. 'We have Mr Drake with us now.'

Quick to her feet, Kay stood in front of the haughty woman. 'Have we really? How splendid. Excuse me.' She pushed her aside and stormed out of the room, making her way to the Chairman's chambers.

Drake and the Chairman, Mr Thompson, stared blankly at Kay as she burst into the office. 'Everyone, it seems, has decided to get in early today. I wonder why?'

Paying no attention to the pleas from Doreen and Mr Grieves who were on her heels, Kay moved towards Drake. 'You're a liar. And I think you might be a thief as well.'

'Now then, Kay . . .' Mr Grieves's voice went over her head.

'And d'yer know what happens to a liar and a thief where I come from? You know, the other side of the tracks, where only the lowest of the low live?'

'I should think an old lag would have no trouble finding refuge in those Dickensian backstreets,' Drake flashed a knowing smile at the Chairman, 'code of silence and camaraderie.'

'You gormless overgrown *maggot*!' Kay slowly shook her head and found herself laughing at him. 'Dickensian? It's time you woke up, cretin.' Not wanting to spend any more time in his company, she stepped forward, grabbed him by the lapels of his jacket and with strength borrowed from her anger, pushed him across the office, knocking an antique statue flying. '*We* get arrested! Even if we're innocent! Now get up! Get up and tell the truth, you spineless bastard!'

As Drake started to raise himself on to his elbows, Mr Grieves stepped forward, but Doreen grabbed his arm. 'Leave her,' she murmured. 'She knows more than we do.'

'You saw me alter that book and you know it!' Kay lunged towards

Drake again, grabbing his tie and glaring into his eyes. 'Tell them the truth, you sodding coward! *Tell them*!'

'I have told them.' Curling his top lip, Drake pushed his face close to hers. 'You're no better than your scum family,' he sneered.

A flash of fury shot through Kay and before she could stop herself, she drew back her arm, clenched her fist and used all her power to land a punch square on his face. Overcome with anger and humiliation, Drake shot forward and grabbed Kay's hair, pulling until her head almost touched the floor. 'Apologize, you slut!'

'That's enough!' Grieves pushed Miss Jamieson out of his way. 'Let go of her, Drake, before I—'

'*Stephen*! Out here! Now!' The booming voice of Drake's father took them all by surprise. 'Move!'

Everyone's attention turned on the red-faced man standing in the doorway. 'I'll deal with this,' he said, assuming command. 'In *private*!'

The colour draining from his face, Stephen Drake pulled himself to his feet, pushed his shoulders back and tried to cover his fear. It was clear to everyone that his father reigned supreme. He instantly filled the room with his oppressive presence.

'And who are you, sir, to come barging into my office?' Mr Thompson was not the least pleased.

'Stephen's father,' he returned curtly, ending it.

'From the Met?' Kay smiled knowingly. 'Here to save your son's skin, no doubt.' She ignored the urgent look on Mr Grieves's face, warning her to take heed.

'I'll show the gentlemen into the boardroom,' Rebecca Jamieson smiled benignly as she led the way out of the Director's chambers. 'We hadn't realized you were dealing with this case—'

'I'm not!' he said definitively as he followed her out of the room.

Once Mr Thompson had ushered everyone except Kay out of his office, he closed the door and sighed. 'It'll be much easier in the long run if you tell the truth, you know.'

With her back to him, Kay asked if she could have a glass of water. Filled with disappointment that he really believed she was guilty, the anger which had fuelled her actions earlier began to drain away and she made no effort to stop the tears.

'We shan't press charges, and *if* the police are prepared to drop the matter, we'll settle for your confession. Of course it will mean your finding employment elsewhere, and I can't promise to give you a clean reference.'

Taking the glass of water from him, Kay felt like giving in, saying that she had taken the money, and putting an end to the whole thing. It might be easier to confess than to fight. She could walk away from the building. Away from the accusing faces.

'Crime really doesn't pay, you know. I should have thought you would have learned that from your brother who spent time in prison.'

'I haven't got a brother,' she murmured.

'Oh, well, your uncle then.' He waved his hand impatiently.

Her uncle. So that had come out too. While she had been in Spain believing that her colleagues were struggling along without her, people had been delving into her private family business, discussing her uncle. What right had they to do that? What right had they to accuse her of stealing when she had never once taken a penny that didn't belong to her? Who did these people think they were?

'Does your wife know you've been fornicating with your secretary?' She smiled into his shocked face. Fornicating. She liked that word. She remembered it from senior school. It had been the cause of a humorous debate between the teasing adolescent boys in her class and the naïve student teacher who thought they had been interested in her religious knowledge lesson.

'You could end up in court for that, you know,' Kay continued. 'If Jamieson's old man filed for a divorce you'd be—'

'That's enough!' His red angry face looked fit to burst. 'You insolent wench!'

'Not very nice, is it, Mr Thompson? To be accused of something you haven't done? How would you feel if your wife believed the lie and stopped trusting you?' By the expression on the Chairman's face, Kay had a feeling she might have touched a nerve.

A tapping on the door stopped her getting in too deep. She could hardly believe herself, speaking to the Chairman like that. She would have apologized if Rebecca Jamieson's sickly smiling face had not appeared.

'Would you come to the boardroom please, Kay.' The polite request was delivered as if it were an order.

'No, I won't. I've had enough. You go and play detectives if it gives you a thrill. *I* am going home!'

'I don't think that would be wise.' Again the sickly smile.

'Oh, get out of here, both of you. I'm fed up to the back teeth with it.' Mr Thompson poured himself a whisky, keeping his back to them.

Kay pushed her way past Miss Jamieson and strode along the corridor towards the boardroom. Again she was filled with determination to prove her innocence, if only to put Jamieson in her place. Kay hadn't bargained for the scene that awaited her in the plush, oak-panelled room.

Stooping beside his thickset father, Stephen Drake was a different person. His cockiness had been replaced by a bent head and a twisted expression. 'I didn't mean to get you in trouble,' he said quietly.

'We can't tell *talk* from *mutter*!' His father barked into his ear, causing Drake to shudder. 'And *stand up straight*!'

As his ashen face lifted to Kay's, she was overwhelmed with pity, and felt like telling him not to let himself be dictated to by his father, but the great bully of a man scared her too.

'I'm sorry for what I've put you through,' Drake inhaled slowly, doing his best to conduct himself with some self-respect. 'I'll set the record straight,' he said.

Kay's mind was racing. Why was she feeling guilty? Drake had deliberately lied, not giving a thought to the fact that she might have faced a prison sentence. Now he was offering to set the record straight, as if he were doing her a favour. As if *she* should be grateful. And the worst of it was, she did feel a sickening sense of gratitude. Looking from him to his father, Kay knew where to lay the blame: at the feet of this overbearing man who stood before her. The father, who was returning her scorn with a grimace, was at the root of the trouble. He was sending her a message. She was a loser.

'I always knew,' Rebecca Jamieson chimed in, startling Kay who had not heard her come in. 'Under the magnifying glass that M *was* clearly an M, not a seven. We felt sure you were innocent all along.'

'You lying cow! They told me at the station, *you* thought I did it. You *regretted* taking on someone from a housing estate. And this boy, as you called him, must be innocent, because he comes from a good family. Because *his* father is a high-ranking officer in the Met!'

'Yes, well,' she smirked foolishly, 'you can hardly blame us for wondering.'

Without pausing for a second, Kay slapped the secretary's arrogant face and enjoyed the tingling it left in the palm of her hand. 'Now fuck off. All of you!'

As if suddenly struck dumb, the three of them stared at Kay as, turning her back on them, she let out a low whimper and hugged herself. Unable to cope with this display of emotion, they each scuttled faint-heartedly from the room, leaving her to it.

An excited buzz was spreading outside the boardroom door, but Kay moved to the large window and stared out.

'He admitted it!' Doreen's voice rang through her brain. Why was everyone so overjoyed? Had they believed she'd done it? Didn't they realize that the truth would come out in the end? Now it was Marge from the switchboard who was shouting for joy. And Ivy the tea lady.

Turning from the window, she gazed at the frosted panelled glass wall, which separated the room from the corridor and Kay from her colleagues grouped together outside, enjoying the euphoria of a crisis resolved. She felt as if she were acting in a film. A movie in which she was the star. Why were they reacting like this? Why weren't they angry? Or feeling like her, sad and let down? Why *did* she feel so hurt, so betrayed? It was a different pain inside now.

A large notepad and pen lying on the long, highly polished table caught Kay's eye. Sitting down on a padded chair, she picked up the biro and wrote in large letters THEY THOUGHT IT WAS ME. She looked up from the pad to the window, and feeling strangely drawn to it, she dragged herself from the chair.

Gazing down at the busy street, thoughts came flying at her. *Wouldn't it serve them right if I jumped? The crowd would soon gather round my broken body. Someone from Thompson's would hear the commotion and look out. Word would spread. I would be dead, and it would be their fault. No more having to face Drake or the police. No more threats of a prison sentence for forgery.*

Behind her, Kay heard the creaking of the heavy mahogany door as Mr Grieves pushed it open. 'Doreen said you'd be in here.'

Keeping her back to him, Kay kept her eyes on the street below. 'They thought I stole that money,' she repeated quietly.

'No, Kay.' He sounded choked. 'None of us believed it. That's why Doreen and I were in early. We searched the office from top to bottom.'

She could feel him moving towards her. 'Please don't come any closer.' Even to herself, Kay's voice sounded different, toneless.

'Doreen's fetching some sweet tea for you.'

'I don't want anything.' Kay opened the window and leaned out. The people below looked so small. The street noise was inviting.

'Why don't we sit down for a while?' Grieves was trying his best.

'Will you please tell Doreen I don't want any tea.' Kay spoke in a monotone. 'Would you please go.'

'No, Kay, I won't.' His voice was quiet but firm. 'You've been through a lot. I dare say you're still in a state of shock. I think we all are.'

'No. You don't know what it feels like. Otherwise you wouldn't be here. You'd want to be on your own.'

'Is that honestly what you want? A few minutes by yourself?'

She turned to him and smiled as she cried. 'Yeah. It's OK. I'm not gonna . . .' She looked at the open window. 'I'm not brave enough. If someone else came along and took the life from me, that would be different.' She wiped her face with the back of her hand. 'Eternal sleep,' she grinned. 'I wouldn't say no.'

Ignoring Kay's request for solitude, Grieves moved closer and placed one arm around her shoulders. 'I wish you could feel as relieved as I do about that confession.'

Pleased that he hadn't left the room, Kay allowed her head to rest against his shoulder. 'Part of me feels good about it, but the rest of me?' She looked thoughtfully into his grey eyes, 'It's having to face everyone. They all know about it.'

'Oh, I'm sure they do. And you can bet that within the hour they'll also know about Drake's confession.' He smiled into her tear-stained face. 'It seems a shame to let them celebrate without you and, well, with your permission, I would like to demand that some of today is taken up with a meeting, in the canteen. I think the Chairman should make a public apology. On behalf of the firm, of course.'

'He wouldn't go for that.'

'Oh, I think he will. No choice really. I should think several of the staff have been toying with the idea of walking out. But if you were given a public apology . . .'

Kay screwed her face up and forced back tears. 'That would be—' she took a deep breath and exhaled slowly, 'that would be—' as much as she tried, she couldn't finish the sentence.

'You'd like that?' Grieves smiled broadly.

She nodded, her lips squeezed shut.

'Good. I'll see to it now.' He turned to leave and then stopped. 'Do you want to be present?' Her half-smiling, pained face said it all, and a slow nod of approval filled him with righteous indignation.

'We'll set the records straight, don't you worry.'

'There *is* something else.' Kay chewed on the inside of her cheek and wondered whether to continue.

'I know about your other extra employment, Kay. Doreen told me in confidence. It won't go any further.'

Kay sighed with relief. She was pleased he knew. 'What if Mr Thompson finds out?' She wiped a tear from her neck.

'I'll deal with that if and when it comes up. I don't think you have anything to worry about.' He winked at her and left the room.

Trying not to look too worried, Laura leaned on the balcony wall pretending she was taking the air and enjoying the last of the late afternoon sun. She stubbed out a cigarette-end in the earth of the flower-filled window-boxes as she saw Jack striding through the playground, on his way back from a dockers' meeting. His unmistakable lean body and broad shoulders filled her with warmth. She gave him a wave and wondered how he had managed to get through the day.

'Kay back yet?' Jack tried to sound casual.

'No. Should be along any minute.' She followed him into the kitchen. 'How'd the meeting go?'

'OK.' He looked sheepishly at her. 'I s'pose Kay would 'ave phoned if that firm was giving her a hard time?'

'Of course she would.' She turned her back on him and covered her face with her hands.

'I wish I could say something to make you feel better, Laura, but I can't. I've been worried sick all day. And wild. Bloody wild, I'll tell yer.'

Sitting down opposite him at the Formica table, Laura lit another cigarette. 'They won't put her away, surely?'

'Who knows what they'll do. I'll tell you what, though—' Jack stopped dead in his tracks as he caught sight of Kay passing by the kitchen window. 'Here she is! Try to think of something else to talk about, for Christ's sake.'

'Why? Don't you think she'll want to talk about it?'

'I don't know what to think any more, tell the truth,' Jack said, staring down at the floor. He expected Kay to look depressed and drained, and tried to fix a smile on his face.

'Guess what?' Kay beamed as she stood in the doorway of the kitchen. 'He's confessed! I've had a public apology *and* the police are not gonna press charges over the passport form!' She paused for a breather. 'Kept my passport though. Said I've got to wait until next year till I apply for another one. Let me off with a stiff warning.' She spread her hands and hunched her shoulders, mimicking Pamela's Jewish father, to Jack and Laura's amusement. 'You could say *something*?'

'This isn't one of your silly jokes, is it?'

'No,' Kay dropped on to a chair, 'it's over.' She clicked her fingers. 'Just like that.' Then, realizing that her hand was still painful from punching Drake, she hid her discomfort. She would relate that scene later. 'What's for tea?'

'Dad's gonna get a Chinese take-away. And what d'yer mean, he confessed? Who confessed?'

'It's a long story. Can't I tell you tomorrow?'

'You're not having us on, are you?' Jack's eyes narrowed and he cocked his head to one side.

'Nope.' She stood up and kissed him on the forehead. 'It's over. I will tell you all about it. But not yet, eh?' Her eyes filled with tears again, but she managed to compose herself. 'I've really had it.' Reaching out for Laura, she gave her a big hug. 'I'm sorry I caused all that trouble. You know, signing the passport form. It was stupid. Immature.'

'Kay! Who confessed?' Jack's face was taking on an angry, determined look.

'The bloke who took it!'

'Yeah fine, but *who* took it?'

'I don't want to talk about it. It's over and done with!'

Laura looked at her daughter curiously. She seemed different, older. Her mind flashed to the holiday in Spain. 'Did you meet anyone nice on the Costa Brava?'

'What made you ask that?' Kay sounded both defensive and pleased that she had been asked.

'Just wondered.'

'I did as it happened. His name's Chris. He lives out there. Got his own bakery.'

'How old is he?' Jack's voice took on a different tone.

'Twenty-two,' she said, knowing he was in fact twenty-four.

Jack slowly nodded. 'Just as well you left him behind then. He's too old for you.' He looked her straight in the eye and made it clear that he meant what he said. 'Now then, sit down and fill me in on what happened today.'

'Oh please, Dad! I've had enough. Can't I just go round Pamela's and forget about it? Just for tonight? Pamela's mum'll feed me. You know what they're like for food.'

'Well if you'd rather 'ave herrings than sweet and sour pork.' Jack teased.

'Jewish people don't eat herrings *all* the time . . .'

'They smell like they do.'

'That's *so* insulting!'

'Your dad's tormenting you, Kay. You should know him by now.' She tried not to smile back at Jack.

'Go on, get going and ask Pamela's mother if she's made one of her nice poppy-seed cakes this week.'

'Now what was it you always told me? *Those who ask, don't get . . .*'

'I didn't ask you to ask, did I?' he grinned.

'*And those who don't ask, don't want.* I'm sure it went something like that.' Now Kay sounded as if she were talking to herself as she picked up her handbag and made for the door.

'I always gave you a tanner when you asked for a threepenny bit, though!' Jack called after her.

'Well,' Laura sighed, 'that's that then! We've been worrying ourselves sick all day, and she's been in seventh heaven.'

'Yeah. Puts years on you, don't it?' Jack looked genuinely concerned about himself. 'Why has Kay made me feel old all of a sudden?'

'Bernard! Bernard! Put up the closed sign will you? Supper is ready!' Pamela's mother shook her head at Kay. 'That man is so slow . . . It's a very sad thing. He reaches forty and settles for being old.'

'Why must you shout, Lillian?' Pamela's father stood in the doorway between the shop and the living quarters.

'Why? Because you are stone-deaf.' She shrugged at the girls. 'I would have thought that was obvious.'

'But if I am stone-deaf, why shout? Why not chalk messages on the blackboard?' Bernard winked at Pamela and Kay who were managing to keep a straight face. 'You don't look very brown, Kay.'

'Kay was arrested over the weekend.' Pamela couldn't contain it any longer. A silence fell as her parents gazed impassively at Kay.

'I was charged as well. They let me out on bail.'

Lillian and Bernard slowly and simultaneously lowered themselves into their chairs. 'Go on,' Lillian said, while scooping and serving fried fish. 'What happened?'

Kay told them the entire story from beginning to end, and the way they had treated her like royalty at Thompson's that day. She carefully skipped the bit about forging her passport form. She told them everything that Laura and Jack had wanted to know. Somehow it just seemed easier with this family. She knew they wouldn't continually throw questions at her, or butt in. They were listeners. At least to visitors. Not to each other. Not often.

'So what happened to the registered envelope?' Bernard asked after a respectful pause. Everyone waited while Kay searched for an answer.

'I don't know.'

'Would you like to know?'

'I would. I really would.' She became thoughtful. 'I think I typed the name and address on it. I remember the name.'

'What time of the day was it?' Bernard asked, in his usual calm manner.

'The afternoon. Before tea-break.'

'And this list? It was in alphabetical order?'

Kay thought about it. 'Yeah.'

'And his name?'

'Mr Woods.'

Bernard smiled quietly at her and ate a little more fish.

'I did type it. Just before tea-break,' Kay said, as it all came flooding back. 'It was the last one! I typed his *just* before the bell went!' She placed her knife and fork down. 'Do you think someone came in and stole the registered envelope?'

Bernard chuckled. 'Who wants an empty soiled envelope?' He took some potato salad.

'Well, what else could have happened to it?'

'What do you do the minute, or second, before you leave your desk to go to the canteen?' He looked at her with his brown, sleepy eyes.

Kay thought about it. 'I push my typewriter to the back of the desk. Don't ask me why.'

'Why?' Bernard looked from one to the other, hoping to get a reaction to his humour.

'It's a habit.' Kay shrugged in true Jewish style. Something she slipped into when in their company.

Disappointed that all three of them had missed his joke, he pressed on. 'Is there a gap?' He motioned with his fork.

Kay's face suddenly lit up as she remembered. 'Yes, there is! I sometimes push my biscuit crumbs down there to get rid of 'em.'

'Well, there we have it. Tomorrow you ask your boss to look. Let him find it. Tell him Mr Simmonds helped you remember, eh?'

'I will!' Kay grinned, 'I'll definitely tell him.'

'Pamela, why aren't you eating?' Lillian gazed at her daughter's full plate.

'I'm not hungry.'

'So?'

'If she's not hungry, Lillian, why must she eat?' Ignoring the scornful look from his wife, Bernard turned to Kay.

'When did you last visit your grandpa?'

'I don't know. Just before our holiday, I think. Why?'

'I saw him yesterday. In Petticoat Lane. The old man looked lonely. We had a chat.'

'He hasn't been in the shop lately as a matter of fact,' Lillian said. 'He always has the same thing: four rollmops and some cream cheese. Maybe he's gone off soused herrings. I don't think he came in for three weeks now; yes, it must be three weeks. Pamela, if you're not going to eat that, stop messing with it.'

'He asked me about the Brady Street Club.'

The three of them waited for him to finish what he was saying but he just shrugged.

Irritated by her father's measured nature, Pamela sighed loudly. 'Well don't just leave it in the air. What was he asking?'

He gazed at all three of them in disbelief, 'It's not obvious?' There was an impatient pause. 'He asked me if he could be involved in some way.' He turned to Lillian. 'I think he misses the youth club.'

'But my grandfather's nearly seventy!'

'Once you've been involved with young people you get hooked.'

'Why can't he spend some time at the Brady Club then?' Pamela folded her napkin and looked sideways at him.

'Because he's not Jewish.' There was a touch of regret in his voice. 'I don't make the rules, Pamela.'

Preoccupied with her grandfather, Kay's mind wandered from the conversation. When she really thought about it she realized that she hadn't been in to see him for nearly a month, and he lived so close by. Suddenly filled with guilt, she pictured him in his tiny cottage going through his daily routine, which was centred around feeding himself and keeping himself and the house clean. His daily visit to the local was probably more for company than anything else.

'I think I'll go now, see if he's all right. You coming, Pam?'

'Hang on a minute. I have to speak with my parents.'

Bernard peered at her. 'She's after something, Lillian – hide the cheque-book.'

Pamela raised an eyebrow and gave him one of her famous glares.

'So talk.' Lillian looked concerned.

'I'll wait until you've finished eating.'

'It's dirty talk?' She almost dropped her fork. 'I said something was wrong with this girl.' She narrowed her eyes, 'Did you get a period yesterday?'

'Oh, for heaven's sake!' She threw her fork down. 'Yes, I *did*!'

Lillian breathed a small sigh of relief. 'For small mercies.'

'I want to move out. Get myself a studio flat.'

Another silence filled the room and Kay almost choked on her lemonade as she watched the changing expressions on Lillian's face.

'You don't need a flat. You've got the best room.' She spoke in a determined, no-nonsense tone. 'A four-foot bed, an easy chair. A lovely carpet. Curtains that meet.'

'I want my independence.'

'At seventeen?' Bernard found it amusing.

'My grandfather's got a spare room,' Kay said, matter-of-factly.

'Has he? Right! What're we waiting for, then?' Pamela kissed her bemused father on the forehead and tried to catch her mother's left cheek, but Lillian pulled away. 'It'll kill two birds with one stone. Company for the old man and independence for me.'

'I was only saying—' Kay shrugged at Pamela's parents.

'It's a strange joke?' Lillian asked, once they had left.

'It's no more than a fancy,' Bernard reached across and patted her hand, 'it will pass. Stop worrying.'

Linking arms, Kay and Pamela strolled along the Whitechapel Road enjoying the early-evening buzz. There were only a few stalls left, clearing away, but still the 'waste' had a feeling of market day about it. People were rushing to and fro chasing buses, and an ambulance was racing along the main road with its emergency light and bell piercing through the air, making its way to the London Hospital.

'Everyone looks so pale and scrawny,' Kay said, looking around at the passers-by.

'I know. We've got to get back there before next year, Kay. I'm dying inside.'

'And where's the money coming from? You're in debt to your parents as it is. Now you want to get a flat. That'll cost you. Even if you did move in with my grandfather, you'd still have to pay him something for your board and lodging.'

'I don't want a flat. I only said that. Give them something serious to worry about so that when I do ask if I can go back to Spain this year . . . when I "give in" over wanting my independence . . .'

'You conniving *cow*!' Kay began to laugh, but stopped the instant she remembered that her passport had been taken away. 'I won't be able to go,' she said miserably.

'I know. I can't help it, Kay. I've got to go back. I can't stop thinking about Charles.'

'Well you know what? I think we should be celebrating.' Kay was desperate to change the subject away from what now seemed like paradise. 'I'm a free woman! Come on.' She marched her friend forward. 'We're going to see an old friend of mine. You'll love him.'

Strolling along Vallance Road, they checked the numbers looking for Terry Button's house, and were surprised when a dark blue Jaguar pulled up beside them.

'I thought that was you, babe. Who you looking for?'

Peering into the car, Kay recognized Bert's brothers, Frank and Freddie, in the front seats. 'My friend lives along here somewhere. Terry Button. Don't suppose you know him?'

'Terry Button?' Frank turned to his passenger in the back seat. 'Ring any bells, Reg?'

'Yeah, as it 'appens.' A knowing smile spread across the tanned face as he looked up at Kay. 'You'll find him in the Sun. He's got a lovely voice.' He looked away and smiled. 'Terri with an i.'

'Why?' Pamela looked puzzled.

'No . . . an *i*,' Reggie joked.

'The lead singer?' Freddie said with a wry smile.

'Give the girls a lift. Save 'em walking.' Reggie's quiet, serious voice caught Kay's attention. She couldn't help thinking how good-looking he was, with thick black hair and eyebrows to match. There was something about him. A mysterious, almost menacing quality.

She opened the back door and slid along the seat up close to Reggie, making room for Pamela. 'I love the smell of leather in cars.'

'Goes well with that perfume you're wearing.' Reggie winked at Kay.

'Thanks. It's Coty, *L'aimant*.' Kay liked the look of him even more close up. His mohair suit and gold cuff-links were quite impressive. She found herself wishing he were a bit younger.

'Bit like a getaway car really,' said Pamela, mock innocent. The remark was a real killer. It suddenly went very quiet.

'How was Spain then?' Frank asked, looking at her in his mirror. 'Your friend's got more colour than you 'ave.'

'Don't tell her that or she'll sulk. I'm Pam*elia* by the way.' This slight variation on her name was a new one to Kay.

Reggie leaned forward and offered her his hand. 'Reggie. All right?'

'I think you'd better call us Uncle as well, Pam*elia*.' Freddie managed to keep a straight face.

'No, that's all right. You're Kay's uncles, not mine.' She could slip so easily into her sophisticated act.

'Spain was great!' Kay said. 'A bit too hot at times.'

'It was only ninety degrees.' Pamela combed her fingers through her long dark hair.

The men found that mildly amusing but kept it to themselves as they cruised along Roman Road. 'How long 'ave you known Terri?' Reggie asked Kay.

'Oh, years. We used to go down hoppin' on the same farm. Haven't seen him since the last time we went. I don't s'pose he's changed much.' She tried to imagine him two years older.

'I wouldn't bank on it,' Reggie said quietly, with a touch of concern in his voice.

'We were very close,' she looked into Reggie's deep brown eyes. 'We shared secrets.'

Reggie gave her a knowing smile, showing his admiration for her tact. 'The boys are gonna drop me off just along here, girls, so I shan't be having the pleasure of your lovely company.' He checked the time on his

Rolex watch. 'It's a pity those two are your uncles.'

'As I said before,' Pamela cut in, leaning forward and smiling at him, 'they're not mine.'

'And that you're both so young,' he continued. 'This'll do, Frank.'

Screeching to a halt, Frankie put the car into neutral. 'See you later, Reg.'

'You're not coming to the Sun then?' Kay smiled, making it sound like an invitation. She knew her uncles would be disturbed by it but she couldn't help herself. She could feel herself drawn in by Reggie's presence.

'Bit of business to attend to.' Reggie gave the boys a show of his hand and Kay a flirtatious wink. 'If you're still footloose in five years, I'll take you to the best restaurant in town! That's a promise.'

'Why five years?' she called out of the window.

'You'll be five years older!'

Dropping back in the comfortable seat, Kay grinned at Pamela, who was sulking. 'Reggie, eh? Talk about chemistry.' She ignored the mocking laughter from her uncles. 'A thousand invisible silver darts flashed between us . . .' she recited melodramatically, trying to make light of the sudden crush she had on a total stranger.

Frank and Freddie found it amusing. 'Don't mention his name to your dad, babe, will yer.'

'Why?' Pamela quite fancied him too. 'He was really polite.'

'Don't they get on then?' Kay should have known her uncles wouldn't give much away.

'You could say that,' Freddie chuckled.

Walking into the pub, Kay felt as if she had entered another world. Terry was on the stage, belting out 'Kiss Me Honey Honey Kiss Me' and singing it beautifully. Even though he wore a long black evening dress and had dyed his hair auburn, still she recognized him. When her uncle Frank asked what she wanted to drink, she heard herself ask for a sweet Martini as if someone else were voicing her request.

She heard her uncles talking across her. 'I don't think she did know his deepest secret.' Frank was laughing.

'You'd better make hers a double,' Freddie added.

Settling herself into a chair, Kay fixed her eyes on her friend. He had changed, that was clear. Not his face – his figure. Or was it all padding? He looked taller, slimmer.

'What's wrong with you? Have you seen a ghost, or what?' Pamela looked from Kay to Terry. 'Surely you've seen a drag queen before?'

'Don't call him that.'

'Why not? What's wrong with drag queen?'

'His name is Terry, OK?'

Terry finished the number and gracefully drank in the applause, and then announced the arrival of a long-lost friend. Signalling to the stage-hand, he indicated to him to throw the spotlight on Kay. Before she could object, she was floodlit.

'My best friend of many years: Miss Kay Armstrong!' Terry proclaimed joyfully.

Deeply embarrassed, Kay could feel herself blushing. 'I'll kill you for this,' she mouthed to Terry as he approached, arms outstretched.

Hanging on to each other, gripping tight, they seemed locked together, Kay almost overpowered by his French perfume. People's eyes were on them, but neither cared.

'Kay . . .' Terry's voice, now quiet, was heavy with remorse. 'Stay with me. Don't go. Please don't walk out.'

Kay gently pulled back and looked into his brimming eyes. 'Why would I do that, you silly cow?' she grinned.

Laughing, he posed for her: 'What d'yer think then? Better than my old jeans and wellies, or what?' His eyes held secret doubt.

'Terry. Shut up.' Kay hugged him again, whispering into his ear. 'It's what's inside that counts.'

Terry let out a sigh and slowly shook his head. 'I dreaded you walking in 'ere one day. Seeing me.'

'What d'yer want to drink, Terri?' Frank called from the bar.

'No, it's all right, thanks!'

'Go on, have one, Tel. He's my uncle.'

Terry turned towards the bar. 'He's your *uncle*?' He looked impressed. 'OK, thanks, I will! G and T please, love!'

'He's not . . .' Kay suddenly felt embarrassed, 'you know. He's married.' She felt herself go hot around the neck.

'Leave off, Kay. I'm not after everything in pants you know. It's me, Terry. And I've got a friend, OK? I'm no different to you when it comes to relationships.' He wiped the lipstick from the corner of his mouth. 'I'm not a tart, and I only dress like this when I'm performing.'

Kay widened her eyes questioningly.

'Performing on the stage!'

Kay's lips parted in surprise.

'*Singing*!' he laughed. 'Mind you, I have been asked to do a bit of striptease. Not 'ere. In a nightclub.'

'And?' Kay hoped for the right answer.

'Would you?' The humour stopped there.

'No I wouldn't.'

'And neither would I!'

'Our drinks are up, come on. Come and meet my other best friend.'

Seated round a corner table, Kay, Pamela, Terry and the two uncles got on famously. They talked about everything from hop-picking to the future of the London docks to unions and management. 'Don't talk to *me* about management,' Kay said after her second Martini. 'I'm up to here with it.'

'Listen,' Terry suddenly said, 'I'd love to sit and listen to your opinion on the subject, Kay, but I must get changed before Ray comes in. He 'ates seeing me in drag.'

'Ray? *The* Ray?' She was referring to an old friend of Terry's who threatened to punch him when he learned that Terry wasn't attracted to girls.

'Yeah,' Terry shrugged. 'I know. It was 'is way of not accepting what he was feeling. I should 'ave known really. He was always going on about how this one or that one was . . . you know. Once he saw it wasn't the end of the world for me . . .' he shrugged.

Kay remembered the naked midnight dip in the Medway. Ray had been mouthing off about fancying her. It obviously hadn't been her fierce warnings which had kept him at bay. Suddenly his behaviour, which used to exasperate her, made sense. Ray had been trying to disprove something.

'Shame,' Kay murmured, 'we might have got on a lot better if he'd admitted it.'

Leaving them to it, Terry swanned off to a back room to change. Watching him, Kay couldn't help thinking how he looked every bit a woman.

'Anyway, where was I?' Kay asked.

'Management, babe, and why you're celebrating tonight.' Her curly-headed uncle chuckled.

Once again she related the story, pleased to offload it and flattered that her uncles showed interest. She knew Pamela was bored, wishing they could be with younger company, but that was tough. Kay had been through a lot and thought she deserved some attention.

'So what d'yer wanna do about it?' Freddie spoke in a matter-of-fact tone but there was a suggestion of revenge in his voice.

'Nothing. Forget it, I suppose.' She shrugged and sipped her drink.

'It wasn't Friday the thirteenth was it?' Frank grinned.

'It was a Friday, yeah. But not the thirteenth.'

And that was enough. From her brief résumé, the brothers had worked out that the cash for the wages was collected from the local bank fortnightly and on a Friday.

'You're right, Kay babe. It's best to forget about it,' Freddie said, looking at his watch. 'Time we made a move, Frank.'

'You girls be all right walking back by yourselves? Or d'yer wanna lift?'

'We know these backstreets like the backs of our hands,' Kay said reassuringly, 'and besides, I want to see Terry before I go.'

'Mind how you *do* go,' Frank tousled Kay's hair. 'Goodbye, Pam*elia*. I expect we'll see you again,' he teased. 'That's if you can bear to stay in this cold, grey country.'

'Say hallo to your mum and dad for us, and your aunt Liz. Tell her we'll be round to see 'er soon.' Freddie winked at Kay and followed his brother out of the pub.

'You've got some dubious relations, Kay,' Pamela frowned. 'They look like criminals to me.'

'Silly cow. They're in import–export. I think they've got their own firm, or they've got top positions in one, according to my dad. I remember him and Uncle Bert arguing about them once. They're not short of cash,' she added proudly.

'Anyone can see that. You should have asked them to lend you the money for Spain.'

'Kay, this is Ray. Ray, this silly cow is Kay from hop-picking – looking a lot more grown-up and sophisticated . . . and this is her friend Pamela.' Terry looked just like his old self in his jeans and white T-shirt, with most of his make-up wiped off.

'Hallo, Ray,' Kay reached out and shook his hand.

'Well. Where shall we go then?' Ray looked pleased to be in their company.

'You name it,' Pamela said, admiring Ray's good looks, feeling sorry that he preferred boys to girls.

'We can't afford the Kentucky but there's other little nightclubs. We could club-crawl.' Terry grinned.

'Kentucky club,' Kay said thoughtfully. 'Where 'ave I heard that before?'

'From your uncles. That's where they'll be heading.'

'I said they were criminals. Only villains, film stars and politicians go to the Kentucky,' Pamela said in her high-handed way.

Making their way out of the Sun, Kay stopped in her tracks. 'Hang about you lot, we're broke. I've only got three pounds to last me the rest of the week.'

'The night's on us.' Terry turned to Ray, 'I haven't seen her for over two years.'

'Yeah, all right,' Ray nodded. 'But don't start asking for doubles.'

Chapter Ten

It was four weeks since the missing salary episode, and everyone at Thompson's appeared to have forgotten all about it. Everyone except Kay. Sitting at her desk, pulling and stretching a paper-clip until it became a single wire, she wondered what she would say when she handed in her notice. She shaped the wire into a spiral, pushed the two ends together and created a ring to slip on her finger. Her mind filled with Chris. She couldn't imagine getting through the year without seeing him.

Pushing herself around in her swivel chair, she turned her face towards the sun streaming in through the window, and tried to visualize herself on a white sandy beach, lying next to Chris's tanned body, holding his hand, waiting for him to turn over on to his stomach the way he did, and kiss her.

'I'm ready to sign today's letters, Kay.' Mr Grieves's voice drifted across the partition.

She could feel Chris's strong hand easing its way under the small of her back, and his muscular arm turning and lifting her on to his sweat-beaded chest.

'I've got one more memo to dictate, but that needn't be typed until tomorrow.'

He was kissing her neck now and pushing the palm of his hand across her sun-warmed stomach . . .

'Kay!' Grieves's face appeared above the glass partition. Kay looked from the grey-suited bulky body, distorted by frosted glass, up to his bespectacled face. 'My letters?'

'Mr Grieves . . .' Kay had left the beach but she wasn't quite back in the present. Somewhere in between. She gazed into his puzzled face. 'I'm leaving,' she said flatly. 'Who should I hand my notice to?'

A bemused smile crossing his face, Grieves raised an eyebrow. 'Why do you want to leave, Kay?'

She picked up the black folder containing the letters for signing and walked around to his side of the partition. 'Because I hate it here now.'

'You don't mean that.' Grieves leaned back in his chair and clicked the end of his biro several times.

'Do I have to give a week's notice, or is it a month?'

'If you are serious, I think we should have a private word.' He threw his pen down on the table, conveying his impatience.

'No, sorry. I'm not interested in company policy to persuade staff to stay on. I've made up my mind.' She offered him the black folder. 'We're all mad to work 'ere.'

'What's brought this on?' He opened the folder and began signing the letters with a flurry of speed.

Kay folded her arms and looked up thoughtfully at the ceiling. 'Well I suppose it could have started to dawn on me when I was accused of stealing that there might be better places to work.'

'Yes, I thought that might be at the bottom of this.' He sounded pleased, as if it were something he could talk to her about, make her see sense.

'I've been window-shopping, down the Brook Street Bureau. I can earn more money, get better conditions, good prospects.'

Grieves nudged his bifocals down his nose and looked up at her. 'You really mean to do it?'

'You make it sound like suicide.'

He pushed himself around in his chair and looked out at the modern office block opposite. 'It feels a bit like that. I wonder why?'

Taken aback by his tone, as if he were speaking to an equal instead of a junior, Kay felt warmness towards him. 'To leave here and go out there, you mean?'

He turned to her and gave a hint of a nod. 'Something like that.'

That line proved too near the mark. Grieves turned his attention again to his signing.

Kay couldn't be sure but she thought he sounded a bit choked. 'Would one week's notice be OK?'

Clearing his throat, Grieves said he would check with Rebecca Jamieson and let Kay know tomorrow, after she'd had a night to think it over.

'You don't want to rush into this,' he sighed, as if he were saying something he didn't really believe. 'We'll have another word in the morning.'

Kay nodded slowly and smiled. He was a funny man. Strict one minute and soft as anything the next. Yes, she would miss him too.

A slight feeling of doubt began nagging at Kay as she prepared for the next day. Friday. Pay-day. She looked up at the registered envelope that had been retrieved from behind the desk and was now stuck on the wall for everyone to see.

The small, dusty blue van had been parked in Clerkenwell Road for an hour by the time Kay strolled by the next morning on her way to work. She was thinking about the way she might play games with Jamieson when she smiled patronizingly at her, saying that Kay would be hard-pressed to find another company as friendly as Thompson's. She had heard about the rehearsed company speech from one of her friends when she tried to leave. A rise of one pound a week and empty praise were all it had taken to persuade her to stay.

'I'm a bit pushed this morning, Kay,' Grieves said as she stood before him. 'I'll have a word with Management after lunch.'

'Fine.' Kay was in no hurry. Her mind was made up. As she turned away, he asked her not to let it distract her from her work.

'Don't worry. It won't happen twice.' She didn't try to keep the bitterness out of her voice as she walked away and out of the office.

And that's exactly why I'm leaving! She pushed open the door to the ladies' room and pulled a packet of five Weights from her cardigan pocket. *Bloody cheek.* It wasn't her fault. Anyone could have made that mistake. She lit a cigarette and stared out of the window at the street below. The dark blue van was still parked in the street, but meant nothing to her. *There he goes. James, upright in his three-piece suit, on his way to collect the wages.* Suddenly, without warning, Kay found herself crying, in anger, not self-pity. She paced the floor. 'It's not fair,' she told the room. 'It shouldn't have happened! I hate them. I hate this place. I hope it burns down!' Dropping on to a chair, she stubbed out her cigarette with the heel of her shoe, not caring about the mess it made on the cold tiled floor.

'Mr Grieves is asking for you, Kay,' Doreen stood with her back against the door, keeping it open. 'We've all got a lot to do today.'

'I know. I wish I had the same enthusiasm I used to have. I can't help it, Doreen. That office. This building. It closes in on me. Sometimes I feel as if I'm suffocating.'

Laughing and shaking her head, Doreen waved her towards the door. 'I think you've missed your cue in life, Kay. You should have been an actress.'

'There's still time,' Kay forced a smile, 'I'm not exactly old.'

'Come on, be a good girl. You always said Friday was your best day. Think of the party tomorrow night. That should put some life into you.'

Walking back along the corridor to their office, Kay told Doreen that she was going to hand in her notice. She was a bit disappointed when the only reaction was slight annoyance that she would have to train someone all over again.

'I wish I had known a year ago you had no intention of staying,' Doreen said as she sat down at her own desk. 'There were two others after that position.' She began typing. 'Now they're established in Bought Ledger and Cost Office.'

Kay felt a flush of anger when Doreen mentioned Bought Ledger. 'That's where Drake worked, till he was transferred to one of the subsidiary companies, after that embarrassing little episode! It would have been a different story if I'd been the guilty one. But then, *I'm* only a docker's daughter!'

She pulled the cover off her typewriter and shoved it in the small cupboard next to her. 'I suppose they've given Drake promotion at the same time for his troubles brought on by the silly mistake of a fellow employee!'

'If you could pop round, Kay? I would like to dictate a couple of memos.' Grieves was obviously in a mood and didn't want to hear her grievances. There was no smile in his voice today.

Collecting her notepad, Kay accidentally knocked against James's chair which fell forward, knocking his filing tray on to the floor.

'Leave it, Kay!' The impatient voice warned her to do as she was told and not argue.

'I'm sorry,' she said, leaning on the partition, looking down at Mr Grieves. 'I couldn't help it.'

Scratching his neck, he frowned. 'I realize that. We'll get on then, shall we?'

Kay felt an overwhelming desire to run out of the office, away from the building. It was stifling her again. She looked out of the window, trying to remind herself that fresh air and sunshine were still out there and always would be, even though the sun didn't shine as much here as it did in Spain.

Glancing down she saw something which caused her to freeze to the spot and then break into a sweat as she saw two men with stockings pulled over their heads jump out of the dark blue van. One of them had a cosh.

'Mr Grieves! *Quick!* They're going for James!'

Grieves was at the window in a flash. The men weren't using the cosh, just threatening James who was handing over the holdall containing the money for the salaries which had just been drawn from the bank.

Kay felt as if she were watching a film that was over in seconds. The robbers were back in the van and roaring along Clerkenwell Road before any passers-by had a chance to realize what was going on. As she stood between Doreen and Mr Grieves, it seemed as if all three of them had suddenly turned to stone.

Snatches of conversation flashed across Kay's mind as she remembered the evening in the pub with her uncles. *So what d'yer wanna do about it, Kay . . . You've got some dubious relations, Kay. They look like criminals to me . . . Only villains, film stars and politicians go to the Kentucky . . . Wasn't Friday the thirteenth, was it? No. But it was a Friday. We get paid fortnightly.*

Kay remembered the look that had passed between the two men. It had crossed her mind that they been talking to her with something else on their minds. But never, not in a thousand years, had she thought that they were already planning to square the accounts. It all suddenly fell into place. Some of the things her dad had said about her uncles and the way they had always seemed to have money to throw around. They *were* villains. They really were.

Leaning against the window-sill, Kay left everyone else to the drama, finding it difficult to stop herself smiling. Would they dare to interrogate her again? Would they dare to accuse her of being an insider? She looked out of the window again at the crowd who had gathered around James. The hero. It would probably add colour to his grey image. No, they would never dream that it was her people who had performed that swift, professional snatch. And if they did? Kay was no longer smiling but quietly laughing. If they did have any reason to suspect her, she felt confident Frank and Freddie would have left no trace of a clue.

When Kay officially handed in her notice that day, she thought Rebecca Jamieson might have detected the smugness in her voice. She had given her a long, puzzled look, but had said nothing.

Chapter Eleven

Wearing her favourite light blue button-through shift dress and matching sling-back shoes, Kay made her way along Lombard Street on a sweltering June afternoon. Weaving her way between pedestrians she arrived at the address on the slip of paper given to her by the employment bureau, and felt her heart sink. She peered in through one of the windows and saw that the ugly Victorian building was even worse inside.

Telling herself she had nothing to lose, Kay entered the dim reception area and made her way towards a long dark desk, deciding that she would go through with the interview now that she was here, but would not accept the position for which she was applying. This was another world. An alien world, where the staff walked around like sad robots with half-smiles fixed on their pale faces. It was as if all colour had been left at the door. Black, white and grey surrounded her. Not the starkly contrasting black and white décor that Kay loved, but a heavy, old-fashioned drab interior.

'Mr Trillington will be down shortly.' The middle-aged woman spoke without looking up. 'If you would like to take a seat.' She swept a long red fingernail across the nape of her thin neck, capturing a few loose strands and slipping them under a tight French pleat of silver-grey hair.

'What's it like working here?' Kay wasn't really interested, she just wanted to see what was under the layers that seemed to prevent this woman from communicating.

Glancing briefly at Kay, she wound a sheet of paper into her grey typewriter. 'I shouldn't worry too much about that.' There was enough smugness in her voice to last a working lifetime.

'I wasn't.' Kay carefully leaned forward and lifted a hair from the grey padded shoulder. 'It's just that you don't seem full of the joys of spring.'

'Really?' Shooting her a ferocious look, the woman answered the internal telephone system.

'This carpet needs fumigating.' Kay slowly shook her head. 'It smells of stale cigarette smoke and yet still the moths lay their eggs.' She leaned on the edge of the archaic desktop and looked into the woman's face. 'Doesn't it bother anyone? This building smells like an old metal ashtray.'

'Mr Trillington will see you now. Third floor, second door on the left.'

'Thank you.' Kay stood for a moment, wondering whether to bother. 'This is only the second interview I've ever been to. I really wasn't asking you for much. Just a few words. Anything that just might have made me feel a bit more at ease.' Kay was surprised at her own audacity.

Studiously examining her notebook, the receptionist looked as if she might be a touch embarrassed. 'Knock before you enter.'

During the lightning tour of the offices, seen through windows from the long dark corridor, Kay did her best to be polite and hide her boredom.

'Why do all the girls and women wear black and white? Is it a rule?' she asked, as they stood outside the typing pool, staring in.

'It's not exactly compulsory.' Trillington nervously scratched his nose and smiled down at her. 'We're a very conservative firm and a very busy one. It wouldn't do to have valuable time wasted.' He folded his arms and curled his bottom lip over. 'I'm talking about the male members of staff, of course. Can't expect them not to be interested in women. Bit of an old dog myself. I'm afraid your sort of colours wouldn't do at all. They'd spend most of their time ogling. Then of course there's your hair.'

Kay checked her reflection in a darker part of the window. Her new short bob turned perfectly under her chin and the thick fringe was dead straight and sat level with her eyebrows. So what was wrong?

'I'm afraid you simply wouldn't fit in. But you seem a bright girl; I expect you've worked that out for yourself. Nothing to do with you, of course. Just your appearance. The blonde "sex kitten",' he smiled. 'The directors would throw a fit if I took you on.'

Sex kitten? He couldn't, as far as Kay was concerned, have insulted her more. She hated the label blondes were given, especially if, like her, they happened to be five foot eight. 'My hair's natural.' She found herself making excuses and feeling ashamed. 'And I'm too thin to be classed as a sex kitten.' She could feel the blood rushing to her face again and hated herself for being embarrassed when she should be giving this pompous git a piece of her mind.

'Those girls,' she could hear the tremor in her voice and cleared her throat, 'they may be wearing traditional black and white but they look like tarts. Their skirts are too tight and too short and the fact that they wear their blouse collars up makes them look as if they're Teddy girls. And they're wearing too much make-up.'

Trillington placed one arm around her waist and steered her away from the window back along the corridor towards his office. 'Come and take the weight off your feet. I'll explain about personal appearance. The difference between what you might wear when you go out with a boyfriend and what you ought to wear when—'

'No thanks.' Kay pulled away from his clammy hand. 'I think I can work that out for myself.'

Looking at his watch, he raised an eyebrow. 'Almost noon. I think I could get away with an early lunch.' He winked at Kay. 'A drink and a quick sandwich sound OK?'

She could hardly believe her ears. A man who must be old enough to be her father and from a different class was asking her out to lunch?

'Unless you want to come back after business hours.' He lifted her chin with his forefinger so she had to look into his leering eyes.

Pushing his hand away she shot him a look of disgust and turned away, her low stiletto heels thudding on the dust-filled carpet. And as she walked quickly down the stairs she willed herself not to break down. 'I won't cry,' she said aloud, 'I won't.'

For most of her life Kay had been told she was too sensitive, bursting into tears at the least thing. But not this time. And, she was determined, not ever again. At least she had Thompson's to thank for that. She had made a resolution when she walked out of the building for the last time that she would never cry again, unless someone she loved were to die. She would allow herself tears then, but not for anything or anyone else would she ever weaken. Her crying days were over.

Sitting outside a small Italian café Kay enjoyed the sun on her face while she waited to be served. She was reminded of Spain and began to fantasize about her future, living with Chris in that small fishing village. For five weeks, since returning to England to face the music, she had quietly begged God to let there be a letter from Chris when she returned from work. So far there had been nothing. Not a word. She had written and posted the first letter.

Maybe they were all the same? Out of sight, out of mind. She had given up on Zacchi a long time ago.

She sipped her coffee and wondered if it was time yet to make a secret appointment with Doctor Brynberg. She was now three weeks late and seriously worried. Would her family ever believe that she had gone out there a virgin and had only made love with Chris twice?

Ignoring the butterflies in her stomach, Kay pushed open the glass swing doors leading into the reception of Waterman's Publishing. Her second interview that day. The first had managed to crush her self-esteem and she wondered how she would react if she were put down a second time.

This time she decided to try harder with her accent. She recalled her teacher drilling into her and the other girls on the commerce course that a 't' was on the end of a word for a reason, and that they must sound it. She had been just as pedantic too about not dropping aitches.

'My name is Kay Armstrong.' She assumed the voice she used when working on the switchboard at Thompson's. 'I have an appointment at two o'clock.' She quickly checked the piece of paper for the personnel officer's name.

'Oh right, yeah,' the young girl checked her diary. 'Mrs Jarold's expecting yer. She's gonna be tied up for ten minutes though. D'yer wanna cuppa coffee while yer wait?' Pushing back her chair the curly-headed receptionist stood up. 'It tastes like camel's piss smells, but if you eat a square of chocolate with it,' she shrugged and grimaced.

'It's OK,' Kay laughed, 'I've just had a cappuccino. Is it all right if I have a cigarette while I'm waiting?' She had dropped her telephonist's voice and compromised, not slipping back completely into her everyday East End tones.

'Not s'posed to smoke in Reception, but I'll keep my eye out for Mr Branson. He's 'ead of staff. Struts about like a peacock with a slipped disc. We've got a smoking room but it's on the second floor.'

'I'll wait till later. Thanks anyway.'

'No. Go on. It's bloody nerve-rackin' goin' for interviews. You wanna fag – have one!'

'No, honestly, I'm not a proper smoker. Just like one now and again.' She sat down on the edge of the red and white sofa and placed her handbag on the glass-topped table. 'What's it like working here?'

'Fucking brilliant, I tell yer. Some of the journalists.' She rolled her eyes and puckered her full pink lips. 'Keep arm's length with the married ones though. They'd 'ave you in the corridor if they could.' She picked up her emery board and filed a broken fingernail.

'I'm being transferred to the subscriptions department. They need a fast typist, or so they said.' She leaned forward and lowered her voice. 'I think Mr Branson told Mrs Jarold that I'm a bit too common for Reception. Fucking cheek. I got caught right out last week though. Couldn't be bothered to go into the cloakroom to do me hair, so I used that big pink mirror.

'There I was, backcombing away like mad, trying to straighten this lot. Me hair was sticking out all over the place and in walks two really important clients. And guess who was with 'em?'

'Mr Branson?'

'Bang on. I tell yer, it was really embarrassing. For the men I mean. Didn't know where to put their faces.' She unscrewed the lid of her nail varnish and carefully painted over the repaired nail. 'It didn't bovver me. I 'ad me make-up on so I knew me face was all right when I took their coats. Cashmere they was. Think they were quite important as it 'appens. Still, there you go. I'd rather be in Subs anyway. The blokes are a right laugh and I quite fancy the driver, Roger. You wait till you see 'im.'

The interview went well. Kay liked Mrs Jarold and from what she could tell the feeling was mutual, and she passed her typing test with flying colours. She was then offered the position either of Receptionist or Production Assistant on the fortnightly magazine *Stock Market*, where she would be working closely with the journalists. Her role would be to ensure that copy was properly typed up and in on time. She opted for Receptionist but asked if she could type copy as well. The one thing Kay hated most was to be bored.

As she stepped on to the train at Moorgate underground a sudden wave of pleasure flowed through her. Her salary had shot up overnight from seven pounds ten shillings to twelve pounds ten a week, and she would get luncheon vouchers on top. But more importantly, she had been treated with respect at the interview.

The train pulled away; just one stop to go, Bethnal Green. Kay felt as if she had been given another start in life; a career she felt sure would hold excellent prospects. Working for a publisher alongside writers was a dream she hadn't imagined could ever happen. Catching sight of her reflection in the train window she decided that her new hairstyle was a success. She liked it, now that she was getting used to it. It had been rather a shock when the scissors were first taken to her long hair.

Suddenly aware of her silly smile, she felt embarrassed at admiring her reflection. She cast her eyes along the car to check if anyone had been watching and noticed the smartly dressed drunk who was hanging on to a rail for dear life. She wondered where in the world he came from. Not the East End, that was for sure. But then, had it not been for his three-piece suit and silver-topped walking stick, the thought would not have crossed her mind.

'Clothes maketh the man' was something her art teacher always used to say. If clothes made this man, then alcohol had certainly done the opposite. His red face and glassy eyes reminded her of the meths drinkers who sometimes lay in the gutter, blood seeping from bandaged heads, outside the Salvation Army hostel in Whitechapel.

Instead of going home after her interview Kay found herself unlatching the gate leading into Delamar Place. Since Pamela's parents had pointed out, and probably deliberately, that her grandfather was a lonely old man, she had made a point of seeing more of him and had gained much by it. Laura had always said he was a rough diamond, and up until recently Kay had not really understood what her mother meant. Now she knew. She had got to know Billy more during the past couple of weeks than in all her seventeen years.

'I'm pleased about your job, Kay,' Billy said, handing his granddaughter a cup of tea, 'but I can't say it eases my mind.'

'Tell me what's *on* your mind and perhaps I can ease it for yer.' She dipped a chocolate Bourbon into her tea.

'I think you know.' He sank into his cushioned armchair and waited.

'Know what?' Kay could feel her heart begin to beat faster. Surely he hadn't picked up on her worst fears?

Billy said nothing; he was wise enough to know that a short silence could say more than a stream of words. He sipped his tea and stared down at the floor.

'You tell me what you think it is and I'll tell you if you're hot, warm or cold. A new version of I Spy.'

Still he said nothing, pretending to be interested in a worn patch on the arm of his chair.

'You're not clever, Billy. I can see right through you.'

'Oh, yeah?'

'Yes.' She leaned back in her chair and kicked her shoes off. 'I'm quite happy to sit and enjoy this silence.'

'Good.'

Listening to the loud tick of the large wooden clock on Billy's shelf, Kay began to count the seconds to see how long he could sit it out. She knew he loved to chat, and it hadn't slipped her notice that he had brought out his oldest photograph album. The one he had promised to show her when he found it. The one that was full of pictures of his daughter, Laura, who, apart from her dark hair, looked so much like Kay.

She counted two hundred and fifty seconds and was beginning to get cross with him for the casual way he sat there, unperturbed.

'OK, so I'm worried about something, am I?' she said finally. 'So what? Everyone has something to beef about.' She was slipping into his language again.

Billy swallowed the remains of his tea, carefully placed the bone-china cup on the saucer, sat back again and folded his arms. This time he looked tenderly into her face and shook his head. His expression said it all. He knew she had been a silly girl.

'You haven't said anything to Mum, 'ave yer?' she murmured, ashamed.

Pursing his lips, Billy shook his head defiantly. 'That's something you're gonna have to do, Kay, and soon.' He raised his eyebrows. 'I suppose it did happen in that bloody foreign country?' There was hope in his voice that he might be wrong.

Kay nodded and covered her face with her hands. 'He *was* English though – well, practically – and he *was* the first.'

'You don't have to tell me that, Kay. I saw the difference in your face when you got back. I can't tell you what the look is, but I saw it in your mother's face when your dad had first carried her through the bluebells.'

'Dad'll go mad.' Kay's mind was suddenly filled with Jack; the way he still treated her like his baby girl.

'Your dad knows already. Well, not about . . .' he nodded towards her stomach. 'He's kept the letters back. Didn't read any of 'em. But he's not daft. He knows they're love letters.'

'He did *what*?' Kay could hardly believe her ears. 'Are you telling me that Chris has written to me?'

'Don't be too hard on him, Kay. He was hoping it would blow over and you'd forget him if you thought he'd forgotten you.'

'That's horrible! How could he do that to me?' She was about to cry and remembered her resolve not to. Taking a deep breath she stood up, keeping her back to Billy. 'He'll think I don't care. He'll think I was just using him.'

A loud banging on the door stopped her dead. They both knew it would be Laura come to check up on him on her way home from Hammond's.

'Don't say anything. Not a word.' Kay stormed out of the room.

Opening the door to her mother, Kay forced herself to smile. 'I got the second interview I went for!'

'What did you do wrong on the first one?' Laura teased, and opened her arms to Kay who sprang into them.

'I've just had a phone call from your dad.' Laura walked arm in arm with Kay along the passage. 'You've got a visitor.'

'Where's today's paper, then?' Billy asked as Laura bent down to kiss his head. 'And where's Liz got to? This is the second time I cut up some fruit bread for the pair of you.'

'She's tired, Dad. Had a busy day. It was our floor manager's birthday and they made a bit of a fuss in the canteen. She's been with the firm for fifteen years.'

'Mum! You said I had a visitor.'

'And you've still got one.' Laura's broad smile was catching. Kay and her grandfather looked at each other and grinned.

'Male or female?' Kay asked, knowing somehow it was male and yet not understanding why her parents weren't hitting the roof. Chris might speak perfect English, but he had Spanish eyes all right.

'Male. Dark hair. Very attractive.'

'Chris?' Kay couldn't believe it.

'No, love. I think his name is Zacchi.' Laura couldn't contain herself. She was as excited as Kay should have been.

'Zacchi?' She could hardly believe it. 'But how do you know it's him?'

'Because your dad said so.'

'And he doesn't mind him turning up?'

'No. He sounded quite chuffed.'

Grabbing her handbag, Kay ran from the cottage out of the courtyard and through the backstreets, almost knocking over a woman as she stepped out of Higgins's, the corner shop. 'Sorry!' she yelled back, not stopping until she finally arrived at the stairs leading up to the second-floor flat where Zacchi would be waiting. She leaned on the white-tiled wall and caught her breath.

'Where've you been, Kay? He's been 'ere for about two hours.' Jack seemed far from pleased.

'Looking for a job, Dad. It does take time, you know.'

'I've run out of things to talk about,' he whispered.

'What does he look like?'

'What d'yer think he looks like? An old man? It's only been just over two years.'

'Nearly three, actually.'

'Anyway, go and see for yourself. I'll put the kettle on. He's in the front room.'

'Dad!' Kay whispered.

He turned and looked at her. 'What?'

'Do I look all right?'

''Course you do.'

'Not too – you know, smart?'

Smiling, he stroked her hair and admired her face. 'You look lovely. Now go in and see 'im.'

Slowly pushing open the door to the living room, Kay tried to stop herself grinning like an idiot.

'Hallo, Zac.'

Spinning round on the heels of his black cowboy boots, Zacchi faced her, looking shy and awkward in his Italian suit. 'You've had your hair cut,' was all he managed to say.

'Yeah. On Saturday.'

'I like it,' he smiled. 'It suits you.'

'Thanks.'

There was a pause while each wondered what to say next. Kay was completely lost for words. There was so much to talk about, but she couldn't think of anything to say. He did look different. Especially in a suit. She hadn't expected that.

'We've left the road,' Zacchi suddenly said. 'Joined the settled travellers.'

'You're kidding?'

'No. It's getting more difficult now, finding places to stop, seasonal work. Gypsies are out of fashion.' He flashed her a smile.

'That's terrible, Zacchi. Your family must hate it.'

Shrugging, he looked out of the window. 'It's not all bad. It means the young ones can go to school.' He turned to face her. 'We're not in a council house, not yet. We're on a site with other travellers. It's a bit like living on the common. Hop-picking.'

'Can't knock that.' Kay was wandering from the conversation again, looking into that familiar handsome face and those dark blue eyes. His wavy hair was just as thick and shiny, maybe a bit shorter.

Zacchi played with a cuff-link on his shirtsleeve. 'I don't suppose you feel like going for a walk?'

'I thought you'd never ask.'

Popping his head round the door, Jack asked Kay if she wanted tea or coffee. He didn't look too perturbed when she told him they were going out.

'Thanks for your hospitality, Mr Armstrong,' Zacchi said, shaking Jack's hand.

'That's all right, son. And good luck with your new job.' He winked at him and squeezed Zacchi's hand in a fatherly fashion. 'You'll soon get used to the nine-to-five routine.'

Strolling hand in hand they walked under the railway arch, heading for Bethnal Green park. It amused Zacchi the way Kay's voice suddenly had an echo, and before long they were making whooping war cries between bursts of laughter.

'This isn't the way I imagined it would be.' Zacchi put his arm around Kay's shoulder and kissed her lightly on the cheek. 'I didn't really know what to expect, but I never dreamed we'd be standing under an arch making silly echoes.'

'I never imagined you in a suit.'

'No. Neither did I. It goes with the job.'

'What's that?'

He took her hand again and for the first time looked relaxed and happy. 'It's all your fault! I've spent the past two years studying to take an O-level in English – while we were still on the road. It started with my buying a dictionary so I could look up some impressive words when I wrote to you.'

'But you never did write, Zacchi.'

'No. I decided to wait.' He pulled her close to him. 'And here I am.'

'You still haven't told me what your job is.'

'Well, because of my years spent travelling and because I seem to have a way with words, and . . .'

'The poetry! Of course, I'd forgotten you wrote all those lovely poems.'

'The pay's not brilliant but it's really good, having my own weekly column . . .' He waited for her reaction.

'I don't suppose you've got any of your poems with you? The ones you wrote specially for me, for instance?'

'. . . "Travelling the Dusty Road – Around Britain". The circulation figures have gone up since they took me on.'

'What are you talking about, Zacchi?'

'I'm a feature writer on the local rag, the Walthamstow *Guardian*.'

Kay stared at him, hardly able to take it in. Zacchi, a professional journalist? Her gypsy boyfriend doing something she had always secretly wanted to do? 'Honestly, Zac? You're not pulling my leg?'

'No I'm not,' he laughed, 'but if you're offering . . .'

Feeling herself blush, she looked away, her mind suddenly full of the time when she almost lost her virginity to him. Then, remembering her own sorry state of affairs, she went quiet.

'I was joking, Kay.'

'I know.' She didn't want to think about that side of their relationship which, as far as she could see, had been ruined by her holiday romance.

Turning into the gateway leading to the park, Kay suggested they sit on the low wall that surrounded the large paddling pond. 'That's old Sid,' she smiled, nodding towards an elderly man handing out tracts to passers-by. 'Bible Sid. He'll start singing a hymn soon and if we're lucky, dancing too.'

Zacchi took Kay's hand and stroked her fingers with the tip of his thumb. 'I said I would come for you, one day—'

'I told you, didn't I?' she interrupted. 'There he goes. The kids love him.' They looked across at the smiling old man.

'Don't the parents worry?'

'No, never. Sid's been around since I can remember. He's harmless. Never begs. Never asks for anything. Some people reckon he's really a millionaire, an eccentric. It wouldn't surprise me.'

'I still feel the same about you, Kay.' He gazed at her face. 'Why won't you look at me?'

'Zacchi—' She felt herself blushing again and wondered if she would ever grow out of it. 'There's something—'

'Don't you mean some*one*? Someone else?'

Kay dropped her head back and sighed. 'It's hopeless, Zac.'

'Why?' His voice, as ever, was sincere.

'I went to Spain earlier this year. For a holiday. I met someone. Chris. He looked so much like you.' She bit her bottom lip and wondered if she should stop there.

'He's the first real boyfriend since you.' She said it quickly. 'And I'm afraid this time I didn't stop when I should have.' There. It was out. The ball was in his court.

He slowly withdrew his hand from hers, and she could feel his body tense even though they weren't touching. She wanted to say how sorry she was and yet somehow that would have been disloyal to Chris, who she did, or at least she thought she did, love. Now that Zacchi was close to her again, she wasn't sure.

'I've been tempted enough times,' he said, 'but it would have been for sex and nothing else. I chose to bury myself in my study and writing instead. I was daft enough to believe you might wait for me.'

'Well that's a bit much, isn't it? Nearly three years and not a word from you! As far as I was concerned you'd wiped me out!'

'It wasn't that easy for me.' His voice was shot through with disappointment.

'Well why *didn't* you write?' she cried, not caring about two women who were sitting close by, listening intently.

'I did write!' He lowered his voice. 'I just couldn't bring myself to send the letters. I don't know why. I don't know.'

Narrowing her eyes, Kay studied his face. 'I don't think I believe you.'

'Thanks.'

They sat there while Sid drew people towards him on the opposite side of the pond. Kay began to feel as if she were sitting next to a stranger. Part of her wanted to suggest they make their way back, and another part wanted to stay with him and rekindle the special feelings they had shared.

'I had a lot of girlfriends before you, Kay. Some I liked a lot more than others. I even thought I loved a couple of them. Then I met you. And I realized what love meant.' He slowly shook his head. 'I loved you so much, a day didn't go by when I wasn't making plans. Thinking about the future, reliving the past, helped me live the present. And if you think that sounds too corny, then you'll know why I couldn't bring myself to post the love letters I wrote you.'

'I felt the same,' Kay kept her head lowered. 'The difference was that I didn't have an address to write to. I had to wait until you contacted me.

I had to get through every day trying to hold the smell of your spicy soap in my mind.'

Zacchi chuckled and shook his head. 'That soap meant more to you than I did.'

'At least you took the trouble to use it today,' she murmured, trying not to smile.

'I had to twist my uncle's arm to get it. You can't buy it in the shops. My grandmother made it to an old family recipe.'

'And she doesn't any more?'

'No. She died last year. That's when my family decided to settle down. We burned her wagon. It's an old gypsy custom.'

'I'm sorry, Zacchi. It must have been traumatic giving up your way of life.'

'It was. But we're adjusting. So long as we stick together, we'll be OK.' He was bending over now, resting his elbows on his knees, his head lowered.

'My uncle Bert died, too. Earlier this year.' Kay could feel the old familiar sadness sweep over her.

'That must have been hard for your aunt Liz.'

Kay was touched that he still remembered her family. 'She's still getting over it. We all are.'

'I'm still in love with you, Kay.'

Covering her face with her hands, Kay willed herself not to cry. 'The trouble is—' she stopped. The words stuck in her throat. How could she tell him she might be having Chris's baby?

'Go on.' His voice was serious, almost as if he had picked up on the gravity of the situation.

'You'll hate me,' she warned.

'Maybe.'

'I think I might be pregnant.'

Zacchi wanted to hear no more. He stood up, and keeping his back to her, composed himself and walked away. Kay made no move to leave. She sat staring into the pond, at the ripples made by a few children who were still paddling.

When she finally checked the clock hanging on the wall of the umbrella factory just outside the park, it was five minutes to seven. The park keeper would be locking the gates in five minutes. She had been sitting there for over an hour and it had seemed like seconds.

Sid had moved to her side of the pond and sat near by, his Bible and hymn-book on his lap. They were the only two there. As she gazed blankly at him, he turned his head sideways and smiled back at her. Then, without thinking, she walked up to him and sat down.

'Hallo, Sid,' she said quietly.

'There's no point worrying. If it's going to happen, it will,' he said, not looking at her.

'It already has.'

'I don't see a happening.' He studied the air around them.

'How could you see what's inside me?' she said, hoping he wouldn't realize what it was she had allowed to slip out.

'If it's inside – it hasn't happened. When it's outside, and you can see it, touch it—'

'Do you know what I'm talking about?'

'It's more important that *you* do.' He stood up, doffing his battered trilby. Then, with one hand flat on his Bible he smiled. 'Thou shalt not kill.'

Kay sat by herself for the last couple of minutes. Sid always left her with a feeling of comfort inside, a safe feeling. Even when she was a child and listened to him with the rest of the crowd, he was special, and somehow managed to find his way into people's hearts.

Thou shalt not kill. His voice hung in her mind. He needn't have worried. That was the last thing she intended to do. If there was a baby growing inside, she would feed it until it was ready to come out into the big wide world. Then she would love it and protect it.

With her hand on her stomach, she wondered if it might be a girl or a boy. She was no longer filled with worry, but with a warmth which she would share with no one until she was sure. She would make an appointment with the doctor before going home.

'He seemed decent enough,' Jack said from behind his newspaper. 'Get rid of that earring, and you'd never guess he was a gyppo.'

'That'd be a shame. It's what I find most attractive about him,' Kay retorted, knowing that was the best way to deal with her dad when he pretended he was racist.

'You'll be buying a wagon next and going on the road.'

'Chance would be a fine thing.'

Jack bent back his newspaper and looked quizzically at her. 'You think you'd enjoy not being able to take a bath when you wanted, do you?'

Not wishing to get into a no-win argument, Kay changed the subject. 'Do you think I could have my letters now? You know, the ones from Spain?'

'Don't know what you're talking about.' He shook his paper and hid his face.

'I've got a friend in the sorting office, so I know there's been letters for me. And I want them!'

'Top drawer in the sideboard. You should 'ave asked before now, I'd forgotten about them.'

'Liar!' She stormed out of the kitchen.

'If you think you're going out there to see a Spaniard, you've got another think coming! Why can't you go out with a local boy? Make life a bit easier, wouldn't it?' he called after her.

In the privacy of her room, Kay sat on the edge of the bed and began to open her letters. She had put them in date order, and opened the first one. It was full of love and promise. Chris wanted her to go back out there for a holiday in the autumn. He even offered to pay half her expenses. The second letter was full of questions. Why hadn't she answered? Had she met someone else? Maybe she had written and the letter had gone astray? The third was all disappointment; the fourth and fifth angry, hurt and desperate.

'How could you have done this?' The tears were pouring down her cheeks. 'He's practically suicidal!'

'I couldn't see the point!' Jack spat back, aloof.

'We loved each other! Isn't that enough? Does there have to be a point?' Kay knew she was hysterical, but the tone of Chris's last letter had been so awful all she wanted was to be with him, to tell him what had happened; to tell him she did love him.

'If you'd met him, you'd never treat him like this!' She gripped the letters angrily in one hand, waving them in Jack's sorry face. 'Read them! Read what you've put him through, and then tell me you were right!'

Jack covered his face with his hands. 'All right, babe. I was wrong. I'm sorry, I shouldn't 'ave done it.' He sighed loudly. 'I can be a silly bastard at times.' He reached out and pulled Kay close, patting her back the way he used to when she was a baby.

'I didn't wanna lose you. I don't want you living a million miles away.'

'It's not even three *hours* away.'

'Yeah, I s'pose that's one way of looking at it.' He gazed into her face. 'You're not scheming up any more wild ideas, are yer? Forging a passport once was bloody risky, a second time would mean prison.'

'I wouldn't do that. I can wait till next year. But at least he should know why I can't go till then.'

'Who is he, anyway? I don't know a thing about 'im.' Jack found it difficult not to show his frustration.

'He was born and bred in this country. He doesn't even have a Spanish accent. And he went to a good school. Better than the one I went to!'

'So what's he doing out there then?' Jack looked relieved.

'It's his family's village. His grandparents are there and some of his other relatives. He's got a small bakery. It's what he's always wanted.'

'He's what?' Jack's eyes narrowed.

'Bought his own bakery.' Kay read his mind. 'He's only twenty-two, Dad, and he bought it from an uncle, so it didn't cost the earth.' She gave him a wink to lighten things. 'You should taste his hot bread, Dad. It's out of this world. And the cakes.'

'I suppose you'd better phone 'im,' Jack said indifferently.

'Phone?' Kay could hardly believe it. It would cost a fortune.

'Well it's cheaper than going out there, innit? Go on.' He tapped one of the letters she held in her hand. 'Look. He's put the number in the corner.'

'You really mean it?' She felt like screaming for joy.

'Yeah, go on. But keep it short!'

'Well, where is he?' Laura unpacked some shopping from her bag on to the kitchen table.

'Who?' Jack knew very well who, but he was in one of his mischievous moods.

'Zacchi of course.'

'Dunno. They went out for a walk; she came back by herself.' He shrugged. 'Then she spent over an hour on the phone to Spain.'

'She did *what*?'

'Well, five minutes anyway. It felt like an hour. Christ knows what it cost.'

'Jack. What's going on. What has Zacchi coming here got to do with her phoning Spain?'

'Search me. She's in her room. Go and ask 'er.'

'I think I will.' Laura marched out of the kitchen and rapped on her door.

'Not now!' came the sorry reply.

'Kay? What's wrong?'

'I'll tell you later, Mum! I need to be by myself.'

'She's not crying, is she?' Jack joined Laura at Kay's door. They both stood there wondering what to do next.

'He doesn't want to know me any more. I couldn't tell him that Dad hid the letters, so I lied and said I'd been too ill to write. He didn't believe me!'

'I warned you.' Laura pointed a finger into Jack's face. 'I said something like this would happen!' She stormed into the kitchen.

'Hiding your daughter's letters! You and your stupid Victorian attitudes! Don't blame me if she ups and leaves!'

Jack turned his back on her and stared out of the window at nothing. 'Of all the nerve. Who does he think he is, doesn't wanna know? Doesn't wanna know our Kay? I'll strangle the little bastard.'

'Yeah, that's it, Jack. Turn it around. Put the blame somewhere else. Like you always do!'

He turned to face her, his eyes fiery with anger. She'd never seen him look so menacing. 'Good job he's miles away,' she murmured, half smiling.

'I'll phone 'im. Yeah. That's it. Go and get one of them letters. The number'll be on it.' Jack tapped a roll-up on the lid of his tin. 'I'll soon knock the little drip off his pedestal.'

'No!' Laura was unhesitating. 'Definitely no!'

Jack spread his hands in the air and shrugged. 'I can't just leave it, Laura. Either I phone, or I push my fist through a window.'

'You'll do neither. Because both would be costly, and I'm not gonna add to the expense that boy's cost us already!' She hoped that would bring Jack's temper down enough to make him see reason.

'So what then?' he demanded pathetically.

'So we leave it. I'm afraid she's gonna have to learn to deal with her own heartaches. Everyone has to in the end. You've got to learn to let her go, Jack.'

Drawing hard on his cigarette, he nodded. 'You're a lot of help.'

'How d'yer think I feel? I wasn't cast in iron, you know.'

'I know.' He stretched out one arm and pulled her to him. 'When does it end, eh? The pain we go through with kids?'

'Never, according to Liz. She still worries about her David and his snooty wife.'

'Yeah, but it's different with us and our Kay.'

'Everyone thinks that about their own. We all love the little sods too much for our own good.'

'Yeah. You can say that again.'

Sitting on Pamela's bed with the pillows propped behind her, Kay waited for her friend to put the finishing touches to her make-up. She hadn't told her about the visit from Zacchi that day, or the call to Spain. She would wait until she had her full attention.

'So when do you start this new and exciting job?' Mouth gaping, Pamela brushed on more mascara.

'Tomorrow.'

'Blimey. Don't give you much time to dwell on it, do they?'

'I didn't ask for time, I wanted to start straight away. No point sitting around being bored.'

'I dunno,' Pamela admired her reflection. 'Some people have all the luck.' She turned to face Kay. 'You don't seem very excited. I'll go in your place if you like and you can take my boring old job. If I 'ave to fill in another claims form I'll go mad.'

'Are you ready yet?' Kay was beginning to lose patience. She had been there for over an hour while Pamela titivated herself. They were, after all, only going for a drink in the Black Boy and it being a Monday, it was unlikely that any of the usual crowd would be there.

'Does this new lipstick suit?' Pamela puckered her pale apricot lips.

'I prefer the pink you usually wear.'

'You don't like it.' She picked up a tissue ready to wipe it off.

'I do! I just prefer you in pink. I'll get used to it. Now leave it alone!'

'Sorry for breathing.'

'Well, what d'yer expect? I want to go *out*,' she snapped. Lowering her voice, she trailed her finger round a flowing leaf on Pamela's bedspread. 'I've got loads to tell yer.'

'Like what?' Pamela pulled on a baggy mohair cardigan. The deep purple made her big brown eyes stand out more than ever.

'Like who my visitor was today. And who I spoke to on the phone – long distance.' Kay suddenly felt lighter. As pleased as punch.

Unable to stop a cocky smile spreading across her face, she began to chuckle. Pamela stared at her forlornly. 'I've got their number,' Kay sang tauntingly.

'You liar!'

'Suit yourself.' Kay slipped down from the pillows and stretched herself out on the bed. 'It was as if he were standing in the same room,' she said, full of swank.

'Where'd you get his number from then, Miss Clever-drawers?'

'From one of the letters he sent me.'

Pamela turned back to the mirror and carefully wiped off the apricot lipstick. 'I'm sure,' she murmured.

'He sent four in all.' Kay's mind clouded over as she remembered how her dad had ruined their relationship. 'My dad kept the letters back,' she said. 'He thought he was doing it in my best interests.'

'Kay!' Pamela sounded angry. 'Stop messing about. You know how depressed I've been not hearing from Charles!'

'He lost your address. Chris wrote that Charles asked if I would get you to write.' Kay pulled a piece of paper from her pocket. 'Here. I've written it down for yer.'

Snatching it from her friend, Pamela screeched with joy until her mother appeared in the doorway. 'What's happened?' She turned to Kay. 'You told her she looked like a model with that new lipstick?'

'Charles lost my address!' She brought her face close to her mother's. 'He lost it. That's why he hasn't been in touch.' She kissed the piece of paper. 'I knew he loved me.'

Lillian raised her eyebrows and shrugged. 'I suppose he's a goy?'

'He's Spanish! And if I have to, I'll convert to Catholicism!'

'Sure you will.' With a smug half-smile on her face, Lillian closed the door behind her, leaving the girls to themselves.

'If I said that to my mum or dad, they'd hit the roof.'

'Why? This faith, that faith, what's the difference? We're all flesh and blood underneath.' She kissed the piece of paper again. 'Give me his phone number! I must talk to him.'

'I don't have it. Only Chris's. And I'm certainly not giving that to you. Not after what he said to me.' Kay turned her back on Pamela and wondered why she didn't actually feel sad any more. She wondered why it was Zacchi's face that filled her mind instead.

'What d'yer mean?' Pamela circled the bed. 'Kay, what did he say?'

'He's gone back with his fiancé. A local girl. I was on the rebound.' Kay sat up and hugged her knees. 'He blamed it on the fact that he wrote four letters for my one. Said he had suffered so much pain, and when she appeared in the doorway one day he realized how much he had loved her.'

'I can't believe it,' Pamela shook her head. 'You're not messing about, either, are you.'

'It's OK. I've done my crying. And that's what gets me really mad. I vowed I wasn't gonna let anyone make me cry again and I did. I hate him for that.' She turned the signet ring on her right hand. 'Zacchi was so warm and oh, I dunno, kind of loving, in a way.'

'Zacchi?' Pamela looked totally confused. 'Today is Monday, isn't it. And I did see you yesterday? And none of this had happened then?'

'All in a day!' Kay forced a smile. 'I gained a new career and lost two boyfriends. Not bad, eh?'

'Lost?'

'Yeah. Come on, let's go for a drink. I'll tell you on the way.'

Walking along the Mile End Road, Kay filled Pamela in, except on the one worry that she was keeping to herself. She couldn't bring herself to tell her best friend her worst fears, or about her visit to the doctor. The two pills he had given her were in an envelope in her handbag. She was to take them that evening and if she wasn't pregnant, her period would come the next day or so. She was almost too scared to take them in case nothing happened.

It was the best thing that could have happened, Tommy and Micky being in the Black Boy. They looked handsome leaning against the bar, each enjoying a pint. Kay looked from them to Pamela. 'Look who's here.'

She felt sure they would take her mind off Zacchi, even though she found herself wishing he would walk in.

'Oh, you made it then,' Pamela said in her haughty way.

'Wouldn't miss it for the world,' said Tommy, looking at Kay.

'You might 'ave told me!' Kay was caught off guard, and was embarrassed that he wouldn't take his eyes off her.

'Haven't seen you around lately,' Tommy slipped between Kay and Pamela, trying to separate her from the group.

'Life's been a bit hectic since Spain,' Kay smiled shyly back at him.

'What she means is that we've been spending time seeing how the other half live.' Pamela showed a limp wrist. 'Her friend Terry's been showing us the town.'

'Oh yeah? Gay, was it?' Micky threw his head back and laughed. 'Hope we're not too butch for yer!'

'No.' Kay looked them up and down, an impertinent smirk on her face.

Enjoying her sense of humour, Tommy walked over to the jukebox while his friend ordered the drinks. Kay watched him as he studied the labels and thought what a coincidence it would be if he chose the same song as Chris had done in Spain.

'This is just for you.' He winked at Kay as Bobby Vee's voice filled the room with 'Rubber Ball'.

Lying in bed that night, Kay lined up in her imagination the three young men she had spoken to that day and measured each against the other. Zacchi definitely came out on top but he was the only one who knew her secret, so she didn't want to face him again. Tommy came second for his good looks and the modern way he dressed. And Chris came last. Had he not told her rather belatedly that he had been engaged before they met, he would have come out on top and she would be making plans to fly out there the following year, 1963, quite possibly with his baby in her arms.

Deciding not to take the pills that night for fear of anything spoiling her first day at her new job she turned over, buried her head in her pillow and quietly prayed that everything would turn out all right. It had been a long, eventful day and within a minute of closing her eyes, Kay fell into a deep sleep.

'The Managing Director wishes to meet you, Kay. Please follow me.' Rebecca Jamieson was wearing a smart, tight-fitting black dress and a beautiful diamond necklace. 'Let's not keep him waiting.'

Jamieson had left Thompson's and was now working for Waterman's. Kay pushed her chair back ready to stand, but on looking down was shocked to see that she had forgotten to put on the skirt she had laid out the night before and was wearing only one stocking. The suspenders from the horrid old-fashioned pink roll-on were dangling down one leg, the elastic so old and loose that the button and clip almost touched her knee.

Leaning on the reception desk, Jamieson pushed her head closer to Kay. 'You're going to have to stand up, you know. You can't hide behind that desk all day. Get up! Now!'

Hot and panicky, Kay pleaded with her, but the words in her mind were not the ones that left her mouth. She was saying the wrong things and her head felt as if it were on fire and would burst into flames. Dripping with perspiration she wiped her legs with her damp dress and was horrified to see the dark red liquid oozing from her and dripping onto the light carpet.

'Get up! The Chairman is coming.' There was an evil sickly smile on Jamieson's face.

'No! Please, no! It hurts! I'm in pain! I want my mother! Please phone for my mother!'

'Your mother is in the next office. She doesn't want to see you.'

Kay looked through a window, and could see Laura. She called out to her, but she just threw her a look of disgust and carried on with her work. 'MUMMY! MUMMY, PLEASE! HELP ME!'

'Kay ..? Oh Kay, baby, it's all right.' Laura was at Kay's bedside in a flash, cradling and rocking her daughter. 'Just a nightmare, love. Just a silly dream.'

'Mum! I've got cramp! It's worse than I've *ever* had before.' Kay gripped Laura's arm as a searing pain shot through her womb.

Shocked by Kay's harrowing scream, Laura whipped back the bedcovers to see that her daughter was lying in a pool of sticky blood. Grabbing her mother by the arms again, Kay caught her breath as her stomach contracted and another pain pierced her.

'All right, baby, all right. Just lie still. Don't move.' Realising the gravity of the situation, Laura felt herself shiver.

'It's just a heavy period, isn't it?' Kay dragged the covers back over herself and dropped back onto her pillow, looking deathly white.

'I expect so.' Laura spun around as Jack arrived. 'Don't ask questions,' Laura warned 'just sit there and hold her hand.'

'Where are you going?' Jack's eyes were heavy with sleep.

'To phone the doctor!'

Another cry from Kay snapped Jack into action. He was by her side and holding her before he could think.

'It's a late period, dad, that's all.' Kay went limp in his arms.

Smiling bravely into her face, he stroked Kay's perspiration-damp hair. 'Try to relax, eh?' He closed his hand around hers and prayed that the worse hadn't happened. 'I'll run you a nice warm bath in a minute.'

While they waited for the emergency doctor to arrive, Laura busied herself, making Kay as comfortable as she could, after changing the sheets. Jack had been sent into the kitchen where he could let go of his bottled-up emotion in private and make them all some hot, sweet tea.

'It's more than just blood, isn't it, Mum?' Kay turned her head away as Laura carefully slid the heavily soiled sheet into a plastic bag.

'Try not to think about it.'

'I've never known pain like that before. You *will* tell the doctor how bad it was!' She arched her back again and struggled with another minor contraction. 'In case it gets bad again,' she managed to say.

Laura looked into Kay's drawn face. 'How bad is it now?'

'Worse than a normal period.' She laid back and sighed with relief as the pain subsided. 'It was as if a knife was—'

'Yeah all right.' Laura didn't want to hear the rest. She glanced at the small alarm clock on Kay's bedside table and was just about to say that the doctor should be here by now when the doorbell rang.

'It's barely termed as a miscarriage, Mrs. Armstrong but your daughter was five or six weeks pregnant. It looks as if she's passed as many clots as she's likely to and the flow seems to be easing. A few days bed-rest and she'll be fine. Just keep her warm and comfortable.'

Laura nodded, avoiding the doctor's eyes. 'We didn't . . . Kay didn't . . .' She took a deep breath. 'It's not an abortion.' She blurted out the words quickly, wanting to get that bit over with.

The doctor smiled. 'I realise that. We *can* tell you know. I doubt if she has had intercourse more than two or three times in her life.'

'Well, that's something to be thankful for, I suppose.'

'At seventeen? I would have thought so. These days.'

Once the doctor had gone and Kay had been given pain killers, Laura braced herself to face Jack. Now he really would have to accept the fact that his baby-girl had experienced full womanhood. Like it or not.

Wrapped in her towelling dressing gown, curled up in an armchair, Kay thanked her lucky stars. One way or another, Mother Nature had seen fit to map out the following year or so of her life.

'I'll have to go to work, Kay, but Dad'll get you anything you want. He'll only be gone a couple of hours.' Laura handed her a milky drink.

'Did Mrs Jarold really sound OK about my not turning up?'

'Yes, for the third time. I told her you had a stomach bug as well as a period and that you wouldn't be taking a day off every month. She was fine about it. OK?' She kissed Kay on the forehead. 'Stop worrying.'

'Thanks, Mum.'

'You'll be all right, then?'

'Yeah.' She waved a library book. 'It'll be nice to get in some reading.'

'Charles Dickens again?' Laura sounded pleased. 'You'll be so well read, we soon won't be able to talk to you.'

'Did I tell you that Zacchi's a feature writer?'

Standing by the door, Laura smiled back at Kay. 'Yes, love, you did. And I'm just as proud of him as you are.'

Once alone, Kay laid her book down on the arm of her chair and closed her eyes, thinking about Zacchi. She tried to put herself in his place and imagine how she would have felt if he had told her he had met someone else and that she was having his baby. She would have hated it.

Full of remorse at having broken her promise to wait for him, she decided to write a letter saying she was sorry. With pen poised, she tried to think of the right words to say. For ten minutes she sat staring at the blank page until it dawned on her why she wasn't scribbling away like mad. She was sorry she hadn't waited . . . but she didn't think she should apologize. Zacchi should have written to her. How was she to know if he was ever going to contact her after two and a half years? No: he was to blame, not her. She would not write.

Tossing the pen and notepad to the floor, she continued to read *The Old Curiosity Shop*. If Zacchi was half as interested in her as she was in him, he would get in touch. If not, at least she knew where she stood.

Ten minutes later, Kay was asking Directory Inquiries for the number of the Walthamstow *Guardian*.

Not knowing quite what to say to him once she was put through, Kay found herself asking why he had walked away from her the day before.

'If you don't know, there's no point in my trying to explain,' he said flatly.

'I'm not pregnant, by the way,' she blurted, 'if that's what bothered you!'

There was a pause. 'Why did you say you were then?'

'I thought I was. Today proved different. I'm at home. I couldn't go to work and it was my first day as well.'

'Did you love him?' Zacchi was never one for mincing his words.

'I thought I did till you turned up.'

'I'll come and see you at the weekend.' Still there was no enthusiasm in his voice. 'Saturday morning, around eleven. I hope you feel better soon.' With that he replaced the receiver.

Feeling frustrated, Kay slammed the phone down. She had hardly said anything to him. She hadn't said how sorry she was, or how she couldn't stop thinking about him. Saturday seemed a lifetime away.

Chapter Twelve

At the end of her first week as receptionist/copy typist at Waterman's, Kay was feeling pleased with herself. Standing in front of the large pink-tinted mirror in Reception, she admired the new Italian suit she had bought in Petticoat Lane that lunch-time.

'Prince of Wales check. It suits you.' Mrs Jarold's sunny face smiled in the mirror as she stood behind Kay. The Staff Liaison Officer had taken a liking to Kay and Kay to her.

'You've made an good impression, you know. The editor of *Stock Market* wants to know if you can be transferred to his department.'

'Really?' Kay beamed, but then remembered that her shorthand wasn't as good as it could be. 'I don't suppose he uses a dictaphone?'

A look of concern came to Mrs Jarold's face. 'I thought you could work with one?'

'I can. I was worried in case he might want a shorthand typist.'

'Ah,' the smile returned to her face. 'No, my boss is the only old-fashioned one here. So? What do you think?'

Kay wasn't sure. She really enjoyed dealing with clients and having a bit of fun with the journalists when they dropped by for a chat. She would miss that. And the *Stock Market* wasn't exactly the most exciting journal.

'Can I let you know on Monday?'

'Of course you can.' She pushed open the smoked glass main door. 'I suppose I had better tell you that the *Mirror* has asked for you as well.' She winked at Kay. 'But don't let it go to your head.'

Staring after her as she walked out of the building, Kay couldn't help feeling thrilled.

'Have a good weekend!' A tall, dark-haired attractive woman in her early thirties passed Kay on her way out of the building.

'Excuse me!' Kay called after her.

Stopping in her tracks, she turned to face Kay. 'Yes?'

'Don't you work for *Female Weekly*?'

'Excellent memory! You've only been to our department once. We must have made an impression,' she smiled.

'Yeah, you did. There's kind of a buzz.'

'Glad you picked up on it. We're not always buzzing, though. It's a nightmare the day before we go to print. Tempers get a bit frayed to say the least.' She pushed the door open with her shoulder and gave Kay a show of her hand. 'See you Monday.'

That was it: that was her goal. Kay would ask if there were any chance of her working her way towards being part of *Female Weekly*'s team. She would turn down *Stock Market* and continue in Reception until a vacancy came up. It was a strange feeling, but she just knew by instinct that she would find her niche on that busy weekly, should the opportunity arise.

Squeezing into the stuffy carriage on the underground, this time Kay didn't mind being squashed like a sardine. She couldn't wait to tell her parents about the new job offers. Her mind went back to Thompson's and found herself believing in fate. If it hadn't been for that terrible incident she would never have left. She would still be working in that backwater instead of experiencing a thriving, lively company.

Her thoughts began to race. Maybe she would go to evening classes and learn about journalism. Maybe she could be trained as an editor. She had already done a bit of proofreading for one of the journalists and she had only been working there four days. If she could achieve that much in such a short time, what could she achieve in a lifetime? Or at least before she settled into marriage and having children. She couldn't remember a time when she felt as happy and optimistic.

Walking home through Bethnal Green park, passing a couple of heavy drinkers who were sleeping it off, she wondered what it would be like to have her own flat in another part of town. Not that she didn't like living in the East End, but London was a big place and Kay had often felt the desire to live in other areas. A whole new life was out there, and in her mind's eye she likened it to a large cut-crystal globe, each facet showing a different Technicolor film, a hundred worlds existing at the same time.

'Hallo, babe. Your mum said you would be along any minute.' Frank and Freddie were walking down the stairs as Kay was on her way up. 'Like your new haircut. Suits yer,' her curly-headed uncle grinned.

'We was hoping to see you, Kay,' Frank said, slipping his hand into an inside pocket. 'This is for you.' He handed her a thick white envelope.

'What is it?' She had a horrible feeling she knew.

'It fell off the back of a van. Enjoy spending it but don't let Mum or Dad know. They'd do their nuts.'

Laughing quietly, Frank carried on down the stairs. 'I take it there was no comeback for you?' he asked, a hopeful look on his face.

Trying to stop herself grinning, Kay slowly shook her head. 'I can't take this.'

'Now don't be a silly girl! That place deserved what it got and you deserve that. You don't have to spend it straight away, all at once, like. Wait till you see something you want.'

Leaving her speechless, they disappeared down the next flight of stairs. 'If you wanna bring your friends to the Kentucky, make it a Monday when it's quiet.' Frank's voice echoed in the stairwell.

Leaning over the green-painted metal banisters, Kay called down to them. 'Will Reg be there?'

'Probably . . . with his fiancée!'

Going directly to her room, Kay sat on the edge of the bed and drew a wad of bank notes out of the envelope. She felt a deep thrill as she began counting. Two hundred and fifty pounds. She swept her fingers across the fanned notes and wondered if she dared use it.

Hearing footsteps in the passage, she pushed the money back into the envelope and tossed it on top of the wardrobe.

'I thought I heard you come in,' Laura stood in the doorway. 'Zacchi phoned. Said he won't be able to make it tomorrow after all. He's got to cover a story.'

'You reckon?' Kay could feel herself sink. 'I'm not the same fifteen-year-old he fell in love with.'

Laura let out a throaty chuckle. 'Anyone'd think you were an old woman.' Stroking Kay's hair, she tried to stop herself smiling. 'So he's coming tonight instead.'

'Mum, that's not funny! You could have said.'

'I just did.'

'Yeah. Bit late though.'

''Cos you let your mum see how much you like him?' Laura teased. 'You won't need any tea.' Cocking her head to one side, she affected a cut-glass accent. 'He's taking you out to dinner. Do you want me to run you a bath? While I press whatever madam decides to wear?'

'My herring-bone suit and white short sleeves'll be all right, won't it? Or the pink and navy?'

Leaving the room, Laura told her not to worry – whatever she wore, she would knock Zacchi for six, if she hadn't already.

Knock him for six. The words rang around her head. Maybe that was the order of the day? She looked at herself in the full-length mirror and doubt clouded her mind. *I'm not the same though, am I. I'm not a virgin any more. He's probably taking me out to dinner to tell me it's over before it all starts up again. He's probably guessed that I* was *pregnant.*

Opening the drawer of her dressing table, she took out the false eyelashes she had bought but never worn. Tonight they would get an airing. If Pamela could wear them, so could she.

Pamela! She suddenly remembered. 'Mum!' She stepped into the passage. 'I'm supposed to be going to the Black Boy with Pam!'

'Phone her! She'll understand!' Showing her face in the kitchen doorway, Laura shrugged. 'It had to happen sometime, Kay. You're both gonna get dates, and not always in a foursome.

'Did you pass Frank and Freddie by the way? They left just before you came in.'

Kay slipped back into her bedroom. 'They just said hallo and goodbye.'

'I'm not sure why they came, really,' Laura called back. 'Probably wanted to see your dad about something.'

'Dunno!'

Pleased that she had managed to get the false eyelashes on without making her eyes water, Kay applied a touch of mascara, remembering that Zacchi didn't think much of painted faces. She slicked on just a touch of ice-pink lipstick.

'He's here, Kay!' yelled Laura from the kitchen. Seconds later there was a knock at the door.

Zacchi stood on the doorstep looking as handsome as ever. 'I'm ready, but you can come in if you like.'

'I've waited too long to share you with anyone else.' He held out his hand and smiled.

Arm in arm, their stormy parting forgotten, they walked slowly through the backstreets. It was as if the three-year gap had never been. 'Where do you want to go?' Zacchi asked.

'Don't mind.'

Then without warning, he grabbed her by both arms and pulled her to him, not caring about the passers-by. They melted into a long kiss. 'I was mad to think there wouldn't be anyone else, Kay.'

'I did wait, Zac, I really did. But being in Spain and him looking so much like you—'

'That's history. Now it's just you and me.'

'Do you know what I would really like to do? Show you around the East End. Show you that it's not quite as Dickensian as people think.'

'If you must,' he groaned.

Carrying two cups of tea to a table in the canteen at Hammond's, Laura waited for Liz to join her. She always took her tea-break when her sister-in-law was not so busy. That way they could sit and natter.

'You seemed a bit quiet at lunch-time.' Laura bit off the corner of her biscuit and waited.

'Did I?' Liz kept her eyes down. 'Bit tired, that's all.'

'Sure?'

'Yes, Laura. I'm sure. Stop digging.'

'There is something to dig for, then?'

Shaking her head and smiling, Liz sipped her tea. 'You're getting as bad as me.'

'Good. Well then?' Laura smiled, but she couldn't stop the nagging feeling. Liz had looked downcast for a couple of days now.

'You know Joe's retiring at the end of this month, don't you?'

'You already told me that. You're not fretting over it, surely?'

'No. Not over that. It's just that . . .' Liz sat back in her chair and pursed her lips. 'He's not all he's made out to be.'

That came as no surprise. Laura had always known that Joe liked the women, and if Liz hadn't been mourning for Bert when she met him, she would have given her a word of warning. As it was, it seemed best to leave it and hope for the best.

'He's a gold-digger,' Liz said at last. 'Thought I had a packet to come from the insurance policies. Ever since I told him that wasn't the case, he's been a bit standoffish.'

'Just as well you found out when you did.' Laura tried not to let her anger get the better of her for the sake of Liz's pride.

'I thought I'd found a friend. Someone I could talk to, a soul mate. Another person to watch television with. Maybe go to the pictures with, now and then.'

'You can always come round to us, Liz, you know that.'

'You know what's worse? The feeling of being used. I should 'ave known better. I'm no spring chicken.' She pulled her little blue tin out, checked that no one was watching and sprinkled some snuff on the back of her hand.

'I passed him on the stairs this morning; he was charming the woman who comes in to clean the telephones. I wouldn't mind betting she's a widow as well.'

'His type ain't worth upsetting yourself for, Liz.' Laura tried to think of something to lift her. 'I'll tell you what,' she smiled. 'My dad's missed you popping in to see him.'

'Poor old Billy,' Liz laughed. 'Missing someone like me? Must be desperate.'

'Come on, Liz. You don't mean that. You know the pair of you can make each other laugh about nothing.'

'Yeah, that's true. I'll drop in after work. Take him a couple of buns.'

'Good. And try not to think about Joe,' Laura stood up. 'He's a loser, Liz – if only he knew it.'

Walking out of the canteen, Laura stopped in the doorway and looked back at Liz. Telepathy or not, she knew that there was a question on Liz's mind, so she walked slowly back and stood next to her.

'You don't think your dad would wanna move in with me, do you?'

'No chance, Liz. But I know he'd love it if you took his spare room. My old bedroom.'

There was a pause as Liz thought about it. 'It's a smashing little cottage,' she said softly.

'Shut away from the rest of the world behind that old green door in the wall,' Laura persuaded.

'I suppose he does get on with the neighbours?'

'They're all pensioners, Liz. All worked for the brewery. They all know each other. It'd be like hop-picking without the hardships.'

'And you think Billy'd go for that? Me moving around in his little house?'

'Ask him.'

Laura hadn't seen Jack look so happy in a very long time. Now, in the middle of July, the London dock strike was over and the men were going back to work the next day. While he wasn't that pleased with the outcome it was obvious that he, like hundreds of other men, was sick of just passing the time of day.

Pressing the collar of his shirt, Laura felt a rush of admiration for him. He was giving the blade of his docker's hook a good polish.

'You did well. All of yer. You let this country know the strength of the dockers.'

'Maybe,' Jack said, trying to hide his true feelings. He couldn't wait to get back to the dockside, and she knew it. 'There's gonna be an investigation by a government-sponsored committee next week. At least it's woken 'em up a bit. If we hadn't have agreed to go back, they would have had to move troops in, you know, to move the perishables.' There was a touch of pride in his voice.

'Well, maybe they'll think twice now before they take on outside labour.'

'You can bet your life on it.' Changing the subject, he brought the conversation around to Liz.

'I saw your dad down the waste today. At the fruit and veg stall. Looked happy as a sandboy, picking out a fresh cauliflower.' Jack chuckled. 'D'yer reckon they'll get married, or what?'

''Course they won't. She's gonna be his lodger and that's all they want.' She hung his shirt on a hanger and checked the cuffs. 'That's all that matters at the end of the day, a bit of company. Someone to say goodnight to.'

'I never did trust that bloke of hers. Taking her to seance meetings. She wouldn't listen, though.'

'No, and neither would you if the boot was on the other foot.'

'Kay's late in,' he said, looking at his watch.

'She's nearly eighteen, Jack, and it's only just gone half past eleven.'

'Half past eleven,' he said, staring out. 'I always had to get you back home by ten.'

'Yeah well, times have changed, thank God. You can do the same thing at midnight as you can before ten. As you well know,' she half smiled.

'I never laid a hand on you till you begged me.'

'Bloody cheek! Me, beg? That'll be the day.'

'Yes you did. With your eyes.' He laid down his sharpening stone. 'Coming to bed?'

Laura pulled the plug out of the socket and stood the iron on the tiled fireplace to cool down. 'I thought you'd never ask.'

'What d'yer think about this gypsy, then?' Jack said.

'Oh, don't keep calling him that, Jack, it's not funny. He's a good kid and she likes him a lot.'

'That's what worries me.'

'He doesn't live in Spain . . .' She had been saving that one.

'That's true,' he said, rubbing his eyes. 'What am I gonna do about this money, Laura?'

'I can't keep up with you. Your mind flashes from one thing to another. What money?'

'The envelopes, for Liz.'

'You should have given them to her by now.'

'I know. I can't bring myself to, though. I suppose I don't want her to have it.' He stood up and stretched. 'Scum money.'

'Oh, shut up. You don't know it's from drugs. You're just guessing. Anyway, you should leave it to Liz to decide. You're not her keeper.'

'Yeah. I s'pose you're right. I'll pop round there after work tomorrow.'

Laura folded the ironing-board and leaned it against the wall. 'I know what I'd do with it.'

He looked at her and waited.

'I'd book a cruise for her and Billy. Tell her you had a good win on the dogs. She won't ask any questions. Neither will Dad.'

'You serious?'

'Yes, Jack, I am. Sod it! Why shouldn't the pair of them see a bit of the world? If that money goes back to the boys it'll just get pissed away.'

'Oy, oy, oy! Language,' Jack scolded.

Laura knew he hated to hear her being coarse, but she knew how to distract him. 'It's true though. You know it is.' She moved close to him and rested her hands on his broad shoulders. 'Where's the harm in it, eh? Try to think of it as unearned income that the taxman won't get his hands on.'

'You mean it, don't yer?'

'Both of them have worked hard all their lives. As hard as any self-made millionaire. So why shouldn't they have a thin slice of what the rich enjoy most of the time?'

'Well,' Jack grinned, 'put like that, what can I say?' He put his strong hands on her small waist, pulled her to him and kissed her with passion.

They would have made love on the rug if the doorbell hadn't brought them down from the heady heights.

'She's forgotten her key again,' Laura couldn't help laughing. 'I'll see her in. You go and warm up the bed.'

Sitting on the edge of the sofa, Laura waited patiently for Kay to stop crying. She knew it was no use trying to comfort her. She had seen her like this before. She'd stop soon enough.

'What will I *do*?' Kay could hardly speak. 'A whole month! Four weeks.' She buried her head in Laura's shoulder and wailed louder.

Suppressing a smile, Laura tried to see the sad side of it, but it seemed impossible. Zacchi had been commissioned to travel through France and Spain, finding and following Romany travellers, and collecting material for a book about them.

'It'll soon pass, Kay.' Laura could have bitten her tongue. She knew that was the last thing her daughter needed to hear.

'How am I gonna live without him?' Kay looked pleadingly at her out of red, swollen eyes.

Her fingers pressed against her mouth, Laura managed to ask if Kay would like a hot milky drink. Thankfully she did, which gave her a chance to get into the kitchen where she could be alone to let out the pent-up laughter. *My God!* She slowly shook her head. *Did I ever feel like that about anyone?* Then she remembered the feeling of emptiness each year that came when she left Richard in Kent.

Knowing Jack was waiting for her in bed, she suddenly felt guilty for thinking about another man. She wondered if Richard would ever fade from her memory.

'You coming to bed, Laura, or what?' Half asleep, Jack stood in the kitchen doorway.

'Kay's upset. Zacchi's got to go away for a month; they want him to write a book. She's sobbing her heart out in there.'

Jack looked at her blankly. 'A month's not that long, is it?'

'She reckons she won't be able to live without him.' Laura managed to sound serious in case he got annoyed with her for treating it lightly.

'Four weeks?' Jack raised an eyebrow and grinned.

'Jack, don't. If she hears you . . .'

With his hand on his mouth, he practically ran along the passage and into the bedroom where Laura could be sure he would bury his face in his pillow to muffle his laughter.

Pouring the hot milk on to Horlicks in Kay's mug, Laura wondered what she could say to her baby to cheer her up. She remembered the blue box in the sideboard.

Curled up on the sofa, Kay sipped her drink between small, spasmodic sobs. 'Thanks, Mum. This is lovely.'

Sitting next to her, Laura held out a hand and offered Kay the ring box. 'This was your grandfather's, your dad's dad. Aunt Liz won't mind if you have it. It's not that valuable, but it is gold.'

Kay took it and pushed the lid up with her thumb. 'This is a man's ring, Mum.'

'Of course it is. I told yer. It was your grandad's. That stone's an onyx.'

'Why are you giving it to me?'

'So that you can give it to Zacchi.'

A smile lit up her face. 'Are you sure?'

'I've never been surer. While he's wearing that, part of you will be with him.'

As she lay next to Jack in bed, Laura hoped he wouldn't hit the roof when she told him about his dad's ring.

'You asleep?' she whispered in his ear, and then kissed his cheek.

'Give my leg a massage, will yer. It's gone dead.'

Slipping her hand down his thigh, Laura began to giggle. 'You lying sod! You've been lying there thinking about me.'

'No I haven't. I've been dreaming about Sophia Loren.'

Turning over, she switched off the bedside lamp and then climbed out of bed.

'Where are you going?' Jack was suddenly awake.

'Just opening the curtains a bit. I want to see you in the lamplight.'

A deep sigh escaped him as he reached out for her.

'Everything seems to be turning out all right then,' Laura said. 'With our Kay, I mean. Happy in love and happy at work.'

'Yeah, but that don't mean she won't do an about-turn all of a sudden. Little cow. I've never known anyone so unpredictable.'

'No?' Laura slipped in beside him. 'I think she's a chip off the old block.' She kissed him lightly on the mouth.

'Your block – not mine,' he joked, and pulled her on top of him.

At Waterman's, Kay got what she had asked for. Once word was out that she could not only type fast but accurately, the journalists threw handwritten copy at her, and she was forever being asked to help someone out with the dictaphone. She was also bombarded with offers to go to the pub after work.

'So who's the lucky fellow?' John from *Stock Market* handed Kay a vodka and tonic.

'What makes you think there is one?' Kay was flirting with him, but it was expected with this lot.

'You're not interested in any of *us*,' he said with a touch of hope in his smile.

'His name's Zacchi. He's a travel writer.'

'What kind of a name's that?'

'He's a Romany.' Her back stiffened as she shot him a warning glance, before he started being offensive.

'Tall, dark and handsome?'

'Not quite as tall as you. Probably not as handsome.'

'But?'

'But . . . he's got it.' Kay sipped her drink. 'Whatever *it* is.'

'You mean you don't know?'

'Does any of us?'

John thought about that, then shrugged. 'So where is he tonight, while you're out with all the journos?'

Fed up with being jostled by the pub crowd, Kay looked around for somewhere to sit. 'He's travelling in France.'

'Over there,' John cut in, 'in the corner. Push your way through. I'll follow.'

Once they were settled, John's manner seemed to change. He was more at ease. 'My fiancée's taking our bridesmaids for a fitting,' he said, unable to keep the pride out of his voice.

'You're getting married!' Why Kay should feel so pleased for him she had no idea. They had hardly spoken at work. Polite greetings as he passed on his way in and out of Reception was all that had passed between them, except when he gave her copy to type up.

'You look relieved,' he smiled and drank his beer.

'I suppose I am really. Don't know why, though.'

'You feel safe,' he teased. 'I'm not the lecher you thought I was.'

She had to admit to herself that he was right. They could talk easily now. The guard was down. No need to read into every line. 'How long have you been engaged?'

'Three years. On and off. Five times off.'

'And now you're sure?'

'As much as I'll ever be. What about you, yours serious?'

Kay was impressed that he seemed genuinely interested. 'Very. But it's early days.' She looked into his face. 'Can you tell me something?'

John raised an eyebrow. 'Depends.'

'Why do blokes usually talk to us girls as if you're chatting us up? I don't mean now. Now we're talking normally.'

'We have proof of nothing but our own existence,' he cut in.

'Come again?'

'Ego. Over-concerned about our image,' he said thoughtfully. 'Or . . . scared of coming across as boring?'

'But the chat-up lines and the tone you use, all the eye contact, that *is* boring. All you can see is the method. The man's hidden.'

'There's your answer. Think about it.' He finished his beer, placed the glass on the table and looked into her bemused face. 'Now then, how about you getting a round?'

Taken aback, she found herself laughing. 'That's the first time a bloke has ever asked me!'

'You're one of us now.'

'Good.' She took that as the best compliment ever paid. 'What's yours?'

'Gin and tonic, please.'

'OK.' Kay looked at the crowded bar. There were a few women, but it was mostly men she'd have to find her way through. 'I don't suppose—'

'You want me to get them in?'

'Would you?' She handed him a ten-shilling note and felt herself blush. 'I'm not used to this.'

Taking the money, he suddenly stroked her face, and withdrew his hand like lightning. 'Sorry.' He jokingly put up both hands as if in surrender.

'It's OK. Don't push it though,' she joked.

While she waited for him to bring the drinks, gazing at the red and gold wallpaper, Kay tried to clarify her feelings. She thought about Zacchi and how much she loved him. She thought about Chris and remembered how she had felt. Now there was John. She was beginning to like him a lot and felt guilty that she was enjoying his company.

'A penny for them?' He placed their drinks down and handed her the change.

'You really want to know?'

'Can't wait,' he leaned back in his chair.

'Well . . . I was wondering about love.'

'Oh *that*,' he let out a small embarrassed chuckle. 'Not to be confused with sexual attraction.'

'Right. So how do we know when it's the real thing?'

'You shouldn't have to ask. You just know.'

Kay became pensive. Somehow, deep down, she felt he must be right. 'Can two people of the opposite sex have a strong liking for each other without . . .' she shrugged, 'you know.'

'Of course. And so can two people of the same sex.' He offered her a cigarette. 'It's affection.'

'And affection's not love?' She waved away the packet.

'No. It's when all the emotions are going that love ends up on the table.' He leaned forward. 'And we blocked sexual attraction when we spoke about our *betrothed*.' He lit his cigarette. 'Got it?'

'I think so. What you're saying is . . . we can love more than one person, but we only really love the one.'

'At the time,' he broke in. 'I love Pauline – that's her name – and I love my sisters, sometimes. I also love my parents. Some of my colleagues. My friends. And now you.'

Kay looked at him worriedly. If he was so clever, so philosophical about it, why had he singled her out instead of grouping her together with his friends?

'You, my new friend and colleague,' he reassured, reading her thoughts.

'You're such a clever dick,' she laughed.

'No. I had to read up on it. Sort myself out. I'm the one who's getting married, don't forget. I had to be sure. And you know what the bottom line was? The questions I asked myself? Would I want this person to bear my children? Did I want part of me and her to make a whole?' He sipped his drink and sighed. 'That was when I knew. This was for real and for good.'

Wondering why she felt a sudden pang of jealousy, Kay decided it was time for her to leave. She looked at her watch and faked her surprise at the time. 'My mum'll go mad! I said I would be going straight home tonight.'

'Phone her.' John sounded very casual about it. 'Your parents'll have to get used to it. We spend most of our time in the pub. It's part of the job. Where we pick up our little tips.'

Before she had time to decide, Jeannie arrived. 'Hi! What're you two up to?'

'Hallo, how's tricks?' John eyed her slim, shapely body.

'I wouldn't know. I never play them.' She turned to Kay and winked. 'I hope he hasn't been trying to turn your head?'

'If discussing bridesmaids is turning a head, the answer's yes,' he grinned sardonically.

'Oh, well done you,' she said to Kay. 'When they begin to tell you about the domestic, it means you've been initiated. Welcome to the club.' Jeannie pulled up a chair and squeezed it into a tiny gap around the table.

'Of course you'll be treated quite differently now. One of the chaps. Expect lots of jokes and no more real lustful looks.'

'You make us sound undesirable! Mine's a gin and tonic.'

'You know where the bar is.' She pulled a pound note out of her pocket. 'Get one for Kay. Whisky mac for yours truly.'

'You've done well for yourself.' She eased herself forward, allowing just enough room for John to pass. 'It usually takes longer for them to accept you as one of *them*.'

'What kind of jokes should I expect?' Kay was beginning to like the idea of being part of this new life.

'Oh, all sorts. They'll hide your handbag in the Gents'. Glue your coffee mug to the blotting pad, that sort of thing. Until the next new girl comes along.' She lit a cigarette and kept it dangling from the corner of her mouth while she pulled a tiny face mirror from her handbag.

'Do you enjoy working in Reception, Kay?' she said, checking her reflection.

'They keep me busy. I like that.'

'Well let me know when you've had enough. We need someone to sort us out.'

'I enjoyed the article I typed up for you last week. I didn't realize you were allowed to write about something as serious as that and show the humorous side of it as well.'

'Life and death, love. Get too heavy and you're pulled. And I'm not talking bed.' She took a long draw on her cigarette. 'If you read our mag, you'll see what I mean.'

'I keep meaning to. Don't seem to get the time.'

'Ever thought about scribbling?' Jeannie peered into Kay's face. 'You never know, you might be good.'

'I suppose everyone's had that dream,' Kay shrugged, 'but I'm just a girl from the East End. In my school the teachers were there more to keep order than to teach. My holes have got a little grammar in them, you might say.'

'Grammar! That's the least of your problems. That, my love, can be taught. Talent cannot.'

'Talking about me again?' John set down a tray of drinks.

'Kay's going to write a feature for *Female Weekly*. What It's Like Living in the East End.'

'Am I?'

'Deadline Wednesday, five o'clock. That gives you the weekend plus three days. No more than a thousand words, double-spaced. Tell us about the wheeling and dealing; the pub life; poverty, and—' she closed her eyes '—Oh, yes,' she smiled, 'the lack of education and rule in schools.'

'OK,' Kay swallowed half her drink, 'you're on. One condition though. You check my spelling on the first draft.'

John roared with laughter. 'She's the worst speller in the whole building. Give it to me, I'll sort it.'

Looking questioningly at Jeannie, Kay was a little surprised to see that she was nodding.

'He's right, the cheeky bastard. And he's probably the best guide you could get. Even though it pains me to say so.'

Within minutes of Jeannie joining them, others arrived and were duly introduced to Kay. Some she had already seen to say hallo to at work, and others who wrote for other publications. Drinks were offered one after the other, and more than one conversation went on at a time. Most of which went over Kay's head. But she enjoyed it all the same; the buzz was fantastic, and she made up her mind there and then that this was the world for her. She would catch up. She would read up. Soon she would know what they were talking about and understand all the in-house jokes.

Feeling more than light-headed, she made her way to the tube and wondered if her parents would smell the drink on her breath. It was nine-thirty. She thanked her lucky stars that a night in had been the intention, otherwise a very angry Pam*elia* would be waiting for her.

* * *

'Hallo, Liz. Did you fetch the haddock?' Billy asked as he closed his front door behind her.

'Yeah. Richard Wood was up the market so I bought it from 'im. Cheaper and a bit fresher. I could do with a cup of tea.'

'I'll put the kettle on. Take the weight off your feet.' He pulled a kitchen chair out from under his green-painted table.

'I don't know,' Liz kicked off her shoes and relaxed. 'I used to love the sunshine, but give me a light cloudy day any time.'

'Laura's old room don't get a lot of sunshine, you know. Time it gets round to the back of the house it's gone down too far.' He shovelled tea into the aluminium teapot. 'I thought I'd give the walls a coat of primrose to brighten it up a bit. I don't know what you think about this brilliant white that's in. For the paintwork, I mean.'

'Jack said he'd do any decorating for yer, Billy. You don't 'ave to push yourself,' Liz said, yawning and rubbing her eyes.

'It keeps me busy. And how come you're so tired? You 'ad a lie-in today, surely? Your day off?'

'Yeah, I know. But I was up at six all the same. Sorting out my things. Where does it all come from, eh?'

'You were married a long time, Lizzie.' He handed her a cup of tea. 'When's the second-hand dealer meant to be giving you a price?'

'Charlie's coming round at seven.' Sipping her tea, Liz looked over her cup at him. 'You sure we're doing the right thing?'

''Course we are. Makes sense. One set of bills instead of two.'

'Yeah, but, oh, I don't know.' She shook her head. 'I just 'ope you won't regret it, that's all. You must 'ave got used to having the place to yerself.'

'You can always get used to loneliness, gal. That doesn't mean to say you like it. What time shall I cook the haddock?'

'About one'll do.' Liz looked at the small orange clock on the kitchen dresser. Five past ten. 'That's fast, innit?'

'Yeah. Ten minutes. Don't ask me why I like to keep it that way, I still haven't worked it out. Need anything down the waste?'

Liz thought about it. 'I wouldn't mind treating myself to a new dressing gown. I wonder if that knock-down stall's out this week?'

'Bound to be. We'll go once we've drunk this. Wanna biscuit?'

'No. I had a big bowl of porridge this morning. I'm still in the habit of making enough for two.' She lowered her eyes, appreciating the silence.

That was the good thing about her and Billy. They had known each other long enough to realize when to keep quiet.

'How about a nice lemon housecoat? To go with your new bedroom,' Billy grinned as he pulled on his cap.

'No. I fancy a pale blue candlewick,' said Liz with conviction as she pulled the old gate shut behind them. 'If not pale blue, then rose pink.'

'It's your money,' he said, striding along Cleveland Way, swinging his arms.

'Slow down, Billy, for Gawd's sake.' Liz had been trying to keep up with him. 'I'm nearly out of breath already. And my throat's dry.'

'I'll treat you to a nice cold sarsaparilla from Becky's sweet shop.'

Liz stopped in her tracks. 'If you don't slow down, I'm going back! I mean it, Billy,' she said, shaking her head at him. 'You're gonna have to get out of that habit of walking fast when you're out with me.'

'All right, gal,' he said, waiting for her. 'Don't get your knickers in a twist. I was rushing to get this bet on, that's all.'

'Oh, right. Go on then, I'll catch you up. I don't want you to miss it. Expect you've been studying form since five this morning.'

'Paper didn't come till half past six. Shall I put one on for you?' he called back over his shoulder.

'Yeah, go on then. A dollar to win on whatever you've picked!'

'A dollar? Bit steep, innit?' He stood on the pavement, pushed his cap back and rubbed his chin. 'If you're gonna spend that much, why not go for a treble?'

'All right. You sort 'em out. But a treble win! I don't wanna place-bet. Not worth it.'

Laughing quietly to himself, Billy walked on, a bit slower. Liz knew he was giving himself time to think about this morning's study, remembering which horses were in good form.

Arriving outside the betting shop, she perched herself on the low window-sill and was content to watch the Saturday shoppers go by. Facing Hammond's side entrance, she was pleased not to be in there working. Monday would come around soon enough.

'Hallo, Liz.' Milly's cheery voice broke into her thoughts. 'I'm just going in to see Laura. I know she finishes at twelve, so I mustn't stop.'

Liz blinked twice as she turned to face her friend whom she hadn't seen in ages. 'Talk about a face from the past,' she chuckled.

'I always go down the waste on a Saturday, Liz. It's you who's out of your territory. Bethnal Green market going downhill, is it?'

'No, I'm just waiting for Billy. Laura's dad. He's in there,' she tilted her head towards the door. 'How's tricks then? Georgie's leg still playing him up?'

'No. Did him the world of good, that little stretch inside. He's a changed man. They knocked the loafer out of him, I'll tell yer.' She looked and sounded happier than Liz had ever seen her. 'I miss 'oppin', though, don't you?'

Realizing that Milly couldn't have heard her bad news, Liz braced herself. 'My Bert passed away you know,' she said quietly.

'Oh, Liz. Surely not? Not Bert?' Her eyes filled up in seconds.

'Yeah,' Liz sighed. 'It was a bit of a shock. Heart. Died in his sleep, more or less . . . you know.' Liz swallowed hard.

'I'm sorry, love.' Milly shook her head. 'When I think of the bastards who are walking about and shouldn't be.'

'Do you ever see Mrs Brown?' Liz was quick to change the subject. She hardly needed reminding that Bert should still be by her side.

'Yeah, poor cow. Walks about as if she's in another world. He left her in the end you know. Gawd knows where to. Still, she's better off I suppose. At least she's not covered in bruises any more. Can't be easy though, bringing up four kids on her own.'

'So why you going in to see my Laura, then? Gonna treat yourself to a nice new frock?'

'As it 'appens. My Brianny's getting married, can you believe? We've booked the room above the Artichoke. Got a band and everything. Her family's from Tonbridge. Little bit on the posh side, so I wanna make a good impression, see?'

''Course you do, Milly, and why not?'

Checking the narrow road for traffic, Milly looked back. 'Why don't you and Laura come for half hour? It'll be like old times.'

'What about Jack? He's still around, you know,' Liz smiled.

'Yeah, 'course, I just thought you might feel . . . oh, I dunno.'

'I'll bring Billy with me if that makes you feel better.'

'Do that.' She stepped out into the road. 'Billy, eh? Didn't take you long, did it,' she teased.

Liz smiled but inside she hurt. The remark cut deep. But then she would have to contend with more of that in the future, especially once she had moved into his cottage. But she could cope with it. She knew why she and Billy needed to share the same roof. Loneliness could turn a good day into a nightmare, and there were lots of days ahead of them both. God willing.

'Our Kay seems to be all right now,' Billy said as he and Liz strolled along the waste.

'What's that supposed to mean?' Liz was sharp enough to realize he might be trying to tell her something.

'I was a bit concerned. When she came back from that Spanish holiday of hers, she looked drawn in the face, as if she had something on her mind.'

'She fell in love, Billy. What d'yer expect?'

'That's what worried me.'

'In case her lover-boy had been dipping his lolly in the sherbet, you mean?'

'Something like that, yeah,' he laughed. 'You can be crude at times, Liz, you know that?'

'It's honesty in my book. Anyway, she's all right. Not in the club, if that's what's worrying yer.'

'You know that, do you?'

'Yes, Billy. I do.'

'That's all right then. All we have to hope is that she behaves herself with that gypsy.' He nodded towards the delicatessen. 'I just wanna pop in and get a couple of Barron's New Green cucumbers to go with our fried fish.'

Waiting outside for him, enjoying the sun on her face, Liz spotted Kay's best friend Pamela walking towards her. She was grinning like a Cheshire cat.

'What you looking so pleased about?' Liz said.

'My boyfriend's coming over from Spain, for a holiday. Next week. Don't tell Kay though, I want it to be a surprise. I want to watch her face when we all turn up on her doorstep.'

'All?'

'Charles, that's my young man's name, and Chris . . . Kay's friend.'

'Let's hope Zacchi doesn't get jealous.'

'Zacchi won't be here though, will he? He'll be out of the country while Chris's in it. Perfect timing.'

'So long as it's not two-timing.' Liz was feeling rattled at Pamela's attitude.

Shrugging, Pamela made to step into her parents' delicatessen. 'Why are you standing out here anyway?'

Liz nodded towards Billy who was paying for his pickled cucumbers. 'Kay's grandfather's doing a bit of shopping.'

Pamela looked thoughtful. 'You're gonna move into his spare room, aren't you? Never too old, eh?' she smiled, leaving Liz open-mouthed.

Feeling her anger rising, Liz inhaled slowly. Had Pamela not slipped out of her hands so quickly, she would have given her a piece of her mind about showing respect to her elders. One thing was becoming very clear: Liz was going to have to accept the fact that people jumped to the obvious conclusions about her and Billy.

'Come on,' Liz walked ahead as her friend joined her. 'I fancy a walk around the art gallery.'

'You what?' Billy shoved the well-wrapped pickles into his jacket pocket.

'The Whitechapel art gallery. It's cool, peaceful and there are nice pictures to look at.'

'Fair enough,' he took her by the hand and led her through the doors. 'This feels a bit like courting to me,' he smiled.

'Don't start that, Billy. We're friends. Don't spoil it.'

'It was a joke, Liz. I'm too old for all that.'

'You reckon?' Liz threw him a mischievous look. 'I wouldn't bank on it.'

Instead of making her way towards her and Pamela's favourite coffee bar, Kay found herself walking along Bethnal Green, heading for the second-hand office equipment shop. She had decided to borrow ten pounds from the envelope to buy herself a typewriter.

Sitting down at the desk, she tried out the used Underwood machine. It took her back to her school days and the commerce course. It was identical to the one on which she had learned to type. She remembered her teacher fighting to have proper desks and typewriters brought in.

'You won't find anything cheaper in that condition.' The owner of the small office equipment shop ran his hand through a thick mop of frizzy, light brown hair. 'And since you're such a pretty face, I'll throw in a spare ribbon.' He crossed his thick, heavily freckled arms and cupped his reddish beard, giving her a fatherly wink.

'Done,' Kay smiled shyly. She felt like yelling for joy. Her own typewriter! Now she could tuck herself away in her room and write whenever she felt like it.

'Gonna write a book, are yer?' he smiled.

'Who knows?' She swept her hand across the keys. 'I always wanted to, when I was little. I begged my dad to buy me a John Bull printing set. He got me a little printing gadget instead. He thought it would be better because it was more up to date.' She looked back at the shop owner, 'I needed a hand-held printing set.'

'The ones with rubber letters all in a row?'

'And you cut them up and used tweezers to space them into the words you wanted to make up and print.'

'Be a lot quicker with this.' He tapped out *I am a writer!* 'Never forget that, and you'll soon 'ave other people believing it.'

Kay felt a tingling in her fingertips. 'I wish it was true.'

'It is true. It's written all over you.' He pointed a friendly finger in her face. 'It's up to you. There's no law to stop you. And every day has twenty-four hours.'

'You sound as if you know something about it.' Kay was warming to him by the second.

'There are three novels gathering dust on my shelf. A collection of my poems and a few short stories. One day I'll send something off to a publisher,' he said, obviously embarrassed.

'Can I read one of the novels?' Kay asked.

'No one ever gets to see the rubbish I write.' There was an underlying tone of disappointment in his blunt voice.

'OK, but what if I do manage to type a book?'

'*Write* a book,' he corrected.

'OK, write a book. We could swap and read each other's. I'll promise to tell you honestly if I think it's good or not – if you'll do the same for mine.'

'How to lose a friend!' he laughed.

'I've never met anyone who's actually written a novel. I work with journalists, but three novels, poetry, short stories! You must be good.'

'Well, I think I am, but . . .' he shrugged and spread his hands. 'Tell you what, come back next Saturday and I'll have sorted out a short story for you to take away and read. So long as you don't nick my ideas.'

'That'd be great. A good excuse to come back in here as well.' She spun herself around on the typist's chair. 'I love the smell of oil and ink and metal, and all these different typewriters. Some look as if they've come out of the ark.'

'They'll be worth a lot of money in the future. Collector's pieces.'

'You reckon?' Kay shook her head and laughed at him. 'I doubt it.'

Proudly carrying her typewriter in its case, Kay walked into the living room to find Laura and Jack sitting quietly with their heads lowered. There was a heavy atmosphere in the room.

'You'd best sit down, Kay,' Laura murmured. 'There's something your dad wants to talk to you about.' She gave Jack a nudge with her foot to urge him.

Folding the letter which had brought the news, Jack leaned back in his armchair and sighed. 'Take the weight off your feet then,' he smiled sheepishly at her, wondering how she would react to his thunderbolt.

Sitting on the edge of the sofa, Kay looked from her dad to her mum and back to her dad again. 'What's happened now?'

'It's more a case of what happened nearly three years ago.'

Jack took his tobacco tin from his cardigan pocket. 'I know it didn't escape your notice that Mum and me went through a bad patch.'

'It could hardly escape my notice, Dad. It went on for years before it all came to a head.' She didn't want those memories to come flooding back. 'I thought that was all in the past. Dead and buried?'

'It is, babe. As far as your mum and me are concerned. We've never been as happy together as we are now.' His voice trailed off.

'So what, then?' She knew it was serious from his face.

'Well . . .' Jack was finding it difficult to choose the right words. 'I was—' he shook his head, 'I've been a silly boy.'

'You're not a boy, Dad!'

'No. OK. Fair enough. When your mum and me were sleeping in separate rooms there was a reason for it. I was full of guilt, OK? I was having an affair with someone called—'

'I don't want to know her name!' Kay clenched her fists, forcing herself not to get emotional. 'I knew about her at the time, so it's not news now! And you know that, so what's different?'

'You've got a half-brother.'

It didn't go in, not at first. Kay deliberately blocked it. She felt a sudden surge of hate for her father. Hate and disgust. 'I'm going to my room,' she stood up, not looking at either of them.

'Sit down!' Jack ordered. 'Sit down and listen! And stop acting the madam!' His face was red and the veins on his neck stood out as if ready to burst.

'I'm not acting! I hate you!' she screamed. 'You make me feel sick. Dirty! I wish I had nothing to do with you!'

'That's enough, Kay!' Laura yelled. 'You high-and-mighty little cow. Do as your dad says and sit back down *now*!'

Reluctantly, Kay threw herself on to the sofa, crossed her arms and legs and glared at Jack. 'I'm listening!'

'Your brother's—'

'I haven't got a brother!'

'Your brother is two and a half years old.' Jack spoke slowly, emphasizing each word, daring her not to deny him. 'And he's a dead ringer for you.'

'And that's supposed to make me feel better, is it?'

'I'm not asking you to feel anything, Kay. I know this has come as a shock.'

'You should have told me before now.' She stood up and paced the floor. 'How dare you not tell me I've got a brother? What right have you to keep that from me?' Kay felt as if she were going to explode. She couldn't believe how insensitive they could be.

'Sit *down*, Kay,' Laura pleaded. She was finding it difficult too. 'Your dad's really upset about this letter he got today.'

'I'm not gonna sit down.' She breathed hard. 'What letter?'

'It's from the child's mother.' Jack carefully avoided calling Patsy by her name. He knew exactly why Kay didn't want to hear it.

'She's getting married, and her boyfriend refuses to take on someone else's—' Jack swallowed hard, looking at the letter in his hand, 'bastard,' he murmured, heavy with guilt.

'Bloody cheek. How dare any one say that about an innocent two-year-old?'

'The thing is, little Jac—'

'Little *who*? You named him after you?' Now she did feel the effect of the shock. It struck instantly. As if someone had tapped the top of her head with a wand and said *Freeze!*

'There's a little boy,' she spoke in a monotone, not moving, not looking, staring ahead, 'who looks like me. My brother. I have a brother. And his name is the same as my dad's. You've been loving him all this time.'

The tears were warm as they rolled down her cheeks, cold by the time they reached her neck.

'But I had to be kept out of it. You didn't want me to see my brother?' She looked at Jack, appealing. 'Why did you do that? Why have you kept us apart? You must love him a lot. You called him Jack. You named him after you. You didn't name me after Mum.' She could hardly focus through her tears.

'*She* called him that, not me!' Jack clenched his teeth. 'And now she's dumped him in a *home*.' Covering his face, Jack began to cry.

Kay had never seen her dad like this before. Loud wailing sounds were coming from him. His body was shaking, almost going into convulsions. Then she remembered coming round after the drowning accident in Kent. She had heard him crying then. It was the same desperate sobbing.

'They've put the poor little sod out, Kay,' he looked up at her, 'dumped him. She's got 'er way in the end. She wanted to get rid of him from the start.' He felt a sharp kick from Laura, and could have bit his tongue.

'No!'

Laura found her voice again. 'A small children's home in Leicester.'

'How could she do a thing like that?'

'She's not all bad. Poor cow probably had no choice. He must have given her an ultimatum. And when you love someone . . .'

'So you want to know how I feel about you taking him?' Kay said.

'No.' Jack shook his head. 'She's made it very clear that she wants him kept in the neighbourhood so that she and the grandparents can visit him at weekends.' He mopped his face with his handkerchief and made an effort to compose himself.

'She wants to have her cake and eat it. Well, we're not just gonna leave it like that, are we?' Kay looked from one parent to the other.

'We'll try applying to the authorities to foster him but it'll take ages, and there's not much of a chance that we'll get him. Mostly because of us living out of the area.'

'So while we've got a home to offer, a loving family, a room of his own, he has to stay in a home?' Kay raised her eyebrows. 'They need their brains tested if they think we're gonna put up with that.'

'It'll take months, years of fighting and meanwhile, that little kid finds himself in a strange place full of people he doesn't know.' Jack's eyes were blazing. 'It beats me how anyone can do that!'

'Especially to a little darling like Jac,' Laura hung her head.

'You've been seeing him too?' Another blow for Kay.

'Only the once. I found a letter in your dad's jacket pocket. I went to Leicester to punch her in the face, but when I got there . . . saw that little tot in his play-pen . . .' Laura found she could barely speak. 'And he is the image of you, Kay. I could hardly believe it.'

'Right,' Kay said, her voice full of determination. 'You two are obviously too upset to do anything, so I suppose it's up to me. I'll get him out.'

'You can't do that,' Jack smiled at her through his tears. 'The law's an ass and all that, but try fighting it.'

'I don't give a *fuck* about the law any more! I've had it up to here with the law and its double standards!'

'Oh, Kay, please don't swear. Don't get bitter,' Laura pleaded.

But Kay could not be stopped. 'Sometimes we have to ignore what's written as wrong – when we know it's right. And that's just what I intend to do.'

Jack frowned at her. 'What's on your mind, babe?'

'You'll see.' She left the room, slamming the door behind her.

'D'yer think Kay took it to heart, you know, when I talked about Patsy wanting to get rid of—'

'Oh, shut up, Jack. She's put it out of her mind – why can't you do the same?'

Jack leaned back in his chair and closed his eyes. 'Because I'm still gutted over it, that's why. I know what I'd like to do to that Spaniard.'

'And I thought you were ready to forgive and forget. Silly me!'

'I'll never forget. Never. Just let him show his face, that's all!'

Chapter Thirteen

Standing in the doorway of *Female Weekly*, Kay saw before her yet another new and exciting world. The sound of electric typewriters clacking busily, the whirr of the photocopying machine and the conversation of people in the office and on the telephone conducting interviews sent a thrill of possibility to Kay's core. She caught sight of Jeannie across the room and cautiously wove her way around workers and desks to join her.

'I suppose you're too busy to talk to me?' Kay said, worried she might be disturbing her train of thought.

Switching off her machine, Jeannie leaned back in her chair and smiled. 'Don't tell me you've finished the article already?'

'No. I haven't even started it.'

Her superior's expression changed instantly. Without uttering a word, she was asking Kay what, in that case, was she doing there.

'Can I sit down?'

Looking at her watch, she narrowed her eyes. 'Five minutes. I'm running late.'

Pulling the chair close so no one would hear, Kay leaned forward. 'I've given it a lot of thought over the weekend, and I honestly don't think that writing about life in the East End will make good copy. We're not that much different from anyone else.'

'Have you spent time in other parts of London, seeing the way other people go through their days?'

'No. And that's another thing. I've got nothing to compare our way of life with.'

'That's the point.' Jeannie examined her fingernails and shrugged. 'Oh well, it was just an idea.'

'I do have another one,' said Kay quickly, before Jeannie's forefinger hit the on switch of the typewriter.

'Go on. But be brief,' she warned.

'I've read a couple of the magazines now, so I've got more of an idea of the house style. The kind of stories you—'

'You're waffling,' she said, in a singsong voice.

'OK. I want to write an article about a seventeen-year-old who suddenly discovers she's got a brother, and what it feels like to know that he's in a children's home.'

Jeannie reached for a packet of cigarettes, a look of interest on her face. 'You?'

'Yeah. I only just found out.'

'And you're prepared to give us the story?'

'I don't see why not. My name won't go in, will it?'

'Not if you don't want it to. We can change all the names. But it's the only way to get yourself known as a feature writer.'

'That's not why I'm doing it. Maybe the next article, but not this one.' Kay could hardly believe herself. She sounded positive: any self-consciousness had gone.

'Why do you want to do it?'

Kay took a deep breath. She was beginning to feel slightly emotional. 'If I can let other parents know the harm they're doing when they make such decisions—'

'Your parents put him in there?'

'No, I mean—*his* parents. His mother.' Kay rolled her eyes. 'He's my father's illegitimate son.'

'Ah.'

'The other woman's getting married and her bloke won't take on someone else's son. Mum and Dad want to adopt him, but she wants him in a home in Leicester near her, so she can visit him.' Kay eyed Jeannie's packet of cigarettes.

'Help yourself.'

'Thanks. I'm going to do something about it. But that'll be the next instalment.'

'Fine.' Jeannie pushed against the desk with her foot and spun around slowly in her swivel chair. 'And what exactly had you in mind?'

'I'm going to Leicester. Get him out of that home and bring him back.'

Slowly shaking her head, Jeannie made it very clear that it was a bad idea. 'The law takes a dim view of kidnapping.'

Determined not to be swayed, Kay avoided making eye contact. 'I've got a couple of uncles who I think will help. They can drive me there, wait while I go in, then drive us both back to Stepney.'

'You've been reading too many bad paperbacks,' she said, not mincing her words.

Angrily Kay stubbed out her cigarette in the ashtray. She hadn't meant to disclose her plan, and was annoyed with herself.

Too late to retract it, she could only hope that the editor would dismiss it. 'I'll just write up the bit about my finding out about him, then.'

'I'm not interested.' She switched on her machine and began to type.

'Why not? You were at first.'

'Yep. It sounded good. Our readers would have loved it.'

'So?'

'I don't want one of our writers getting mixed up in what you have in mind. We can do without that kind of publicity, thank you.' She looked up at Kay. 'A member of *Female Weekly* going to prison?'

'Don't be daft. Prison?' Kay smiled nervously. That word had been bandied about too much of late.

'Listen. Don't even think about it. Drive it out of that silly head of yours. Go for plans B or C.'

Kay looked at her, puzzled. She hadn't mentioned any other plans – she didn't *have* any other plans. Jeannie was half smiling, waiting for the penny to drop.

'You mean I should have thought of other ways?'

An impatient sigh escaped her. 'Something like that, yes.'

Kay shrugged forlornly. 'I couldn't think of any other way. I've gone over it so many times.'

'Look. Write your article and meanwhile, I'll give it some thought. Legal thought.'

'Fighting for an adoption could take *years*!' Kay knew she was out of order talking to her senior like that, but something inside was beginning to snap.

'And meanwhile that poor little two-year-old is with strangers! It's my baby brother we're talking about—' Her voice cracked and she had to turn away.

A comforting, feeling arm went around her shoulder. 'We'll think of something, Kay, don't upset yourself. She can't be made of stone, his mother. And if she is, we could always wield the threat of the power of the pen.'

'You mean you'd write to her?'

'No, silly! I'll see if I can set up a meeting. Don't worry, I'll be gentle. I'm a good journo. I know how to handle people. Especially women. She'll see us, I promise you.'

'I'd got it all planned out, as well. I was gonna rush in and carry him off.'

'And scare the bloody life out of the poor kid?'

Kay suddenly felt foolish. 'Doesn't know me from Adam, does he? It was a pretty dumb idea.'

'No it wasn't. It was lovely, thoughtful gesture. And when I tell my fiancé about it, he'll want to marry you instead of me.'

'Oh no, please don't tell anyone!' Kay felt her world changing again, slipping out of her control.

'We'll need him,' Jeannie said, lowering her voice. 'He'll find all the ins and outs for us. He's an investigative journalist and a bloody good one.'

Turning back to her work, she added brightly, 'Welcome to our inner circle. The one outside work and pub sessions. Join us for dinner tomorrow night, OK?'

Kay nodded and retreated, believing she had found another friend.

'And get the article in on time!' she called out as Kay was leaving the office.

'What was all that about?' asked a tall, thin woman draped in layers of mauve and black. 'You're not getting her to write about life as a docker's daughter, are you?' she smiled sarcastically.

'The kid's just discovering she's a writer. I don't suppose you can remember what that felt like?' Jeannie said, putting the seasoned journalist in her place. 'Too long ago, I would have thought.'

Drawing on a long ebony cigarette-holder, the woman blew a smoke ring into the air. 'She can hardly string a sentence together, let alone write a decent feature.'

'You think so? We'll see.' She began to type again. 'She might end up Chief Editor – before she goes on to other things.'

Surprised and pleased with Kay's first feature article, Jeannie decided to hold it back until a sound plan had been worked out regarding the meeting with Patsy.

'I won't alter your story, Kay. Just turn a few sentences around for the sake of grammar. Once you've seen what I've done, you'll know for the next time. I have a feeling you're a quick learner.'

'What about my spelling?' Kay whispered. She didn't want any staff passing through Reception to overhear.

'John went through it for me. I'm afraid even your spelling mistakes had spelling mistakes.'

'Oh God, how *embarrassing*.' Kay suddenly wished she had never had ideas above her station.

'Don't be silly! You're a good writer. Spelling comes once you've learned a few of the rules. Take a dictionary to bed instead of a paperback. I did. It worked wonders.' She winked at Kay and left her to go back to the *Female Weekly* office.

You're a good writer . . . The words drifted through Kay's mind, once, twice, three times. She couldn't stop smiling as the bearded face of the man in the office equipment shop came into her thoughts. Remembering the line he'd typed on her machine she clenched her fists and yelled, *'Yes!'*

Now that she had handed in her article she felt a sense of loss. Nothing else for it, she told herself, I'll just have to make a start on that novel. She leaned back in her chair and began planning. It would be a psychological thriller about a woman betrayed. She would wander the streets at night tracking down men who were out looking for women instead of at home with their wives and children. Her heroine wouldn't kill the men, she would just terrorize them; maybe cut off a lock of their hair as a warning. A warning that should she catch them out again, she would hack off all their hair. *The Woman in Black* is what she would call her first novel. Or better still, *The Woman Who Terrifies . . .*

'Couldn't type up this copy for me, could you, Kay?' John's voice brought her back to earth. 'Dreaming about that gypsy of yours again?' he teased.

Feeling herself blush, she told him how clever he was, reading her thoughts like that.

'Pop it on my desk when you've done. You up for a drink after work?'

'No, not tonight. Apparently Pamela's arranged some kind of a surprise date.' She lifted her nose.

'Two-timing, eh?'

'What if I was?'

'Enjoy it while you may,' he grinned. 'If you fancy 'em, bed 'em, that's what I say.'

Kay tried not to look shocked. 'You don't mean that?'

'Of course I do.' He was very matter-of-fact.

'You mean, if you met a girl, say, in the pub tonight, and she and you – well, you know – sparks flying and all that.'

'Yes,' he grinned, cutting in.

'But you're already getting married?'

'So?'

'You *can't* love two people at once.'

'Who said anything about that? I don't have to fall for every girl I fancy.' He perched himself on the corner of her desk. 'I'm not in love with you, am I?'

'Don't be stupid.'

'Well, there you are then. I fancied you rotten at first. Then I found I really liked you. But that's all. It stops there.' He pushed his face up close to hers. 'You don't have to love those you like a lot. You can have friends of the opposite sex. It's not against the law.' He stood up, shook his head and walked away chuckling.

Hating him for being so cocksure, she secretly stuck two fingers up to him. He certainly had a way of making her think. She had always believed that if you began to like a boy you stayed with him until you fell in love. If you didn't fall in love, you said goodbye. But now she was seeing things in another light. Each friend, male or female, was just part of her world. Different mates for different reasons. Love was something else.

She looked down at the copy John had left her. He had scribbled across the top in red pen *To be typed by the sexiest girl in the whole bloody building*. And for some reason she felt flattered instead of affronted. He hadn't meant anything by it other than a bit of fun. It dawned on her that she had been taking life, and people, far too seriously.

Feeding a sheet of paper into her typewriter, she tried to guess what the surprise date was that Pamela had lined up. Probably Tommy and Micky were going to take them to the Prospect of Whitby at last. She had begged them enough times in the past to change their regular pub-crawl and enjoy a drink overlooking the Thames.

'But my twin-tub does boil up the whites, Billy! And it's a lot less trouble than that old boiler.' Having lost over the refrigerator, Liz was determined to have her way and install her washing-machine into his old-fashioned kitchen.

'That's as may be, Liz. But I'm used to that copper. And anyway we can hardly get it carted away. It'd cost a bomb to move it.'

'We won't need to. We can plant some lovely indoor bulbs. My machine'll go over there, in that corner, near the butler sink.'

'Indoor bulbs?' His blue eyes twinkled at the thought of it.

'Yeah. One of my friends did it when she modernized. It looks lovely. Brightens up her old scullery, I can tell yer.' She was winning him over and knew it.

'Now then, what about getting rid of this old gas stove?'

'But there's nothing wrong with it. Clean as a whistle, and does my Sunday joint a treat.'

'Yeah, but mine's electric,' Liz said proudly.

'I'm not having electric and that's definite!' Billy marched out of the scullery. 'You can fetch your washing-machine in, but that's all!'

Looking out of the window on to his tiny back garden, Liz suddenly felt very happy. It was full of lupins, Canterbury bells and roses. Her eyes went from the rich black earth to the old brick wall that was covered in purple clematis.

'If you wanna make yourself at home, you could put the kettle on the gas stove,' Billy called from the living room. 'Matches are on the shelf above it. Cups are in the dresser!'

Liz couldn't help smiling. This was a breakthrough. So far he had always insisted that he made the tea. She couldn't think why. 'Two sugars?'

'Two and half!' he corrected, yelling above the sound of the television he had just switched on. 'The six o'clock news'll be on in a minute, if you wanna see it!'

'I do, Billy, yeah. You gonna 'ave a piece of this angel cake?'

'No, ta, I'm not keen. A couple of digestives'll do me!'

Pouring boiling water into the teapot, Liz began to feel more and more at home. Waiting for the tea to brew, she became pensive. Moving in with Billy felt right. And she knew that Bert would be chuffed to bits if he could see her. She felt sad that that night would be the last she would spend in her own two-up, two-down. Tomorrow was the official moving-in day. Jack had borrowed a van from a friend and was going to bring her bits and pieces over during Saturday. Most of the larger pieces had been sold off to the second-hand dealer.

'Do you play cards, Billy?' Liz asked, handing him his tea.

'Haven't done for years.' He sat back and thought about it. 'Three card brag. Pontoon. Rummy. Three of One and Four of the Other, as young Kay used to call it.' He dipped his biscuit into his tea. 'I dunno, Liz, you keep bringing memories back,' he chuckled.

'Only there's a couple of friends of mine who like to play. Perhaps we could invite them over one night in the week, for a game?' Liz knew it was rather early on to suggest changing his routine, but she felt it best to start as she meant to go on. Billy was set in his ways and he could be a bit on the stubborn side.

'Could do, yeah. Leave it a for a couple of weeks though, eh? Till I get used to having you around the place.'

'Yeah, all right.' Liz smiled inwardly. At least he was willing to try.

'We'll 'ave to sort out the finances, Liz. I don't want anything for the rent but perhaps you could chuck a little bit in for groceries. What d'yer reckon?'

'I'll pay half the rent, half the electric, half the gas. And half for the shopping. You can buy your own tobacco and I'll pay for my own sweets. I always keep a tin of Quality Street in the cupboard and I buy a half-pound of chocolate off the stall on Saturdays. Other than that, I don't need much else.'

'You're not paying my rent,' he said, insistent.

'Yes I am.'

'Oh, no.'

'Oh, yes.'

'I said no, Liz!'

'And I said yes, Billy!'

Shifting about in his chair, Billy shook his head. 'Jack warned me you were obstinate,' he murmured.

'Good. That's settled then.' She sat back in the armchair and focused on the television. 'That's a good picture, Billy, much better than mine.' She knew how to get round him.

'I get it serviced regularly so it'll always go. Bit like my bowels. A dose of Epsom salts every night to keep myself open,' he grinned.

Liz found that amusing. She had never heard anyone compare themselves to a television set before.

Feeling relaxed, she lay back and let the six o'clock news go over her head, while her mind filled with her son, his wife and their lack of interest in having children. Liz longed for a grandchild and at sixty, she reckoned she was entitled to one. If David didn't get a move on, his wife would soon be past safe child-bearing age.

'What d'yer reckon about Kay and this Zacchi, then, Billy? Fancy gypsies for in-laws, do you?'

'Don't bother me, so long as she's happy. He seems nice enough. Clean. Very clean. Gets a good shine on his shoes as well. That says a lot. Why, you're not prejudiced, are yer?'

'Hardly. If the truth be known, there's gypsy in our family line, and not all that far back neither. No. It'll be strange seeing Gypsy Rose again. I expect we'll meet up now. She always said we would.' Liz smiled and drifted off into a light sleep as sunny hop-picking days came flooding back. Anyone looking into that small living room could be forgiven for thinking that seventy-year-old Billy and his new lodger, Liz, had been living there together for decades. All that was missing was a cat curled up at their feet. Liz would soon see to that though. Her fifteen-year-old mog, Blackie, would be moving in with her the next day.

'Kay'll give you a hand with your packing if you ask her,' Billy said.

'I wouldn't dream of it. My niece 'as got 'er own life to get on with. She's gonna be a writer, you know.'

'Oh yeah?' It made Billy feel uncomfortable, Liz talking about his granddaughter as if she were as close to Kay as he was. 'What makes you say that?'

'Don't know. Just feel it in my bones, that's all.'

'Let's 'ope you're right. She can look after us in our old age.'

Liz liked that. At last Billy had stopped thinking of himself as slipping into the grave. There was life in the old boy yet.

While Liz and Billy were fantasizing about Kay, she was on her way to the date Pamela had set up for them. Strolling along with all the time in the world, she enjoyed the warmth of the late sun as it began to go down. It had been a flaming hot day and the tar on the narrow road felt soft underfoot as she crossed from one side of Brady Street to the other. Pamela had insisted she meet her outside the Whitechapel art gallery on the dot of eight.

Kay passed a young woman who was studying a tricycle in a toy shop window, while wiping some ice-cream from the chin of her small child in a pushchair, and it made her wonder what her brother looked like. She had been thinking about him on and off since she discovered that she wasn't an only child. She had begun to miss him. Miss the little boy she had never met! It seemed silly to her but she just couldn't help what she was feeling inside; a feeling of loss. She had a brother, and she wanted to hold him. She wanted that more than anything else in the world.

As much as Kay realized that her original idea of walking into the children's home and carrying Jac off had been a reckless one, she couldn't quite get it out of her mind. Jeannie had been right to suggest they handle it her way. Kay felt sure of that but even so, she was anxious to do something, and soon. She couldn't help worrying that little Jac might be very unhappy at being dumped in a strange place with strange people.

In no real mood for fun, Kay approached the art gallery wishing she had never agreed on the rendezvous. She missed Zacchi and would rather have been at home in her room, typing the short story she had begun to write. At the moment she much preferred to be in a world of her own creation than the real one.

'Fifteen minutes late!' Pamela looked angry and nervous.

'So?' Kay was beginning to wonder about the surprise her friend had in store. 'Where's the fire?'

'In here,' a familiar voice spoke from behind her.

Spinning around, Kay came face to face with Chris's smile. He had his hand on his heart. 'I just couldn't put out the flame.'

Arm in arm with Charles, who had also stepped out from the shadows, Pamela was laughing. 'Look at her face! Anyone'd think she'd seen a ghost! A very tanned ghost.'

'You should have told me,' Kay snapped at her friend. 'You're not clever!'

'Someone doesn't seem very pleased to see me,' Chris dropped his head to one side and looked into her face. 'Maybe I shouldn't have flown all this way? Maybe you should have written Return to Sender on my letters?' There was a touch of anger in his voice. 'Instead of making up stories about your dad holding them back!'

'It was true! And where's your fiancée? Being fitted up for her wedding dress?'

'You really did fall for that one?' He took Kay by the arm and led her away. 'We'll meet you in the Beggar's in half an hour,' he called back to Pamela and Charles.

'If you were lying then you could be lying now!' Kay caught a whiff of the familiar aftershave he wore and felt her heart beat more rapidly.

'Maybe you haven't experienced hurt pride? You do anything to hide it. Anything. Until time helps to dull the pain.' He looked away, pretending to be interested in dogs fighting across the busy Whitechapel Road.

'I wasn't lying, Chris. My dad really did keep the letters from me. He thought I might go rushing off to Spain to live.'

'What's so terrible about that?'

'I'm an only child.' She felt her heart sink as she said the words but it wasn't the right time to go into all of that. Nevertheless, the two-year-old flooded back into her thoughts no matter how hard she tried not to think about him. Then the other loss filled her mind. Chris's baby.

'You're really upset.' He squeezed her hand. 'I'm sorry. I shouldn't have lied about loving someone else.' He flashed a smile. 'To tell the truth, I've never had to do the chasing before.'

'No, I can understand that.' She gave in and smiled at him. 'You're too bloody attractive for your own good.'

'And you're not?'

'I don't know what I am. I've never really thought about it. I think more about what I feel than what I look like. And if beauty's judged on that, I'm very dull.'

'You don't mean that, so why say it?' A frown replaced his smile.

'No, I don't mean that, you're right. But I did up until recently.'

'What happened to change it?' He pushed open the door of the Blind Beggar.

'Quite a lot actually. I was kind of pushed into leaving one job and starting another. It was the best thing that's ever happened to me, as it turned out.' Her mind was still full of the miscarriage. Her secret.

'What about us? Doesn't that compare?' Chris leaned on the bar and tried to catch the barmaid's attention.

'No. That was much more special. More special than anything.' Determined to start as she meant to go on, Kay took a breath and said, '*Was*.'

He cupped his face with one hand, pushing his elbow on to the bar, and looked straight ahead, studying the bottles of spirits above the optics. It was obvious to Kay he knew exactly what she was saying.

'It's not that I feel any different. You affect me exactly the same way, if not more. But I mistook it for love when it was, I don't know, chemistry.'

'Thanks a bundle.' Still he wouldn't look at her.

'I didn't mean it was only that. I did fall in love, but wasn't it just a holiday romance?'

'You'd best get out while you're ahead.' There was humour in his voice. 'What do you want to drink?'

'I can't be in love with two of you, surely?'

He faced her and raised an eyebrow. 'I never realized you were boss-eyed – two of me? That's orignal.'

'You remember I told you about Zacchi? Well he came back.'

'Hoo-bloody-ray. Three cheers for the gypsy!' He turned his back to the bar and leaned on it. 'So it's one door closes, another one opens?' He looked angry. 'And I'm out in the cold.'

'It's not like that,' Kay was feeling more wretched by the minute.

'No? Well what is it then? What am I supposed to think, or feel?'

She looked into his warm brown eyes and all the old feelings came flooding back. 'I don't know.'

'I'm here for a week. Then it's back to work. Back to the bakery. Either we carry on where we left off or end it. It's up to you. You've got six days to think about it.'

In bed that night, Kay tried to weigh everything up. She tried to analyse the two weeks with Chris in Spain, and then how she and Zacchi were together again, after nearly three years.

Closing her eyes, Kay tried to clear her mind of all that was worrying and upsetting her. As she began to doze off, the noise of trains and traffic moved further into the distance and the imagined face of Zacchi filled her with a comforting feeling. Soon he would be back. She hadn't realized just how much she was missing him.

She wondered whether she would have felt comfortable taking him with her to the dinner party at Jeannie's if he had been around. What should she wear, and who else would be there? More importantly, she feared she might feel right out of her depth.

'Jeannie – you've done it again! This goulash is even better than Tibor serves in the Budapest, and that's saying something.' Bill, a commercial artist, lifted his glass of Bull's Blood and winked at the proud hostess.

'I do my best,' Jeannie was in her element.

'It's really nice,' Kay smiled shyly. 'I've never tasted it before.'

There was a brief hush as all attention was turned to her. 'You mean you haven't been to the Budapest or the Gay Hussar?' Bill's Hungarian wife raised an eyebrow and smiled.

'Oh, oh!' Bill laughed. 'Susie looks as if she's just found a new disciple.'

'The next time we go, you must come. And in return, you could take us to a pie and mash shop in the East End. I love the East End.' Susie turned to the others. 'Cockneys are truly wonderful people.'

With trepidation Kay told Susie she would be pleased to take them on a pub-crawl if they wanted. All eight guests thought that a wonderful idea, and raised their glasses to Kay who was already feeling tipsy from the wine. Jeannie's fiancé, Rob, turned out to be a lot of fun as well as a really nice person. Sitting next to Kay on the green velvet Victorian *chaise longue*, he explained a few things about writing fiction as well as good copy. His friend Harold, a playwright, threw in a couple of tips about characterization and dialogue. They had obviously been filled in by Jeannie about Kay wanting to write, and having some talent in that direction.

'*Monsieur Hulot's Holiday* is a fine example of good use of the camera. Hardly any dialogue, but full of innuendo and subtext. Have you seen it, Kay?' Rob asked.

'No, I haven't. I haven't seen that many films since I was a child. My aunt Liz used to sell ice-cream at the local cinema, so I could always get in free. I loved it.'

'Paris Pullman. That's the place.' Bill turned to the others. 'We could go now!'

A chorus of *No!* resounded through the room. Everyone was enjoying themselves enough not to want to go out.

'I've never heard of the Paris Pullman. Is it a theatre?'

'No, love. It's one of the best little cinemas in town.'

'We'll take you there too. After we've eaten at—'

'The Budapest!' they all yelled, poking fun at Susie.

'Well I don't know about you lot, but I'm making a move,' said a petite redhead called Christine. 'I want to be down Portobello good and early. I'm very low on stock.'

'Ah, speaking of which, Chris darling,' Rob placed his arm around her slim waist. 'I've seen a lovely little stripped pine table in your window which would double up as a writing-desk for yours truly . . .'

'Thirty pounds to you,' she kissed him lightly on the cheek.

'Make it twenty-four and you've got a sale.'

'When can you collect?'

'And I saw a pair of Vicky serving spoons.' Jeannie gently pulled Rob away from Christine. 'If you're to have the table, my love . . .' she said, seducing him with her green almond-shaped eyes.

'I know the ones you mean. Silver plate, I'm afraid. Bit pricey.'

'How pricey?'

'Eighteen.'

Conversation bubbled and rose between the eight guests as Kay sat with her feet tucked under her, on an enormous old worn African pouffe. She was out of the action now. They were discussing antiques and the best auction rooms where you could still pick up a bargain. She was more than happy to sit and watch in the lovely Georgian sitting room of Jeannie's flat, which was crammed full of interesting furniture, rugs and pictures, a mix of attractive old furniture and genuine antiques.

Picking up her hand-painted pottery cup, she remembered the Whitechapel art gallery where she used to go on Saturday mornings. She had never quite got the hang of the potter's wheel. Running her finger round the rim of the chunky cup, she thought how nice it would be to own a set like this one. Greyish-mauve with delicately painted leaves.

'Carnaby Street, love. And not as expensive as it looks. Tiny shop where they throw the pots themselves. First on the left after Liberty's on the right.' Rob winked at her, and she couldn't help laughing at him. He was as drunk as her dad and uncles got when they had a beer party.

'What are we gonna do about this brother of yours, eh? That is the question!'

'I'm not allowed to kidnap him.' Kay wondered why she had said that; she wasn't thinking it. Maybe it was the wine, not to mention the liqueurs.

'Oh no. Mustn't do that.' He tapped his nose. 'I'll think of something, worry not!'

'I've got the address now, of his mother. I know where she lives. I got it out of my mum, eventually.'

'Did you now? Clever girl. The art of good journalism is—'

'Stop boring her, Rob.' Jeannie smiled down at Kay. 'You look all in, love.'

'I think I'm drunk. I could fall asleep on the spot.'

'Well, no need for that. Come on. I'll see you safely to the boxroom.'

Having said her goodbyes, and accepted all kinds of invites to dinner, Kay was pleased to be alone in the tiny guest room. The single, old brass bed felt very welcoming as she slipped between crisp white sheets. Two minutes later, she was fast asleep.

Kay could not be sure whether it was the chime from the grandfather clock in the hall or the loud laughter coming from below that had woken her, and she peered at her watch. It was almost two-thirty in the morning.

Creeping out of her room and heading for the bathroom, she picked up a strange but somehow familiar smell drifting up the stairs. It reminded her of the bonfires her grandfather made in the back garden when he was burning dead leaves.

From the lower half of the staircase she could see the group through an open door. They certainly knew how to enjoy themselves, talking and laughing, some more hysterical than others. Jeannie and Rob were sitting cross-legged on the floor, listening with amusement to Bill relating a story from his travels in India the previous year.

There were more empty wine bottles on the coffee table and a bottle of whisky, two-thirds empty. Kay guessed they were all a bit tiddly, hence the excellent party mood. Sitting herself down on the stairs, she sniffed the air. It was a good smell. She liked it. Looking back at the group, she saw Jeannie draw long and hard on a cigarette and then pass it to Bill. The penny dropped. This was no ordinary smoke. It was a reefer.

Feeling like a spy, she quickly made her way back to her room and threw herself on the bed. So this is what they got up to. Drugs! She wondered why it didn't shock her the way she expected it to. Maybe it was because they all looked and sounded so happy.

If her dad could see what they were up to he would throw a fit and drag her away. Just as well he would never know.

As her head sank back into the feather pillow she felt strangely flattered to be there. It was a pity they didn't trust her enough to smoke while she was in the sitting room. Maybe another time they might invite her to join them?

Turning over and settling down again, she was more than pleased to be a guest in this other world which was so different from her own. She had no doubt that Zacchi would fit in perfectly. Susie the Hungarian had gone on quite a bit about gypsies and how much she admired their way of life and their ancestry.

Yes, Kay found herself thinking: it was Zacchi who would fit in, and not Chris. It was becoming clearer by the day which one of them she was really in love with.

The Friday evening before Zacchi was due home, Kay and Pamela went to the Black Boy with their friends. Tommy and Micky were there, as usual, chatting up the girls.

'So whose house are we gonna go back to then?' Micky was ready for a party.

'Not mine. The old man's decided to return to the nest – unfortunately.' A tall, broad-shouldered mod piped up.

'Your old lady still on 'oliday, Tommy?'

'Yep.'

'Well then?'

'Nope,' he looked across at Kay and winked. 'I've got other plans.'

The small crowd let out a chorus of catcalls and whistles which angered Kay. 'I hope you're not referring to me. I'm not in the habit of visiting strange men's homes.'

'No? Oh well,' he shrugged, 'I just had this feeling.'

'Well get rid of it then,' Kay smiled, 'my boyfriend's due back tomorrow.' She tried her best not to put Tommy down.

It didn't take long before the incident was forgotten, at least by most of the crowd. The chatting up continued to the sound of the jukebox and Bobby Vee, singing 'Run to Him,' filled the bar.

Amused by Tommy's sense of humour at choosing the record, Kay gave him a broad smile.

'Can't win 'em all!' Tommy shrugged, making his way towards her.

'I'm just an old-fashioned girl who doesn't two-time,' Kay said.

'That's what I like about you. You're decent.'

Kay looked around to see where Pamela had got to. She was across the room having what looked like an intimate conversation with one of the other boys. So much for her undying love for Charles.

As Tommy drank his pint, Kay noticed his attention drawn to the bar door as it opened. Within seconds a hush had settled on the group. Turning to see who had walked in, Kay was delighted to see Terry and Ray. She was just about to wave them over when a tall eighteen-year-old blocked her view. He was standing close to Terry and indicating with his thumb that he and his friend should leave. Terry and Ray stood their ground and an argument began to break out. Unable to get through the mob that had moved forward, Kay felt her pulse quicken.

Pulling on Tommy's sleeve she shouted at him, but he wasn't listening. 'They're my friends!' she yelled at one of the men behind the bar.

'It only takes one to set the rest of them off,' he shrugged.

Trapped on the wrong side of the small crowd which was gathering around Terry and Ray, Kay used all her strength to push her way through until she almost fell through the door and on to the ground outside.

Still cursing and screaming at the mob to leave them be, she grabbed at one of their jackets. A strong arm swung backwards at her, hitting the side of her face. Defiantly, she went back again and yelled for Tommy who turned and glared at her.

'Get inside!' He looked fit to kill. No longer the handsome smiling face she had warmed to, but a very different, ugly person.

Through the crowd she could see that Terry was on the floor, that they were kicking him. Ray was being held back by two others, having to watch his mate take a hiding. She could see Terry's face as it screwed up in agony as one kick after the other went in. When she saw a black shoe ramming into his head she let out a shrill scream, which was lost in the roar of wild abuse.

Blood was oozing thickly from Terry's ear and his eyes were closed. Still they continued to kick until the sound of a police car could be heard in the distance.

Sobbing, Kay grabbed Tommy's arm as, with the others, he turned to run. 'Why did you do that? I don't understand!'

Pulling away from her, he spat on the ground in disgust and ran from the scene, disappearing down an alley.

'His head, Kay! His head!' Ray was kneeling beside Terry and crying. 'Look at his head.'

Wiping her tears with the back of her hand, Kay nodded. 'He'll be all right, he'll be all right,' she mumbled over and over, wanting desperately to believe it.

The blood trickling from Terry's ear began to flow more heavily, and then came in short, dark red bursts. She looked from Terry to Ray, unable to move, while Ray's face was turning white before her eyes. When he passed out and dropped to the floor she could do nothing but stare at their limp bodies on the pavement, the sound of bells ringing loud as the police arrived.

'You can't lie in bed crying all day, Kay,' Jack quietly scolded. He didn't know how to comfort her when he was so full of anger himself. Laura had taken the news badly and had gone to see Terry's mother, hoping to hear that he had survived the savage attack.

'You should have been there . . . you can't imagine how quickly they changed. My friends changed from really nice blokes to a vicious mob. It was like they became animals.'

Jack sat on the edge of her bed and stroked her hair. 'I know, babe. I've seen it before, worse luck. I can't explain it to you. No one can. Animal instincts, I suppose.' He sighed heavily. 'But I do know this much. If me and a few others had been passing by, we would have given them flash boys an 'idin'. The difference is we'd 'ave used our fists and not our feet.'

'I begged Tommy, but it was as if he couldn't hear or didn't want to. I can't believe how he changed in seconds.'

'How about a nice hot cup of sweet tea?' Jack was finding the conversation too much.

'I think Terry's gonna die, Dad.'

'Now don't say that! Of course he's not!'

'You didn't see what a mess they made of his head. Never mind the rest of his body.'

'Your mother'll be back soon with the news. If you get yourself up, have a nice bath, then I'll take you to the hospital to see him. How's that sound?'

'If he doesn't die, he'll have brain damage.' Kay stared up at the ceiling.

'Now stop it!' Jack shouted. 'Get up and get dressed. Do something positive, instead of lying there feeling sorry for yourself!'

Once outside her room, Jack drew his hand across his face and gritted his teeth. It wouldn't do for him to shed tears. Not right then.

'I'll make some toast as well! Your mother'll kill me if I let you starve—' He just stopped himself from saying *to death*.

When Kay opened the door to Zacchi later that day, she fell into his arms and wept on his shoulder. He had telephoned from Dover earlier on, and all she had managed to say in between sobs was that something terrible had happened to Terry.

'I could do with a cup of tea.' He was too moved at seeing her grief to give her words of comfort. Her lovely face was swollen and her silky blonde hair was all over the place and damp with tears.

'They kicked Terry's head,' her voice was a whisper in his ear. 'My friends almost kicked the life out of him.'

Gently withdrawing himself from her arms, he looked into her face.

'Kay?' Again he could not find the words.

'They didn't kill him.' She pulled a handkerchief from her sleeve and blew her red nose. 'He's in hospital though. Intensive care.'

'Are we allowed to visit?' he said quietly.

'I think so. I'm not sure. Let's go anyway, Zac, please?'

''Course we'll go.' He walked her into the kitchen. 'I bought this bottle of duty-free for your parents.' He held the bottle hopefully.

Kay smiled. 'Brandy. Yeah, they won't mind if we open it. You've only just missed 'em. They've popped round the Eagle for a quick drink. This 'as really gutted them.'

'I'm sure.' Zacchi turned away and filled the kettle. 'It's not easy to take in, is it?'

Sitting down, Kay felt a wave of comfort. It was good to have him back. She wanted to tell him how much she had missed him. But it didn't seem the right time.

'We'll go after we've had coffee, then?'

'Yep. After coffee.' Zacchi knew she couldn't wait to see how her friend was but he also knew she needed to relax a little before they left. 'They might not let us in. You should be prepared for that.'

''Course they will,' she snapped at him, as if by saying it he was siding with authority.

'I have to obey orders,' the slim, dark-haired nurse was sorry. 'I daren't let you go in. Only his next of kin. Leave it a couple of days.'

'But I'm like his sister! Just ask him if he wants to see me. Please! Just go and ask him.'

Looking from Kay to Zacchi, she shrugged. 'Wouldn't be much point. He hasn't regained consciousness.' She backed away and gave a reassuring smile. 'Phone tomorrow evening, around this time. Ask for Nurse Derrick. I'll tell you how he is then. OK?'

'Will he live?' Kay could not contain herself. 'He's not gonna die, is he?' She was daring the nurse to say yes.

'Try not to think the worst. There's a chapel on the second floor. Why not pray for him?'

The sound of the nurse's heels on the marble floor echoed as she walked quickly away down the corridor. *Pray for him . . . Pray for him . . . Pray for him . . .* The words ran through Kay's brain. She looked pleadingly into Zacchi's eyes.

'Come on,' he managed, 'we'll go for a walk.'

Arriving at Bethnal Green Park an hour before the gates were due to close, Kay was secretly pleased to see that old Sid was there, enjoying an ice-cream.

'OK if we join you?' Kay knew it would be and sat close beside him on the sun-heated wall, with just his big black Bible between them.

'That's some accordion you're got there,' said Zacchi, and he swept his fingers over the ornate polished brass edging that glinted in the evening sun.

Sid studied Zacchi's face and then smiled. A twinkle returned to his blue eyes and the guarded look dissolved. 'Romany?' he said.

'That obvious?' Zacchi took an instant liking to the old man.

Turning his attention to Kay, Sid pursed his lips and waited, as she twisted a handkerchief in her hands.

'My friend's in hospital,' she said. 'On the danger list.'

'Does he know anything about it?'

'He's unconscious, if that's what you mean.'

'Then he probably doesn't.' Sid wiped ice-cream from his fingers on one of the rolled-up newspapers that were stuffed inside his old gabardine mackintosh.

'He might not survive.'

Sid's mischievous, knowing laughter stopped Kay in her tracks. Sometimes he could be irritating. She bit her lip while he picked up his accordion and began to play softly.

'How can you laugh, Sid?' She was begging him to say something that would make her feel better.

'Would he want us to cry?'

'Maybe!'

'No. If he is hovering between this world and the next, he'll be able to see you. And it's my humble opinion that if he had a voice, he would tell you the real meaning of death and birth and life, body and soul.' Before Kay could ask any more questions, Sid began to play and sing.

> Lead us, heavenly Father, lead us
> O'er the world's tempestuous sea;
> Guard us, guide us, keep us, feed us,
> For we have no help but thee;
> Yet possessing every blessing,
> If our God our Father be . . .

Without any prompting from Sid, Kay joined in on the second verse. Zacchi was too moved to sing, and the hair on his neck stood up. Once that verse was finished, Sid began to walk away, his voice filling the empty park grounds.

> Spirit of our God, descending,
> Fill our hearts with heavenly joy,
> Love with every passion blending,
> Pleasure that can never cloy;
> Thus provided, pardoned, guided,
> Nothing can our peace destroy

'He's special all right. You're lucky to have him in your part of the world,' said Zacchi.

'He's always been here.'

'No, not always. Since as far back as you can remember. He must be in his seventies, and you're only seventeen.'

'That's true. I hadn't thought about that. He doesn't have a cockney accent, as it 'appens,' she remarked.

'Doesn't have any accent. The man from nowhere.' Zacchi grabbed Kay's hand. 'Come on, before we get locked in for the night.'

Taking his hand in hers she pulled him towards her, and as they clung together, drawing comfort, Kay realized that Zacchi had become the mainstay of her existence. She couldn't imagine herself without him. He was part of her, and of her world.

Nuzzling into his neck she kissed him lightly. 'I love you,' she murmured.

Cupping her face, Zacchi looked more serious than she had ever seen him. He sighed and nodded briefly. It was his way of saying he loved her too. 'Where to now?'

'Hackney?'

'Kay, this is my first day back. Can't we just sit in the nearest pub garden?'

'If I sit still, I'll start thinking about last night and Terry, I know I will.'

'OK. So who lives in Hackney?' He sounded bored and tired.

'It's only a fifteen-minute walk. And I've got loads to tell you.' She took his hand and led him along towards the library. 'You'll never guess what I've got.'

'Go on then. Shock me.'

'A little brother,' she grinned.

Looking puzzled at her, he frowned until his dark eyebrows met. 'You're sure about that, are you? I've only been away two weeks and the last time I saw your mother she looked very slim.'

'Half-brother. Dad's been a naughty boy.'

He let out a low whistle. 'Yes, well, that's fairly shocking. How did you find out?'

By the time they had reached the Bethnal Green museum she had filled him in on everything; her first plan to snatch Jac, and the second more sensible one of Jeannie's, to use the power of the pen.

'We thought that if I went to see her and explained why he should be with us and not in a home she might see sense, and if she doesn't, tell her how bad it would look in a national newspaper— '

'National newspaper?' Zacchi cut in.

'So, I'd be telling a white lie. Jeannie said it would go in *Female Weekly* so it's not that much of a fib, is it? We just thought it would sound more threatening if it was a daily.'

'You're evil.'

'And she's not? Putting a two-and-a-half-year-old in a home, with strangers? When he could be with his blood-father?'

Zacchi eyed her suspiciously. 'So who is it lives in Hackney?'

'Don't worry, not her. She's up in Leicester. We're going to see a very good friend of mine who I used to see on the bus when I worked at Thompson's. I miss her.'

As they turned into Tanner Street, Kay began to tell Zacchi about the dinner party she'd been to in the week. Her new arty friends in Hampstead. How they were both invited the following Friday to one of the guests' flats for dinner somewhere in Chelsea. He was an abstract painter and she a sculptor.

'Count me out thanks.' Zacchi sounded resolute.

'What do you mean, count you out? Don't be so bloody pompous!'

'I've met their kind, they bore the life out of me. So you go and have nice long debates about life, the universe and art. See how long you last.' He winked cheekily at her.

'I like them, Zacchi. I really enjoy being in their company. It's got to be better than just standing in a pub listening to the jukebox.'

'What did they give you to eat, then?' he smirked.

'Hungarian goulash. With small dumplings and cucumber salad. God, you can be annoying.' She pulled her hand out of his. 'You think you're above it all. I don't suppose you'll like Juanita either!' She pressed her finger on the black and white porcelain bell.

The door slowly opened and a very tall, very good-looking, broad-shouldered young man stood smiling at them, as if quite aware of his beautiful row of even, sparkling white teeth.

'Hey, you brought a chaperone!'

'Sorry?' Kay thought he must be mixing her with someone else.

'We don't eat white girls, you know. Come in.' Malcolm stood aside, bowed and waved them in.

'Mum and Dad should be back in an hour. Tea or cold drink?'

'Nothing, thanks.' She cleared her throat. 'Do you know who I am?'

'The lovely Kay. The daughter she should have had – you see what I'm saying? Never mind the white skin.' He turned to Zacchi. 'We've all been waiting to meet her. All three sons. Shame about you – know what I mean?' he grinned.

'Who plays the guitar?' Zacchi asked, ignoring the flirting going on between Malcolm and Kay.

Eyeing a soft armchair, Kay was tempted to push her shoes off and drop into it. 'Do you mind if I sit down? I feel as if I've walked miles.'

'My pleasure.' Picking up his guitar, he lovingly drew his fingers across the strings. 'It's mine. You see what I'm saying? My woman. The only woman I've had the pleasure of . . .' he lightly strummed a few chords.

'If you can believe that,' Kay rolled her eyes. 'Give us a song, then.' She looked across at Zacchi. 'Don't suppose you still keep the old mouth-organ in your pocket?'

'New mouth-organ.'

'Hey! Fab. Let's make some music.' Malcolm threw the guitar strap over his shoulder.

Curling her legs under her, Kay felt very much at home. She liked the way the room was furnished, it reminded her of Juanita. The well-polished second-hand oak furniture was simple, and the embroidered chair-back covers on the three-piece suite brightened up the dark green upholstery.

'What can you play?' she asked.

'You name it.' Malcolm hugged his guitar.

'You want me to choose?' She was enjoying being made to feel special. It was just what she needed.

'Be my guest.' He took a bow.

'That'll do for a starter.'

'"Be My Guest?" OK.' He turned to Zacchi. 'Know it?'

'You play – I'll come in.'

Within minutes, the room was filled with lively music and song. It was one of Kay's favourites. Turning her attention to the door which was slowly opening, she was amused to see Malcolm's brother dance his way in. It didn't take him long to pick up the tune on the piano and belt out the words.

A bit later, while they were performing 'Teddy Bear', Kay remembered Terry. This was one of his favourite Elvis Presley numbers which he used to sing accompanying himself on his guitar.

While the two brothers and Zacchi were hamming it up for fun, Kay felt a pang of guilt. Her best friend was lying in hospital, his life in the balance, and she was enjoying herself.

'I want to go now, Zac.' She stood up and tried to get his attention. 'Zacchi, I want to go.'

Involved now and enjoying themselves, they circled her, singing and playing louder and louder.

'I'll wait outside, OK?' she tried to smile. 'I've got a headache,' she said, searching for an excuse.

Once outside, Kay leaned on the brick wall and waited, while they finished the song and started on another – which was obviously meant for her. The chorus drifted out through the open door.

Qué sera, sera . . . They could never know just how much their mock crooning was causing her pain. Not wishing to dampen their spirits, she walked slowly away.

'I was getting a kick out of that,' Zacchi said, arriving by her side out of breath. 'Why did you leave?'

'I'm sorry, Zac. I needed some air.'

'Now that's what I call good company.'

'I know. I had a feeling it would be OK. I took to Juanita when we first met, as well. It was as if we'd known each other for years.'

'Bit like when we first spoke,' Zacchi lifted her hand and gently kissed it. 'Terry'll be all right, you'll see.'

Pressing her lips together she nodded. There was no need for explanations. He knew what she was going through.

* * *

The following day, unable to lie in as she normally did on Sundays, Kay was up at the crack of dawn drafting out a letter to Patsy. She was taking Zacchi's advice and writing to ask if she would please think about letting her family adopt Jac. She promised they would send the fare so that Patsy could visit every week for a year. She would send it all, one sum of money, which she had been left by an uncle.

Glancing up at the top of her wardrobe, she felt relieved to have found what she believed was an acceptable way of disposing of Frank and Freddie's envelope. Finishing the letter, she urged:

> I feel as if we are related in a kind of way, you being the mother of my brother. I hope we can meet. I would be on the next train if I thought you wouldn't mind. A day doesn't go by when I'm not thinking about my brother. I wish my dad had told me before now. Before good news became bad news. I'm referring to Jac being in a home amongst strangers.
>
> My very best wishes,
>
> Kay Armstrong

She looked across at her typewriter on her dressing table and wondered whether to type it out or rewrite it in her best handwriting. She decided on the latter.

By nine o'clock both Laura and Jack were up and Kay was on her way out to post the letter which was hidden in her jeans pocket. 'I'm going round Terry's. See if there's any news.'

Laura frowned, throwing some strips of bacon into the frying pan. 'I'm not sure that's a good idea, Kay. His mum wasn't the least bit pleased to see me yesterday. Well, that was the impression I got, anyway.'

'She always was a bit moody.' Kay grabbed an apple from the fruit dish. 'Probably be all right today. I'll buy her a box of Dairy Milk on the way.'

Stepping out into the quiet, sunny morning lifted Kay. As she pushed the doorbell and waited for Terry's mother to answer, she felt good having posted her letter, and looked forward to the response, if any. One way or another it would get things moving. If Patsy's reply was negative, she would put plan B into action. She would take a train to Leicester and see her in person. If that didn't work, she would carry out Jeannie's plan of threatening to write the article.

'You've got a nerve showing up here.' Terry's mum caught her off guard. 'It's because of you that my son's where he is now.' She stepped back and looked ready to slam the door shut.

Kay could hardly believe her ears. 'But I had nothing to do with it!' She pushed her hand against the closing door. 'Please don't—'

'You and your flash friends. He would never 'ave gone to that pub if it wasn't for you. Why couldn't you have stayed away, left him be? If the truth were known, you're partly to blame for the way he's turned out anyway. Picking blackberries with you when he should have been kicking a ball about!'

'Terry's the way he is because that's the way he was born. He knows that, and so should you by now!' Knowing she had overstepped the mark she tried to apologize, but the door slammed shut between them.

Determined to have her way, she grabbed the iron knocker and banged it three times. When the door abruptly opened again she pushed her shoulder against it and forced a foot forward. 'If you shut the door on me again, you'll crush my leg.'

'Just go away and leave me to mourn my son!'

Kay swallowed hard. Mourn her son? 'What are you saying?' She just managed to get the words out.

'You surely don't expect him to pull through this, do you? A cat tied to a tree and stoned would stand more chance!'

'You mustn't say that. Terry will live, I know he will.'

'And when it's time to bury him? Where's the money gonna come from, eh? I don't even have enough to buy a cheap coffin!' Mrs Button grabbed the edge of the door for support as her legs buckled under her.

In a flash Kay was there, catching her before she fell to the floor, pulling her inside and closing the door behind them. She ran into the front room and grabbed a couple of cushions from the sofa, placing one under her head and one under her knees.

'It's OK, Mrs Button. I'll get you a glass of water. You'll be fine. You fainted, that's all.'

Mrs Button moaned and rolled her eyes as Kay backed into the kitchen. Filling a glass, she forced back the tears. It wouldn't help to get emotional.

Supporting her head, Kay brought the glass to her lips. 'Sip this. You'll soon feel better.'

'Can you help me into the front room? I'd rather be sitting up, in an armchair.'

Once she had settled Mrs Button and made her comfortable, Kay went into the kitchen to make them both a cup of sweet weak tea. Waiting for the kettle to boil, she scanned the small back room. Apart from all the crockery on the blue-and-yellow-painted units, in one corner on the Formica surface was a tray with two of everything. Two dinner plates, two cups, two saucers, two tea plates, two soup bowls.

'Oh, Terry . . .' Kay murmured. 'You mustn't die. You mustn't.' A shrill whistle made her jump as steam forced its way out of the spout.

'I didn't mean what I said earlier, love. I'm all at sixes and sevens.' As Mrs Button looked at her, Kay couldn't help noticing her eyelids which were rapidly twitching above her tired eyes.

'Do you think they'd let me see him today? If I went in with you?' Kay hugged her cup of tea and hoped she might say yes.

'No. They're very strict about that sort of thing. Daft really. I could do with someone by my side.' Her voice trailed off and her eyes filled with tears. 'There's only my sister, and she's emigrated to Canada. God knows where Terry's dad is.'

'Why don't you ask the police if they can trace him?' Kay couldn't imagine herself lying critically ill and her dad not being there.

'We'll see.' Terry's mum let her head drop back in the cushioned armchair. Staring up at the ceiling, she slipped deep into her own thoughts.

'Is there anything I can do?' Kay asked.

No reply came. It was as if she hadn't spoken. As if she wasn't there. 'I could stay overnight if you wanted?'

Still the tired face showed no sign of response. The woman looked drained and beaten. Kay tried to stop herself thinking the worst. If Terry didn't survive the beating, his mother would have nothing to live for, and it showed.

Looking around the room, it was evident that they had not had an easy time of it. The floor was covered in a cheap brown lino which, though highly polished, showed signs of age. There were cracks and worn patches and a threadbare rug did nothing to make the room look cosy. The skimpy, faded gold and white curtains on each side of the bay window were unlined and Kay doubted that once drawn together they would meet.

Her mind went to the envelope and the money she had promised to Patsy. She felt suddenly guilty at having had such a comfortable upbringing. Her family had never really wanted for anything, in comparison to the existence she had seen in Terry's home.

Kay didn't want to leave the woman by herself, but she could see that staying would not only be a waste of time but an intrusion. Mrs Button wanted no one but her son and Kay could do nothing for her there. Nothing could be said or done to make either of them feel any better.

Walking home through the backstreets, Kay decided that until she was allowed to visit, any information about Terry would have to be drawn from the nurse she had spoken to the previous day. She would phone her for updates on his condition.

Life seemed so unfair. Her friend Terry was the very person she had chosen to tell about the way she felt inside about losing her baby. It would have been easier somehow, talking to him. Pamela would not have not let her forget it as easily as he would. Now she would have to keep it bottled up inside for a while longer - until he was up and smiling again.

Chapter Fourteen

Three weeks had passed since Kay first wrote to Patsy, and they had exchanged several letters. Bernard and Lillian found it strange that mail care of them had been arriving for Kay, but said nothing, after their first interrogation with Pamela. She had told them it was very personal and private – a confidential family matter.

'There's nothing else for it but to go up there,' Kay said, as they sat in Pamela's bedroom.

'Rather you than me.' Pamela was more interested in the *Melody Maker* she was reading.

'I don't suppose you fancy coming with me?'

'No.'

'Thanks. I always knew I could count on you.' Kay was beginning to wonder if she and her childhood friend were drifting away from each other. They seemed to have different attitudes about everything lately. Pamela hadn't even been with her to see Terry in hospital.

'I don't know why you don't drop it. She doesn't want the kid to move in with your family, surely that's obvious by now.' She didn't look up from her paper.

'Think I'll go tomorrow, get the early train. Go straight to the children's home. Say I'm a cousin or something.'

Looking defiantly at Kay, Pamela pushed her hair away from her face. 'You said you would come up west with me!'

'I think this is a little more important than you buying a new dress.'

'Well I don't! I want it for the party tomorrow night. We haven't been out since Terry's . . . you know.' She pretended to be absorbed in something she saw in the paper. 'If you're not seeing your precious Zacchi, you're brooding over him.'

'I do not brood over Terry. I happen to think he's better off where he is at the moment, than out here.'

'You're only saying that so you don't have to face the truth. He's on his deathbed and you know it.'

Lighting herself a cigarette, Kay leaned back on Pamela's bed. 'I'm longing to see my little brother.' She tried to blow a smoke ring towards the ceiling. 'They say he looks just like me.'

'Oh, bloody well go then! Get it over with.' Pamela was sick of hearing it.

'I intend to. Might even bring him back with me.'

'Don't talk rubbish.' She licked her finger and flicked a page over. 'When are we supposed to appear in court then?'

'I don't know.' It was the last thing Kay wanted to think about.

'I suppose we'll get a letter?'

'Yes.'

'Put the bastards away once and for all.' She gazed up at Kay, a different expression on her face. 'What made them do it?'

'I don't want to talk about it, Pam. I don't want to think about it, OK?' Her voice was remote with tension. 'Anyway, we might not have to go. There were other witnesses. My dad's trying to get us out of it.'

'Why? I'll go! I don't care. I'll bloody well tell them what happened. Wicked gits. I'll never forget what they did—'

'Shut up!' Kay clenched her fists. 'Mention it again and I'll put my hand through a window!' She glared at her friend, daring her to answer back.

'OK, OK! Fair enough. Calm down.'

'Terry's all right. He's not in as much pain now. Right?'

'Yeah, yeah, you're right, of course you are,' Pamela smiled and held out her hand, but Kay edged away.

'I'll be round on Sunday.'

'What about the party tomorrow night?' Pamela was losing her patience.

'Count me out. I'm not in the mood for dancing. Anyway, you never know what kind of people you're mixing with. Not any more, anyway.'

Kay and Laura were in the kitchen idly looking through a mail-order catalogue when Jack's piercing cry shot through the flat. Looking up, they waited to hear what might follow. Nothing came. A haunting silence filled the place.

Shrugging at Kay, Laura cautiously left the kitchen and went into the living room. 'What now?' she asked, dreading the answer.

As Jack sat there, head turned away, she caught sight of the headlines on the newspaper in his hands.

VICIOUS ATTACK LEADS TO SUICIDE.

Jack jumped up from his armchair and stormed out of the living room, throwing Laura into shock. She stood paralysed.

Once on the back balcony, the newspaper still in his clenched fist, Jack punched the brick wall over and over, crying and cursing until his knuckles bled. Staring at his fist he shouted out loud. 'Bastards! Bastards! Bastards!'

Kay rushed past Laura and stood in the veranda doorway.

'What is it, Dad? What's happened?'

Slowly raising his head, Jack's face twisted as he began to cry. 'Kay . . . I'm sorry, babe,' he shook his head. 'I don't know what else to say.' He handed them the newspaper and walked into the living room crouching down on the edge of an armchair.

Reading the lead story, Kay's face was slack with disbelief. 'He was terrified of coming out of hospital,' she murmured. 'He slashed his wrists.' She dropped the paper on the floor and walked out of the room and out of the flat.

Heading for nowhere in particular, Kay just kept walking. Thoughts seemed to be flying over her head instead of through it.

Nothing to think about. Not the past, not the present, not the future. No one. No one must be in her mind. They must all be cleared out. Friends, family, colleagues. An empty space. Empty room. Her head must be like an empty room. Only she would be there, standing alone. On a platform ordering everyone out. One by one they go. Out of the door, everyone. Only herself in the big, empty silent room. None to be allowed back in. Not then. Not ever. She would stay there for ever. By herself . . . by herself . . . by herself. Until she was ready to let new friends in. Jeannie and other people. Other people who led uncomplicated lives. Her legs would be strong. They would support her. She would walk around the empty room. Around the room. Around and around the room . . . By herself. Up and down. By herself.

'I couldn't believe it. I wasn't going fast, just biking along. And she walked out. I don't know how I missed her. She just seemed to drop down in front of me.' The man stood on the doorstep, his pale face pleading with Laura to believe him. 'I promise yer, I didn't knock her down. I think she's coming round now. Nearly gave me heart attack an' all!'

'Bring her in,' Laura waved the small group of curious children away from the door. Having seen Kay being carried by the stranger, they wanted to be part of the drama.

Laying her gently down on the sofa, the man shook his head. 'Scared the life out of me, I tell yer.'

'What happened?' Kay moaned.

'She didn't look right you know. It was like she was sleepwalking or something.' He was becoming less defensive by the second. 'I mean, if she's ill I don't think . . . I mean I could have bloody killed her!'

'Look, I would offer you a cup of tea but we've had a bit of a shock. A tragedy.' Laura hoped he would just go.

'That ginger-headed kid'll tell you. She saw what happened. I don't know how I managed to swerve in time! My bike's bound to have some scratches.' Remembering his bike gave him something else to think about. 'That balcony looks out on the road, don't it?' He rushed out to check what was happening below.

'Mum . . .' Kay was trying to focus, get her bearings.

'It's all right. Lie back and rest.' Laura's attention was half on her, half on the hyperactive cyclist, with his mac flapping around him.

Rushing through the room, the man almost tripped over his own feet. 'Bloody kids all round it now. Little sods. Bound to nick me pump!' His voice disappeared with him as he rushed through the flat.

'Who was that?'

'I have no idea, Kay.' Laura tried to keep a straight face. 'You OK?'

'Is Terry really dead?' her glazed eyes questioning.

'Yeah.' Laura parted her lips and took in a deep breath. She was lost for words. What could she say?

'It's all right, I'm not gonna cry. I'm really not.' Kay raised herself on one elbow. 'I tried to. For the first time in my life I actually tried to cry instead of trying to stop. I'm all dried up. Terry's dead. So? He's better out of it anyway. No one in their right mind would choose to be born, would they? Not if they knew what you have to put up with. And yet we kick and fight against leaving. Mad. We're all mad.'

She sat up and stared at nothing. 'I would swap places with Terry like a shot.' Feeling weak, she flopped back on to a cushion.

'You don't mean that.' Laura was unsure how to deal with Kay's mood.

'Oh, I do. Yeah. Sorry, Mum. But I do.' She smiled, closed her eyes and left Laura to do the crying.

* * *

After what seemed the longest night in her life, Kay sat in the kitchen with Laura. Neither of them had slept much, and when one did manage to doze off she was disturbed by the other moving around the flat. It wasn't until five o'clock that they were up at the same time.

'I had no idea, Mum. If you'd have seen their living room. Just a few sticks of furniture.' Kay remembered what Terry's mother had said about the funeral. 'She won't even be able to afford a decent coffin.'

'Yes she will. I've seen to it. Yesterday afternoon.'

'How d'yer mean?'

Laura rubbed her eyes and decided it was time to tell Kay a few home truths about some of her relations. 'Freddie and Frank gave your dad some money for Aunt Liz. Well, that's who they said it was for.' She sipped her tea and studied Kay's face for a reaction. There was none.

'The money they come by . . . well, it's not exactly kosher.' Again she looked for a response.

'What are you trying to say?' Kay sounded more impatient than surprised.

'Well they're, you know, small-time thieves.'

'Yeah? So?'

'Well we didn't think your aunt Liz'd want to take it—'

''Course she would!' Kay was on the edge of swearing at her mother for being soft.

'I popped an envelope – two hundred pounds – into Mrs Button's letter-box. Just wrote that it was from a well-wisher.' She expected a raised eyebrow from Kay.

'I'm glad you did that, but I'm not sure it's fair on Aunt Liz. You should have asked her first.'

Laura found it strange taking advice from her daughter. The tables had certainly turned in the past few months. 'There were two envelopes handed over. The other one's got three hundred pounds in it.'

'Oh, that's all right then.' Kay swallowed the rest of her tea.

'It doesn't bother you? Your uncles being crooks?'

'No, why should it? At least they don't go round kicking people's heads in.' She poured herself another cup of tea. 'I really like Freddie and Frank. They're good-hearted and generous. I'm not bothered where they get their money from.'

Laura's heart sank as she listened to her daughter who seemed to be getting more hardened by the minute. She felt sure it was the shock of Terry's death, besides everything else that had happened so far that year.

'They invited me and Pamela to the Kentucky club. I might go.' Kay was being deliberately rebellious. She knew it would upset and worry Laura.

'I can't stop you from doing what you want, Kay, but I will say this. If you do start going down the wrong pathways, it won't be so easy to find your way back to your normal way of living.'

Kay half smiled. 'What's wrong with that?' She had no intention of turning against her uncles. The reverse, in fact. She had been invited to the Kentucky and that was where she would go. If her uncles could so easily repay one debt, they could repay another. Those flash bastards whom she had thought to be her mates were not going to get away with causing the death of her best and closest friend.

Sitting on the edge of her bed, Kay waited for eight-thirty to come round on her small alarm clock. She thought that was probably the time they would be drinking at the club. A drink before they went for a Chinese meal, is what she imagined.

Approaching the unassuming building she could feel her heart pumping faster, and as she got closer she was puzzled by the exterior of the Kentucky club. Surely this wasn't it? She had expected bright lights and glitter. Film stars and politicians is what Pamela had said. Famous and important people in a place like this?

Beside a small door, she could not miss the sign in black-painted letters, *No. 106A Kentucky Club. Strictly members only.* Smiling to herself but with her heart still thumping, she knocked on the door and was surprised by a sudden movement from the wide letter-box as a make-shift shutter was pulled to one side. Bending down, she tried to sound positive. 'I want to see my uncles. Frank and Freddie.' In a flash the door opened and there stood three men, bouncers. They showed no trace of a smile as they stared her out. Behind them she saw the sign *All guests must be signed in.*

'My name's Kay Armstrong and I want to see my uncles.'

'They're not here, love. But you can come in and wait.' No trace of compassion in their voices, never mind the endearment.

Stepping inside the bar, she looked around at the seedy club. The smell reminded her of the horrid building in the City where she had gone for an interview. Old metal ashtrays, she thought. Old metal ashtrays and bad lighting. The dark red-embossed flock wallpaper reminded her of the small corner pub where she had once gone to pay her dad's union dues when he had the flu.

In the smoky room, amidst the many smartly dressed bodies, she thought she recognized some of the guests. Famous faces were laughing and talking. Is this it, she thought, is this really how the rich and famous like to spend an evening?

'Give Kay a drink.' One of the bouncers had followed her through. 'She's waiting for Freddie and Frank.'

'No, it's OK. I'm not staying.' She backed towards the open door.

'Any message?'

'No. You don't even have to say I came. It's OK now. I've just remembered I don't need to ask them what I thought I needed to . . .' She had to get out of there. There was a feeling in the air. A strange feeling of importance, fear and something else she couldn't identify.

Once outside, she leaned on a wall and breathed deep lungfuls of fresh air. 'Sorry, Terry,' she murmured, 'I can't do it.'

With tears streaming down her face she made her way through the backstreets, past the brewery and towards the safety of her home. Still she found herself thinking that Terry was better off out of it. If he went to clubs anything like the one she had just been to, his life could not have been that rich. Law and justice, she decided, would have to seal the fate of the boys who almost kicked the life out of him.

There was no doubt in her mind now. She would have to get away from this sordid part of the world. There had to be better places. Had to be.

When she arrived at the block of flats she sat down on a stone step and cried for the friend she would never see again. She wished over and over that she could turn back the clock. Maybe give him different advice, when they were hop-picking. Safer advice, like don't let anyone know. Hide behind a grey suit. Do anything to stay safe, to stay *alive*.

One thing she did know. Life really was what you made it. And tomorrow she would do her best to make her brother's life happier, come what may.

Standing on the doorstep, the morning sun warming her, Kay felt her anxiety begin to lessen. She could hear the sound of children playing in the garden behind the large Victorian house and wondered if little Jac was one of those laughing. Full of apprehension, she pressed her finger on the doorbell and prayed that she was doing the right thing.

The matron, a woman in her early thirties, looked her up and down as she stood in the doorway of the entrance hall. 'Can I help you?' Her face broke into a warm smile.

A surge of embarrassment rushed through Kay as she struggled to find the right words. 'I wonder if I could come in and talk to someone?'

'To do with—?' The matron's smile was instantly replaced with a look of concern.

'My cousin,' she lied without thinking. 'He lives here.'

'Name?'

'Kay Armstrong.' She felt as if she were being interviewed.

'I'm sorry. We have no one here by that name.' Her bright but firm tone conveyed the message that she wanted to end the conversation then and there.

Smiling nervously, Kay shook her head. 'No. That's my name. The little boy's called Jac. I was in the area and thought I might pay him a visit.'

'You'd best come in. Though I warn you, we don't allow visitors without parental consent.' She led Kay into a large, old-fashioned room. It wasn't how she had imagined it would be. The curtains with sunflowers printed on them were faded and reminded her of those which used to hang in her grandparents' cottage when she was small, and the green carpet, although spotlessly clean, had several worn patches.

'Would you like a cup of tea while you're waiting?' The matron smiled.

'Yes I would, thanks.'

'Don't hold out too much hope, will you. We'll have to speak to his mother on the phone before we can go forward.' She closed the door behind her and left Kay wondering if she had made a mistake in coming. Trying to imagine what Jac looked like, she warmed again to the thought of having a brother. She felt strongly that she had every right to see him.

Sitting down in one of the armchairs, Kay gazed out of the glass french doors and watched the gardener as he dug over a flower-bed. He reminded her of her grandfather, Billy.

'Good news and bad news,' Matron said as she handed her a cup of tea. 'Mrs Hemmingway doesn't want you to see the boy, but she is on her way here. She wants to meet you.' She sat down opposite Kay. 'Mr

Watson, our resident house-uncle, will bring the boy's mother in once she arrives.'

'I suppose she told you who I really am – Jac's sister?'

'Half-sister,' she corrected.

'I'm sorry, but I don't see it like that. He's my dad's son and that makes me his sister as far as I'm concerned. Neither of us are half a person.'

'True,' she smiled again. 'It's always a difficult one —'

'You mean this isn't the first time you've had someone like me knocking on the door?'

'Similar cases. We usually manage to work something out, but it takes time. Be prepared for that.'

'We'll see,' Kay murmured.

'How long have you known about Jac?'

'Not long, a few weeks. I've been writing to his mother. I've asked her if my mum and dad could adopt him. We've got a spare room and even though we live in flats, there's plenty of playing area. Grass as well as tarmac.'

The matron looked back at Kay with sympathy in her eyes, as if she were trying for the impossible.

'I can't wait to see him.' Kay sighed and leaned back in the armchair. 'It's strange. I can't explain it, but ever since I was told, it's as if I've always known, deep down. It might have something to do with my baby brother who died at three months old. I was five or six at the time. I don't really remember, but sometimes I think I do. If that makes sense.'

Both Kay and the matron looked up as the door opened and the house-uncle appeared, followed by Patsy, who looked less than pleased. 'I told you in my letter not to come here,' she said at once.

'Please,' Kay felt a familiar, unwanted mood rising. 'I just want to say hallo to him.' Her tears streamed down despite herself. 'You don't know what it's like.' She wiped her eyes with both hands. 'I think about him all the time; dream about him, have nightmares that he's locked up in a cupboard.' She tried to stop but the words tumbled from her as if she had no control, and her body began to shake.

'I—' she tried to speak but then couldn't get the words out.

'My God. I didn't think she would be *this* concerned,' Patsy said.

'Miss Armstrong is more than upset,' the Matron placed one arm around Kay's shoulder and did her best to comfort her.

'My friend—' Kay tried again, but it was no use. She looked into the Matron's face, desperate to tell her about Terry. 'My friend—'

'It's OK. Just try to relax. I'm sure Doctor will give you something to calm you.' She glanced up at the house-uncle hoping to get his attention, but he was gazing trancelike at Kay, moved by her sorrow.

'Has something else happened,' the Matron asked, 'apart from finding out about your brother?'

Kay could only nod and make whimpering sounds.

'Wait until you feel better. Then tell me.' She gently held her trembling hands. 'It will pass, I promise you. Just let go for now. Don't try to stop. It's your body reacting. I expect you've been bottling things up.'

'I don't want you to fetch Jac, not now – not with me like this,' Kay managed to stammer.

'You've got yourself in a real state over this, haven't you?' Patsy smiled.

Kay tried to return her smile, but her face felt numb. She sipped her tea, thankful for the warm liquid on her dry throat. After a few silent minutes, she began to feel slightly better. 'I'm sorry about this.'

'No more than I am,' Patsy looked ashamed. 'I've been a bit selfish. Just thinking of number one.' She turned to the house-uncle. 'I had no idea they felt this strongly about Jac.'

'Dad's really cut up about it.'

'Poor Jack. He's not a bad bloke. I just tried to make myself think that way to ease the hurt. I did love him, you know.'

It wasn't what Kay wanted to hear, but it was better than being yelled at, which is what she had half expected.

'Once you've pulled yourself together, we'll bring our Jac in. I think you're gonna be in for a surprise,' she chuckled.

'Mum said he looks like me.' Kay's puffy eyelids and flushed cheeks made her look younger than her seventeen years.

'He does.'

'Are you sure this is what you want, Patsy?' The house-uncle asked, hoping it was.

'It is, actually. Now that I've seen this young lady. She is my Jac's big sister, after all's said and done.'

'Who's that?' Jac pushed a chubby finger in Kay's face, making her laugh.

'*That* is your big sister,' Patsy said with a touch of pride in her voice.

'Isn't,' Jack said quietly, a strange look on his face.

'Oh, yes it is. You gonna give your sister Kay a kiss then?'

Without any prompting, Jac leaned forward and landed a big wet kiss on Kay's mouth.

'Coming?' Kay held out her arms.

'No!'

'I'll go away again.'

'No!'

'I will . . .'

Throwing himself into Kay's arms, he almost knocked Patsy off balance and thought it was hilarious when she pretended it was worse and landed on her bottom.

The three of them spent an hour together, walking around the grounds, playing chase with Jac and swinging him by his arms. An earlier rainstorm had passed, and the sun was warming the wet grass again.

'You can see why I don't want him to be miles away from me. This way I get to see him when I like.'

'Does he mind being here? I would have thought he'd miss his own home.'

Patsy sighed. 'Not at first. It was a novelty, like full-time nursery school. He's been a bit quiet the last couple of visits, mind. He probably thinks this is just a little holiday and that he'll be coming home soon.'

'What will you do if he starts crying when you leave? I couldn't bear that.'

'I don't know, to be perfectly honest. I'll just have to wait and see. It's no worse than boarding school, and plenty of children go there. And look at this place. It's much better than the place we live in, I can tell you.'

'And you wouldn't consider him living with—'

'No.' Patsy wasn't prepared to discuss it. 'But you can visit him, providing you let me know you're coming.'

'Sounds fair.' Kay scooped Jac up again and kissed him on the cheek. 'I'm going home now. But I'll be back to see you, Master Jac.'

'Master Jac,' he giggled, and playfully slapped Kay's face.

'What do you want me to do with the money? Keep it until you come back, or send it by registered post?'

'Keep it for now.' Kay looked at her watch. 'I'm gonna have to run, or I'll miss my train.'

After hugs all round, Kay left the house, smiling and waving and promising she'd see them again soon.

'Kay! What's the flat like, anyway?' Patsy suddenly called after her.

'Nice. And plenty of room to play. See you!'

Waiting on the platform for her train, Kay wondered why Patsy had asked about the flat. Maybe she was having second thoughts about Jac going down for a weekend visit.

Zacchi had turned up unexpectedly at Jack and Laura's flat, and was slightly miffed that neither of Kay's parents seemed to know where she was. He waited two hours before deciding to leave.

'I'll phone later this evening, see if she's back.'

'OK, son. I'm sorry about this. Seems daft us not knowing where she's got to. We assumed she was round Pamela's. I'll tell her to stay in and wait for your call once she does come in. OK?' Jack gave Zacchi a friendly punch on the shoulder.

After seeing Zacchi out, Jack returned to the kitchen in a black mood. 'What does she think she's playing at?'

'Don't start, Jack. I've had enough. She's got other friends, you know. Zacchi said something about Juanita, someone she used to meet on the bus. Maybe that's where she is.'

'I've no doubt. What *I'm* saying is she should tell us if she's gonna be gone all day!'

Laura bit the end of a thumbnail, something she had never done in her life. 'I've got a horrible feeling we're gonna be saying goodbye to Kay soon.'

Jack got himself a glass of water. 'What makes you say that?' The tone of his voice said it all. He felt exactly the same.

'She's gonna go. Move out. Away from here.' She pulled her thumb away from her mouth and tucked her hands under her arms. 'She's crossed that line between depending on us and needing to live her own life.'

'Yeah, I know. She's young though, Laura. Eighteen next week. What age is that?'

'I think Zacchi knows it too. She's gonna slip through his net as well, you see if I'm wrong.'

Listening to the dripping of the cold tap that Jack hadn't turned off properly, they sat in the otherwise quiet kitchen. It had been a heavy, stormy day and now, in the late afternoon, black clouds filled the sky darkening the kitchen, but neither Jack nor Laura could be bothered to switch on the light.

When Kay finally came into the kitchen as if it had been just another day, Jack shocked her by slamming his fist down on the kitchen table, his pale face pinched with fury.

'You 'ad no right to go behind my back! First your mother and then you! What am I around 'ere? A fucking ghost or what?' he yelled.

'I was only trying to put right what you've messed up!' Kay shouted back at him. 'I should have been told about Jac! Keeping my letters from me is one thing,' she clenched her fists and screamed, 'it's not fair!'

Drying her hands on a tea towel, Laura stood between them. 'Have either of you given a thought to what I might be going through?' She threw the tea towel on to the table and turned on Kay.

'Your father's right. You shouldn't have gone without talking to us about it. It wasn't clever!' She took a deep breath, spun around and turned on Jack. 'And as for you, playing silly games, knowing full well I was planning to go to Leicester and not letting on.' She walked out of the kitchen. 'I'm packing my bags and leaving you to it, both of you! Because *I* have had enough!'

The remark took the wind out of both Jack and Kay's sails. They knew Laura well enough to know this might not be an empty threat. Once she made up her mind to do something, she carried it through.

'Now see what you've done?' Jack balled an empty tobacco packet in his fist. 'You'd better go and talk her round before she does something silly.'

'Look me in the eye and say that, you sod!' Kay snapped back.

Jack made a sudden jerking movement towards her but thought better of it. 'Get out of 'ere before I give you a right-hander!' He hurled the green and gold wrapping across the room.

'No! *You* get out of here and do something positive for a change.'

Inhaling deeply, Jack looked fit to burst. 'Like what?'

'Apologizing to Mum for giving another woman the son that she would have liked, for a start!'

Pushing both hands through his hair, Jack leaned forward, resting his elbows on his knees. 'Leave me alone,' he murmured and then shouted louder than she had ever heard him. 'Leave me fucking alone!'

'We did. And look where that got us!' With that insolent remark, Kay moved like lightning across the kitchen, heading for the door. She knew it was time to lock herself in her bedroom.

With her weekend bag firmly in one hand, Laura stormed out of the flat. She had no idea where she was heading. Maybe Harlow. Not Billy's cottage, that was for sure. The last thing she needed was to be told by her dad that her place was in the home.

Making her way through the backstreets, Jack's misdeeds flew through her mind. He had played the field back in the old days and had got away with it scot-free. She remembered Patsy's words; *Jack made love to me more times than you've given him a hot dinner.*

Seething, she walked briskly across the Mile End Road, daring the traffic to come anywhere near her. Having reached the other side in one piece, she reacted to an angry motorist by showing him two fingers.

'Hallo, Laura, mate.' Milly stood in her door full of smiles, wearing a flimsy pink housecoat and holding a green chiffon scarf. 'I've bin trying out my vacuum cleaner. Come and watch this,' she giggled. Following her friend through the brightly decorated passage, Laura couldn't help smiling. Nothing seemed to surprise Milly. Hadn't she seen her overnight suitcase?

'I only got it yesterday. Can't bring myself to suck any dirt into it.' Holding the delicate scarf in front of the brush, she pressed the switch on the vacuum cleaner and was overjoyed when the scarf disappeared into the machine.

'A kid with a new toy,' Laura smiled.

'I know.' She unzipped the cloth bag and pulled out the scarf with a flourish. 'Hey Presto!'

'You're mad.'

'Stopping long, are yer?' Milly asked, eyeing the small suitcase.

'I wouldn't mind hiding for a couple of days. Pigeons have come home to roost.' She shrugged and smiled.

''Course you can stop. Do Jack good to wonder where you've got to. I take it you didn't tell 'im?'

'I didn't know where I was going myself till I got here.'

'Oh, I'd love to do something like that.' She switched on the electric kettle. 'Especially when George and Brianny get going. He's not been out five minutes and they've clashed already.'

Pushing her shoes off, Laura lay back in an armchair. 'And you really don't mind my staying?'

''Course I don't. Be company for me. 'Ow many sugars?'

'Two. How's the wedding arrangements going?'

'Lovely. I've got myself a nice turquoise number – hat to match. I can't wait to get all dressed up, to tell the truth.'

'What about Georgie?'

'Dunno really. He shows a bit of interest sometimes, when I remind 'im that he's getting rid of his son.' She placed a cup of tea in front of Laura and sat down. 'He's changed a bit. It's all the sex he's getting now. Won't leave me alone. Thinks he's a young man again.'

'Not jumping off the wardrobe, is he?' Laura was beginning to enjoy herself. This was what she needed. A little break from all her worries.

'No, but—'

'Mum!' Brianny burst into the kitchen. 'Dad's only gone and nicked my best Ben Sherman shirt! That's twice this week!'

Laura laughed so much she had to cross her legs. Georgie Smith in a Ben Sherman – she couldn't imagine it. 'He's not wearing winkle-pickers as well, is he?' she managed to say.

'Yeah, as it 'appens,' Milly sipped her tea. 'Bought 'em off a stall down Chris Street market last week.'

'I warned 'im,' Brianny barked, 'I said I'd 'ave his suede tie if he did it again!'

'I hear you're getting married, Brianny?' Laura was longing to find out a bit more about his fiancée.

'Yeah, worse luck. Bloody country bumpkin, ain't she.' He narrowed his eyes and grinned. 'You remember – Richard Wright's little maid, Janet.' He left the room whistling.

'They been together all this time?' Laura tried not to let Richard creep into her mind.

'Yeah. Love, eh? Still, she's a good kid. She'll keep a nice front door and step. Helped me polish my windows last week as well.' Milly snatched a Rich Tea out of the biscuit barrel. 'You'll never guess who she's invited to the wedding?'

'You are joking?' Laura knew exactly who Milly was referring to. Her face said it all.

'They're coming as well.' She looked serious for a second. 'That's why I wanna look my best. Lord and lady of the manor coming to my son's wedding! Turn-up for the books, eh?'

'So Richard Wright did employ Brianny after all?' she said casually.

'Up until a few months ago when Brianny's uncle offered him work in London. He'd had enough of country life – thank Gawd.' She pulled a tiny patterned handkerchief from her pocket and wiped crumbs from the corners of her mouth. 'Getting in practise for the big day,' she giggled.

'You knew the Wrights were coming when you invited me and Liz, I suppose?'

''Course. That's why I didn't ask Jack.'

Once Milly had let Laura know that she had learned about her romance from Brianny, the floodgates opened. Laura told Milly everything and she was all ears.

'You don't still love 'im, surely?' Milly wanted more.

'No, I don't. And to tell the truth, I don't think I ever did.' She became pensive. 'I've been weighing things up this last couple of weeks, once I knew about little Jac.' She pulled her cigarettes out of her handbag and offered one to Milly.

'We weren't in love. It was unreal. We needed each other just then, that's all. We'd both arrived at a difficult patch in our lives—'

'Give over, Laura,' Milly managed to grin even though a cigarette was dangling from the side of her mouth. 'You were madly in love, the pair of you. And just about everyone on the hop fields knew it.'

'You reckon?' Laura felt herself sink again. 'I don't know. I don't know anything any more.'

'What's gonna 'appen about Jack's kid then?' Milly had a way with words no one could match. Every line was spoken as if the words were from a song. 'Gonna dump 'im on yer, is she?'

'Chance would be a fine thing, no. And that's what all the upset's about really . . . well, that and other things that have been happening lately. Horrible things.'

Milly bent her head and her eyes filled with tears. 'Yeah, I know. Poor Terry, eh? Your Kay must 'ave taken that badly.'

'Fucking 'ell, Mum!' The freckled face appeared in the doorway again. 'Dad's took me suede jacket an' all!'

'See?' Milly shrugged at Laura, 'I told yer.' She tapped one side of her head. 'Gone mad. Thinks he's nineteen instead of turned forty. You're in for a treat. He'll be back from the pub soon.'

'I'm going down there. Pull it off 'is bloody back.' Brianny grabbed some biscuits and disappeared, banging the front door behind him.

It was Milly who started to laugh first, and Laura couldn't wait for

Georgie to walk through the door wearing his new look.

Her fingers flying over the keys of her typewriter, Kay was in another world. The article she had begun writing the week before had somehow turned into a short story and was now developing into a novel. More and more ideas had come to her as the main plot developed. She had started to type to take her mind off the way she had upset her mum enough to make her walk out. She was also trying to block out the picture that kept flashing through her mind of the little boy she had left behind. Last but not least, she wanted to be free from her feelings about Terry.

> The room where the orphans played was light and cheerful and looked out on to a small garden. Sarah pulled the sunflower-patterned curtains slightly to one side and was reminded once again of her childhood. The young man digging the garden looked just like her brother John, who had joined the merchant navy.
>
> 'Her Ladyship will see you now.' The austere face of Mrs Johnson showed no signs of a smile.
>
> 'How many children are there?' Sarah regretted the words as soon as they were said. She knew by the woman's reaction that it was not her place to ask and the atmosphere at Wynchling Manor was enough for anyone to realize that not only children but staff must speak only when spoken to.

Pausing to read what she had written, Kay wound back the sheet of paper in the typewriter, moved along to the word *slightly* and typed a row of x's through it.

'Kay? You coming out of there now, or what?' Jack tried to sound indifferent.

She was up and unlocking her door in no time. 'It's going really well. I don't want to stop.' Her face was glowing. She splayed her fingers and wiggled them. 'I couldn't stop,' she grinned. 'I feel as if I could go on and on writing, in my other world.'

'Yeah, well, maybe we'd best sit down and look at what's 'appening in this one.' Jack went back into the kitchen.

'I can't believe it's nine o'clock already!' Kay rummaged around in the cupboard. 'I s'pose you're worried about Mum?'

'No. I couldn't care less. She won't have gone far. Probably having a chin-wag with Liz.'

'So what did you want then?' Finding a jar of peanut butter, she opened a drawer and took out the bread knife.

'Just wondered if you was all right in there, that's all,' Jack didn't sound too convincing.

'Do you want a slice of bread and butter? There's some cheese in the fridge.'

'No thanks. I'm not hungry.' He poured himself a glass of milk. 'So what's all these hints you've been giving out lately, about moving out?'

'Jeannie at work's got a friend who's got a studio flat for rent. In Highgate. Three pounds fifty a week.' Kay reeled it off quickly while she had him listening.

'And who's gonna do your washing? Cook your dinners?'

'Me, of course.'

'And what about Zac? Where does he fit in with all this?' Jack seemed almost to be coming round to the idea.

'Things won't be any different to what they are now. He'll get a train over there instead of here, that's all.'

'You mum won't like it, Kay. I'll tell you that now.'

'What about you? You gonna stick up for me?' She studied his face and waited.

'I s'pose I'll have to. Little cow. You're gonna go one of these days, in any case. No matter what I say.'

'I don't do it on purpose, you know. I mean I'm not deliberately setting out to cause trouble or anything.'

'No?' Jack flashed her a smile.

'I'm *not*!'

'You're a natural rebel, babe. You don't even know you're doing it. Promise me one thing, though.' He looked her straight in the eye.

'What?'

'If you ever decide you wanna get married before you're twenty-one, you won't forge my signature on the marriage certificate form.'

'You've put the idea in my head now,' she grinned.

'No, I mean it, Kay. That would really cut me up. I don't think I could forgive you if you did that.'

'Well I won't then. See, Dad, all you have to do is talk these things over with me—'

'But you're only a kid!' He was getting angry again. 'I shouldn't have to—'

'Dad!' Kay cut in. 'It doesn't matter how old or young I am. You mustn't – oh, I don't know! I can't stand to feel as if I'm not free to come and go as I please. I've got to feel free! Otherwise it's like I'm suffocating.'

'You're overdoing it, but all right! All right. I'll try to let you fly if you must. But I tell you what, Kay. You're not gonna be able to make these demands when you get married. You can kiss your freedom goodbye then.'

'It doesn't have to be that way! Two people can . . .' Kay's voice trailed off as the sound of a woman talking to a child drifted through the open kitchen window. Both of them recognized the accent but could hardly believe their ears. Dumbstruck, they waited for the sound of the doorbell. Instead they heard three short, sharp raps on the knocker.

'You gonna answer that?' Jack had suddenly lost his nerve.

'Is that who I think it is?'

'We won't know till you answer it, Kay – will we?'

'There she is, then,' Patsy said to Jac as Kay stood in the street doorway. 'Your big sister.' She looked at Kay and managed a smile. 'He cried once you'd gone. Cried for you, I mean.'

'I can't believe you're here!' Kay laughed as Jac put his chubby arms out to her and almost leapt from Patsy's arms. She was suddenly caught between the devil and the deep blue sea. Her mum could arrive back any minute.

'Dad's in. I don't suppose . . .?'

'Why not,' Patsy sighed and braced herself.

'Yeah,' Kay grinned broadly, 'why not?'

Leading the way, she hugged Jac and smothered his face with kisses. 'Look who the wind's blown in, Dad.'

So wrapped up in the moment, it had escaped Kay that Jack was looking at the son he hadn't seen for nearly two and a half years.

'What's going on, Patsy?' He spoke as if little Jac were still a well-kept secret.

'Is that all you can say?' Kay kissed Jac's smiling face again. 'This funny man is your daddy. And mine. You gonna say hallo?'

'No.' Jac placed his hands either side of Kay's face and pushed her cheeks together.

'You gonna give him a kiss?'

'No.'

Jack couldn't take it in. He looked drained and ready for his bed.

Turning to Patsy, Kay pulled her into the kitchen.

'Hallo, Jack,' she said, shyly.

Swallowing hard, Jack sucked on his bottom lip and kept his eyes down. 'You OK?'

The little boy answered for her. 'Hallo – Jack!' he giggled, which started Kay and Patsy off. 'Hallo, Jack!' Jac loved having an audience. Pointing one chubby finger at himself he said, 'Me Jac!'

Smiling through tears, Jack looked up at his small son. 'So am I.' He leaned forward and offered his hand. 'How d'yer do?'

Jac took his hand and shook it in a very grown-up fashion.

'Pleased to meet you.' He glanced sheepishly at Patsy. 'You didn't come all this way by train, did yer?'

'No. Tom drove me. He's waiting downstairs. I just thought maybe . . . try it for a week. Think of it as a little holiday.' She stroked her son's hair.

'Why don't you fetch What's-his-name up? Tom?'

'You must be joking. He's scared of what you might do to him.'

'What am I gonna do, Patsy? I've got no grudge against the man. Why should I?'

'Because he won't bring up your son?'

'Can't blame 'im for that. I'd be the same in 'is shoes.'

'You would not, Jack, and you know it.' Patsy caught his eye and a smile passed between them.

'So I'm allowed him for a week then?'

'If Jac likes it, he can stay a bit longer.' She wiped the dribble from her son's chin. 'Do you think you'll like it, then?'

'No garden!' Jac exclaimed splaying his hands.

'Five minutes walk away. A very big garden. It's called Barmy Park and it's got swings as well.' Jack put his arms out to Jac. 'Come on. Come to your dad while your sister makes us all a cup of tea. We'll go and tell Tom to come up, shall we?'

'Yes.' Jac thought that was a good idea. 'Yes!' He looked into his father's face and repeated what he had heard so many times from Patsy. 'Got Jac's eyes!'

'No,' Patsy laughed, 'you have got your daddy's eyes.'

'No!' He pressed a finger on to each of his lids and almost whispered, 'My eyes.'

'Go on then, go to your sister. I won't be a minute.' Placing Jac in

Kay's arms, Jack grinned at her. 'Still gonna move out, are yer?'

'I didn't say straight away! Maybe in six months or so.' Kay put a tissue up to Jac's nose and told him to blow.

Once Jack had left the flat to fetch Tom, Patsy sighed with relief and sat down. 'Where's your mother?' She sat erect, preparing herself for a confrontation.

'Don't ask.' Kay smiled.

'Fair enough,' Patsy shoved her hand into her pale lilac summer coat. 'I've brought the envelope back.'

'No. I mean it, Patsy. Use it for the fare money so you can come down regularly. It's only fair on Jac. And anyway, Mum and Dad don't know about it. A couple of my relations treated me. Let's leave it at that.'

'Well, I'm not going to argue with you. Thanks.' She slipped it back in her pocket. 'I only hope I'm doing the right thing, that's all.'

'It's not carved in stone.' Kay shrugged. 'If it doesn't work out . . . Come on. Let's show Jac where he'll be sleeping. Bring his bags.'

'These are full of toys and teddy bears. The back seat of the car's full of boxes and bags of his clothes. I didn't want to bring them up in case—'

'You didn't like the look of the flat?'

'Something like that, yeah. Your mum's in for a shock when she gets back.'

'You're not kidding.' Kay let out a sigh of relief. 'She'll be pleased, Patsy. It'll be good for her.'

No sooner had Jack left than he was back. 'Tom's a funny sort of bloke, ain't he, Patsy? Kept shaking my 'and but wouldn't come up!' Jack sounded pleased about it.

'He's all right. You leave him be.' Patsy gave Jack a look of scorn. 'I'm going now. I'll phone tomorrow, see if he's settled.'

Bending down to kiss Jac goodbye, she was taken aback when he turned away and snuggled up against his new sister.

'Kiss Mummy, Jac. Don't be silly!' Kay's mildly scolding voice worked. He gave Patsy a hug and kiss.

'Be a good boy and I'll see you very soon. OK?' Swallowing hard and rolling her eyes at Kay, Patsy forced back her tears.

Jac put his thumb up. 'OK!'

'Right. I'll be on my way.' She turned to Jack and gave him a teasing smile. 'You've still got great shoulders.'

* * *

'I'm not sure I can go along with this,' Georgie Smith said, tucking into his supper of cold meat, bread and pickle. 'You should be at home with your old man, Laura.'

'She's stopping and that's final.' Milly clinked her glass of port and lemon against Laura's. 'And you can do the same for me one day,' she gave Georgie a mock warning look.

'I'll tell you what, George. I'll phone and let Jack know where I am. How's that?'

'That's more like it,' he said. 'Now then, what's on the telly?'

Leaning back in her chair, Laura decided there and then that she would only stop overnight. That would be enough time for Jack and Kay to have a chat and sort themselves out.

'What's your birth sign, Laura?' Milly was studying the horoscopes in the Sunday paper.

'Virgo.'

Milly began to read. *'You are seldom at your best this time of the year. However, you will soon realize that nothing you have gone through has been wasted or in vain. Yesterday's lessons are tomorrow's guidelines.'*

'Thanks, Milly. That makes me feel a lot better.'

'Load of bloody rubbish,' Georgie switched on the television set. 'Life's what you make it.'

Laura smiled to herself. He was dead right there. Her mind was full of Kay and what she would make of her life. It was plain enough that she was on course for a change.

'I don't suppose you fancy giving me a lift home do you, George?'

He stared at his watch. 'It's gone eleven!'

'I know but, you know . . .'

Milly yawned. 'I knew she wouldn't make it through the night. Go on, get going. But come and see me again. I've enjoyed tonight. Had a good laugh. Done my stomach good, that 'as.'

After thanking Georgie and waving him off, Laura walked slowly up the concrete stairs and could almost hear the echo of her own breath, as well as her footsteps. She couldn't wait to see Jack's face. He would be worried and upset. His self-esteem had been a bit on the low side.

Not surprised to see the lights were still on at that late hour, she turned the key and closed the door quietly behind her in case Kay was in bed, and made for the living room.

'Oh, you're back then?'

Laura looked from Jack to Kay. They didn't look too worried. The reverse, in fact.

'I thought, you know, you just might have been a bit concerned!' Laura cursed herself for coming back too soon. She should have stayed the night and given them both something to think about.

Getting up, Jack took Laura by the arm. 'I've got something to show you.'

With one finger on his lips, he carefully opened the spare-bedroom door. A small night-light was on and the soft glow just allowed them to see Jac with his thumb in his mouth and an old brown toy dog under one arm. He was sound asleep.

Laura crept forward and gazed down at him. With her hand firmly over her mouth she looked to Jack for an answer. He just shrugged, pressed his lips together and did his utmost not to cry, but a tear was in each eye and beginning to trickle down.

Kissing Laura and Jack goodnight, Kay went to her room without saying a word. She knew that this was probably one of the greatest experiences they would ever have; the best thing in the world for them was to share it together, without her. Besides which, she couldn't wait to get back to her story which was almost certainly going to include Jac. She could write down her innermost feelings and maybe one day her mum and dad would read what had really been going on.

'Can't you advise us where to go? This is all foreign to us. We haven't been further than the Isle of Sheppey.'

'Isle of Wight,' Billy corrected. 'I always took Laura and her mother to the Isle of Wight when she was small. I've never much fancied Sheppey.'

The travel agent leaned back in the chair, narrowed his eyes and suggested a tour. 'I'm thinking of Austria. Mountains and lakes. Holland and the tulip fields. Clean air, not too hot. Flowers everywhere. Springtime.'

'Tulips from Amsterdam . . .' Billy was warming to the idea.

'How far is it?' Liz was beginning to wish she hadn't accepted Jack and Laura's offer. The Isle of Sheppey would have suited her.

'I take it you do have passports?' The travel agent seemed to be in a world of his own.

'No. But our Kay can fill us in on what to do. She's been abroad. Went to Spain, if you don't mind! Cheeky cow forged her passport form.'

'That's it, tell the whole bloody world!' Liz shot Billy a look to kill.

'Why not take a brochure and have a browse at your leisure?' The man smiled benignly at them.

'What about foreign money? How do we go about that?' Liz asked.

'We can arrange currency for you.' He pushed a colourful brochure in front of them. 'Please come back when you've found something you like.' He looked at his watch and raised his eyebrows.

'Dutch people, innit? Over there?'

'Ye – es. In the main, in Holland.'

Liz flicked through the shiny pages. 'So we'd get from one place to another by coach?'

'Mmmm. That's usually the way.'

'And stop in different hotels?'

'Yes. You'll be moving on from place to place.'

'And how much is this gonna cost?' Billy had no intention of leaving until the man had answered all his questions.

Having little faith that his time spent with this couple would achieve a sale, the travel agent pulled the brochure towards him and turned to a page near the back. 'All the prices, for the different tours, are listed here.' He showed them a pink insert.

'Mmmm. The small print,' Liz said suspiciously. She sniffed and looked at Billy. 'I don't know what you've got against Sheppey.'

'OK,' Billy suddenly said to the man. 'You're on. We'll take it. Two to Austria. We'll leave it to you to sort the coaches and that. Send us a bill with all the charges on.' He reeled off his address and slapped his cap back on. 'We'll get the passports sorted out.'

Pushing his hand into the travel agent's palm, he gripped it tight and shook heartily. 'Thanks for all your 'elp.'

'It doesn't quite work that way.' The bemused man tried to keep a straight face. 'You choose, and we—'

'Stone me. D'yer want our business or not? Just pick what you think'd suit us. Come on, Liz, let's get going. My belly's rumbling.' He gave the man a show of his hand. 'You've got an honest face. We trust you to sort something out. All the best.'

Surprised by this sudden sweeping conclusion, Liz could only shrug at the man behind the desk. 'I s'pose that's it, then?'

'It would appear so.' He looked far from pleased.

'Make sure we're in separate rooms, only we're not married,' she smiled, and followed Billy out.

Tucking into their dinner in the pie shop, Billy grimaced at a family with five children who were making a racket. 'I'd show 'em my belt if they were mine.'

'You never used it on Laura, surely?'

'Never 'ad to. Any cheek and my hand went to the buckle. She soon came round. Never 'ad to lay a finger on 'er. A look was enough.'

'I bet it was.' Liz dipped a forkful of pie into the liquor.

'So where d'yer reckon this money did come from then? If it wasn't a win on the dogs?'

'I know where it came from, Billy. I know full well. Bert's brothers. The Brothers Bung, as I used to call 'em. It's not the first time they've bunged me a little treat on the quiet. Bert would 'ave blown 'is top if he'd 'ave known. Pride, eh?'

'Jack's just as bad. Let 'im try eating pride. Soon lose weight.'

'What sort of foreign food d'yer reckon they eat out there in Austria?'

'Dunno. Kangaroos, perhaps?'

'Silly bleeder. That's Australia.'

'Is it? Oh well . . . you never know.'

Liz waited for him to finish his sentence but it became apparent that he had. 'You never know what?'

'We might go out there an' all, one day. Australia. I expect that's where our Kay'll end up.'

Willing herself not to laugh at him, she asked why Australia.

''Cos that's the furthest bloody corner of the world, innit?'

Sitting cross-legged by Terry's freshly dug grave, Kay ran her fingers over the flowers and dried wild hops she had brought with her, and wondered why she felt so light inside.

'You don't know how pleased I am to see you here.' It was Ray. He looked tired and drawn. 'Of all people you're the only one he really cared about, apart from his mum.'

Kay reached out and took Ray's hand. 'Come and sit down. It feels OK. And it's as close as we're gonna get.'

'So what now?' Ray said, settling himself down beside her.

'I don't know. One day at a time, I suppose?'

'Yeah. That's it. One day at a time.' He smiled at her and nodded. 'Thanks for being here.'

'And you,' she took his slim hand in hers and squeezed it. 'We'll be OK. We'll be fine.'

'So long as this weather holds out,' he said, admiring the blue sky dotted with cotton wool clouds.

'Yep. So long as that sun keeps on keeping on, eh?' She leaned her head on his shoulder and he responded by rubbing his cheek on her blonde silky hair.

'How's Zacchi?'

'Oh, he's OK. Wrote a nice poem for Terry. I'll let you have a copy.'

'Will you talk to me about him, Kay? All those years when you played together down hoppin' – all of it?'

''Course I will. But not now though, eh? In time. Bit by bit. Until we can laugh at him again. That's when we'll know we're over it. It will happen. It's beginning to already with my uncle Bert. I can think about him now, the way he really was. And it's OK.'

'That's good.'

'Did I tell you I've got a little brother now?'

'No. I didn't know that.'

'Yeah, he's lovely. And he looks like me.'

'I've got a little sister. She can be a cow sometimes . . . nearly three and bossy already.'

'But you wouldn't be without her.'

'No. I wouldn't be without her.'

Kay trailed one finger across the dark mound of rich earth and remembered Sid in the park and what he had said about Terry when he was in hospital. *If he is hovering between this world and the next he'll be able to see you . . .*

Kay had a strong feeling that Terry was hovering close to them now, and smiling. She couldn't describe it, but she felt his warm happy presence and from the way Ray was relaxed with his face to the sun, she imagined he too could feel that Terry had not quite made that final departure.

Her mind was full of that black tin hoppers' hut on the common, the white sheets smelling of washing powder and starch. His mum's faded curtain. The small Primus stove and the oil-lamp nailed to a wooden stretcher on the wall. It was as if it still existed. But of course it didn't. The hut, like all the others on the common, had been smashed to the ground and grass was growing where Terry's mum's polished lino used to lie.

But still in Kay's mind the hut was as real now as it was then. And so was Terry. Nothing could destroy what was in her mind. The memory of him would be with her for ever. And one day she would be able to think back and enjoy their times together all over again, no matter which part of the world she chose to live in.

Looking around and admiring the small, well-kept patches of garden dotted between the white marble tombstones, Ray slowly nodded. 'It's funny; I never imagined a graveyard to be like this. It's really peaceful and, I dunno . . . alive. All these flowers.'

'Yeah. I know what you mean.'

Enjoying the tranquillity, the two of them sat there in the warmth of the sun, allowing time and space to move in and begin to soothe the knots of pain inside.

They were by no means alone. Others were there. Some removing fading flowers and replacing them with fresh ones. The bereaved, quietly getting on and dealing with their loss in their own way. One or two were tearful, but on the whole most of the relatives and friends looked happy – some were even smiling as they chatted to each other between the graves.

'We'll be all right,' Kay murmured, and locked her fingers in Ray's. 'We'll be fine. You'll see.'